Praise fo
and H...

"Simply the best writer I've come across in years."

—*New York Times* bestselling author Laura Kinsale

"Fans of Hall's amazing debut, *Glitterland*, and the breadth of the author's work since will demand this latest."

—*Library Journal* on *How to Bang a Billionaire*

"5 Stars! Top Pick! Fantastic. Funny and full of feelz."

—Night Owl Reviews on *How to Bang a Billionaire*

"Desert Isle Keeper. *How to Bang a Billionaire* is an entertaining read from beginning to the HFN ending, with the Prologue and the end scenes in Scotland pure undiluted Alexis Hall. Yes, of course, I shall be buying books two and three when they are released. Enjoy."

—All About Romance on *How to Bang a Billionaire*

"A complex, poignant look at modern love, loneliness and sexual identity."

—*Washington Post* on *For Real*

"Hall blends pleasure and pain, both erotic and emotional, to create an engrossing romance with sharpness hidden in the sweetly traditional power-exchange relationship."

—*Publishers Weekly*, starred review, on *For Real*

How to Blow It
with a Billionaire

ALSO BY ALEXIS HALL

How to Bang a Billionaire

How to Blow It with a Billionaire

ALEXIS HALL

FOREVER
YOURS

New York   Boston

Copyright © 2017 by Alexis Hall
Excerpt from next book copyright © 2017 by Alexis Hall
Cover design by Brian Lemus
Cover copyright © 2017 by Hachette Book Group, Inc.
Hachette Book Group supports the right to free expression and the value of copyright. The purpose of copyright is to encourage writers and artists to produce the creative works that enrich our culture.

Forever Yours
Hachette Book Group
1290 Avenue of the Americas
New York, NY 10104
forever-romance.com
twitter.com/foreverromance

First Edition: December 2017

Forever Yours is an imprint of Grand Central Publishing.
The Forever Yours name and logo are trademarks of Hachette Book Group, Inc.

The publisher is not responsible for websites (or their content) that are not owned by the publisher.

The Hachette Speakers Bureau provides a wide range of authors for speaking events. To find out more, go to www.hachettespeakersbureau.com or call (866) 376-6591.

ISBN 978-1-4555-7136-9 (ebook edition)
ISBN 978-1-4555-7135-2 (print on demand edition)

E3

To CMC, you are still the fucking best.

Love is merely a madness; and, I tell you, deserves as well a dark house and a whip as madmen do; and the reason why they are not so punish'd and cured is that the lunacy is so ordinary that the whippers are in love too.

—*As You Like It*, William Shakespeare

How to Blow It with a Billionaire

PROLOGUE

*F*ifteen years, Arthur. And sometimes I still can't quite believe you're dead. Your son is so like you in some ways—passionate, obstinate, ambitious—and in others not at all. He has such dark needs. A twist of sexual cruelty as integral to his nature as gold through marble. You would not have understood him. Not the way I do. To you I was nothing but an experiment, an impulse of fondness and alcohol, cast aside for that doe-eyed whore you married, relegated to the ranks of mere friend. But Caspian is mine in ways you could never be. We made him together. Your final gift to me. My reward for half a lifetime of unregarded love.

I did not plan what happened between us. But he came to me, the rage and grief in him an irresistible reflection of my own. He thought he wanted to punish you, but all he truly needed was to mourn. I, however, had needs too. I will admit that manipulating your son into bed is hardly an accomplishment worthy of my abilities. Nor any true testament to my taste. But what are rules to men like us? Petty middle-class limitations placed upon those with the capacity for greatness. *And, Arthur, he has your eyes. Blue as forever.*

He was so enticing. So young and restless and full of pain. It was not like loving you at all. It was far superior. He was everything you could have been, were you only less hidebound, less conventional. Less excruciatingly kind. And what are you now? Nothing but an absent father. When I am his teacher, his lover, and his friend. Of course, he has his dalliances. It does him good, I think, to test the limits of the ties that bind us. And, as the loosed hawk returns always to the hand of its master, so will Caspian to me.

Ah, but sometimes he tries my patience. I offered him a gift—the perfect subject for his desires—and he uses him like a secretary. Nathaniel Priest should have been a passing folly. Instead he nearly ruined what I gave so much to create. And now this boy. This boy of no consequence.

While I would infinitely prefer Caspian to return of his own volition, perhaps it is time to remind him where, and to whom, he belongs. Of course, I would never stoop to an instrument as blunt or as unreliable as force. Rather, I am the loving vivisectionist of Caspian's soul. I have shaped and reshaped him with incalculable cuts, and I can bring him back to me whenever I will it. All I have to do is show him who he truly is.

CHAPTER 1

So I had this totally crazy dream. I dreamed I met a billionaire called Caspian Hart and he kind of liked me. Well, liked me enough to put me up in a ludicrously expensive London flat but not enough to trust me, talk to me, or spend any time with me. A sufficiently self-esteem-tanking level of liking that I ended up running back to my family's place in Scotland. But, also, a sufficiently *something* level of liking that he wound up following me. And telling me a bunch of things which made me realize that not only did my level-of-liking scale need serious recalibration, but I liked him enough to give it another go.

Except, oh wait, that wasn't a dream.

It had really happened.

And there was Caspian himself, tucked into the corner where the bed met the window, watching the distant sea. He was pale in the cool, blue-tinted morning and a little tousled—that one wayward lock of his fallen free again. The smile he gave me, as

I emerged from the duvet, was slightly shy, as if he wasn't sure how to greet me.

"Good morning." I stretched with abandon, spine arching, toes uncurling. "Did you sleep okay?"

"I'm fine. I saw the sunrise."

"Really?" It was a little hard to imagine. Or maybe not? He was probably the only person I knew who would have the patience to do something like that: watching and waiting as the light cracked wide the night. Lonely, though. With me snuggled and oblivious right there beside him. "Um, maybe you should have woken me? Or…I don't know. I might have been grumpy."

"I didn't want to wake you. You looked, frankly, terribly cute."

I looked what now? I wrinkled my nose, unimpressed. "Cute in a way that makes you want to do bad things to me?"

"Oh yes."

He crooked a finger and—after a second of *OMG, will I taste of mornings* based hesitation—I dived under the duvet, surfacing again between his knees. He wrapped his arms around me, hauled me up, and kissed me, not roughly exactly, but without mercy. Prizing my mouth open like the lid of a treasure box and taking possession. These simple caresses infinitely preferable to whatever drug I'd taken with Ellery in London. No feverish ecstasies but a deep, heavy, and all-consuming bliss. A spell to turn me to butter.

He was smooth and silken against me—his hair surprisingly soft, though I could also feel the wicked tightening of his nipples and the hot pressure of his cock. He smelled of warmth, if that was a thing that was possible. A cozy, sleep-clinging scent of skin, with only the faintest trace of sweetness from his cologne. This unexpected nakedness that was just him.

He made a low sound at the back of his throat—almost a growl—and flipped me. I went gladly, though the bed made a godawful telltale creaking as I landed on my back amid the pillows and rucked-up sheets. I wasn't even sure Caspian noticed, let alone cared, as he came down on top of me.

I'd been kissed and delightfully manhandled enough by him that I had a pretty good notion of what he might like. So I stretched my hands over my head. Giving him my surrender. The safety and the dark thrill of it.

His eyes glinted. Turned stormy.

And he reached up, dragging a finger from my wrist to my shoulder, making me very aware of that line of pulled-tight skin, all exposed and unprotected and held that way by nothing but the desire to please him.

As he settled between my thighs I couldn't help arching my spine and tilting my hips, making very, very explicit all the places of my body I was up for yielding.

"God, Arden." I was always suspicious of the phrase *ground out* when I saw it in books, but it seemed to apply to Caspian's words right then. Especially if you also took into account what he was doing on top of me. "You're such a…"

"Wanton?" I offered, tightening my calves around him.

"Tease."

Tease. My cock gave an eager jump.

I loved this kind of talk but it was tricky. There were lines in my head even I didn't properly know how to navigate. And I'd found asking people to call me names tended not to go so well.

It seemed to make them either act weird or get nasty. Neither of which I was into.

But tease…that was lovely. Made my toes curl with the naughty delight of being *bad*.

And Caspian said it just right too.

In this sexy-angry way.

As if being a tease was something wicked, not something wrong.

I was already swooning slightly—because of that, and also because his cock was pressed right against the warm, tingly space beneath my balls. But then he twisted a hand in my hair, yanking my head back, and my overthrow was complete.

The breath shuddered in my throat.

The fear was animal, instinctive, and so very sweet.

He leaned down even further and licked a long, wet stripe up my trembly, stubble-speckled Adam's apple.

I made a sound.

I guess you could have called it a whimper.

His teeth found the tender places under my jaw. Playful little nips that didn't really hurt so much as *spark*.

And then he pressed his open mouth to the side of my neck and—

Oh oh oh.

Something at once familiar and surprising about that damp suction and the blunt edge of his teeth: pleasure with a hot heart of pain.

It was sufficiently sanity-consuming that I forgot myself, moaning shamelessly as I curled my palm around the back of his neck, holding him to me. That strange and glorious push-pull of *yes-no-doitharder*.

My skin was as fiery-achy as my cock by the time he drew back.

He stared down at me, mouth red and eyes wild. "What the hell am I doing?"

"Um." I touched my fingers gently to the throbbing circle he had left on my neck. "Giving me a hickey, I think."

He winced. "I'm so sorry. I'm not some brutish adolescent. I don't know what came over me."

It *was* the teeniest bit ridiculous.

Caspian Hart—billionaire, sophisticate, chess grandmaster— and me with what was probably a glowing red-purple bruise. The proud teenage symbol for "getting some." Which, embarrassingly enough, I'd missed out on when I was an actual teenager, on account of being literally the only gay in the village. And English to boot.

I'd made up for it at university—although, now I thought about it, while I'd occasionally been bitten (with varying degrees of conviction), I'd never received an actual, one hundred percent genuine, bona-fide hickey.

Turned out, I was oddly glad it was Caspian.

And I liked—more than liked—that he wanted to *mark* me.

Unfortunately, he was looking a little bit traumatized about it.

"No, no," I said quickly. "It was lovely." I twisted my head helpfully. "Do it again."

He laughed, and kissed the bite so that it lit up like a flare and made me gasp. "I think I might have been wrong when I called you a tease."

"I'm not a tease?" I just about managed not to pout but I couldn't keep the disappointment from my voice.

"I think perhaps"—he'd gone all husky again—"you're worse."

I brightened. "Coquette?"

He didn't answer. Only tongued at a wildly sensitive spot beneath my ear.

"Uhh." I swallowed. "Minx?"

He shook his head.

"T-tart?" It was getting increasingly difficult to think of, well, anything. But every suggestion sent a pulse of whiskey-rough arousal through me.

"Worse," he whispered.

And, God help me, it felt like a caress. Like a compliment.

I tried to breathe and realized I was already panting. "Um…"

His eyes had that "all the better to eat you with, my dear" gleam as they found mine. Pinned me as surely as his body. "What are you, Arden?"

I wanted to say it so badly. Have him brand me with it like a badge of honor and sexual freedom.

But I was sort of…scared and squirmy at the same time. In case it wasn't true. Or it would be different outside the safety of my head.

"Arden." There was a low note of warning in his voice this time. It sounded so deliciously dangerous that I nearly came.

And then—bam—whatever was holding me back wasn't there anymore.

Broken or yielded or simply vanished.

"I'm a slut," I gasped out. "Am I a slut?"

He slid a possessive hand up the naked underside of my thigh. "Yes. Yes, you are. A very depraved, wayward little imp of a slut."

"Oh god." I squirmed frantically. "W-what happens to… slutty little imps?"

"What do you think happens to slutty little imps?"

My tongue flicked across my lips and, wow, they were dry. Almost as if every spare ounce of fluid I possessed had already leaked out my cock. "Do they…do they get punished?"

Which was when he rolled away. Taking all his heat and strength and the promise of erotic cruelty.

Before I could panic or complain, he covered his face with his hands and gave a deeply gorgeous groan. "Get dressed, Arden. I need to get you to London. I need to get you to London right now."

"Might take a while. Trains are really ropey at the weekend."

"Then it's fortunate I have a plane waiting at Inverness."

"You have a—" Of course he did. "Oh wow. But we've still got to get to Inverness."

"I hired a car."

"You can drive?" I blurted out.

He gave me a reproving look, softened by the hint of amusement in his eyes. "And I can tie my own shoelaces too."

Being whisked to London in a billionaire's private jet made such a ludicrous contrast to my miserable, lonely, to say nothing of lengthy, journey up.

But I guess that was life with Caspian Hart. And life without him.

CHAPTER 2

Despite our eagerness, it actually took a while to get on the road because Mum made us breakfast.

And sex was all very well but *pancakes*.

Caspian went for the lightest sprinkling of sugar and a twist of lemon juice. While I went for syrup. And cream. And strawberries. And chocolate. And—okay, yes. Everything. I went for everything.

I couldn't help but notice the way he was watching my lips.

It's possible they were a little bit glisteny.

And sticky.

He was looking all tormented by the time I was chasing the last swirl of syrup from my plate with a fingertip. And I seriously hoped I was going to pay for this later.

It didn't take me too long to pack on account of the fact I'd been living out of my suitcase since I got home. Then we said our goodbyes to my folks and headed to his car.

It was this silver hatchback thing. Very "family of four on a daytrip." So unlike his fleet of billionairemobiles.

Caspian must have noticed my amusement because he explained somewhat grumpily, "This is what was available in Inverness."

"You didn't think to get chauffeured up in comfort?"

"And have an audience for what could very likely have been a futile twelve-hundred-mile round trip?"

I still wasn't sure if it was terrifying or reassuring that you could have all the beauty, wealth, and power in the world, and still be uncertain about a boy. But, then again, if you were a total dick to the boy, you probably deserved to be uncertain.

Anyway, it had all worked out: happy endings ho.

We dropped off the car at Inverness and headed into the airport. When Caspian had told me he had a plane waiting, I hadn't quite realized what it would be like. What it meant to be a man who owned a private jet.

The terrifying value of his time.

Time he was currently spending with me.

It was an overwhelming thought. Knocking me silent as we were whisked across the concourse and then ushered into a plush private waiting room.

I had just enough knowledge of cars to be able to recognize status vehicles when I saw them, but private jets were completely beyond my sphere of experience. I wouldn't have been able to tell you the difference between a Gulfstream and a Bombardier if my life depended on it.

So all I could really say about Caspian's, as I gazed at it through the viewing windows, was that it looked like a plane.

With wings and engines and wheels and everything else you'd expect.

In barely a handful of minutes, our passports were checked in the most cursory fashion imaginable. And then we were let out onto the runway, me dragging along my entirely disregarded luggage. If I'd ever fancied terrorism or drug-dealing, this would have been a fantastic opportunity.

The chill hit me almost immediately, sharpened by the rough edge of the wind. I shivered and Caspian wrapped his coat about my shoulders. It was probably a demeaning sort of gallantry that I, as a liberated twenty-first-century man, should have resisted. But I didn't feel demeaned. I felt cherished. And the thought made me blush.

"Why don't you ever have a coat?" he asked.

I shrugged.

"Do you have some objection to dressing for the climate?"

"I have an aesthetic one." I had a duffel coat Mum's girlfriend Hazel had found in a charity shop, but it made me look, and smell, like an aging yak with personal grooming issues.

"Come on." Caspian took my free hand and hurried me across the runway.

All around us the sky gleamed. His palm was warm and his fingers were strong. The wind was making carnage of my hair. It was hard for me to hold on to the idea that this was normal life for Caspian. When it felt so utterly surreal to me.

As we boarded, it was "Good afternoon, Mr. Hart." Someone took my case. And then I was led into a space that would have impressed me if it had been a hotel. Tastefully decorated in shades of brown and cream and gold, it was essentially just a living room—soft carpets, sofas, cozy armchairs, a wall-mounted flat-screen—except it flew.

It motherfucking *flew*.

Only the windows, and something about the heavy quality of the light, betrayed the fact we were on a plane.

I must have had an "I don't think I'm in Kansas in anymore" look on my face because Caspian steered me gently into a chair. He was telling me useful things about where the bathroom was and what to do in case of an emergency but I was too dazed to really take it in. Words like *office* and *conference room* and *master bedroom* kept shooting past me in bullet time.

Although I definitely perked up at *bedroom*.

Soon enough, we were trundling down the runway. The world smearing a bit as we picked up speed. I'd once mentioned to my friend Nik that I had no idea how planes went from being on the ground to being in the air. So he'd told me. The bastard. And that had taken some of the fun out of it. But this was still my favorite part of flying: the moment just before takeoff, when what was about to happen seemed absolutely impossible.

I loved the tilty feeling in my stomach, the instinct to hold my breath. The way you could sort of sense somehow, in the responses of your own body, the unimaginable, unbelievable grace of all that metal.

"Are you all right?" Caspian asked. "You aren't afraid?"

"You know, maybe you should have checked before we got on the plane." He looked so horrified that I took pity on him. "I'm fine. It's just…I'm not used to this literally high-flying lifestyle."

There was a slightly weird pause.

And I found myself almost wishing we were back in the

relative normality of a hired hatchback, or in my family's home, where we'd found this…I didn't know what to call it…this *ease*. This burgeoning sense of an us.

I'd liked being so close to him. Having so much of his attention. And I'd liked the secretive parts of himself he'd seemed willing to share with me—things I'd previously only glimpsed, or suspected, or hoped for. The Caspian Hart who played chess. Who was antisocially competitive. Who washed the dishes. Tickled my feet.

Right now, though, he was nowhere to be seen.

The man sitting on the sofa in his private jet seemed so far out of my league as to belong to an entirely different sport.

He crooked a finger at me and I shuddered with a kind of fearful longing. "Come here, Arden."

He said it softly but there was no doubt that it was a command.

And I suddenly remembered that I loved this side of him too. That it was all part of him: the playfulness and the arrogance, the kindness and the cruelty. That he wasn't really remote at all, if you knew how to reach him.

If you weren't afraid.

I found myself eyeing the expanse of carpet between us, filled with the oddest compulsion to crawl.

I imagined the rub of the fibers beneath my palms. The ache in my knees. The way he would watch me, the hunger flaring in his eyes. And when I got to him I would push his legs apart and—

Oh, fuck imagining.

I slid off my chair and dropped to the floor. Making sure to arch my back, raise my arse, bowing my body in supplication. Invitation.

Caspian's reaction was way better than any fantasy. The gasp he uttered sounded almost shocked. And, God, the look on his face. Desire and this terrifying gratitude. As if I'd given him something wonderful.

Maybe it should have been humiliating. Crawling to someone's feet. But, honestly, I felt sexy as hell. Very aware of myself: the roll of my shoulders, the curve of my spine, the shapes I could make, sensuous and brazen and all for him.

Caspian was shaking when I got there. His head thrown back, lips damp and parted to admit his harsh, unsteady breaths.

I rubbed my cheek against the inside of his knee, then up a little higher. The denim was rough but he was hot, hot, hot underneath. And he smelled amazing. Not a trace of cologne left. Just his skin and the promise of sex.

Before I could get much further, his hands closed around my upper arms and he yanked me into his lap. His mouth was frantic against mine. His passion unrestrained to the point of need. Making me squirm and whimper and surrender. Leaving me bruised and breathless and dizzy on pleasure.

He shoved a hand into my hair, pulling hard enough to melt me. "Tell me again. What are you, Arden?"

"I'm a...I'm a slut."

"No, you're not." He pulled harder. Pain this time, but so good, so sweet.

I moaned helplessly, confused and blissed out and sensation lost. "I'm not?"

"You're *my* slut."

I garbled something along the lines of *yesyesyesoyesplease*.

"And what happens to my slut?"

I opened lust-heavy eyes. Stared deep into his. Found words. Important words. Put them in a sensible order. "Anything you want."

He pushed me gently to my feet. My legs had apparently gone all shaky.

"Strip," he told me.

I couldn't help glancing toward the front of the plane. When I'd offered anything he wanted, I hadn't quite realized he'd take it right now.

"We won't be disturbed."

He sounded certain but I couldn't shake the mental image of a horrified air hostess—did you get those on private jets?—finding me all naked in the middle of her day job. I liked performing for Caspian, exposing myself to him, but exhibitionism was not my thing. In fact, even the idea of casting some stranger in the role of nonconsenting voyeur was wangwiltingly embarrassing.

"Arden?"

Oops. I must have been lost in my own head. "Um. Yes?"

His eyes met mine, pale in the silvery light that filled the cabin, and softly gleaming. "Will you trust me?"

It was the last thing I'd expected, somehow. I guess I'd thought he'd command me. Force me even. And I probably wouldn't have minded. But I had no defense whatsoever against…against being asked. It was neither plea nor demand but God, it was intoxicating. And it slipped between the edges of my heart, twisting it open like an oyster.

"Yes," I whispered.

The moment I said it, I knew I meant it.

And suddenly I found myself thinking about the story of Sir Gawain and Lady Ragnelle. Not that I was hideously cursed. Or that we were being forced into matrimony because the King of England had made a deeply spurious promise to some random woman he met in the woods.

But still. Caspian had given me my sovereynté.

And now I was ready to surrender it to him.

My hands were unsexily damp as I peeled off my T-shirt and it was only when I was wriggling my jeans down that I remembered shoes were a thing I was wearing. So I had to stop, with everything bunched around my thighs, and hop about for a bit. By the time I was finally done I was all warm and flustered and pretty much the opposite of attractive.

And so … so *naked*.

It shouldn't have been a big deal. Caspian had seen me before—he'd fucked me for fuck's sake, a bunch of times—but it had never felt like this. As if my skin was too thin and my heart too hot.

All I could think was: what if he's laughing at me.

But no. When I managed to meet his gaze, there was no mockery in it. No exasperation at my failure to spontaneously launch into an alluring striptease. Just this fierce, glittery excitement, that was, in itself, exciting. Definitely worth getting starkers for at thirty-five thousand feet.

My cock, which had been retreating like it didn't want to know me, was definitely back in the game.

Caspian held out a hand—the gesture slightly formal, the

way you might invite someone to dance—and I took it instinctively, not really sure what to expect. Which was probably for the best because what happened next was...well, it wasn't the sort of thing that happened in Jane Austen.

(Though maybe Fanny would do it to a penitent Henry Crawford.)

Basically, Caspian tugged me closer and...*arranged* me, I guess, over his lap. He wasn't rough and I was a little dazed, so I wasn't entirely sure how I went from standing to...not doing that.

Whenever I'd seen this type of thing in pictures or, y'know, porn, it looked a lot less comfortable, the subject hanging there, precariously balanced on tiptoes and fingertips. But Caspian got me up on the sofa and positioned over his thighs, letting me brace myself on my knees and forearms. It felt...natural, actually. Except for the part where my arse was cheerfully right in the air.

It was just on the bearable edge of embarrassing. The ideal mixture of exposure and arousal to make me squirmy. The worst thing was not being able to see his face anymore. I needed the reassurance that he was definitely finding this hot and not ridiculous.

At that moment, his palm glided over my upraised buttocks and I was suddenly too busy shuddering and moaning to worry anymore. Maybe it was the vulnerability of the position, but even that light touch was crazy intense—heat and pleasure spilling across my skin, along with a rush of rising goose bumps. His fingers followed, tenderly skimming the groove of my spine until he reached the taut plane between my shoulder blades and stroked me there. He found nerves I never knew I had and lit them up like stars, sharp and bright and sweet.

I couldn't help wriggling. It was good, it was so good, being touched that way by Caspian, but also a little bit tormenty at the same time. I hadn't realized something gentle could ache like something harsh, and it unhinged me a bit.

But then his other hand came down on the back of my neck, cupping my nape, all warmth and pressure and the promise of control, and the tension leaked right out of me, leaving me fizzy and liquid in his lap. He squeezed and I just gurgled in this pathetically eager way.

"Have I told you," he murmured, "how bewitching you are?"

I guess I would have balked if he'd tried *beautiful*. I wasn't unappealing but compared to Caspian Hart I was entirely fucking ordinary. But bewitching, it turned out, I could get behind, since it was as much about my effect on him as it was about me. I liked the idea a lot: this power had been given me, to please him.

He caressing fingers returned to my arse, slipping into the soft valley between my cheeks and reminding me abruptly exactly how my current position presented me: no longer with peach-like discretion, but spread wide and wanton for his looking and his touching.

I was glad my face was tucked away because I was bright red. It wasn't as if I hadn't had people get up close and personal with my bum before but I was starting to discover that context really made a difference. The very personal activities you indulged in in the dark were one thing. Being laid out not-very-virgin-sacrifice style in broad daylight was pretty explicitly another.

And then there was the fact Caspian was still clothed and I was about as bare as it was possible to be.

But, the truth was, I loved it. Especially because, amid the roughness of denim beneath my thighs, I could feel how gloriously hard he was. I'd been jerking off to fantasies vaguely reminiscent of this for as long as I could remember but I hadn't accounted for the charge that came from knowing he was just as into this as I was. That it wasn't just something he did, or something I gave, it was something we *shared*.

Which didn't mean I wasn't also nervous about it. And getting more so as he…uh…got acquainted with the territory, his hand mapping the curve from the tops of my thighs to the (occasionally rather admired) dimples at the base of my spine.

"Um," I squeaked. "You have done this before, right?"

"Yes." He stopped stroking me. His palm just resting there, possessive and protective and vaguely threatening, all at the same time. "Have you?"

Occasionally my lovers had taken a swipe at my arse while nailing it, but as much as I'd enjoyed that sort of play, it hadn't remotely prepared me for this. "Not technically, no. But"—I pulled in an unsteady breath, suddenly terrified he was going to change his mind, and I'd have stuck my posterior in his face for nothing—"don't let it stop you."

"Believe me, the only thing that can stop me is you. Tell me what you want."

Ahhhhh.

I wished yet again that I could see his face but then I was also glad I couldn't because it reminded me that the last time I'd felt physically closest to him, when the things I'd done for his pleasure had seemed most intimate, he'd only been a voice on the phone.

And that was how I found the courage to tell him.

Well, the courage to burrow into the sofa and then tell him: "I want you to spank me."

He made a soft, lust-rough noise, but his voice was amazingly steady: "Show me how much you want it. Ask me."

"Oh God." I twitched and dripped and nearly combusted with arousal. "Will you spank me, Mr. Hart? I really"—help, breath, words—"I really want you to."

His other hand tightened on my neck and I swear to God I could feel his pulse pounding in his wrist. "It would be my pleasure."

And then he…he did it. His palm cracked against my arse—the noise more startling than the pain and the impact more noticeable than either. I juddered forward a bit, though he kept me anchored, and swallowed a gasp. I'd known what was about to happen but it was still shocking for some reason.

He gave me a moment to process but my brain was kind of stuck on *he hit me* when he did it again—same spot, almost exactly, sending a flare of heat across my skin. The third time made me yelp and it was such a ridiculously undignified sound that I was giggling by the fourth. Then giggle-yelping as it went on. Not because it didn't hurt—since it soon did, building from a swiftly fading sting to a deep, hot ache—but because it hurt in this totally giddy-making way. Some combination of the helplessness and the attention and the intimacy of his naked hand.

And, oh God, the *freedom* of it.

Of just being able to lie there and writhe and make silly

noises and feel all the things: pain and arousal and fear and pleasure and this wild, wild joy.

Caspian was trembling, his strikes falling with a little less precision than they had originally and his breath sounding harsh in the spaces between. Which was a touch worrying.

"A-ah," I managed to gasp out, "am I doing it right?"

He made this sound, probably a laugh, though it was ragged. Shot through with things I didn't have the wherewithal right then to interpret. "I don't care. Don't stop."

He was stroking me again: long gentle sweeps of his palms over my too-warm, too-sensitive flesh until it seemed like every last drop of blood in my body had gone south for the winter and redistributed itself evenly between my arse and my cock. The hurt was still there but through some strange alchemy of sex and trust, right then it was indistinguishable from passion.

I wailed and bucked against him in a semi-delirious and fully shameless attempt to make him touch me. He laughed again at that, a less broken sound this time. Not mocking, but softly teasing, even a little wonderstruck. His fingers brushed against my hole and I cried out frantically, all my giggling vanquished.

"God. Please. *Please.*"

He dipped inside and I reared up and swallowed him with my arse like Moby Dick. For a brief second it was the most beautiful, the most perfect feeling in the world: his finger pressing into me, a very slight stretch and this cool-water pleasure in the middle of the fire he had forced into my skin. And then it was just not enough, not nearly enough, relief becoming frustration becoming fresh and fiercer need.

I couldn't tell if he was giving me cruelty or mercy but I

wasn't entirely sure I cared. Trying not to think about how profoundly debauched I was going to look, I spread my legs as wide as I could get them, and…well…yeah, fucked myself on his fingers. It wasn't much—mainly a sort of desperate rocking—but as self-torture went it was irresistible, teeny-tiny starbursts exploding behind my eyes with every *very nearly* nudge in the vicinity of my prostate.

I probably couldn't have got off that way, but I was damn committed to trying. And he let me for a little while, his other hand still curled against my neck, petting me, making me feel tormented and indulged and cared for all at once. I tightened as he withdrew, greedily trying to keep him but, of course, I couldn't. And so I was reduced to whimpering and twitching my arse pitifully at him instead.

"Ready for more?" he asked, tracing tantalizing circles where he had left me wanting.

I could barely breathe, my whole body strung tight and poised on his fingertip. "More?"

"That was just the warm-up."

CHAPTER 3

*W*_{arm-up?}

"H-holy shit." I tried to imagine what else he could do to me—but my brain was dopamine dazed and came up blank.

He withdrew and his touch became soothing again, which I was pretty sure I didn't want at all. "We can stop at any time. You've already given me more than—"

"No." I flattened my forearms to the sofa and shoved my hips up. "Take it all. Take everything."

For a moment, he was so still I thought he was going to say no or something. But then he shifted his grip from my neck, laying his palm flat across my shoulders in a way that felt both ominous and reassuring. And when he hit me this time, it hurt in such a real way that I heard myself say "Ow" in a ridiculously surprised tone of voice. It would have been funny—pain hurts, no shit Sherlock—but it was like his hand had knocked everything out of me except the capacity to respond. A few strikes later and even "ow" was gone. Instead, these breathy cries were being jolted out of me. Sort of like being expertly fucked. But not. But yes.

And it was relentless. His hand coming down on me to the rhythm of his choosing. This pain that was both in my control and out of it. I knew with a faith I thought I'd put aside when I no longer believed in fairy tales that if I told him to stop—if I really meant it—he would. And, sometimes, I almost wanted to. Not so much because what was happening was unbearable but because it was simply overwhelming. The pure physicality of it. The way he had me all pinned down and splayed out. The sweat and tears—oh wow, I was actually crying—stinging my lips. The *sound* of each strike, loud and clear and undeniable. A question demanding an answer given in suffering and submission.

And, God, did I give it. Gasping and sobbing and writhing under his hands. Begging incoherently for him to…fuck, I didn't know what I wanted, only that I wanted to beg for the simple pleasure of begging. Knowing it would make no difference. That I could scream and cry and struggle and he'd use me however he wanted. And, for some reason, in my slutty little brain that wasn't bad at all. It was awesome.

Liberating and sexy and scary and exactly what I'd longed for. It wasn't like my fantasies—it was a lot messier and my reactions were more complicated—but it was way better. And weirdly, something I never would have imagined: how peaceful it would be, right at the heart of all that tumult. How safe I would feel. How cherished.

It made me arch into the blows, not welcoming the pain so much as everything it brought with it: adrenaline and intimacy and this deep sense of acceptance. Of being beyond strength or weakness or shame. And trusting it was okay to be there. That Caspian was with me.

That he had me.

I was so blissfully lost that it took me a moment or two to realize it was over. That the roaring in my ears was my own heartbeat. My knees slid out from under me I flopped into Caspian's lap like a fish.

"Ohmigod."

I didn't know how long I lay there. Minutes, hours, ages of the world, while the sun tarnished and the stars fell.

Wow I was floaty.

When my breathing had steadied, and the sweat dried on my back, Caspian drew me up and gathered me to him. He arranged me so I was straddling him, my weight distributed away from my arse, which was a relief because even the air moving against it felt rough. But he could have knotted me into a pretzel for all I was capable of resisting right then. I was mercury between his hands.

Well, for the most part. My cock was very much the opposite of mercury. Granite or marble or iron. Something really fucking hard. I blinked down at myself, slightly bewildered at the sight I presented: impressively large and shiny-slick with precome, straining pleadingly from between my spread-wide thighs.

Caspian caught me gently by the chin and made me look at him. Maybe it was my state of befuddlement or the way the light was…doing something, but his eyes looked wet.

"Was I okay?" I asked, voice coming out all hoarse and excitingly abused.

For a moment, we were just gazing at each other, intense and awkward at the same time. If anything, he seemed shocked—a flush of arousal staining those flawlessly sculpted cheekbones of his.

"You…you're perfect. Absolutely perfect. God, you have no idea."

He leaned in and kissed me gently, almost reverently. I fully intended to be graceful about it but for some reason his lips on mine triggered a *cry havoc* reaction and I …attacked him. Turned what I'm sure could have been a beautiful moment into a tongue-tangling, teeth-clashing mess.

But he let me. He let me eat his face like a clueless teenager until everything was hot and slick and our mouths tasted coppery with too much kissing. The world was still kind of distant—out of focus even, a little bit photoshopped—but Caspian was everything real.

I clung to him, dug my fingers into him and my teeth, and he held me tight and didn't flinch or try to calm me. I realized I was making desperate, throaty little mewls, almost as if he was spanking me again, but he took those too, giving me in return these soft, dazed gasps.

It was a bit shocking, actually. I'd got used to him being miserly with his sounds and restrained in his pleasure. But this was different. A glimpse of the man who had fucked my throat that night on a balcony in Oxford.

The man I had always known was there.

And wanted. Wanted to call mine.

It was me, in the end, who broke the kiss. Any more and I would probably have died of ever-increasing lust: a moth hurling myself repeatedly into Caspian's, er, flame. I collapsed against him, panting.

He was also breathing hard, his heart thundering under mine. And his mouth looked all ravaged, which gave me a filthy, possessive thrill.

"Y'know," I said, "I'm really super horny right now."

He laughed and, while making someone laugh had never been high on my sexual agenda before, just then it was absolutely right. He sounded so…happy. And also a little wicked, his eyes alight with that touch of cruelty I found inexpressibly enticing.

He urged me upright on my knees and pushed a hand between our bodies, fumbling with his belt and his zipper. An arch and a shimmy and, a moment later, his cock—his ever-gorgeous, flatteringly hard cock—was free.

I think I might have actually licked my lips. And I would definitely have said a friendly hello, with my hand if nothing else, if Caspian hadn't distracted me by easing a sachet of lube out of the pocket of his jeans.

He'd just been carrying that?

I couldn't tell if the forward-fuck-planning was flattering or arrogant. Or maybe it was both, and that was why I liked it.

He tore it open with his teeth—if I'd tried to do that, I'd have ended up with a mouthful of lube—and slicked up his cock. And, oh wow, I could have watched him do that forever: his long, elegant fingers working his long, elegant cock until everything glistened.

He tangled his free hand in my hair and yanked my head up, drawing an excited gasp out of me.

"You want it," he told me, steadying himself by the base, "you take it."

"Fuck yes I want it."

He was not...unchallenging, but I was a hundred percent on the case. Honestly, I was so turned on, I could probably have fucked a butternut squash. I eased myself into a good position, adjusted my angle, and sank down upon him—for about two seconds, and then I almost hit the ceiling, howling.

"Oh Jesusfuckingchrist."

My arse had lit up like Rudolph's nose.

How the fuck had I...forgotten? Yet somehow, in the haze of greedy kissing, the hot ache of spanking had become background and I had.

Though from Caspian's glittery smirk he absolutely hadn't.

I blinked the tears out of my eyes. "You bastard."

He smiled and kissed my nose.

I tried it a bunch of ways, getting freshly sweaty and whimpery the more I struggled, but it was like one of the punishments in Tartarus: this perfect prize of a cock I couldn't fuck. I was driving myself wild with frustration, and God knows how he was managing to stay so calm, but I could have done with about three more hands. I simply couldn't brace myself and angle myself and guide his cock past the inferno he'd made of my arse all at the same time. I wanted him so much—I was fucking *dying* from lack of him inside me—but I just didn't know *how*.

Eventually, I surrendered. Rested my brow against his and gave a broken little sob.

"I can't. Please."

His arms came around me. "Let me help you."

"Wait." I jerked upright. "Was that an option?"

"You didn't ask."

I wasn't sure whether to laugh or cry, so I sort of did both and smacked him in the arm. "You bastard."

"You already called me that."

"I'm out of my mind with lust. I'm sorry my insults aren't living up to your exacting standards. But, yes. Please. For the love of God. Please help me."

His hands slid down my back and pulled my buttocks apart. It still hurt but for some reason it hurt differently when he did it. And I shuddered with a kind of weird hurty pleasure and the vague knowledge that my arsehole was on full display to incalculable miles of sky.

Not that it was looking.

But I still felt pretty exposed.

And I loved it.

"So"—I nipped at the side of his jaw, squirming between his hands—"did it turn you on? Watching me totally failing to fuck you?"

His eyes flashed. "It turned me on watching you try."

"You'd better not be trying to teach me a life lesson right now."

He gave me a mean squeeze, starbursts of sensation flaring beneath his fingers, and I squeaked. "The key to success, Arden, is the realization that failure is a temporary condition."

"What's that supposed to mea—"

Before I could finish, he pulled me down upon his cock and the rest of my question vanished into a strangled shriek. I flailed wildly, clutching at his shoulders, shock and excitement and a splash of panic blending into a unique and special cocktail. But he only breached me. He didn't force me. He left the descent under my control—that sweet-harsh glide that burned so very beautifully.

I took him all—took the pain and the pleasure, the stretch and the pressure, the whole gorgeous invasion of it—and he let me see. For once he let me see. The helpless flutter of his eyelashes. The creep of heat across his cheeks. The way his lips parted on a soundless groan. He looked…vulnerable, and a little bit wrecked, softness in his eyes along with the haze of passion.

I threw back my head, full of savage triumph, because I'd made this happen. And this flawless, unreachable man—with all his mysteries and his sadness and his strength—was mine.

He pressed his mouth to my throat, warm and wet, with the scrape of teeth, and I rode him like a rodeo cowboy. Yee-fucking-haw. I was alive with small hurts, aches inside and out, but they felt like fireflies in my skin, barely recognizable as hurt at all. Because everything was igniting into bliss. His hands, his lips, his cock driving into me, rough and hard and fucking perfect. The noises he was making against my skin: reciprocal ecstasy shuddering out of him. And, oh, words. Fierce, tender, slightly muffled words becoming their own prayer: "Arden, oh Arden, my Arden."

I didn't really have breath or brain to reply but my answer was everywhere: in the pulse that beat for him and the body that yielded to him and the pain I'd borne for him. *Yours yours yours yours yours.*

Sweat was slicking down me, gathering in the creases of my groin and behind my knees. And I was probably going to have to take up yoga again or do something about my core strength because—as much as my arse was loving the adventure—the pace was getting punishing. But then Caspian gave this harsh and shattered cry, his hands dragging me down and pinning me in place, his cock so deep in me it felt practically embedded. I screamed, my prostate launching its own little hallelujah chorus as Caspian's teeth plunged into the bit where my neck met my shoulder.

It was the aggression that undid me—seeing him so lost to it, so utterly out of control—the final riff in my sex-rock anthem of rapture. Next thing I knew was a full-body-shaking, mind-obliterating orgasmic white-out—static snowflakes behind my eyes, every nerve I had electric—and my cock went off like a party popper, extravagant ribbons of come shooting between us.

When I was next capable of anything, I said: "Ow ow ow ow ow."

Because suddenly everything that had hurt in a good way was starting to hurt in a bad way. Particularly my arse, which was sore and sticky and throbby, and had a cock in it.

Caspian, who was still trembling, gentled me before I could freak out, since the need to not be in pain had become really rather urgent but my coordination wasn't up to the task. And then he very carefully eased himself out of me.

I tried to stand, only to discover I was head-to-toe spaghetti.

Thankfully Caspian caught me before the floor did, wrapped me up in the scarily pristine cream blanket that had previously been draped over the arm of the sofa, and drew me back onto his lap, somehow managing to position me so I wasn't resting too much weight on my poor bum.

I meant to protest because I was a mess and the blanket was lovely, but it was all soft and cozy, I couldn't quite muster the will. I tucked my head under Caspian's chin and he brushed his fingers against the nape of my neck, so lightly I thought it was an accident at first. But, no, it was a caress. One that carefully roused my sensation-battered flesh to shivers of softly tingling pleasure. If he'd been holding me less tightly I'd have arched greedily into his touch…and probably made a million bits of me immediately start hurting again. But he didn't let me. Just kept me safe and helpless, his kindness as ruthless as his cruelty, and the sweetness of his touch running in rivulets across my skin.

Since my mouth was the only bit of me capable of movement, it opened and emitted a weird, drunken purring.

Caspian's breath stirred the damply curling hair at my brow in a nearly-kiss. "You're as delightful in pleasure as you are in pain."

"I'm good with both," I mumbled.

"You *are* good." He pushed his hand into my hair, his palm curving to fit the base of my skull. "So good."

I was vaguely aware we were talking nonsense to each other. But it didn't matter. The words were less important than the exchange of them. Frankly, he could have been telling me "wibble kerplunk gargle blip" as long as he did it in that tone of dazed admiration.

My brain was cottage cheese at this point so I stopped trying to make it do things. And let myself float off on the magic carpet of his care.

"Arden?" he asked, after a moment or two. At least, I thought

it was a moment or two. I might have been asleep. "You are...
you are all right, aren't you?"

"Whu?"

"You aren't..." He cleared a trace of huskiness from his voice.
"I mean, I didn't..."

"You hurt me, then fucked me, now you're holding me. What
more could a boy want?"

He laughed—or made some shaky sound close to a laugh,
anyway—partially muffling it against the side of my head.

"And you had fun too, right?"

"You gave yourself to me like a gift. Offered without restraint
things I would never have dared ask or hope for. And you were
so beautiful I could hardly believe that you would do this for
me. So yes, Arden. I had fun."

Some of the heat accumulated in my arse redistributed itself,
giving me a serious case of the warm fuzzies. "I'm not...you
know. I'm not beautiful."

"Do you want me to turn you over my lap and spank you
again?"

"Not *right* now."

"Then be quiet."

Nestling close, I hid my smile in his neck. *Then be quiet*
was hardly the three-word declaration of my dreams. But, right
then, it fell upon my ears as tenderly as if it were. He was, after
all, Caspian Hart. Not some tamer beast.

And, anyway, I wasn't very into princes.

CHAPTER 4

I wasn't really aware of being awake or not awake but I guess I must have been not-awake, because I was woken up by Caspian whispering to me: "I'm sorry, sweetheart, but we'll be landing soon."

I whimpered. "Do we have to? Can't we live here forever?"

"On the plane?"

"Yes." I curled into him stubbornly. "We can spend all our time having sex and cuddling"

"We can also do those things on the ground. And with a smaller carbon footprint."

It should have been reassuring—well, it *was* reassuring, since I hadn't seriously expected we'd become joint founders of a flying and fucking commune—but I was feeling fragile. In a way that was completely unlike the raw vulnerability of writhing naked and sobbing over Caspian's knee, and a lot less fun.

"Arden? What's the matter? You haven't…haven't changed your mind, have you?"

He sounded so genuinely anxious that I came in immediately with a "No." And, anyway, it was true.

Well. Mostly.

"Then what's wrong?" he asked.

I stared at my toes. The polish needed touching up. Also maybe Sally Bowles green hadn't been the best color choice—I looked a little gangrenous down there. "I don't know. I think maybe I'm failing London."

"How could you possibly be failing London?"

"Same way I failed Oxford."

"You have no idea whether you failed Oxford." He curled a comforting hand over my knee. "Your results haven't even been released yet. And, when they are, you'll get a 2.1, exactly like everyone else."

He was probably right. You had to fuck up super hard to get out of Oxford with anything less than a 2.2. But that led to a situation in which a lower pass was as good as an admission of failure anyway. "Even if I do get a 2.1, I won't deserve it."

"It's hardly an assessment of your moral character, Arden."

"But I got offered this incredible opportunity. And I *squandered* it."

Caspian sighed. I thought he was about to tell me to grow up and stop whining but, instead, he just drew me closer. "Oxford is only a university," he murmured. "And there are many things besides the academic to learn at university."

"What, like how to go six weeks without doing any laundry?"

"Like what sort of man you wish to become."

"I'm not sure I even figured *that* out."

"Yes. You have."

He leaned down and kissed the tip of my nose. The playful gesture was a strange contrast to the sincerity of the words but I treasured both. Believed in both. Mustered a slightly wavery grin. "Well, I must be doing something right since you like me. But, when it comes to everything else, I don't have a clue."

"You told me you were interested in journalism."

"I am. Except all I've done so far is write a few articles."

"Have you been able to place them?"

A couple of emails had come in during my Kinlochbervie heartbreak exile, except I hadn't really been in any state to appreciate them. "Yes. I mean, mainly online and stuff."

"That's wonderful." Oh God, he sounded all proud of me. "And seems to directly contradict your assertion that you don't know what you're doing."

"I just feel like I'm fucking up another amazing opportunity. You take care of everything and what do I have to show for myself? A satirical review of expensive mineral water brands."

"It's a perfectly reasonable start."

"But I had weeks. I could have learned Mandarin or written the Great American Novel."

"Do you want to learn Mandarin or write the Great American novel."

"Um, not exactly."

That made him laugh, his breath ruffling my hair. And I guess I was being a bit silly.

"I wrote something I thought might work for *Milieu*," I admitted. "But I haven't submitted it yet."

"*Milieu*?"

"Caspiaaaaan." I thunked my forehead against him. "It's a

high-society lifestyle magazine. You're regularly *in* it."

"I pay very little attention to what other people say about me. Besides, I have lawyers who manage these things on my behalf."

I pouted, wounded for *Milieu*. "It's not a gossip rag. We're not talking Twelve Shocking Things About Caspian Hart (You Won't Believe Number 7) type material."

"I see." Except clearly he didn't.

"*Milieu*'s like…this quintessentially British thing, y'know? It's been around since seventeen-o-something. And somehow manages to be glamorous and ridiculous at the same time. I find that combination incredibly charming."

His hand slid between us, his fingers tugging lightly at one of my nipple rings. "I definitely see the appeal."

"I'm not glamorous." I paused. "Wait. Are you saying I'm ridiculous?"

"I'm saying I find your combination of qualities unique and intriguing. And you don't have to explain what you like to me. It's enough that you like it."

"*Milieu*'s probably the closest you can get nowadays to being in an Evelyn Waugh novel. Only without all the war, Catholicism, alcoholism, mental collapse, and dead children. And, anyway, I grew up reading it. I'd absolutely love to be part of it."

"Then why haven't you sent in your article?"

"Well…" I squirmed.

He poked me. Caspian Hart actually poked me.

Which I would have found hilarious if I hadn't been in the middle of a major moop attack. "What if they say no?"

"Then you'll find something else."

"I thought you were only supposed to have one dream."

"That's a sinister lie perpetrated by Hollywood. You can have as many dreams as you dare imagine."

I pulled a dubious face. "That just sounds like a long list of things to mess up."

"To truly want something is to make yourself vulnerable." He gave me one of his most uncertain smiles—the ones I half believed were only for me. "None know that better than I."

He kind of had a point. "I still can't quite believe you came all the way to Kinlochbervie."

"I have crossed continents, risked millions, and ruined lives in pursuit of my business aims. Why do you believe I would do any less for you?"

I couldn't help wondering how the whole situation would have played out if it had been reversed. Probably I'd have hidden under the nearest duvet, emerging only to scavenge for food in ruined supermarkets after the fall of civilization, and Caspian and I would never have seen each other again.

Urgh. I sucked. "I...I'll try to do the same," I said. "I mean, if you ever need me to come for you."

He laughed, not in exactly in a nasty way, only I hadn't made a joke. I guess it had sounded like one given he was, well, him and I was, well, me. And I couldn't quite imagine in what topsy-turvy looking glass world he would need me to play rescuer. Getting into stupid scrapes was my gift, not his.

Reaching for my hand, he tucked it into his. "Send your article to Milieu."

"Okay. Okay. Fine. But when they say no, and I'm crushed and my life is over, I'm blaming you."

"Firstly, they might not say no. Secondly, if they do, you'll find something else."

"What something else?"

"It doesn't matter. Whatever quickens your magnificent heart will eventually bring you success."

"You really believe that?"

He gave me a look so full of warmth and pride that, right then, I could have turned tides. Pulled the stars from the sky. "I do."

"Does, um, multinational banking and financial services make you feel that way?"

"It doesn't have to. I'm not you, Arden."

He sounded sort of quelling and sad. And both were walls, in their way. I gave his cold fingers a little squeeze. "It doesn't mean you have any less right to happiness than I do."

"You make me happy."

I couldn't tell if that was romantic or a lot of responsibility. Maybe both. "Then you better make damn sure we spend more time together in London. No more abandoning me in One Hyde Park."

"Of course not. I shall endeavor to make myself available to you."

"I like the sound of that." I wriggled into a sitting position and tucked my knees up—although considering everything that had happened on this plane, modesty was pretty irrelevant right now. "When?"

"Pardon?"

"When are you going to make yourself available to me? I want names, I want places, I want dates."

His hand went to his mouth, I think covering a smile. "When I said to pursue what inspired you, I didn't mean my schedule."

"It's not your schedule I'm after. It's you."

"Oh." He looked oddly abashed. "Arden."

"What? You can't give me life advice and then go weird when I follow it."

"No I…I simply wasn't expecting you to apply it immediately. And to me."

I shrugged bit self-consciously. "Well, you quicken my heart. And also other bits of—*mmfff.*"

His kiss cut me off, unexpected in its clumsy, close-lipped sweetness.

"When do you want to see me?" he asked.

"How about, say, right now? Today?"

"I'd love to but"—a shadow deepened his eyes to gray—"it's not possible. I have to work."

Of course he did. Caspian's life was nothing but work. I'd known that from the beginning. And while I was capable of immense feats of whininess, there was no way I was setting myself up in opposition to his job. Because if TV had taught me anything, that was how you got murdered: see *Damages*, see *Luther*, see *Scandal*. "Tomorrow?"

"It's a deal. Now come on." He nudged his nose gently against mine. "There's just about time to shower."

If it was an attempt to distract me, it totally worked. "There's a shower?"

He nodded and led me off to the bathroom.

Where there really was a shower.

A *shower.*

On a private jet.

It wasn't big enough for two, unfortunately, but the water pressure was way better than plenty of showers I'd taken in buildings on the ground.

I stood under the spray, wincing as the droplets stung my poor arse, but my muscles appreciated the attention. My knees were still wobbly, though, and my head felt light and stuffy at the same time, like my brain had been entirely replaced with candyfloss.

Happy, shiny candyfloss.

Oh wow.

Was this really my life?

And did Caspian really say all that stuff to me?

And if being fucked on a plane got me into the mile-high club, did being fucked on a plane with its own shower make me a platinum member?

I wasn't sure how much water there was, so once I'd got over a fit of the giggles at the sheer impossibility of everything that had happened to me lately, I got out, toweled myself off carefully, and dressed. I didn't remember Caspian bringing me my clothes but I was so well fucked and so well cared for I probably wouldn't have remembered if a barbershop quartet had parachuted in and performed *Bohemian Rhapsody*. Mainly, I was relieved I didn't have to wander his plane with my junk hanging out.

No sign of Caspian back in the cabin.

Just the indentations we had left on the sofa and what was clearly a splash of my dried come on the floor.

I stared at it in horror. Before rushing back to the bathroom to get warm water and a cloth.

I was on my hands and knees, scrubbing urgently, when Caspian strolled in, pulling a jumper—fresh but otherwise identical to the one he'd been wearing before—over his head.

It reminded me abruptly that, while I'd been about as naked as it was possible to be, he'd been fully clothed as usual. I'd found it hot at the time but now, watching his abs vanish behind a curtain of whisper-soft cashmere, I felt a little cheated. They were quite some abs and I wanted to make an ordinance survey of their valleys. With my tongue.

Caspian, however, was staring at me like I'd gone mad. "What on earth are you doing now?"

"Um. There's…" I pointed.

"Leave it, Arden. Someone will see to it."

"Omigod no."

He looked a little startled at my vehemence.

"I'm working class," I explained, rubbing away at the carpet. "Middle class if you push it. And I absolutely refuse to contribute to a universe where it's someone's job to clean up my come."

He sighed—though I told myself there was more affection in it than exasperation—and walked out.

That threw me a little. Maybe I'd already got too used to the petting and the smiling and the *oh my Arden and your magnificent heart* type sweet talk. But I guess he had…calls to make? Or maybe watching me de-ejaculate his plane was so unsexy he'd felt obliged to remove himself from my vicinity.

Thankfully, he came back a moment or two later and crouched down beside me. He'd brought a bottle of Vanish.

"Uh, what are *you* doing?" I asked, as he plucked the cloth out of my hand.

He sprayed and mopped and very soon all trace of my…of me was gone. Leaving the plush carpet as uniformly ecru as it had been before I spoodged all over it. He glanced up and gave me one of his apparently-becoming-somewhat-less-rare smiles. "If there is to be a universe in which the job of cleaning up your come exists, it might as well be mine."

I laughed and leaned in, hoping for a kiss. "Y'know, you can be weirdly romantic sometimes."

He stiffened (in the whole body, rather than exciting, way) and pulled back, flushing. "I don't know what you mean."

"Caspian, it wasn't an insult."

"No, I know. But"—he got to his feet, which put an end to our tender moment over a come stain—"I can't let you pretend that I'm—"

"Oh what? Pretend that you're kind and funny and sweet? That you look like a god and fuck like the devil?" I rolled onto the floor and lay there on my stomach in the fashion of a kid about to throw a tantrum. I wasn't actually, but the urge to full-body face-palm was strong right then. "Can't you for once just let me enjoy being with you? And trust me to handle the emotional fallout when it comes?"

He nodded, though he still looked slightly freaked out. "I'm sorry. You're right. But you have the most peculiar sense of romance."

I pushed onto my elbow and attempted a sultry look. "I'll take what I can get, Mr. Hart."

He gazed down at me, the curve of his lips softened by

another burgeoning smile. "Come and sit with me, Arden. We're about to descend."

I decamped. I wanted to be in his lap again with his arms around me, touch-needy idiot that I was, but I knew it wasn't fair to push him. I'd promised him that degree of control in Kinlochbervie and he hadn't exactly been measly with his attention. So I squidged up next to him on the sofa instead, and put my hand down between us in what I hoped was an accessible and appealing way.

For a little while we sat quietly.

Then I noticed his hand had somehow ended up right next to mine. And, weirdly, that was okay. Better than okay. It was sort of lovely.

"You bought me Pocky," I reminded him.

"Hardly an act from which myths are spun."

"That doesn't matter." I turned to face him, tucking a knee under me. "It's not the size of the gesture that counts, it's…"

"What you do with it?"

I laughed. Not so much at the joke but at the fact it came from Caspian. He was so…entrancing like this. Shyly playful behind his most severe facade. "What's romantic to me isn't the rote stuff like flowers or chocolate or serenading someone on a balcony at midnight—"

"I will not be serenading you ever."

"Of course not." I grinned. "I'm sure you'd outsource it to a serenading company."

"The best regarded and most exclusive serenading company in the world."

He'd derailed me by being funny, dammit. I made one last

attempt to make my point. "I feel, um, *romanced* when you do things that show that…you know me. As well as care for me."

"That simple, hmm?"

"What about when you rang me the night before your finals?"

"I was desperate to hear your voice again."

"But you knew I'd be scared. And you reached out to me. That was romantic. Just like when you came to Oxford. And to Kinlochbervie."

His eyebrow lifted into its most sardonic arch. "You seem to find a lot of romance in my behaving selfishly."

"I don't know if it was selfish or not. But I do know I needed you and you were there."

"Did you also need Pocky?"

"Hell yes. Matcha chocolate cookie is nearly impossible to get over here."

His expression turned thoughtful. "I suppose I'll have to take your word for it."

"Feel free to look for yourself."

"Not about the Pocky." His hand slid fully over mine and claimed it. "About what makes you happy."

"Generally a good plan in any…um—" Shit. I'd nearly dropped the R-word. The other R-word. "Generally a good plan. Hey, you know what else makes me happy?"

Least plausible cover-up ever. Way to go, Arden.

But he seemed willing to let me get away with it. "What?"

"When you…uh…" I was unexpectedly blushing, though I wasn't sure it was because of what I was saying now or what I'd nearly said before. "…when you call me your slut—"

"Because you find it romantic?"

"Yes. Because it's just for me."

Caspian was silent for what felt like ages. "I think I was right the first time," he murmured.

"What do you mean?"

"You do have a very strange sense of romance."

CHAPTER 5

There was a car waiting for us at Heathrow—a proper billionaire car this time, with a driver—to take us to One Hyde Park. It felt odd coming back. I couldn't have called it a homecoming because I was pretty sure that shining glass monster would never feel like home, but I was in a way more comfortable than I had been the first time I'd stepped into its gold and marble maw.

Now it was a familiar gold and marble maw. Put it that way.

Unfortunately Caspian couldn't stay. I hadn't expected him to, but it didn't stop the swell of disappointment from whichever organ generated the stuff. The balked duct.

He was, however, very nice about leaving. No vanishing abruptly into the night like the hero-villain from a gothic novel. There was only genuine reluctance, an apology, and a kiss on my nose before he left. Which was something he seemed to be making rather a habit of. Not that I was complaining. It was just unexpected.

Even—hah—*romantic*.

And my nose did have this very slight, almost questioning uptilt at the end, like maybe it was waiting for him.

Nasal care dispensed, he wished me a good night and promised to see me soon. I trailed him into the hallway trying not to look too desolate and puppyish, and probably failing hard.

He hesitated in the doorway. For a happy moment, I thought he might be about to change his mind, but all he said was, "You should have a word."

"A word with who?"

"A word," he repeated, looking everywhere but my face. "In case you need…in case you…in case you don't like…"

"Oh, a safeword."

He nodded, a touch of pink rising to his cheeks.

"Why?" Since I couldn't catch his eye, I had to put all my blatant invitation into my voice. "Are you going to do terrible things to me while I beg you to stop?"

Pink was long gone. Now he was very red indeed. And looking so much like he was wishing the ground would swallow him whole that I felt a little bit bad. But then he nodded again. "Assuming, that is, you have no objections."

"None whatsoever." If only he would see my smile. "I absolutely and categorically welcome any depravity you care to practice on me."

"Thank you. But I still think you should have a…a…"

He couldn't even say it. "A safeword."

Another nod.

I'd never seen him so uncertain. It made me want to pull him back into the apartment, wrap him up tight in my arms, and never let him go. But I knew he wouldn't let me.

He cleared his throat. "Arden?"

Shit, I needed an actual word. But my mind had gone completely blank. "I can't think of anything."

"Any word will do." He shifted impatiently. "I understand *red* is traditional."

Red was boring.

The silence stretched out between us. Every single word in the entirety of the human history of language was somewhere else right then.

"I…I know I've probably startled you. Maybe even frightened you. But, Arden, I really don't want to hurt you in any way that—"

Oh God, the look in his eyes. Like a half-tame wolf the second before its spirit broke.

"No," I cried. "No. It's fine. My safeword is…um…Mace Windu."

"It's what?" Caspian asked, finally.

I shrugged. "He's the badass Jedi with the purple lightsaber."

"Yes, I'm aware of that." He sounded faintly affronted that I'd doubted his knowledge of the Jedi Council. "I just don't know why you'd— It doesn't matter. If that's what you'll remember. If it makes you feel safe."

I thought about telling him *he* made me feel safe, but I didn't think he'd believe me. "It's Samuel L. Jackson," I said instead. "Of course I feel motherfucking safe."

Caspian really did leave after that. He had his phone out as he stepped into the elevator, immediately back into work mode.

And I was, once again, alone in One Hyde Park.

But it wasn't so bad. And, God, I was spoiled. There were

homeless people. And here I was, conceding that an extravagant, exclusive apartment in central London was "not so bad."

I unpacked and changed into my whale print lounge trousers
for the sake of my arse. Although not before I'd spent some time
admiring how red and totally owned it looked in the bathroom
mirror.

Then I arranged myself, stomach-down on the bed, and got
to grips with the emails I'd neglected while in Kinlochbervie.
I even made a spreadsheet so I could keep track of what I'd
written, where I'd sent out, and what the outcome was. And,
okay, it was only five lines long but it was still a motherfucking
spreadsheet, motherfuckers. Finally, I settled into brainstorm-
ing up some fresh ideas. Because Caspian was right: even if
Milieu rejected me, there were still countless opportunities for
frivolous-article writing floating about in the universe.

And, no, it wouldn't make me a billionaire or change the
world. But a lot of things that changed the world were actively
bad. And this was what I wanted to do.

I was so caught up in writing—a column pitch for *GQ* enti-
tled "The Ten Most Awesome Things in the World Right Now"
that I thought I could put together monthly and research entirely on the internet—that I almost brain-hazed right through
the ringing of my phone. I scrabbled for it and answered about
a second before I would have lost the call. "Uh, hello?"

"Arden?"

Caspian's voice, perhaps still the part of him most familiar
to me, slipped down my spine like an unexpected caress.
"Gosh…it's you. Hi."

"Did I wake you?"

"N-no. I was just—what time is it?"

"It's late. Nearly midnight, I'm afraid."

I guess I'd stopped expecting more than terse little texts so this was almost as startling as it was gratifying. "Is everything okay?"

"Yes, of course." He sounded slightly flustered.

And then fell silent.

An intriguing possibility crept into my mind. "Is this…I mean…do you miss me?"

"Actually, I thought you might prefer to hear from me personally because I won't be able to see you tomorrow as I'd hoped. I have a conference call that will likely take most of my evening."

"Oh." I'd been back less than a day and we were doing this again? Seriously? And right after all the promises he'd made? Well, okay. The promises he carefully hadn't made. Gah. Still, at least he'd phoned instead of sending one of his heart-crushing little texts.

"In fact, the whole week is looking somewhat overwhelming, and I need to be in Paris on Wednesday. Can we do Friday?"

"Sure. Whatever."

"I'm truly sorry." He sighed. "I would much rather be with you."

On some level, I recognized that he was trying. But it was still too reminiscent of the treatment that had driven me to Kinlochbervie in the first place. "And what if, by the time Friday rolls round, there's something else you absolutely have to do?"

"Sweetheart, I'm the owner and CEO of a multinational corporation. There will be times when I have to work, but I give you my word that I'll be here on Friday come hell, high-water, or the simultaneous collapse of the dollar, the yen, and the euro."

I muttered balefully.

"What was that?"

"Calling me sweetheart. It's cheating."

"I'm sorry. I won't if you don't want me to."

"No, I do. That's the problem." Fuck. I couldn't start an argument now. It couldn't be my first contribution to our newly reconciled relationship. And, besides, this was who Caspian was. There was no point agreeing to bang a billionaire if you took issue with them, y'know, being a billionaire. "Friday's fine. And if the entire global economy implodes I won't mind if you can't make it."

Somehow I knew he was smiling. And when he spoke, his voice was all silk and menace and mirth. "I was thinking you could perhaps arrange for sushi?"

Well. That was definitely promising. And would hopefully console me for the last time I'd attempted to seduce him with dinner and light bondage. "And what will you bring?"

"My tie."

I made an undignified, gleeful squeaking noise. And then flailed desperately after sexy. "I look forward to it, Mr. Hart."

There was another silence. I was fully expecting him to wish me good night and hang up and I would have actually been okay with that since I'd had more of Caspian today than I would have thought possible before Kinlochbervie. But instead he asked: "How's your…how are you feeling?"

"I feel good. My arse feels sore. I think about you every time I try to sit down." I grinned, even though he couldn't see it. "And I'll probably be thinking about you later too."

"Is that so?"

"Oh yes. I'll be thinking of you…very…hard…indeed."

He laughed—uninhibited for once and joyous. "Is this how you've spent your evening?"

"What? No. That's going to be my reward. I've been super productive."

"What have you been doing?"

Wow…this was. Wow. If life was Buzzfeed, it would definitely be near the top of the Arden's Best All Time Moments list. Caspian Hart had hurt me and fucked me, and was now asking about my day. And it was perfect. Like having a real boyfriend. I pushed my laptop aside and swooned into a happy heap on top of the duvet. "I'll tell you but I need to know something first. Where are you right now?"

He hesitated for a moment. "I'm on my balcony," he said warily. "Thinking about having a cigarette. Why?"

"I just wanted to be able to picture you while we talked." And I could: waiting like Rapunzel at the top of some great glass tower, halo-ed in artificial gold from the city that lay at his feet. I wanted to tell him: *you can come back to me.* I wanted to beg: *please don't be alone.* But he already knew that. And at some point he was going to have choose for himself. So I went on lightly, "It's not very exciting. I organized myself and drafted another couple of articles."

"Did you send your piece to *Milieu*?"

Eep. "Technically…no."

"Are no and technically no the same thing?"

"Kind of."

"Is something holding you back?" he asked gently.

"You mean, apart from anxiety, insecurity, and raging imposter syndrome?"

"Yes."

I sighed. "I guess I keep tinkering pointlessly with it?"

Even little silences felt epic on the phone.

Finally, he said: "Would it help if you shared it with me?"

I blinked. "Seriously? You want to read my crappy article?"

"Well, I did. But"—his voice turned teasing—"now you've told me it's crappy, I've changed my mind."

"Hey, I'm just managing your expectations. I…um…I could read it to you. If you have, y'know. The interest."

"Of course. Give me a moment." I heard the click of a lighter. Followed by Caspian's indrawn breath. "How about we make a pact? You read it to me and then submit it to *Milieu*."

"What if you think it's terrible?"

"Unless I think it's terrible. But if I don't think it's terrible, you have to send it."

"Um. All right."

Wait. What was happening?

Had I really offered to read my article to Caspian? And had he really said yes? I was suddenly and completely overwhelmed by self-consciousness. This was a man whose time was so valuable he needed his own plane. Also, what if I sucked? What if I sucked so badly he stopped believing I was charming and special and adorable? What if I put him off wanting to fuck me?

Ahhhhhhh!

But then. Did I trust Caspian or didn't I? In what deranged world did I live in, that I as up for him tying me up and hitting me, but so-so on showing him some words I'd arranged into a particular order? And, hell, if I didn't have the bollocks to share this with someone who was demonstrably on my side, how in God's name was I going to face editors and publishers and a public who would have nothing else to judge me by?

So I did it. I read the damn article to Caspian Hart.

And he was…nice about it. I wished I could have seen his face, but he made soft, amused noises at the bits I'd intended to be funny and, afterward, he told me he liked it with just the right amount of conviction that I got all flustered and glowy. As praise went it was pretty straightforward, but any more and I would have felt patronized. I was under no illusions that what I'd produced was a heartbreaking work of staggering genius. But I hoped it was, well, good enough to entertain someone while they were on the loo or stuck in a queue anyway.

"You have a very engaging voice," Caspian said. "Although, of course, I'm somewhat biased."

I squirmed with pleasure. "Thank you."

"Given this is not my field and I have little experience or expertise to bring to bear, would my feedback have any value to you?"

And that was when I realized he was self-conscious too—in his own way—and wanting to be helpful. It steeled my nerves and made me nod pointlessly into the phone. "Absolutely."

My trepidation wasn't entirely unjustified. You didn't become a billionaire through sensitivity and good karma. I was half expecting him to annihilate me—not maliciously, but by dint of having no conception of how lesser mortals might feel about things. But he was actually perfect. Focused and thoughtful and…gentle, so that rather than leaving me crushed into the dust, I felt weirdly excited about what I'd written. The ways I could refine it and make it even better.

None of his observations were particularly harsh—they just drew my attention in small, careful ways to places where my meaning wasn't quite clear or the structure wasn't quite right. It wasn't anything any other moderately astute reader couldn't have told me. Except it was exactly what I needed. And it was even better because it was Caspian.

I didn't for a moment believe this was how he interacted when he was billionaire-ing. But it still offered a glimpse of that side of him. A man who, for all his cold ways and his locked-up heart, understood people. And how to motivate and inspire them.

"I, ah, I hope it's useful," he finished. "I'm not exactly a literary critic."

"It's wonderful. You're wonderful."

He made a snuffly noise, which I thought might have been embarrassment. And was adorable. Then cleared his throat. "Remember our pact."

"I'm going to make these changes and I'll send it. Promise promise promise."

"Then I should probably say good night."

"I guess you probably should."

Except…neither of us did. We just hung around in the silence like teenagers.

Until Caspian cleared his throat again. "I'll see you on Friday."

"I'm crossing my fingers for the future of the dollar, the euro, and the yen."

"As am I. Good night, Arden."

And then he was gone.

As laid down by the terms of our pact—OMG, Caspian could be the *cutest* sometimes—I gave my article one last edit and then fired it off to *Milieu*.

I really hoped they wanted it. Abandoned hospital rave seemed so them. It was quirky and unusual and—honestly—the whole affair had reeked of privilege. Of exclusivity and payoffs and self-conscious slumming. An ultimately upper-class hobby. I also hoped the fact I'd sent it at 2 a.m. made me look like a wild party animal. Rather than just, say, horrendously unemployed.

Regardless, I felt shiny and accomplished as I put my laptop away and gingerly rolled myself up in the duvet. I did wonder how well I'd sleep, given the requirement to lie on my stomach. But I didn't wonder long.

Because in minutes I was gone. Blissfully, totally gone.

CHAPTER 6

I only woke up because I could smell smoke. Not house-burning-down type smoke. The lightly-toasted skunk-flavored smoke that meant someone had weed nearby.

I rolled over with a muffled moan, which was followed by an entirely unmuffled yell. Ellery was sitting right there, back against the footrest, spliff in her hand.

She took a nonchalant toke. "So you're here."

"Um, you're in my bedroom."

"What is this—a be-more-obvious contest?"

"No, it's a…" I was way too nonconsensually naked for banter. "What are you doing here?"

She shrugged and kept on smoking. For all her half-closed eyes and general stoner air, you didn't have to be Jean Grey to notice she didn't seem entirely happy. She was wearing New Rocks, suspender tights, and a barely there T-shirt dress with the Rolling Stones *Sticky Fingers* tongue on it. From the smudged glitter on her eyelids, she'd probably been out all night. I guess I was lucky she hadn't a brought a bunch of friends with her this time.

"Do you want to crash?" I tried. "Take a shower or something?"

Another shrug. Another drag.

I resisted the urge to flap the smoke away with my hand. "Are you really just going to sit there? Getting high? On my bed?"

Shrug. I was sensing a theme.

"Okay, fine. But I think I might go back to sleep if it's all the same to you."

Since no answer forthcame, I wriggled onto my stomach, tucked myself into the duvet, and stuffed my head under the pillow. I didn't actually believe I would prance off to slumberland with my…uh…okay I was still drawing a blank on what to call whatever I was doing with Caspian…with Caspian's sister sitting right there, but it was better than effortfully extracting whatever the fuck was up Ellery's arse.

"Are you coming to my birthday or what?" she asked, the moment I was settled. "Caspian was supposed to give you an invitation. But probably he didn't bother."

I refused to exit the pillow. "I got it. And I'm definitely coming."

"You didn't RSVP."

"I haven't had time." Also RSVPing scared the crap out of me. What if I did it wrong and everybody was secretly laughing at me?

"If you don't RSVP they won't let you in."

"Ellery, what time is it?"

No reply.

I sighed into the bed. "I'll RSVP today. I promise."

There was a long silence. I was starting to regret my sleep-based strategy because it meant I was essentially stuck facedown with nothing to do until Ellery got bored, passed out, or we both died of old age.

"It's lame."

If Hazel had been here, she'd have thrown back *not as lame as your use of ableist language*, just like she did when I was in my teens. The words sounded so familiar in my head it was almost as if she was there to say them. I thought better of trying them out on Ellery, though. "What is?"

"The party."

That was a pretty low-key way of describing what was likely to be the poshest do of my life. A party was when you went to someone's house with a bottle of £4.99 wine and ended up sitting on the floor because the living room was too small for the twelve people who'd turned up. A masquerade ball was… something else. "It sounds, uh, amazing."

"It's Trudy's thing."

I de-pillowed and turned, settling the bits of me that needed it as carefully as possible. "Trudy?"

She muttered something.

"Huh?"

"My mother." Her already husky voice had acquired that weed-hoarse edge so she sounded like Lauren Bacall in a bad mood.

"Um, you call your mother Trudy?"

She glanced up, her strange blue-green eyes sparking. "Text-book, aren't I?"

"I'm not your counselor."

She unfolded her legs and climbed off the bed, boot buckles jingling. Took the final drag of her joint and then vanished with the roach. Truthfully, I was relieved she didn't just toss it onto the carpet or something.

As soon as she was out of sight, I shot out of bed, pulled on a pair of boxers and the biggest T-shirt I had—which I'd got at a John Grant concert, and the only size they'd had left was apparently elephantine. It said *callipygian* on it, with the definition underneath. Nik had bought it for me. Since it definitely applied.

I was trying to bring order to my hair, which had assumed its usual sleeping position of every-fucking-where when Ellery came back. She lingered in the doorway, toeing at the wall in a not-quite-kicking it way.

"I didn't know where you'd gone," she said finally.

I blinked. "Uh, home? I mean, back to Kinlochbervie, where my family live."

"Did he hurt you? Is that why you had to leave?"

"Well…kind of."

Her hands clenched into fists and now she did kick the wall, making me flinch. "Then you should have stayed away. He hurt his last boyfriend too. He hurts everyone. So they leave."

Oh God. I had no hope of untangling that: layers of perception and interpretation and implication about people I hardly knew in a situation I only partially understood. "I left because we had an argument and I thought he didn't want me here. But it was a moderately-sized misunderstanding and we've sorted it out now."

She glared at me. "I had to ring him."

"Ring who?"

"Caspian. I don't like having to ring my brother. Because I couldn't find you. He told me it was none of my business."

Wow. That was a seriously dick move on Caspian's part.

Which was when I got it. I'd hurt her. Or, rather, I'd acted like she was irrelevant to me, and that had allowed her own stupidhead brother to hurt her. It was a realization that helped banish a lot of my own frustration. "I'm so sorry. Of course it was your business."

"We've only hung out once. I don't care where you go or what you do."

"You know, I'm not going to leave, Ellery." Now I'd figured out what was happening, it was easy to ignore what she was actually saying and try to address what she meant. Or, at least, what I thought was bothering her.

"That's what Nathaniel said."

Nathaniel. *Again.* It was all I could do to keep myself gruntled. "Yeah, well. I'm not him." I seemed to be saying that a lot these days.

"He promised he'd always be there for me." Ellery drove her boot even more viciously at the poor, defenseless, very expensive wall.

I sat down on the edge of the bed in the hope that it might encourage her to stop and sit down too. It didn't. "You got on with him, then?"

"He was okay."

From Ellery this was practically a declaration of undying devotion. And, God, when was I going to stop getting all freaked out over Nathaniel? Every time I heard his name, I got skewered by this spike of bad feels. Sort of general dislike and, well, I guess it was some relation of jealousy. This nasty sense of always following in his footsteps.

I fully intended to be a mature grown-up about it. Unfortunately, what came out of my mouth was: "Did he go to many raves with you?"

Ellery glanced up—her eyes as sharp and bright as her sudden grin. Apparently, in being sullen and pathetic, I'd said the right thing, somehow. "No." She finally stopped beating up the apartment. Slinking back into the room, she flumped onto the floor, knees pulled up to her chin so she was a grumpy knot of boots and legs and elbows. "We did other stuff. It was…I dunno. Like having a proper brother. But Caspian fucked it up."

I didn't want to argue with Ellery. But at the same time, I wouldn't have been much of a friend if I'd twiddled my thumbs while she said unreasonable shit. "You wanted your brother to stay with a guy who didn't make him happy?"

"Nathaniel was good for him."

"By what metric?" She glared at me and I knew I was pushing my luck. But I continued anyway, "Look, it's really hard to understand relationships from the outside. And, besides, you're being super inconsistent right now."

"Super inconsistent?" she repeated, with a sarcastic little lilt.

"Well, either you hate Caspian, in which case you wouldn't care whether he's with someone good for him, or maybe you do care about him at least a little bit. And either Nathaniel was your friend, in which case Caspian should have been irrelevant, or…or he wasn't." Okay, that hadn't gone quite to plan. "Shit, sorry, that sounds bad."

She was tugging at the buckles on her boots, making them catch and clink. "He said it was too complicated. And painful. Hanging out with me when he wasn't—oh whatever. Doesn't matter. Caspian takes everything. He always has."

I couldn't keep arguing with her about people I didn't know and a past that wasn't mine. So I changed tack. Gave her something I *did* understand. And could guarantee. "He won't take me."

"Yeah right."

"It's true. Chicks before dicks."

She gave me a swift, sardonic look from beneath the tangles of her hair. "He's definitely that."

"And I'm really sorry I went running off to Scotland without telling you. I was just messed up and confused. I promise I won't do it again. At least, I won't if you give me your phone number so I can communicate with you instead of waiting for you to randomly turn up."

"Whatever." But she tossed her iPhone at me.

I added my name to her address book and sent myself a text before passing her mobile back.

There was a slightly awkward silence.

She fiddled with her phone a while. It had a gorgeous mother of pearl case that glinted with its own soft rainbows when it caught the light. Not very Ellery. Or maybe very Ellery. It was hard to tell sometimes.

"So." She glanced up, at last. "Want to shoot some people?"

I made a gurgling noise.

She watched me for a little while, and then the corner of her mouth ticked up into a smirk. "I don't like Mondays but not in the mass murder way. I meant on the PS4."

The last time I'd fired up the epic flat-screen in the sitting area had been when Nik was staying. Because, the thing was, home cinema felt ridiculously fucking lonely if there was only you.

"Sure," I said.

We got ourselves settled on the sofa and Ellery got everything set up, finally tossing the second controller into my lap. We played some kind of Call of Duty-alike (actually, it probably *was* Call of Duty) and I was basically terrible—dropping grenades on my own feet, banging into Ellery's character, and wincing every time I had to shoot a person-shaped collection of pixels. By contrast, she was positively surgical, cutting through our enemies, headshot by headshot by headshot.

When she wasn't laughing at me, anyway. She had a good laugh—throaty and uninhibited, just rarely seen in the wild. Strangely, it was when she most reminded me of Caspian.

I ordered a pizza at the point that a sensible-food-having time rolled round. It was Ellery's choice, though she only ate a slice and then did coke off the box.

"Problem?" she asked, catching me staring.

"No. I mean…Um. Drugs are bad, aren't they?"

"This isn't bad. It's some of the purest shit you can get." She swung her legs up onto the sofa and sprawled out, lazy as an alley cat who had beaten up all the other cats and nicked the best spot in the sun. "Sure you don't want some?"

I shook my head. "Aren't you worried you'll get addicted or your nose will fall off or something?"

"Nah. They'll send me back to rehab before I go full Winehouse."

"Good to know."

We were quiet for a bit. It was probably the longest I'd ever seen Ellery sit still.

"Why do you do it?" I blurted out, sounding like Squarey

McSquareson, the Squarest Square in Squaresville. The only place in the universe they still said *square*.

"Do what?"

"You know."

"Ohhhh, you mean getting tweaked. Getting geeked. Blowing out. Making it snow. Hitting a bump. Chillin' with mah white bitches."

I pouted. "I feel mocked and derided."

"You should. Because that's what's happening to you."

"It's not a completely unreasonable question," I mumbled.

"It's boring, which is worse. I do it because it feels good. Obviously."

"But it's not real."

"Have you noticed nobody ever says that about the shitty stuff?"

"I…hadn't thought of it like that."

She gave one of her I'm-almost-too-apathetic-to-express-my-apathy shrugs. "Life is just another come down. Least this way I get to choose."

"Steady on." She'd managed to put me off the pizza. Apparently pepperoni didn't go with ennui. "There must be something else that makes you happy."

"Like what?"

"Um, a beautiful sunset?"

She shot me a look from beneath her half-closed eyes: this sliver of greenish malice. "A beautiful sunset? What the fuck is wrong with you?"

"I panicked, okay?"

No reply.

Wow. In less than ten minutes, I'd achieved an almost one

hundred percent fun to awkward conversation rate. Go me.

Ellery swung her boots off the sofa and stood up.

"I'm going now."

A glance out the nearest window confirmed it was late and dark. And maybe cold. "You can crash here if you like. I promise not to keep saying stupid things."

"Got somewhere to be."

That could have meant anything from shooting up in the toilets of a twenty-four-hour McDonalds or floating down the Thames in a bag. Although probably she was just on her way to some kind of soul-crushingly trendy party.

Anyway, I wasn't her keeper.

She had more than enough of those already.

"You can come if you like?" she offered.

Admittedly, One Hyde Park wasn't the most homey of places. But at least I was allowed to hang out there in my underpants. "Once I've engaged pajama mode I'm kind of locked in."

"I get it. Pajamas are dangerously cozy. Fuck pajamas."

And with that, she was gone.

Since I'd fallen into that weird space where it was too early to go to bed and too late to do anything useful—like attempt to have a career—I decided to fix my toes. Marshalling my bottles of nail polish, I got rid of the remains of the Sally Bowles experiment, and repainted in alternating sparkly purple and silver. While I was glad Caspian couldn't see me, hunched unattractively over my own feet like something from a *National Geographic* pull-out, I was hoping he'd appreciate the end result. After all, he'd told me in Kinlochbervie that he found my taste in self-decoration distracting. Which now I thought about it, didn't sound all that flattering. But the way he'd said it...oh God the way he'd said it. Insta-melt.

Proud of my handiwork, but also conscious that Caspian might not be up for a barrage of needy selfies, I sent it to Nik.

Nothing.

Boo.

And here I thought Nik could always be depended upon to find me cute on demand. What time was it in Boston anyway? Eight? Nine? A quick social media stalk soon revealed he was in the on-campus pub with some of his MIT friends. They looked like they were having fun, huddled round a rickety table and drinking what was probably craft beer. It gave me a weird pang for my barely over university days, though it was mainly the sense of community I missed, not so much the whole being expected to get a degree in English thing.

At that moment my phone buzzed. It was Nik:

Sry, crap reception. Adorbs.

I sent him back a kissy face, feeling mildly bad for having interrupted his evening with my feet, and then went to bed. Lounged around on the edge of sleep, wanking idly, and thinking about Caspian. About Friday.

Which was foreverrrrrr away.

Though, actually, while I generally preferred my gratification undelayed, it wasn't too bad—waiting for Caspian like this. Knowing I meant something to him and that he wanted to be with me as much as I wanted to be with him. There was no more nervy uncertainty, just a warm flutter of anticipation. Maybe we'd be able to spend the whole weekend together. A prospect so sweet it made my newly bright toes curl as I came.

CHAPTER 7

I spent the next day glued to my email. Just in case *Milieu* were all "we loved your article so much we got in touch with you straight away even though that literally never happens."

It hadn't happened.

So I dedicated myself to being moderately productive, which mainly involved restocking my food supplies and writing, and only fretting about *Milieu*/daydreaming about Caspian a little bit. Nik woke up hungover in the middle of my afternoon and we long-distance buddy-watched an episode of *Supergirl*, me curled on the sofa, Nik apparently still in bed and not consistently conscious.

I was back in the study and back at work—go me—when Ellery said, "Come on, we're leaving."

"Oh my God." I finished having a minor heart attack. "Are you ever going to like knock or warn me before turning up?"

She thought about it for a moment. "No."

"But what if you get here and I'm bonking your brother?"

"Then I'll be psychologically traumatized and you should feel bad about yourself."

I abandoned that line of argument as a dud and asked instead, "Where are we going?"

"I told you. Out."

I glanced at the time on my phone, surprised at how quickly the day had passed. I'd damn near worked a nine to five, if you discounted the fact I'd gone shopping, watched TV, and not got up at nine. But, y'know, I was definitely getting there.

"Okay, okay." I closed my laptop. "Let me get changed."

Ellery's own outfit—an off-the-shoulder jumper that simply said DEAD, a floral skirt, black tights, Docs, and a backpack with cat skeletons on it—didn't offer much insight into possible destinations. It suggested something fairly casual but, knowing Ellery, that was probably how she'd dress for tea with the queen. I settled for jeans and my Boy George T-shirt. Another present from Nik, it was just a stylized eye, very blue, with the familiar slash of a brow, a touch of makeup, and a single colored tear sliding from the corner. I mean, the queen liked Boy George, right? She'd offered him an OBE once. Well, allegedly. I flung my velvet jacket over the top, grabbed my phone, and that was me: ready to go.

We headed out of the building and down into the street. It was actually shaping up to be a fairly nice evening. Not exactly warm because, y'know, England, but the sky was swirly blue and a pale silver orb was hanging in it. I'd seen pictures of such a thing on the internet and I think it was the sun. Ellery produced a pair of dark glasses and put them on. They were huge and round and covered her from brows to scowl.

Thus protected from the merest hint of summer, she led me into Hyde Park through the Albert gate. At least, I thought it was the Albert gate—it was sandwiched between a couple of embassies, wide enough to admit a carriage, and there were weird statues of animals on either side of it, which struck me as the sort of thing Victoria was liable to stick her husband's name on. It led to a sandy avenue lined by hazy green trees, broken up every now and again by wrought-iron lampposts.

"Rotten Row," I said, getting all excited.

Ellery turned her head slightly in my direction. "S'not that bad."

"Are you seriously telling me there's something I know about London that you don't?" She didn't answer so I took that as a grudging yes, and went on, "The name's a corruption of *Route du Roi*, and it was the fashionable place for ladies and gentlemen to ride out during the Regency period."

"I'm not into rich people shit."

"Spoken like a true rich person."

That earned me another head-turn, but her mouth wasn't quite as sulky as usual. In fact, I would even have gone so far as to say her expression was amused. "How do you know this stuff?" she asked.

"Georgette Heyer. Obviously."

"Oh." I couldn't see her eyes, but her tone suggested they were rolling. "Romances."

"What's wrong with romances? And don't give me some line about them being trashy or patriarchal or always having the same plot because everything always has the same plot."

"Nah. They're just about people. Can't be fucked with people."

The righteous wind wheezed out of my sails. "Aren't all books fundamentally about people?"

"*Watership Down* is about rabbits."

"Allegorical people rabbits though."

"No, it isn't. They have their own language and faith and culture, and think about things totally differently."

I wasn't sure if I'd genuinely outraged her with my thoughts on *Watership Down*. So I did a conciliatory backpedal for the sake of social harmony. And also because I'd never heard her sound so passionate, and it was kind of adorable. "I guess. And, anyway, that book is really fucked up."

She grinned. "Isn't it?"

We walked on in silence. Turned left at the tennis courts and ended up back on the Kensington Road, between the Albert Memorial and the Royal Albert Hall. This part of London was basically a noncon Albert sandwich whichever way you went.

"Come on."

Ellery stomped off purposefully, looping round to the south side of the concert hall. I'd never actually been this close to it before. It was a tiered cake of a building in red brick and terracotta, wrapped up this decorative frieze about the advancements of Arts and Science and works of industry of all nations. I knew that because it was written right there in huge shiny letters. You had to love the Victorians. I mean, apart from the colonialism. And the bigotry. And the widespread social oppression. Okay, maybe the Victorians sucked.

Once we got to what, I guess, was the front it was clear something epic was going on. There were two lines of people running down each side of the Queen's Steps and, from the general relaxed atmosphere—there were even little clumps of picnickers—it looked like everyone was in it for the long haul. It was probably the most British thing I'd ever seen. Because, say what you will about us as a nation, we sure as hell give good queue.

Up near the front on the right was a little group all playing cards. Though they stopped when Ellery approached and an older woman, with a cluster of white curls, got up from a fishing stool in order to—OMG—*hug* her. And Ellery didn't flip out or bite anyone. It was super weird.

"This is Arden," Ellery said, when she was finally released. "Arden, this is Flossie, Dick, Mikhail, Janet, and John."

I waved a little awkwardly, since I had no idea what these people had to do with each other, or with Ellery. With the exception of Mikhail, they were all in their fifties at least. John, in his tweedy, elbow-patch-sporting jacket, looked like an academic. And Janet like the subject of that Jenny Joseph poem.

Dick peered up from the latest George RR Martin. "Where've you been, Ellery girl? We thought you'd forgotten us."

"Just been busy."

"You've missed out."

"Oh yeah? Highlights?"

Flossie reclaimed her seat. "This German couple took Miskha's spot. But we soon had them put to rights."

"I meant," said the alien being who had replaced Ellery, "musically."

"The Halle, I think. Gave us some smashing Mahler."

Ellery shrugged. Now that was more like her. "Das Lied?"

They nodded.

"Eh. Every time I hear that, I'm like…hurry up and die already. Don't hang there in D forever."

John was polishing his glasses on the edge of his sleeve. "We should have guessed our lonely, half-forgotten Bela would draw you out."

Another Ellery shrug.

"Did you know he was supposed to have composed much of this piece while at a nudist camp?"

"Look that up on Wikipedia, did you?"

John's forehead went pink as the others laughed.

"Anyway"—Ellery pulled out her phone and checked the time—"we'd better get going. Got our own queue to join."

Oh great. We were queuing as well?

My face must have reflected something of my feelings on the subject because Dick smiled up at me. "Never you mind, lad. It's part of the fun."

"You should come with us one day," Flossie was saying to Ellery.

"Nah. Arena's for people who want to be part of something. Gallery's for people who don't."

"You know you're always welcome."

Ellery smiled—and, wow, she looked bizarrely sweet. "Save me a heave."

"If you save us a ho."

Then she caught me by the hand and dragged me off down the steps. And I couldn't say I was any more illuminated. Our queue led all the way from the west side of the Hall, along a street, and past the back of a church.

"We're good," Ellery announced, having sized it up.

"Are we?"

"Oh yes," said the lady in front of us, "I've been right at the bottom of Bremner Road and still got in."

Since something was clearly expected of me, I offered a slightly anxious "yay."

Ellery lowered herself to the ground, crossed her legs, and pulled her backpack into her lap. Then began rummaging around inside it like Mary Poppins had gone seriously off the rails.

Not really knowing what else to do, I plopped down next to her and pulled my knees up to my chin. A suspicion was…not so much forming as being ominously confirmed. "Ellery," I asked, "are we at the Proms?"

"Maybe."

"Why are we at the Proms?"

She shrugged.

My knowledge of the Proms was scanty to put it mildly: they were an annual classical musical festival and the last night of them was a big deal and would be shown on BBC2 or something, with much pomp and circumstance and fireworks. "I thought you weren't into rich people shit."

"Arden." Ellery hooked a finger under her glasses and pulled them down her nose so I could receive the full force of her appalled look. "*Anyone* can go to the Proms. That's the whole point."

"But I don't know anything about classical music."

"It's not about knowledge."

"Right now it seems to be about my arse getting numb. How long do we have to wait?"

There was a lengthy silence. Finally, Ellery took off her sunglasses and folded the arms with a click. "I knew you wouldn't get it."

Should have seen that coming. I stifled a sigh. "How can I get it," I said, as gently as I could, "when you won't tell me anything?"

Silence again.

"Like…" Ellery's newly naked eyes looked oddly vulnerable—their shades softened by the sunlight "…ever since 1890-something the Proms have been about making music available to the people who get told that shit isn't for them. All you have to do is turn up and pay a fiver—well, it's six quid now. And you can go to a concert."

I risked a small smile. "Wow, that's pretty cool."

"She's right," said Unasked for Queue Lady. "This way you get to be part of something that goes back over a hundred years."

Ellery didn't exactly strike me as a raging traditionalist. "I just don't know what we're doing here."

"Because I like it, okay?" Her raised voice startled a couple of pigeons on a nearby wall and they took to the skies with a crackle of wings. "And you asked. You asked what I liked. And I trusted you. So either…fuck off and die. Or have a strawberry."

"Have a what?"

"A strawberry. I brought strawberries." She wrenched open her backpack and pulled out a brown paper bag.

"Oooh. Don't mind if I do." Unasked for Queue Lady leaned over me and helped herself.

"Well, maybe I won't fuck off and die," I said.

Ellery was still flushed and full of scowls. "Yeah, whatever."

"I'm sorry."

"Yeah, whatever."

"Can I have a strawberry?" I made my cutest face.

For a moment, I thought she was going to say no, but then she relented. "Oh all right."

It was probably the closest to forgiveness I was ever going to get. And the strawberry tasted amazing, sparkly sweet and bright as the juice exploded over my tongue.

"What are we going to see…um, hear?" I asked.

"*Bluebeard's Castle.*"

"I shouldn't know that, right?"

Unasked for Queue Lady gave a little hop. "You're in for such a treat, love."

Ellery just put her sunglasses back on, her lips curving into an unreadable smile.

CHAPTER 8

What had started out as the worst queuing experience of my life gradually became one of the best. Not that, in all honesty, there was that much competition. The evening got a flood of last-minute warmth, like a guilty start from the sun just as it was slipping away. I lay with my head on Ellery's lap and she fed me the rest of the strawberries—at least the ones she could wrest from Unasked for Queue Lady.

I couldn't help but notice that lots of other people were drinking wine but Ellery had gone all ascetic on me and only brought water. Probably it was the right call—I wasn't sure whether my capacity to appreciate classical music would be improved or diminished if I was wankered. And, besides, I was slightly floaty anyway—on the balmy evening air and the brush of heat across my skin and the strange liberation of having nothing to do but wait.

We were briefly interrupted by the click-whir-flash of a camera. And I startled out of a not-quite-daydream to find a...well, there was no nice way to say it, a twitchy, rat-like man in a leather jacket taking photos of us from the other side of the street.

"New boyfriend, Ellie?" he called out.

"A friend," she threw back. "Now fuck off."

"Aren't you going to introduce me?"

"Oh suuure. This is Billy Boyle, an independent photojournal-ist. And this"—she flapped a laconic hand in my direction—"is none of your fucking business."

"You know I'll find out anyway."

"And you know I'll set your car on fire."

"I love it when you get feisty." He gave a frankly creepy shiver.

"Okay. Fine. How about you fuck off now and I'll be at Tansy Stourburton's twenty-first on Friday."

"You'll make it worth my while."

"I'm hurt." Ellery gave a magnificent yawn. "It's like you don't know me at all."

Boyle grinned with sharp teeth. "I'll be watching."

"Yeah, yeah. Try not to get cancer."

Unasked for Queue Lady had listened to the exchange with unabashed curiosity. As soon as Boyle had oozed away, she turned to Ellery and asked excitedly, "Are you famous?"

"Nope." Ellery settled her sunglasses more firmly on her nose. "I'm notorious."

A couple of fairly relaxed hours later, there was a judder down the line of people, which was snaking so far beyond us I couldn't see the end anymore, and we were moving. Funneled, with surprising efficiency, through door 10, and into the Royal Albert Hall. Ellery, who had a crumpled tenner and two pound coins already in hand, paid for me.

Then there were stairs.

A lot of stairs.

No, really, so many stairs.

We finally emerged, me wheezing and Ellery barely winded, onto the gallery. It was kind of otherworldly: a corridor of gleaming stone that curled gently around the entire hall. Ellery dragged me into a space between two decorative pillars and…Oh God, we were high, the tiers of seats sloping away from us so sharply it made me feel like I was about to topple over. Even though what I was actually doing was clinging to the rail as if I was on a roller coaster.

Down in the…was it still a mosh pit if you were in a concert hall? Anyway, the people jiggling about down there were pin-heads. And the orchestra might as well have been a flea circus. Other prommers were filtering in behind us and around us, and there was a bit of jostling for the best spaces, but it didn't feel crowded at all—especially in comparison to the audience below, who looked like hundreds and thousands tossed too liberally over an ice cream sundae.

Ellery was stretched out on a travel rug, her backpack tucked under her head. "You sitting down?"

"But I won't be able to see."

"It's music. You listen."

A quick glance around us confirmed that, while some people had chosen to stand by the railing, others had brought cushions and blankets of their own. No wonder Ellery liked it here—it was its own secret world.

After a moment or two, I lay down beside her and rested my head against her shoulder. Considering we were about to spend an hour or more on a stone floor, it was pretty comfortable, and I could still see through the gaps in the railing—mainly the arches on the other side of the gallery, which shone faintly gold, and the strange disks hanging from the ceiling.

"It's like an alien planetscape," I said, pointing.

"They're for the acoustics. Apparently, there used to be an echo, so they put those up in the sixties."

It made sense. Giant floating ceiling mushrooms: the solution you'd come up with if you were high on LSD and sexual liberation.

Various noises floated up to us: the jingle-thonks of an orchestra getting ready and the rustle-creaks of an audience settling down. The lights slowly began to dim.

"Hang on." Ellery thrust a bundle of papers at me. "I brought you a libretto."

"You wha—"

And then a deep voice broke across the darkness: *Once upon a time, where did this happen? Was it outside or within? Once upon a time, there was an old story. But what does it mean, my lords and fine ladies? The song begins and you watch me, watching you, the curtain of your eyelids raised. But where is the stage? Is it outside or within us, my lords and fine ladies?*

The music crept through the words, twisted round them like ivy. A gathering sense of foreboding, sobbed softly over cello strings. Then clarinets…violins…and, oh, I was there. In a dark castle, where the walls wept, and the air tasted of blood. It turned out only the prologue was in English and the rest was…um…something else? But Ellery was right, I didn't need the libretto. Not when I had two voices and a whole orchestra to tell me a too-familiar fairy tale of love and pain.

Despite being up in the gallery, I didn't feel far away from the music at all. I felt surrounded by it. Suffused by it. Like I'd taken emotional heroin and nothing I would experience from this moment forward could ever be so pure a hit. It was perfect, it was overwhelming, it was ridiculously fucking numinous.

The bit in the middle, when Judith opened the fifth door to reveal Bluebeard's kingdom, and the orchestra just...*exploded*—as if the music itself was light—and the mezzo-soprano hit a note I had no idea human beings were capable of producing, I honestly thought my heart would burst. And, afterward, when the sixth door revealed a lake of tears, I started crying too, almost without realizing I was.

I liked it, is what I'm saying.

And, when it was over, and Judith had taken her place among the other wives, and everything was dark again, there was this moment of absolute silence.

Followed by a storm of stamping. And then rapturous applause.

I lay back and tried to remember how to do ordinary things like breathing and thinking and functioning.

Ellery still had her eyes closed, one arm flung above her head. There was something oddly abandoned about the pose. Not exactly sexual because, God knows, I didn't want to think of Caspian's sister like that. But content maybe?

"Well?" she asked.

I gave a shaky laugh. Because there was only one answer really. "It was so good I nearly peed my pants."

"Come on." She grabbed my hand. "Let's get out of here before we get Debussied. Can't stand that syrupy shit."

* * *

I was slightly dazed as I followed Ellery out of the Royal Albert Hall and into the lingering warmth of the night. We wandered silently between the pale white mansions and red-brick towers of Kensington, letting the memory of the music linger.

Next time I paid attention to my surroundings, we were on the Old Brompton Road. This was the closest Kensington got to having a commercial district, but it was still Kensington so that meant incredibly posh flats, boutiques that sold nothing anybody would reasonably want to buy, upmarket restaurants, unnecessarily large branches of Pret A Manger, and somewhere in the middle of it all the pub where *Private Eye* was founded.

Ellery grabbed my hand and pulled me into a late-opening gelato parlor so dinky that I would probably have walked straight past it if I'd been on my own. The sight of the long counter, with the different ice cream flavors all fluffed up like perfect little clouds, and as bright as birds of paradise, made me legit squeak.

It earned me a dubious look from Ellery. "You okay?"

"OMG"—I flailed like a Disney princess about to go to the ball—"yes yes yes."

"Because you look like you're about to die."

"I *have* died. And I've gone to heaven."

Ellery was still mid facepalm as I hustled her over to the menu.

"What's best?" I asked, jumping up and down. "What do you recommend?"

"It's all fine."

It the sort of place where they told you exactly where everything came from: Grand Cru chocolate, Channel Island milk,

Chilean sultanas. Where even the pistachios were superior. And so, of course, I wanted to eat everything.

Ellery ordered a chocolate cone of green tea gelato—though they called it *Tè Verde*. And I finally overcame my greed-paralysis enough to get the stracciatella. Since, as far as I was concerned, the only thing better than chocolate or vanilla was when you were allowed to have chocolate and vanilla together. There might have been a moral in there somewhere.

The place was nearly empty, what with it being close to nine on a Tuesday, so we sat in the bay-window and stuffed our faces. At least, I stuffed my face. Ellery ate ice cream with the same air of mild contempt she brought to everything.

Well, everything except music. As I'd learned today.

"Thank you for this," I said. "It's been the best."

She shrugged. "Yeah."

"So um"—I chased a curl of chocolate with the edge of my spoon—"any particular reason for that opera?"

"Maybe I just like the music."

"And the story was irrelevant?"

She gave me a look I couldn't quite read, her eyes greener than they were blue in this softer light, and less like Caspian than usual. "Well, what do you think?"

At this rate we would be here all night. Like the vultures in *The Jungle Book*, I broke cover. "I think Judith chose her fate."

"Huh. Interesting. Because I think she married a psycho who murdered her."

"I think"—I squirmed—"it's a touch more ambiguous than that."

"He has a torture chamber in his head."

"But also a lake of tears."

She crunched off the end of her cone. "Probably from the people he's tortured."

"Or maybe it's all him: his own pain and grief and darkness. The wives could represent the hopes and dreams he's lost."

"*Or* maybe some castles are dark and there's nothing you can do about it."

"Except, y'know, accept the castle is dark. Instead of worrying about how it isn't light."

"Whatever." Ellery pulled out her phone and checked the time. "Okay. I've got to go."

I glanced at my half-finished ice cream and then at the counter, wondering if I had room for another scoop. Because, fuck me, the stuff was amazing. So rich and sweet and sharp all at the same time. "I might stay here. For the rest of my life."

For a moment, I thought she was going to say something but she just stood there, idly kicking at the leg of her chair.

"It's not like Caspian's going to murder me," I said.

"Yeah, but maybe you deserve a nicer castle."

And, with that, she picked up her backpack and disappeared into the night, leaving me with my stracciatella and some slightly tangled thoughts about my relationship.

Which quickly unraveled into me missing Caspian. Wanting to hold his hand across the table. Share a milkshake with him. Lick the sweetness from his mouth.

That was the thing about billionaire non-boyfriends, though. They could do anything. Be anything. Reshape the whole fucking world.

But you'd probably always be left eating ice cream by yourself.

CHAPTER 9

My Instagram account, which I only intermittently remembered to update, had been a lot more lively since @i_hate_ellery had started tagging me. But I woke to find it was going notify-crazy, with no intervention from her at all. Which, given that my last post had been a suggestive butternut squash I'd seen at the farmers' market down on Bute Street, meant that something else was going on.

Cringing, I opened Google and fed it my own name.

Not a bean, beyond my usual stuff, social media accounts I'd forgotten about, and some of the articles I'd written.

With an increasing swallowed-live-lizard feeling in my stomach, I tried: Eleanor Hart.

And boom.

In every afternoon tea-and-gossip magazine from *Hello!* to goodbye, there we were: me with my head in Ellery's lap as she fed me a strawberry in a fashion that, to those unfamiliar with the inherent sensuality of my strawberry-eating technique, probably looked a bit intimate. The byline was mostly something like "Notorious Wild Child Eleanor Hart Spotted with New Mystery Man at Proms" because the internet murdered brevity the way video killed the radio star.

For a few minutes, I just stared. Tried to figure how I was feeling—if I was scared or angry or violated or confused or all of them. Because if my Instagram was anything to go by, the mystery man ship had sailed. Had *way* sailed.

What the hell was I supposed to do? Only one thing for it, really. I rang Bellerose.

He picked up as swiftly as ever. "Arden."

"Um, I don't know if this is something I should be bothering you with."

"Well, neither will I unless you tell me."

"It's on the internet. Google Ellery."

Then came the tap of his keyboard. And a thoughtful silence. Followed by, "Are you at the apartment?"

"Yes."

"I'll be there in an hour."

I wasn't sure that made me feel better or worse. In any case, it called for trousers. Unfortunately getting dressed couldn't last me sixty minutes and so, by the time Bellerose turned up, I was in knots.

"Am I in trouble?" I blurted out, the moment he was over the threshold.

"Of course not. I wanted you to meet someone." He stepped aside to reveal a slight, elegant, stiletto of man. "This is Alexander Finesilver, of Gisbourne, Finesilver & King. He's the Harts' lawyer."

In all honesty, I didn't find this very reassuring. "Okay?"

"Among other things, he specializes in media litigation and reputation management."

Finesilver smiled at me. And, wow, he was good at smiling. It was positively *bounteous*—warm, genuine, everything you could possibly want in a friendly baring of teeth. "I hope you'll contact me directly if you have any concerns like this again."

And the next thing I knew, he was holding his business card, which was pearl gray and gold, at once opulent and discreet.

"I'm actually pretty concerned right now," I said.

"Understandably, Mr. St. Ives." Another smile.

It was hard to get the measure of him, probably because most people seemed ordinary when Bellerose was standing there like the ridiculous golden Ganymede he was. But Finesilver practically courted it. To shuck your curiosity like water. Pay no attention to the man behind the curtain.

A few minutes later, they were huddled around a laptop on the dining table while I hovered anxiously nearby.

"I don't suppose"—Finesilver glanced up—"you remember anything about when or where these photographs were taken. Or by whom?"

"We were waiting for the Proms. And it was only the one guy. He was sleazy. And…uh…wearing a leather jacket." Arden St. Ives: Witness of the Year. "I think he had brown hair?"

"Sounds like Boyle."

I snapped my fingers. "Yes! That was what Ellery called him."

"Can we try another injunction?" asked Bellerose.

I caught something in Finesilver's eyes—as real and sharp and frightening as the flash of the hidden blade. Everything his smile wasn't. But, when he spoke, his tone was mild enough that I was tempted to convince myself I'd imagined what I'd seen. "It's difficult to make them stick when Miss Hart herself keeps breaking them."

"Obsession can be quite attractive." Bellerose cleared his throat. "Or so I understand."

"He's not her friend."

"Do you think I haven't tried to tell her that?"

"Um." Great, I'd apparently opened my mouth and made words come out of it again. And now they were both staring at me, like lions eyeing up a gazelle across the Serengeti. "They didn't seem very friendly."

"As I'm sure you're aware," murmured Finesilver, "Miss Hart forms complex relationships with those around her."

"I don't know. She did sort of tell him to get cancer and die. That doesn't strike me as *super* complex."

Bellerose's hand curled into a fist on the tabletop. "Arden, this situation is delicate. And Ellery's entanglement with Billy Boyle longstanding. We have put in place several measures to protect her from him. And, in the end, it's Ellery who has broken them all."

He sounded frustrated—and not in the idle, commonplace way he got impatient with me sometimes. This was thorn-in-paw helplessness. Though I didn't think it was for Ellery. Far more likely he was pissed off because there was something he couldn't fix and make neat for Caspian.

"There must be more to it," I said. "I know there's aspects to this situation I don't understand. But Ellery's not...I mean. Ellery doesn't do things for no reason. Even if it's just her reason."

Bellerose's mouth thinned into a mean little line that didn't suit him.

And Finesilver was still radiating an impenetrable field of *trust me, trust me, I'm a nice person.* "I believe she feels in some way connected to him."

"Because he follows her around taking candid photos of her?"

"Because he has done so since she was fifteen years old. And"—he sighed gently—"on one occasion got her to hospital after an overdose."

Oh Ellery. I wanted to hug the living daylights out of her. Which she would have hated.

"I guess"—I shuffled my feet awkwardly—"he can't be all bad, then."

Finesilver's only change of expression was the slight re-angling of a brow. "He took photographs first."

"The matter at hand?" Bellerose turned the screen more toward Finesilver and even less toward me.

Finesilver busied himself with the laptop again. "These are the only photographs circulating and they don't appear to have been picked up by any major outlets. If we do nothing to suggest they might be worth attention, they will be less than flotsam in a day or two."

"And if not?"

"Then," said Finesilver mildly, "I will ensure there is something more newsworthy available to claim attention."

He could do that? Of course he could do that.

"So it's okay?" I asked.

He nodded. "I believe so. Though I will continue to monitor the situation."

"And Caspian isn't cross?"

Uncomprehending silence.

"I mean," I babbled on, "he might not like it if people thought I was, y'know, dating his sister."

Bellerose gave me one of his coolest looks. "He is quite aware of the vagaries of the gutter press."

"Okay. Good. Well, not good but—"

"Though it's possible he might be less circumspect if he thought you were upset. Something I will not be communicating to him." His eyes were steady on mine, and diamond sharp. "Will you?

Wow, he really did not think good things about me. "Of course not. And I'm not actually upset. Just worried Caspian might…see it and not like it."

"Arden, are you laboring under the misapprehension that he spends his afternoons googling you?"

I could have pointed out that Caspian had stalked both my Facebook and my Instagram feed looking for me. But I didn't. Because I had *dignity.*

And then Finesilver slipped back into the conversation with the grace of a fencer. "There's only one potential cause for concern here. And that is if details about Mr. St. Ives came to light that would perhaps be better left unilluminated."

I wasn't sure I liked the sound of that. "What kind of details?"

"Oh, anything that could be perceived in particular ways."

"What he means," explained Bellerose, "is have you done anything illegal, embarrassing, or scandalous?"

Embarrassing and/or scandalous covered about eighty percent of my life, and probably the remaining twenty percent was me being asleep. But it also didn't seem like the sort of embarrassing or scandalous that sold copy. I mean, I fell over in front of billionaires a lot. Did that count? "Not really."

"Are there secrets you shouldn't be keeping. Any skeletons in your closet?"

Well. There was my dad. But he wasn't so much a skeleton in my closet as a boogey man. And not remotely relevant. I sighed heavily. "I guess it was going to come out eventually. When I was at university, I fell in with this elitist crowd of loners, and we were all completely enthralled by our classics professor. He filled us with wild passion for the ways of the ancient Greeks and we started holding these, like, legit *bacchanals*. Unfortunately, we accidentally murdered this random farmer. And then one of our other friends to cover it up. And then our classics professor ran away and someone else committed suicide. And now everything is ruined and we are very sad and I have bad dreams."

"I'll take that as a no, then." Finesilver looked faintly amused.

Bellerose didn't. "Arden, we're trying to help you."

"Actually"—I tucked my hands into the pockets of my jeans—"you're trying to protect Caspian and his family. Which is cool. But not necessarily the same thing as helping me."

Finesilver closed the laptop with a gentle click. "You make my job more difficult. But, as far as your own interests are concerned, that is no bad thing."

It was the weirdest praise I'd ever received. But, hey, I'd take it.

Bellerose seemed less impressed. But, then, I had no idea what *could* impress Bellerose. I think it involved being Caspian Hart.

"By the way," he said as he herded us into the hall, "Caspian asked me to make sure you received a parcel, so I brought it with me, rather than having it couriered. It's by the door."

"Oh, right. Thanks."

I waved them off politely, not entirely sure whether I was reassured by their visit or not and turned my attention to the, well...*parcel* didn't really do it justice. It was a work of art: this heavy, dark cream box, discreetly embossed with a golden logo and tied up with the most austerely masculine bow I'd ever seen in my life. I carried it through into the dining area and put it on the table. What on earth had Caspian sent me?

Well, it wasn't going to open itself. I undid the manribbons and took off the lid. Inside, carefully folded and wrapped in tissue paper, was a coat.

The sort of coat you saw on runways and in white-floored boutiques that only stocked about three garments.

The sort of coat that probably cost more than any car I'd ever own.

The sort of coat that had absolutely no business belonging to someone like me.

There was a square of buttercream-colored card lying on top of it. If nothing else, meeting Caspian had been a comprehensive education in shades of posh. "Thinking of you..." was scrawled across the front. I traced my fingers over the harsh slash of the *T*, the curve of the *o*, the generous loops of *g* and *f*. Caspian's hand? I hoped so. Then, turning it over, I burst out laughing as the message continued:

"...getting cold because you never have a coat."

Oh, it had to be him. And whoever had described lovey-dovey feeling as butterflies was way off base. Because I had swooning eels in my stomach. And I just about managed not to press his card against my heart, like a Jane Austen character receiving a letter. Or dance around with it Disney heroine–style, while bluebirds flew round my head.

Then I remembered the actual present.

I drew the coat carefully from its tissue cocoon, shook it out, and put it on. Of course, it was perfect: a simple black trench coat with a high collar and a belt, clinging to my body so well it could have been tailored to my measurements.

It made me feel beautiful and sexy and invincible. And also terrible for being materialistic enough to love it. But I did.

I totally did.

As I brushed my fingers over the smooth fabric, I tried to convince myself I should turn down the amazing present from my billionaire non-boyfriend. That was the right thing to do, wasn't it? I was pretty sure there were nebulous moral and social rules governing the acceptance of extravagant gifts from rich, (slightly) older men.

But I was already sleeping with the rich, (slightly) older man in question. Enthusiastically and for free. And, proportionally speaking, if you looked at it in terms of annual income, a coat like that was probably the equivalent of a packet of crisps and a pint of Stella to Caspian.

Not a big deal at all.

Except…that wasn't true. Because this wasn't just a post-bang bunch of roses he'd told his assistant to arrange. It was something he'd chosen specially.

While thinking of me.

Well. While thinking I was a Dickensian urchin who would freeze to death come winter.

But hey. It was a thought. It counted.

And now I couldn't tell whether I was trying to talk myself into it or out of it, or whether I felt good or bad or what. Maybe it would have been easier if Caspian had actually been here. He would have been able to tell me I deserved to be lavished in expensive gifts. And I could thank him with my hands and mouth and body.

And then wear the coat.

Great. Now I was having a sexy fantasy that essentially amounted to prostituting myself for tailored outerwear.

This was why I couldn't have nice things.

Knowing how busy he was, I didn't want to interrupt him. So I ended up making my awkward thank-you call in the evening. He picked up with velociraptor swiftness on the second ring.

"Hello, Arden."

"Good evening, Mr. Hart."

"Did you...I mean. I sent you something. I trust it arrived."

Oh bless, he sounded, well, not nervous exactly. But eager and trying to cover it up. And I suddenly felt a whole lot better about the coat. "Yes. Thank you. It's perfect."

"I'm glad you like it."

"Best thing in my entire wardrobe. I won't wear anything else ever again."

"*Anything* else, you say? Now that I'd like to see."

I gave this weird bleaty little laugh because I hadn't been properly prepared for flirting. But I rallied. Made what was probably an ill-advised attempt at sultry. "Come round, then. I'll give you a private viewing."

"You know I'd love to. But I'm waiting for a call from Tokyo, and I prefer to handle such things from my office."

I sighed. "Soon, then?"

"I'll insist on it."

The growl in his voice sent happy little shivers racing down my spine. But it also made me miss him. Even more so when he hung up, and I was alone again in the flat: just me and my gorgeous coat. The last thing I needed was more complicated feelings centered on an item of clothing, but it highlighted the way he could reach into my world whenever he wanted while his remained utterly inaccessible to me.

Blah.

Leaving my Coat of Many Emotions draped over a chair back, I Kiked Nik to see if he wanted to binge-watch *Supergirl* with me, having forgotten it was something like one o'clock in Boston and he was out to lunch with friends. Typical, really, that Nik would travel across the world, without billionaire backing, and be right at home. While I was living only an hour away and still didn't have a clue about anything. I mean, I was glad he was settled and had friends and stuff. But it reminded me that I needed to do the same. Instead of acting like my life was a ten-pound note I'd found in the gutter and couldn't decide whether it was okay to keep.

I couldn't help coming back to what Caspian had said to me on the plane. All that stuff about daring to want things. I'd made it about him at the time—partly because, well, I *did* want him, but also because I wasn't ready to think about it too deeply. Y'know, in case he was right.

Which, to be honest, was looking increasingly likely.

It was extra strange because I'd been full of dreams as a teenager. Mainly big stupid unrealistic dreams, like becoming a world-famous novelist, when, y'know, I had no interest in actually writing novels. Except I'd also dreamed of going to Oxford, and I'd made that happen, and not—when I managed to see past my raging imposter syndrome—just by fluke or by accident. I'd wanted it and worked for it. And yet, having achieved it, all I'd done was fuck around and watch illegal streams of *Pretty Little Liars* with a mostly straight boy I'd half believed I was in love with.

Was that it for me? Had I dreamed myself out?

Except that wasn't true either. Despite having made no effort to get one, I wanted a career. I wanted to write my champagne bubble stories. I wanted to write for *Milieu*, or somewhere like it. But I kept acting like it didn't matter. Same as I treated Oxford like it didn't matter. Because it was easier to say I hadn't tried than admit I wasn't good enough.

That was the thing about Oxford, though. Apart from the top percentile of certified geniuses, most of us got in by believing we were somehow extraordinary. And spent our time there learning how to be average. Everyone dealt with it in different ways: some people worked really hard to scrape a first, some people worked really hard to secure a good 2.1, some people switched universities, or hung themselves from the light fittings. And I guess I'd…given up? Decided it was better to be nothing on my own terms, than found lacking on someone else's.

Even if I knew their terms were fucking insane. I'd been through the educational equivalent of *The Hunger Games* and lived to tell the tale. Making me, at this point, I guess, Haymitch: riddled with survivor's guilt and basically dead inside.

It was no way to live. Especially when you weren't actually the broken puppet of a sadistic dystopia. And more just a nice middle-class boy, who'd turned failure into a monster, and then convinced himself he was too weak to face it.

There'd been a time when Oxford had seen something in me. Enough, at any rate, to offer me a place. And the fact I hadn't been what they'd thought I could be didn't mean I was nothing. It meant I was…

Something else. Me.

A boy Caspian Hart had traveled to Kinlochbervie to prove he wanted.

A couple of hours later, I wandered out onto the balcony. The wood was cold under my feet and the night nipped at me with sharp teeth. Beyond the shadowy trees, the city was alive with lights, turquoise and silver and gold, as uncountable as stars. And one of those lights was Caspian, working late.

It made me feel so close to him and so impossibly distant at the same time. Like I could have my Jane Eyre moment, and whisper his name, and he would hear me and know I was thinking about him. Although if it turned out Caspian was keeping a mentally ill spouse in his attic I was going to be super miffed.

Anyway, I sent him a text instead. A simple *how're things?*

I got back: *Fine, thank you. Almost done.*

My thumb traced *I miss you.* Then *can I come over?* Then *I miss you. Can I come over?* But I didn't hit send on any of them. Instead of bridging the gap between us, his message had made

him seem even further away. Because I suddenly realized I had
no idea what Caspian did when he finished work and wasn't
with me. His body suggested an aggressive gym regime but beyond that? How could I know, when I was consigned to One
Hyde Park like the Lady of Shalott?

Or possibly I was just looking at this the wrong way. I mean
I'd told Caspian I wanted to see more of him, but I'd taken it
as read that he would make it happen. When, actually, I was
the one choosing to wait around. Maybe he was really up in the
tower. And I was supposed to be fighting through his briars,
climbing his hair, breaking his curse, or whatever.

Maybe, in some strange way, he was waiting for me.

My hands were sweaty on the balcony rail. It was scary as
fuck, trying to break through three years of carefully
cultivated…whatever it was. Especially when it had, in its own,
unhealthy little way, kept me safe. Or at the very least from having a nervous breakdown.

But it wasn't helping me now. It was holding me back.

After all, if I believed in Caspian and Caspian believed in me,
couldn't I believe in myself? Just a little bit? I took a deep breath
and made my way back into this apartment. This Prufrock had
at least one peach in his life. And I damn well dared to eat it.

Grabbing the coat Caspian had sent me, I slipped it on with
a giddy little purr because it looked and felt so good. I did
the buttons and turned up the collar and fastened the belt,
and flicked an enigmatic glance at my reflection in the floor-
to-ceiling windows, imagining myself lingering on some misty
street corner in Budapest. Surely, nobody could object to an uninvited visitor if they turned up in such a fabulous garment?

It was a shame, really, about everything underneath it. I was going to be like Oscar Wilde, unable to live up to my blue china. Except with a coat. Unless…

Oh dear. I was having an idea.

Probably a terrible idea.

But Arden 2.0 embraced terrible ideas.

I stripped. Replaced my barbells with a glittery heart captive ring and a titanium rainbow pincher. And then put the coat back on.

Hmm. The basic idea was certainly sound but the execution was lacking. My legs, poking out the bottom, looked particularly pale and unprepossessing. But it was fine. I could work with it.

Rummaging around in my socks and pants drawer, I unearthed an unladdered pair of lace-topped hold-ups and pulled them on.

There. Much better.

I also found a battered black trilby. Got it angled coquettishly across one eye. And, as a final touch, I painted my lips harlot red. That was the actual name of the lipstick and a large part of the reason I'd bought it in the first place.

A peek in the bedroom mirror and…oh wow. Well. That would do.

That would definitely do.

With the stockings and coat and the fuck me lips and the shadow of the hat brim adding a touch of noir…I was a bona fide *homme fatale*.

One last more, um, personal piece of preparation—hoping lube wasn't going to squidge out of me embarrassingly—and I was good to go.

Then I called for a car. Luckily, Caspian's employees were made of stern stuff and Alisha, tonight's chauffeur, didn't bat an eyelash when I slipped into the back of the Maybach, (un)dressed like a slutty lunatic.

It was late enough that the roads were relatively clear, for London anyway, so it only took about fifteen minutes to get to Caspian's office. I watched the roads and buildings flash by in pockets of light and shadow, and the river that curled around them like a dark snake, its back a shifting kaleidoscope of the city's glitter.

"You want me to wait?" Alisha asked as she took us past security, into the underground parking lot, and pulled up outside the lift.

I hesitated, not quite sure how to answer. This had the potential to be the shortest encounter of my life. But Arden 2.0 did not talk himself out of things. "Um, no. It's fine, thanks. I probably won't need you again tonight."

I scrambled out of the car, clutching the mobile Bellerose had given me way back when I'd first moved into One Hyde Park, since it also allowed emergency access to all of Caspian's buildings. Admittedly, I wasn't sure that "fuckstop" was the sort of emergency he'd had in mind, but it was nearly ten o'clock at night. The building was all sealed up and, even if it hadn't been, I could hardly have waltzed up to reception. *Cheap tart in a greatcoat to see Caspian Hart.*

The lift whirred upward for what felt like a long time. And when it finally stopped moving, I stepped out into a silent, shadowy corridor. I vaguely remembered it from the last time I'd launched a one-man assault on Caspian's place of business, but it was different now. Eerie without people round, broken reflections from the city outside skittering across all the darkly shining glass.

Caspian's floor was the only point of light, his often its own soft glow, just past his assistant's thankfully unattended desk.

My heart flailed around in my chest.

Okay. Okay. I was doing this.

CHAPTER 10

My stockinged feet made no noise on the plush carpets as I approached the office. My nerves were fluttery but holding steady.

I was feeling reasonably impressed with myself as I pushed open Caspian's door and went in.

Or rather I fell in.

I didn't even know what I tripped over—my own misplaced optimism I guess—but one minute I was sliding into Caspian's office, all sultry in my sex coat, and the next I was yelping and in a heap on the ground.

"Arden?" If anything romantic had taken place—Caspian's face lighting up with joy at the sight of me, that kind of thing—I was in no position to witness it. He sounded surprised, though, rather than horrified. So that was good. Maybe. "Are you all right?"

I nodded, and rubbed my nose into the carpet. "I meant to do this."

"You did?"

"Absolutely. I was just, y'know, sitting at home, thinking about you working late, how tired you must be and how hard you work in general. And it struck me that what you probably needed was for somebody to turn up uninvited and fall over."

"That's very kind of you."

I still didn't dare look up. "Are you laughing at me?"

"No. I'm…I'm glad to see you."

"Oh God, Do you mean that?"

"Now I'm nodding. Do you need help?"

"Nope." I bounced to my feet, with only a small wince. "I'm good."

Caspian was standing by his desk, washed silver by the light from his computer screen, his face all shadows and angles, and so starkly beautiful that it made this whole venture seem absurd. What in God's name had I been thinking? How was someone like me supposed to seduce someone like him? How had I ever convinced myself I possessed that power? I mean, it was an excellent coat but it wasn't *magic*. And I wasn't a prince.

If anything I was a frog.

A frog in ill-considered lipstick.

"This was supposed to be sexy," I muttered.

"Surely"—his voice had gone silk-soft in the quiet room—"you're familiar enough with my tastes by now to know just how appealing I find the sight of you on the floor."

Well. That was slightly cheering. "Really?"

"Yes, really. Though I like you best at my feet."

I managed to meet his eyes again. They were steely gray in the gloom and gleamed like the glass that surrounded us. My magnificent predator. So fierce and so lost. "I can do that."

My hands were shaky as I reached for my belt.

But, strangely enough, my confidence was back. Maybe he'd been right all along: it wasn't that fragile. It was true that compared to Caspian I was short and skinny and apparently ridiculously clumsy, and as ordinary as ordinary could be. But all it took was the way he looked at me, the things he said to me and wanted me to do for him, the fractures in his self-control, shining like veins in marble, and I felt like the most powerful, desirable, wondrous person on the whole fucking planet.

And, God, I wanted to please him. Give him everything.

Submission. Desire. Suffering. Longing. Safety. With him it all became the same: the same ache, the same need, the same... oh God...the same helpless love.

Button by button I bared myself.

Halfway down, I realized I should probably have turned around and let the coat slip from my body, while I peeped coquettishly over my shoulder.

So what I was having here was a stripping learning experience.

But it didn't seem to matter. Because the moment I flashed lace, Caspian made this amazing sound—all rough and deep and lusty—and was away from his desk so fast, his chair hit the window behind him. He prowled across the room, swift as a panther after prey, and then my coat was a pile on the floor and I was in his arms.

Literally in his arms. Legs round his waist. Lips against his. Like some crazy movie kiss in the pouring rain.

Except for the part where it wasn't raining, and I was naked except for thigh highs and a hat.

But still. I wrapped myself round him, tight as honeysuckle. And kissed and clung and clung and kissed until I was breathless and dizzy and his mouth was a red smear and my eyes were full of stars.

It was only when I felt something solid nudge the backs of my thighs that I realized he'd carried me to his desk. I shoved his laptop out of the way, grabbed him by the tie, and pulled him down on top of me. The glass was gasp-inducingly cold against my unprotected back but he was blissfully warm. I shuddered, caught in a kind of delirious skin-confusion. An ice and fire sandwich.

And then Caspian's mouth closed over my nipple, drowning me in fresh heat. My brain gave up trying to process anything and I just moaned and clutched at his hair. For once he didn't shake me off, tugging my pincher back and forth with his tongue until my veins filled up with lightning and I could hardly bear the pleasure of it.

He glanced up, panting and disheveled.

My lipstick had traveled from my mouth to his to everywhere his mouth had touched me.

Which meant I had painted nipples.

It was the most brazen thing I'd ever seen and I wished I'd thought of it.

"I, er, I take it you don't mind me showing up then?" I asked.

He traced a hot wet stripe up the side of my neck, making my pulse flutter at the realization of its vulnerability. "If I still possessed the capacity for rational thought, I might consider it ill-advised." I wasn't sure I liked that answer. But my own ability to have thinking happen was not so great either right then.

"You look…" He seemed to lose track of what he was saying.

He dragged a hand along the outside of my thigh until he came to the top of my hold-ups. Slipping a single finger beneath the band, he pulled it outward, and then let it go so that it snapped sharply back into place.

It didn't really hurt but it made such a loud crack that I gasped anyway. "I look what?"

"Wicked beyond belief."

I nodded happily. "You should show me my place."

"And where's that?"

"Wherever you want me. Begging for whatever you think I deserve."

"Right now—" His eyes closed for a moment, though not before I caught the flare of passion and cruelty my words had ignited. "I think you deserve to be fucked. I think you deserve to be fucked until all you can do is scream my name."

I could have come on the idea alone.

"God yes," I breathed. "Yes, please."

He gave a shaky laugh. "This is my office, Arden. I keep pens here, not lube. And there are ways I don't want to hurt you."

I'd gone without once before—it hadn't been the worst thing in the world, and it would have probably passed into actively okay if the other guy had been just a touch less eager to plunge his manspear into my succulent dudehole.

But thankfully it wasn't an issue tonight.

"It's okay," I said. "I was a Boy Scout. I came prepared."

I gave him a little push so he was standing between my legs. Then, putting my years of dedicated yoga to good use, I took an ankle in each hand and split myself like a wishbone.

He was staring at me. At...well. A quite specific and

currently very exposed part of me. And having him do that hit me right on that perfect edge between exciting and embarrassing where they got all muddled up. It needed a word. There must have been one in German.

"You were a Boy Scout?" He sounded a bit preoccupied—almost as if that wasn't at all what he was really thinking about.

"For five minutes or whatever. Before they kicked me out for being a raging queer." I smiled at him, in what I hoped was a winning manner, and flexed some intimate muscles in a saucy wink. "Now about that fucking me till I scream thing?"

His glanced up, as swift and sure as a wolf scenting blood, and as ferocious. "Don't move," he told me.

I'd been feeling pretty audacious with the whole do-me move but I hadn't quite anticipated being stuck like that. All laid out for his taking. Bound by his command.

But, holy shenanigans, it was hot.

I whimpered earnestly. "I won't, Mr. Hart."

And was rewarded by a low growl of approval and pleasure from Caspian. I was glad to see him fumble very slightly with his belt as he released his cock. We were both so fired up I thought he'd slam into me like a train. But he came into me neither carefully nor roughly, just relentlessly, filling me up slowly so that I felt every inch of him as he took possession of me.

There was enough lube to ease his way, but the deep stretch was almost an echo of pain, and it made me pant and cling tight to my ankles. By the time he was all the way in I was moaning softly at the back of my throat, my sweat slicking the glass beneath me. I loved this. Holding him inside me. That kind of *oh hey, there's a man in my body*. The slight physical and emotional shock of it. And the way it made me feel vulnerable and strong and right all at the same time.

He pulled out partway, adjusted his angle, and hit my happy spot so perfectly I had to turn my face into my shoulder to smother the epically grateful noise I made.

He caught my chin and pulled my head back. "Don't do that."

"I'm not going to—?"

"There's nobody to hear but me and I want to hear you."

"O-okay."

It turned out, that was straightforward. I wasn't sure how successfully I'd have been able to hold back if I'd tried. He fucked me mercilessly, with a precision and a power that left me an incoherent trembling mess on his desk, my whole body rocking with the thrusts I held myself open for.

Being fucked that way, and helpless to do anything but take it and feel it, was insanely intense. My hands were slippy and my legs were aching and my arse stung a little bit from his thrusts but somehow, that just made everything even better.

Best of all, though, I got to watch. I got to see him pushing into me, framed by the V of my legs, the tender skin of my thighs looking paler than usual in contrast to the dark nylon of the stockings. I got to watch my cock bouncing between us, hard and flushed and shiny with precome, my balls drawn up tight beneath. And I got to watch *him*. Gorgeously unraveled with his tie askew and his hair mussed from my fingers. Perspiration gleaming at his temples and this tight line of concentration between his brows. The strained ecstasy in his half-closed eyes and the softer bliss of his parted lips, like an untouching kiss.

That was when the phone rang.

It gave me such a fright that I arched right off the desk, my arse death-clamping around his cock.

"Whu?" I gasped.

"That would be the call I was expecting." He sounded impressively calm considering he was literally inside me.

"Oh…um…awkward."

I expected he would either pull out or that we'd unconvincingly try to ignore the call. What I didn't expect was that he'd take it.

The only warning he gave me was a stern "Don't move, Arden" before leaning over me to hit the speaker button.

I froze, legs akimbo, trying to hold in a horrified yip.

Caspian said something in…I guess…Japanese? And received a longish reply. While I lay there, terrified of the sound of my own breathing, almost unbearably aware of my body, and trying not to squirm. Or do anything that might reveal what was going on to the person—or, people, fuck, what if it was people?—on the other end of the line.

I couldn't tell if I was panic-stricken or aroused beyond all reason. My cock was definitely on the second team.

Caspian was still talking. Rattling off, I don't know, figures maybe.

Out of the corner of my eye, I caught our reflection in the window. I looked like the virgin sacrifice in a Victorian horror: this pale shape, yielding rapturously beneath the shadow of Caspian. I'd never felt quite so…penetrated. Or so aware of it anyway: the hot stretch and the pressure of him inside me. It made me wish he had fangs to sink into the tender flesh of my bared throat.

Just then, he dragged a finger all the way up the underside of my cock. My mouth fell open on a soundless scream. I was going to come. Or die. Or both. Oh God. Oh God. Oh *God*.

Caspian put a hand over my mouth.

Which I was grateful for...and also found superhot. So it was helpful and not helpful. I thrashed—though given my position, pinned and impaled and teetering on the verge of a deliriously exciting feargasm, it was more of an undignified wriggle. Somehow I got myself under control, my teeth scraping against his palm as I muffled my whimpers.

A pause.

Then Caspian murmured something, his tone politely encouraging, and the conversation resumed. It should have been more incongruous: him dealing with whatever he was dealing with, while I was shuddering helplessly on his cock. But it was the same thing, really, wasn't it—utter command of his universe, from the financial empire he ruled to the lover panting and writhing on his desk.

I honestly thought he'd be at his most remote. I didn't know how else he could be responding with such ease and precision in a language that wasn't even his own. But then he glanced down at me and I didn't think I'd ever seen him quite that out of control, with his hair sweat-heavy over his brow and his cheeks all sex-flushed with heat and exhilaration. His eyes were bright with cruelty but there was something softer too. Something heartbreakingly innocent. Joy, maybe?

It was a good job I was gagged.

I mean, I could probably avoid having a screaming orgasm while he was on speakerphone with Tokyo, but no power on earth would have stopped me blurting out *I love you*. I kissed his hand instead and he smiled at me, this perfect, film-star smile.

Then he started, as if maybe—just maybe—he'd lost track of the discussion the teeniest tiniest bit. Thankfully, he couldn't see me smirking under his palm. He said something fairly sharp in response to whatever the other man was telling him and reached into the interior pocket of his jacket, pulling out a fountain pen of such sleek, gold-edged simplicity it was must have been worth more than my family's house.

Twisting off the lid with a practiced motion, he brought the nib to the planes of my abdomen and scribbled something across my skin. I squinted down my own body trying to see. Numbers? A series of numbers.

It was a weird sensation—a little bit scratchy, a little bit tickly, not really pleasure, not quite pain—but, oh God, the ownership in it. The casual way he marked me and claimed me, turned me into his personal Google keep.

And oh fuck…fuck I was going to lose it completely.

He must have realized. Probably he couldn't have failed to, given my curling toes and the straining muscles in my thighs, the noises he was almost managing to contain in his hand. A few more notes I could barely keep still for and a hasty—I assumed—goodbye. And the line went dead with the sweetest click I'd ever heard in my life.

The moment my mouth was free, I let out this…mortifying banshee wail of sex need. Caspian's pen clacked against the desk. And then he was fucking me, fucking me hard enough to rattle the glass and judder my bones, and it was perfect, the pleasure as inexorable as the hammering of his cock against my prostate, coiling so tight inside me it was like being strangled. In a good way. Maybe. I wasn't sure.

I sucked in a sobbing breath. "Ohgodcaspianpleaseohgod-please." Fuck knew what I was begging for. More. Less. The luxurious liberty of begging itself, I didn't know. I didn't care.

Just…

"Caspian."

Tears leaked from the corners of my eyes. Moisture pooled on my stomach from my cock. I was starting to slide on the desk, driven back with every harsh shove into me. The scent of us—sex and sweat and the last honeyed base notes of Caspian's cologne—hung heavy in the air. And the sounds we made to-gether had turned ugly: the wet slap of skin and the squelch of lube, his ragged breaths and my frantic cries.

But it was all beautiful somehow.

The reality of sex. Rough and raw and glorious.

And when he finally wrapped a hand around my cock, I came hard and instantly, relief pushing me over the edge and then al-most into unconsciousness with the baseball bat of orgasm.

Breath-snatching. Heart-bursting. Like thunder inside me.

Wracking me from fingers to toes. To the ends of my fucking hair.

Muscles just…weren't happening anymore. My hands dropped, my legs fell, curling around Caspian. But he was prob-ably too far gone to notice. He half collapsed on top of me, his face pressed against my neck, and came too, almost silently, in great body-shaking heaves.

I forced my arms into action and got them round him.

Held him tight.

A stolen embrace when he was closest, and most lost, to me.

I was utterly sex-dazed but it wasn't an ideal situation for a languorous afterglow. Caspian was heavy and the glass was hard and my arse had that wet, well-fucked feeling that made me slightly self-conscious about the mess I might be making on his desk.

"You'd better rescue your notes," I mumbled, "because I'm seriously—oh fuck." Whatever he'd written was nothing but sweaty, pale-blue smears. "I'm really sorry. Was…was it important?"

"Yes." A pause. "Which is why I memorized what I needed."

I'd been so ready to feel awful that I ended up giggling instead. "And then wrote on me anyway?"

"I'm afraid"—he looked almost abashed—"I wasn't thinking all that clearly."

"It's okay. It was superhot."

His fingers followed my tattoo over my hip. "But I know I wanted to claim a little piece of you."

"You can claim all of me."

"My beautiful Arden." He smiled at me, but there was something almost sad about it, his hands soft on my body. "In some ways, you are unconquerable. And I wouldn't have it otherwise."

"Write on me again?" I wriggled enticingly…if somewhat stickily.

"Write what?"

"Anything you like. How about *Caspian + Arden 4 Eva* in a big heart?"

That earned me an exasperated look.

I prodded him with my foot. "Please? It doesn't even have to be romantic."

"I'm not literary like you."

"You mean you've never stumbled across some words arranged into an order you quite liked? Ever?"

"It's not that." He picked the pen back up and absently fiddled with it, twisting its lid round and round between his fingers. "I'm afraid I find it rather exposing."

"Caspian, I came to your office practically naked."

"Yes, but you chose to do that."

Oh fuck. He had a point. I was being super pushy—and one person's risky titillation was another person's excruciating nightmare. "I'm sorry. Ignore me. You don't have to."

He leaned down—smooshing our too-hot bodies together in a way that was only okay because we'd just had the best sex ever—and kissed me. "No, I'll do it. I just need to think what to write."

"But I don't want you to do something that makes you uncomfortable."

"You do many uncomfortable things for me."

I blushed, very aware I was sort of…dripping on his desk. "They're things I like doing, though."

"And, in return, there are ways I'm willing to be uncomfortable for you."

He slid the lid off the pen, found a bit of me he liked that wasn't too sweaty, and began to write. I couldn't see much except his head bent over me. But that just made me feel what he was doing all the more intensely. The sharp-delicate pressure made my toes curl. And imagine what it might be like if it was a blade he held.

"What does it say?" I asked when he was done—since all I could make out was a ribbon of blue across my hip and stomach.

He gave me an unreadable smile. "You'll have to wait and see."

That was when I realized I'd spent so long sweating the *arriving* part of this little escapade that I hadn't given any thought at all to the *leaving*. The idea of pulling my gorgeous new coat over my seriously sexed body and limping wetly into a taxi was one gazillion percent the wrong uncomfortable. Did Caspian keep spare clothes in his office? It was a posh building—maybe there would be an onsite employee gym, or something, with a shower I could use.

"What's wrong? Did I hurt you?" Caspian pulled away abruptly. But since, not so very long ago, he would have taken me being post-coitally tense as an invitation to run like hell, this was definitely progress.

I sat up gingerly, pressing my knees together and folding my hands over my dick, in what was a pretty belated act of modesty. "No. Not at all. Just, err, fretting about logistics."

"Logistics?"

"Yeah. I need to get back somehow."

Caspian was silent for a long moment. Apart from the fact there was come and ink on his shirt from where our bodies had pressed against each other, he looked…well…almost put-together. Whereas I was wrecked from eyes to arse.

Then he leaned in and brushed back a lock of hair that had gone off on a frolic of its own when I'd been too busy having sex to keep it under control. "Don't worry about that. You can stay with me."

"Are you sure?" I asked, with fucking extraordinary nonchalance.

From the look on his face, I didn't think he *was* all that sure, but he nodded anyway. And, dammit, I would take it.

"Here." He took off his shirt and wrapped it round me. It was warm from him and smelled of him—quite pungently of him, actually, considering what we'd just been doing—and, being ridiculously expensive, it was soft and smooth against my still over-sensitive skin. Of course it was way too big for me, brushing my stocking tops, but I was totally okay with that. It felt like being in Caspian's arms.

Once I was only partially indecent, he helped me down off the desk. We stared a moment at the imprints we'd left on the glass: smudges of heat and sweat and other fluids.

He didn't quite facepalm but his palm hovered perilously close to his face. "What in God's name was I thinking? This was so unprofessional."

It seemed sensible to brace myself for a cavalcade of regret. I hung my head. "Sorry."

"Don't be silly, Arden. I was as responsible for it as you."

"But I turned up in a...a..." I made an awkward gesture. "...provocative way."

"Yes, and I chose to respond by fucking you on my desk. Which I enjoyed very much."

"Really?" I shot him a silly, happy smile. "You aren't freaking out?"

"No."

"It was still bad of me, though. You should, y'know, probably spank me later."

He laughed and pulled me unexpectedly into something I could only call a hug. Squeezed me so tightly, so desperately, I nearly ran out of breath. "Oh Arden, you're incorrigible."

I nodded into his chest.

"Please, never stop."

"No intention of it," I mumbled. Though what I was thinking was: *please never stop holding me like this.*

Of course he did. And if he hadn't, it would have been awkward, what us having to eat and go to the toilet and have separate lives and things. But I could have taken a little bit more of being hugged like that.

A lot more, to be honest.

CHAPTER 11

Once we were untangled, he led me over to a different lift. The doors were so discreet I hadn't even noticed them the last time I'd been here. And tonight I'd been a bit busy for sightseeing. I was just staring blankly, but the pressure of his hand at the small of my back propelled me forward.

"Make yourself at home," he told me. "I need to clean up and finish my work. But I'll be with you as soon as I can."

It took a moment or two for the implication of his words to sink in. "Wait, you live here?"

"I have several houses. This is one of the places I stay when I need to." Since I was still nonfunctional, he pressed the button for me. "See you soon."

A few seconds later, I was blundering into his apartment. Or rather "one of the places he stayed in." While it had clearly been decorated in a no-expense-spared way Caspian favored, it was nowhere near as opulent as One Hyde Park. In fact, in billionaire terms, it was positively monkish.

No personal touches, but I hadn't really expected it. The austerity, if nothing else, was Caspian: the emphasis on smooth wood and polished stone, the slightly overwhelming sense of space created by the high ceilings and the triple aspect windows. The Sahara noir marble floors—beautiful though they were— were slippery and chill beneath my feet. Which meant my most overriding impression of Caspian's penthouse was that it needed a goddamn rug or two.

I penguin-shuffled into the bathroom, which was yet more marble, relieved, if you could call it that, by granite and gold, and reluctantly divested myself of Caspian's shirt. Then tried to figure what he'd written. Which wasn't actually that straightforward since it was either upside-down (if I used my eyes) or back-to-front (if I used a mirror).

In the end I took a photo with my phone. I was trying to get a good angle on the words, but it turned out to be a pretty good angle on me. I'd twisted round to expose the writing, so my body was all sleek curves and sharp edges. And for once my bony bits and squeezy bits were working in harmony instead of contriving to make me look like a knobbly gazelle. My leg was conveniently in the way of my junk so it wasn't porny—more *suggestive* with the laddered thigh highs, the smudgy bruise shadows on my flanks and the vulnerable ridges of my clavicles. This was so getting a grainy filter and going on Instagram.

I zoomed in so I could see what Caspian had written. It was two lines, curling neatly over my hip a bit like my tattoo: *what will the creature made all of seadrift do on the dry sand of daylight; what will the mind do, each morning, waking?*

Well. So much for an Oxford education. I had no idea what it was from. I could have googled it, of course, but that would've felt like cheating. I touched the loops where the ink was already blurring. Kind of a shame to wash it off straightaway. Except Caspian would be along at some point and I didn't want to greet him smelling like the bargain basement option at a bordello.

He had one of those walk-in shower room type things, with about eighty multidirectional settings for water to blast you unpleasantly in the face. When I found one that wasn't overwhelmingly painful and hitting the right parts of my body, I had a hasty wash and enjoyed unparalleled views of the London skyline. It felt weird to be soaping my bits and staring at the dome of St Paul's but…that was my life now.

Curtains, I was starting to realize, were a poor people invention. If you were rich enough, you just got to move the world out of your way.

As I dried off, I fretted slightly about Caspian being witness to the carnage that was my hair post-shower. But then I remembered I'd vomited on his feet, shown him my arsehole, and begged him, on several occasions, to spank me. So probably he could cope with my duckish floof.

There was, however, still no sign of him, which left me at a loss. He'd said I should make myself comfortable, but I wasn't sure where to start because everything was showroom perfect. And showroom anonymous. I only managed to figure out which bedroom was his because there were suits in the wardrobe. And it felt all kinds of creepy having to look.

I did have a little wander, in case I'd missed where Caspian really lived. But no: all I found was a series of empty, pristine rooms, and a door I couldn't open.

Which was weird, right? Edging into super weird.

Because why was it there? What was behind it? And who the fuck did that? It wasn't even like he'd known I was coming, and thought to himself, *Better secure my priceless collection of Fabergé eggs before Arden accidentally breaks them.*

It was just there. A locked room permanently in his apartment.

I mean, was Caspian a vampire, and this was where he chained up his blood-doll? Or was he your regular, common or garden kidnapper? Maybe he was a masked vigilante and this was where he kept his cape? Or he was one of those conspiracy theorist types and the walls would be covered in maps and newspaper clippings, connected by bits of string.

Or probably it was a room he *happened* to have that *happened* to be inaccessible. And I was massively overreacting. After all, he didn't owe me unfettered access to his past, his heart, or the place where he lived. I wasn't Judith, running about Duke Bluebeard's castle, believing love was the answer to every question, and the key to every lock.

Well, apart from the bit where I was ransacking Caspian's apartment.

Literally looking for a key to a lock.

So I could open a door that was at least eighty percent metaphor at this point.

In any case, I was foiled. And trying to bash my way in cop-show style didn't work either. It just hurt my shoulder. Hurt my shoulder quite a lot, actually.

So I retreated to what I'd concluded was the master bedroom, and slipped under the cool, crisp covers of the huge and ridiculously comfortable bed. Gazed out of the unavoidable windows.

How did Caspian feel as he lay here? Masterful? Like a corporate emperor?

Me, I felt small. Squashed by the vastness of things. And haunted by a room I couldn't get into.

I was so sick of crashing against all the stuff I didn't know about Caspian Hart. Of feeling that however close I got to him there was always another barrier. Secrets he'd never tell me. Parts of him I couldn't reach.

And that…honestly, it sucked. Because all I wanted was to throw wide the chambers of his heart and fill them full of light.

Oh fuck.

I was totally Judith.

Except my Duke would barely let me through the front door. Let alone into his torture chamber or near his lake of tears.

Rolling over, I intended to put my head under the pillow but then I spotted a book on the floor, partly hidden by the spill of the bedclothes. It was a battered paperback, with a pulpy cartoonish cover and big bright lettering that proclaimed it: *Downbelow Station*.

It was so much the last thing I would've expected that I found myself wondering—in what was, admittedly, a slightly messed-up way—if another lover had left it.

Picking it up, I peeked inside. What I think they always called a *bold hand* in Victorian novels had written *To Arthur, with love, L* in the front. Neither the name nor the initial seemed connected to Caspian in any way. Which meant I knew even less about him than I thought. Or he'd picked it up in a charity shop one day. Or it wasn't his at all and the maid—of course he had a maid—had dropped it.

I leaned over the side of the bed, like I was a little kid again, checking for monsters. Nik told me he would pull the duvet over his head and hide. But, me, I always had to look. There were no monsters under Caspian's bed. Not even normal things like fluff or hair. What there was, though, was a battered cardboard box, which I dragged out by one of the flaps.

It was full of books like the one I'd found on the floor, all of them tatty and yellowing, with fairly cheesy cover art. Barring a few classics like Verne and Wells, it was mostly the sort of sci-fi I checked out of after three pages of "Grand Mardok Ooler Thon Thistlethwaite was sitting at his Steinway grand, while the gardleflumps gambolled majestically around the anterior viewport of his nebula class star destroyer." Though some I recognized by being told a lot I should read them: Asimov, Russ, Vonarburg, Bradbury, Heinlein, Bujold, Engh, Le Guin.

I nosed through in search of any more mysterious dedications but came up empty. And finally put the box back where I'd found it. I'd already spent enough time going Sam Spade on Caspian's belongings. *Downbelow Station*, however, seemed fair game, since it had just been lying there. And I desperately needed something to stop my brain eating itself with unanswerable questions.

So I made myself a little nest and snuggled down to read. There weren't any gardleflumps but it was sufficiently dense that Caspian's arrival felt like reprieve. I heard the door open and close, and then the sound of the shower.

Waiting for him in his bed was weirdly nervous-making, not least because I couldn't guarantee the first words out of my mouth wouldn't be *Are you a serial killer or a bigamist and, if not, what the fuck is that locked door about?* Which I didn't think was the best way to initiate that conversation.

Finally, Caspian came into the room, hair damp and raven-sleek, a few drops of water still clinging tantalizingly to his neck and shoulders. He was naked except for the sexy billionaire pants he favored (and I favored too because they framed some of his best bits so very nicely) and he blushed a little when he saw what I was reading.

"I didn't realize I'd left that out," he said.

"I wouldn't have taken you for a sci-fi buff."

"My father was." He climbed into bed beside me and gently coaxed the book from my hands. "This was one of his favorites."

"It's, uh, really serious. I'm not sure I have a clue what's going on."

I felt a bit like the we-both-reached-for-the-gun scene in *Chicago*: my voice was saying things, but they didn't seem to have anything to do with me. Though if I was doing an unconvincing impression of myself, Caspian showed no sign of it. "It's probably best to skip the history chapters at the beginning."

"Why are they there, then?" *Like, for example, the locked door in your apartment?*

"I'm sorry, I don't know." For all his casual act, he touched that tatty paperback with such care as he put it back in the box. "I just know this story so well it feels less like reading. And more like…visiting old friends."

Oh fuck. That was adorable.

And reminded me pretty sharply that Caspian was a human being, not a puzzle I was trying to solve in thirty seconds or less. There'd be plenty of time to ask him about his living arrangements.

Especially now I actually had access to them. Which was a big step for both of us. Even if it had only happened because it would have been majorly harsh to pack me back off to One Hyde Park when I was half naked and covered in come.

Anyway, I didn't want to argue with him. I wanted to do cuddly post-sexing things with him. Afterglow not after-row. And, besides, immediate demands for explanations and no-holds-barred access to all the areas of the property was what a detective did during a murder inquiry. It wasn't how a guest behaved.

At least, not a guest who wanted to be invited back.

"Caspian?" I asked.

"Yes."

"I'm about to kiss you. Is that okay?"

He looked a little bewildered but nodded.

I leaned over. He was very still indeed, his hands curled in his lap. I let my breath brush his lips but, at the last moment, I reared up and kissed his nose instead.

He gave a startled laugh, lashes flickering. "What was that for?"

"You do it to me all the time."

"Your nose invites me. But I meant the kiss." He paused. "Regardless of locale." He'd gone all cool and dry, which made me think he was secretly amused. That, and the hint of a smile in the curve of his mouth.

"I did it because I like you."

"You like me?" he repeated, as if he wasn't quite sure what to do with the information. "Well, that's very flattering, thank you."

He seemed determined not to meet my gaze just then. And I was hopelessly charmed by the way he could be so sophisticated—so full of sexual aggression and refined cruelty—and yet undone by the tiniest of tender gestures.

So I took him gently by the wrist and kissed his fingers too, surprised by the way they trembled against my lips. "Yes, it is. I mean, you already know I admire you. Am slightly intimidated by you sometimes. Fancy the living shit out of you. Can't keep my hands off you. Want to be with you and please you and make you happy." I inched a little closer over the expanse of bed. Enough that I could get a sense of him: his shape, his warmth, the rhythm of his breathing. "But when you talk to me, when you tell me what you're thinking and what matters to you...I remember how much I like you as well."

There was a long silence.

Then: "Go to sleep, Arden. It's getting late."

"Okay."

I was on the edge of dropping off when I felt his hand close around mine in the secret darkness under the covers. I gave his fingers a drowsy squeeze.

"I like you too," he whispered.

I waited a second or two.

Then: "Go to sleep, Caspian. It's getting late."

He laughed at that, his sweet, soft laugh, and it was almost prize enough to guard me from further sleepless speculation about the damn door.

* * *

I awoke a few hours later to an empty bed. Knowing what I did of Caspian's habits, it shouldn't have been a surprise.

But, somehow, it was. And it hurt.

I told myself this didn't mean anything. That it didn't diminish what we'd shared or the fact I was here.

Except it *did* mean something. It meant...I was spending my night alone. And suddenly, out of nowhere, I was lying there with my head full of that fucking photo. The one I'd seen in *Milieu* before I'd run away to Scotland: Caspian and his ex-boyfriend, Nathaniel Whateveritwas, at some fancy event together. It'd been taken long after they'd broken up, and quite a bit before he'd met me...but I wasn't doing the best job of being rational about it. I mean, it wasn't so much that the photo existed. It was how good they'd looked in it. Like they were meant to be together, Nathaniel's hand curled so naturally around Caspian's elbow.

When he would barely let me touch him at all.

Toga-ing myself in the sheet, I went to look for Caspian. He was in the living room, wrapped in a dressing gown and watching the gray-gold dawn as it broke across the city.

The way the window framed him reminded me of the first time I'd come to his office. I'd been furious then but still the sight of him there had touched at me somehow. He'd seemed at once so remote and so beautiful—a cold-eyed tiger in his corporate cage—and I'd yearned to both gentle and unleash him.

Part of me still yearned to do that.

But the rest of me just felt rejected.

Because it was all very well to stand around looking dramatically lonely when you were, in fact, lonely.

But I was *right here*.

Right. The Fuck. Here.

I perched on the arm of a chair. "What's wrong?"

He glanced my way—his eyes all velvet-dark against navy cashmere—and gave me a faint smile. "I'm sorry. I'm a light sleeper and I'm not used to sharing a bed."

"What about when you were with Nathaniel?"

Fuck, why had I said that? The words clattered between us like a frying pan I'd dropped. He didn't flinch but a kind of awful stillness settled over him. And I knew I'd gone too far, pushed too hard. Broken nearly every rule in the *how not to make yourself look like a jealous, insecure harpy (while not-quite dating a billionaire)* book. He would probably never let me get even this close again.

"I'm sorry," I blurted out. "I'm tired. I don't know where that came from."

"Go back to bed, Arden." He didn't say it in a nasty way but that was almost worse. As if I was on the other side of the glass with the rest of the world.

"You could come with me?" I didn't know what else to do so I tried a minxy look. "We don't have to sleep."

He shook his head.

"Can I stay, then?" Wow. That was just pathetic. I felt like a broken traffic light, flicking back and forth at random between signals. In my case: needy, flirty, and pushy.

"It's really not necessary."

"I want to." I joined him at the window, watching the silver towers with their fleeting golden crowns.

If I could manage to shut up for five seconds, maybe he'd relax. Put his arm around me. Draw me in close. Let me snuggle. I wasn't a morning person but if this was what life with Caspian meant…I was game to try.

Then my mouth happened. "Why don't you trust me?"

There was a brief hesitation and then, with devastating patience, "I do trust you. If I didn't, you wouldn't be here."

"And where exactly is here, Caspian?" My brain was screaming at me to stop. But I didn't. Couldn't. And I had no idea if this was coming from my better self or my worst. "In your bed but not in your arms? In your body but not in your heart?"

Oh what was the fuck was I expecting? For music to swell and lightning to flash from the sky as Caspian pulled me into a fierce embrace. Covered my mouth with his and—between deep, desperate kisses—told me in a voice hoarse with passion how much I meant to him. How much he needed me. The light in his dark, the balm of his soul, the jam in his doughnut. Whatever.

He was frowning. "We fucked in my office—which would have been entirely against my better judgment, had you not so comprehensively overthrown it. And now you're staying in a place where only I stay. What more do you want? What more can I give you?"

"How about the truth? Why can't you be with me like you were with Nathaniel? How come you can't sleep at night? What's"—and the words rushed out before I could stop them—"with the locked door?"

"The locked door?"

"Yes." I pointed wildly. "The one over there."

"It's…it's not important."

I made a sound. It wasn't a very dignified sound. Honestly, it was kind of a scream.

"I just meant," he said quickly, "it's a room I don't use anymore."

"Why? What's in there? Your fucking guitar collection?"

He'd gone horribly pale. "No."

"When were you last there?"

"With Nathaniel."

"Show me." I felt like this lurching fleshmonster of a person, sewn together from anger and hurt and confusion. "*Show me.*"

His eyes met mine in the glass, wavery blue shadows that revealed absolutely nothing. I might as well have tried to fish the moon from its reflection in a pond. "As you wish."

He crossed the room to the table where he'd left his keys. Picked them up and tossed them to me. Of course I missed them and had to go scrabbling around on the ground. But I got them, minus five to personal dignity, and bolted for the door before Caspian could change his mind.

He followed me silently into the corridor, arms folded tightly across his chest, leaving me to try all the keys as if I was a contestant on the world's shittiest game show. Finally, though, I found the right one and pushed the door open.

And stepped like Alice into a kinky wonderland.

CHAPTER 12

I mean holy shit. We were talking the real deal, the full shebang: a lavishly furnished, luxury bondage dungeon complete with four-poster bed and implements hanging on the wall. God. So many implements. Cuffs, crops, spreaders, floggers, stuff I didn't even recognize, gleaming softly in the mellow light. Everything was dark leather and dark wood, occasionally relieved by accents of burgundy and gold, opulent and forbidding and sexy as hell. And some of the furniture in there I couldn't even look at for fear of insta-blushing. I hadn't quite realized how many ways there existed to immobilize and expose someone.

Though, let's be clear, I was up for all of them.

"Oh my God." I spun back to Caspian. "I always guessed what you were into, but this is amazing."

"It was built a long time ago."

He sounded slightly distant. I guess he was worried I was going to freak out. And I could sort of see why, since a room like this suggested a commitment to BDSM that went way beyond a little bit of spanking and begging. Maybe I should have been scared, or at least a little bit apprehensive, but I wasn't. I just wasn't. I trusted Caspian. And I wanted to explore this with him. As much for my sake as for his.

"You know, you didn't have to hide your naughty sex room from me," I said.

"I wasn't hiding it. I told you, I don't come here anymore." He wasn't lying about that. The air smelled stale, and nearly every flat surface had accumulated a faint patina of dust. "I keep meaning to have it dismantled, but it seems unduly mortifying to hire someone for the task."

"You must have hired someone to build it," I pointed out.

"I...actually, that wasn't me."

Nathaniel? Except that seemed incredibly unlikely, given what Caspian had told me of their relationship. "So you tripped, fell, and landed on your very own home dungeon?"

"It was a gift. From...a mentor of sorts."

We were getting off track. I went further into the room, running my fingers through the tails of a row of floggers, before perching on the edge of...well...I wasn't sure what it was. Like, if a chair and a chaise and saddle had a threesome and covered the resulting offspring in dark purple velvet. One of those. Though it was only when I was sitting on it that I discovered it also had stirrups. And reins. Oh *my*.

"But"—I gave Caspian my best *come bonk me on your outrageous furniture* look—"we can still play, can't we?"

He didn't seem at all enticed, despite my blandishments. "No."

"What? Why?"

"Because I didn't want to bring you here in the first place."

"You brought Nathaniel."

Caspian made a convulsive gesture, his fingers opening and closing impatiently. "This isn't about him."

"How can it not be?" I cried. "When he got everything and I get compromises. When you can't even spend a full night with me? How long did you make him wait before you let him stay with you? Or before you let him touch you?"

"It was different, Arden. I was different." He gazed at me, almost pleadingly. "I'm trying to learn from my mistakes with him, so I can be better with you."

"So...you won't let me have fun in your sex dungeon as a mark of special favor?"

He glanced round sharply, almost as if he didn't quite recognize where he was. Then said, in a strange, rough voice, "Can't you understand? I don't like being here."

"Because it reminds you of Nathaniel?"

"Yes, but not in the way you think." He took a step across the threshold, but almost immediately retreated, fine tremors running through his body. "All you see right now is a tawdry fantasy. What I see is the room where I hurt someone I loved."

He'd said something like this to me in Kinlochbervie. At the time I'd been a bit too preoccupied with everything going on between us to get caught up in specifics about someone else. But I was finally starting to get it: if I wanted to understand Caspian, I would also have to understand Nathaniel.

"What did you do?" I asked. "Push him too far? Ignore his safeword?"

"It was always too far. Every single time."

"What do you mean?"

"Oh Arden." Caspian put a shaky hand briefly to his eyes. I wasn't sure, but I thought he might have been blinking back tears. "I was twenty-three when I met Nathaniel. The attraction between us was instant, and powerful. He was a light, when I thought only darkness existed. I'd never dreamed someone like him, so good and so unswerving in that goodness, could love someone as sullied as me."

This was everything I'd been asking for. Truth. Openness. And it was fucking awful. Not so much the *idea* that Caspian had once been in love with Nathaniel. I knew that already. But the reality of it? Right in my face? Ouch ouch ouch ouch ouch. "Sounds great."

"I was very…lost back then. Very twisted by the choices I'd made. I believed that love and pain were inextricable." He swept an arm out to encompass the room. "Nathaniel didn't want any of this. But he suffered it for me."

"Wow," I drawled out, in a voice I didn't quite recognize, "must've been hot."

He glanced over at me, visibly startled. "What the— Why would you say that?"

"I don't know. Maybe I don't like hearing about how amazing and wonderful your ex is."

"For God's sake, you asked. Insisted even."

I winced. "Yes, but…I didn't realize how crap it would be. And, for the record, I think it's really fucked up to submit to someone in order to prove you're the better person."

"It was what I thought I needed. So he gave it to me."

"And how did that work out for you?"

"You know it didn't."

I swung my feet onto the…whatever it was I was sitting on. Ended up sprawled out and arched up like I was at the world's lewdest psychologist. So much for looking cool and nonchalant as jealousy gnawed on my liver like Prometheus's eagle. "Couldn't he take it?"

"Actually," said Caspian, very softly. "I couldn't. He made me see this for what it truly was: cruelty from cruelty, and pain from pain. And it became unbearable, subjecting him to such…such debasements. I had to let him go. I didn't deserve to be with him."

"Oh my God." I flailed upright, sheet flying. "Have you listened to yourself? Way to make me feel like absolute shit."

"I'm not sure what's going through your mind, but my previous relationship is—and should be—irrelevant to you."

"But you do remember I like being *subjected to debasements*, right?"

"I…I"—he flushed—"I don't see what that has to do with anything."

"You broke up with Nathaniel the Martyr because you believe the fact you're kinky and he's not makes him too good for you. So what does that make me, Caspian?"

He drew in a sharp breath. "I've treated you with far greater care than I ever showed Nathaniel."

"You mean by keeping me at a distance and refusing to believe me when I tell you that I'm comfortable with my desires, and yours?"

"The reason," he snapped, "you are comfortable is because I have kept myself in check. I have set boundaries and maintained them and protected you from the consequences of both my nature and your naiveté."

I stared at him, shocked momentarily into silence, and thrown into such turmoil I couldn't tell if I was angry or upset or both or neither. Finally, I got my mouth working. "This is such bullshit."

"What is?" Caspian, as he often did after an outburst, had turned to ice.

"You. This. Everything." Or maybe I was just tired. Heaviness rolled over me like I was being dragged through the floor soul first. "You've only gone and Madonna-whored me."

"I don't—"

"You're fucked up about kink because your last boyfriend was a judgmental prick. And you'll never think I'm as good as Nathaniel until I'm as judgmental as him or as fucked up as you."

I gathered my garment, and what precious little of my dignity remained, and pushed past Caspian. There was no game plan here. All I wanted was away. From him and the room where RACK went to die.

Probably there would be crying at some point.

But I didn't actually get very far. Caspian caught up to me in the bedroom.

"Where are you going?" he asked.

It was a good question. "I guess I'm leaving?"

"Now? It's five a.m. You're in a sheet."

I gave him a wild, senseless grin. "One of these is fixable."

"Arden."

"What?"

"I think, perhaps, we have both spoken too hastily tonight. Implied things we did not mean."

"Is that…what the fuck is that? Are you trying to say sorry?"

He raised a fretful hand, then let it fall. "I don't know what I'm trying to say. I can't…think in that place. I'm not…I don't feel…"

That was when I saw he was sweating. And not in a sexy glowing way. More just drenched, and almost feverish. He was trembling too. And looked—unlikely as it seemed for someone so beautiful—absolutely terrible.

"Are you okay?"

I started forward but he jerked away. "Don't touch me."

"I won't." I threw up the surrender gesture. "I promise. But what's wrong?"

"Nothing. I mean"—he made a shaky sound—"I just need to breathe."

"Um. Sit down maybe?" It was hard to help someone when they wouldn't let you near them, but I managed to gently herd him, sheepdog style, toward the bed. "I think you're meant to put your head between your legs if you feel faint."

"No, it's…it feels…It's like being there."

I was still super cross with him. But it wasn't in me to prioritize my own anger over someone else's distress. Not because I was amazing or anything. But because I wasn't a psychopath.

He pressed his fingers against his eyes. "I can't stop remembering. Can't stop seeing. I don't want…I can't make it stop."

"Oh God." I dropped to my knees in front of him, trying to demonstrate closeness without impinging. "I think you're… triggered maybe?"

"Maybe."

Actually take that back about not being a psychopath. I

wished I could whip out my phone and google *what to do when you brutally traumatize your bildom non-boyfriend by trying to kinky sex him in a place full of horrible associations*. What the fuck was wrong with me? I'd gone into free-fall in a void of my own insecurities. I mean, yes, Caspian had said some messed-up stuff that had made me feel hella judged. But how hadn't I noticed how much he was hurting?

Fuck. Okay. I could fix this.

I shuffled forward a tiny bit. "Caspian? That's the past. It's over and done with. You're here now. In the present. With me."

No reaction.

Shit. Shit. Shit. This was beyond difficult.

"Just, y'know, keep breathing. And…like…sort of…feel where you are? The ground under your feet. The bed if you just reach out and touch it. My voice talking to you. And if you open your eyes, you'll see me. Waiting for you."

It took forever. But eventually he lowered his hands. Looked down at me with this strange mixture of wild animal fear and desperate trust. I was pretty sure I was on the verge of a heart attack myself. But I gave him my best *calm, here, and incredibly sorry I made you hang out somewhere damaging for you* face.

"See," I whispered. "All safe."

He did actually seem to be doing better. He wasn't trembling anymore, and there was color in his face again—although he'd gone kind of red. "Yes." He cleared his throat. "I'm…I'm fine now. And I'm sorry you had to see that."

"Jesus. That is not something you have to apologize for."

"Well, I'm hardly proud of it. And I have no cause to react that way."

I almost could see him trying to put himself back together. Except it was the emotional equivalent of that scene in Bambi with the icy pond. "You've lost me."

"I was not the one to endure torment in that room."

"You know"—the words were out before I could stop them—"I'm really not sure about that."

For a moment he stared at me with this terrible emptiness. And then, "Arden, go if you must, but I can't talk about this anymore right now."

I nearly lost my temper again. How could he think I'd leave him after what I'd just seen? Except he must have felt vulnerable enough without being reminded, and the last thing I needed was him mistaking my care for pity. And actually, in that moment, it cost me nothing to sacrifice a little of my pride to salvage his.

"I'd like to stay," I said softly. "If you don't mind."

He shook his head. And most likely I was imagining it for my own benefit, but I thought I saw relief in his eyes.

I gave him a tentative smile. "If it would make you more comfortable, I could sleep in one of the other rooms. Or on the floor since I'd much rather be near you."

"I'm not going to make you sleep on the floor." He sounded a little bit more like himself—which was to say, faintly exasperated with me.

"Will you really be okay sharing, though?"

"I don't know. But I'm"—he swallowed—"quite tired."

I'd never seen anyone struggle over such a basic admission of humanity. "Then get into bed, doofus."

He managed a laugh, and half crawled, half dragged himself

up toward the pillows. Landed in a vaguely vertical sprawl, his face shadowed by the crook of his arm. "I should shower," he mumbled. "I'm disgusting."

"You're fine." I untangled the sheet from my body and settled it over him, then drew up the duvet and—

Okay. It's weird to say I tucked in Caspian Hart. But I did. Before slipping in beside him, top to tail, just like in Kinlochbervie. I felt him tense, then relax. He said something I didn't catch, though it might have been nothing more than my name, and was asleep in minutes.

Annoyingly—despite me also being *quite tired*—my brain wouldn't leave me alone. So I ended up lying there, restless but trying not to move in case I disturbed Caspian, hamster-wheeling through the carnage of our evening. And to think we'd started out so promisingly. Although, actually, in some horrible demonstration of *beware of what you wish for*, I'd got everything I thought I wanted: the truth about Caspian. Though probably not in any way he would himself have chosen to share it with me.

And, God, that was a bitter prize.

It didn't help that my feelings for him were a total mess, as if someone had ripped open the sofa cushion of my heart and scattered the stuffing all over the living room. I was hurt by him and hurting for him. And I wasn't all that impressed with myself either. A lot of my behavior tonight had sprung from a toxic combination of ignorance and my own shit. But, for fuck's sake, it was sexing 101 that you didn't make people do stuff that made them uncomfortable.

Even if you were the one ostensibly surrendering power.

Even if you were a nobody and they were a billionaire.

And even—especially, in fact—if you thought their reasons for being uncomfortable were a big pile of crap.

Most likely, from what Caspian had said, a lot of it came back to Nathaniel. And, obviously, for both selfish and unselfish reasons, I wished he could find peace with his desires. Believe that they weren't the consequence of cruelty or perversion. But who the fuck was I to decide whether his choices were valid not?

It was the first time I'd ever been able to see Nathaniel as something other than my opposite or my enemy. After all, we had a lot in a common.

Since neither of us really understood the man we claimed to care about.

CHAPTER 13

I must have eventually dozed off because when I woke up, the bedroom was full of cold light and Caspian—exquisite in a pearl gray suit and an indigo tie—was sitting on the edge the bed, shaking me gently.

I jerked upright with an undignified wuffle. It was hard not to be slightly discombobulated because seeing Caspian, absolutely composed and back to normal, half made me believe last night had been a really fucked-up dream.

"What time is it?" I asked, blearily.

"Nearly eleven."

He gestured to a line of cups on the bedside table. "I'm afraid I didn't know what to bring you. So I thought I'd try everything. There's tea or coffee or orange juice."

This was not one hundred percent comfortable. Were we seriously just going to pretend nothing had happened?

"Um, juice?" I said. "Coffee makes me hyper. And I've never got into tea."

He gave me a slight smile. "What a terrible confession for an Englishman."

"I know, right? The government will be closing in on me as we speak." My voice rang hollow in my own ears, full of false jollity. But what was the alternative? *Hey Caspian, still fucked in the head?*

He handed me the orange juice and I took a sip, glad to have something to do with my mouth that wouldn't cause an emotional apocalypse. It was annoyingly good. Sun-bright and sweet, with an edge of sharp, not a single fleck of pulp or pith, leaving this citrus-glitter on my tongue.

Typical. Billionaires even had better squeezed fruit products. Orange juice of this caliber: second best wake-up call after a bj.

Caspian was watching me, hands resting in his lap, the epitome of composure but for the hint of tightness at his knuckles.

Fuck. He was going to dump me.

He'd brought me orange juice and now he was dumping me. It was the orange juice of condolence. Or maybe he just thought I wouldn't hit him if I had something in my hand.

He was probably right.

I was trying to work up the courage or cruelty or whatever it took to dash my drink in his face, when he said, "Please don't go back to Kinlochbervie."

I inhaled in shock. Except my mouth was full of liquid so mainly what I did was splutter. Attractively.

"I know," he went on, "after what happened, the way I made you feel, that I have no right to ask. But I don't want Nathaniel, Arden. I want you. I can't change that I loved him once, but you are not, and have never been, in his shadow."

Oh God. It was so much what I needed to hear that I nearly cried. If I'd had any dignity, I would have accepted the reassurance. As it was, I said "R-really?"

"Of course. I'm appalled that I made you doubt it for a moment." He reached out and did this totally movie cheek-cupping thing. And somehow I didn't feel ridiculous. "Love is a complicated experience. And so powerful that it can sometimes become its own justification. Nathaniel gave me hope that I could be a better man. You make me believe that I'm not such a terrible one."

"I don't," I wailed. "I tried to make you do sex things with me that you didn't want to do. That's *awful*."

"I don't believe we came anywhere close to that."

"But I triggered you."

He gave me an incredibly cold look. "Can we please refrain from throwing around this pop psychological jargon?"

"Um, sorry."

"I experienced a regrettable loss of control brought on by circumstance. Certainly not by you."

I opened my mouth, then closed it again. Maybe this was how he needed me to see what had happened. "Okay."

There was a long silence.

While there'd definitely been improvement, things were still not a hundred percent comfortable. I would have put them at maybe fifty-five to sixty. Sixty-two at the outside.

Eventually, Caspian got up and prowled about, like an agitated fashion plate. "I can't believe I'm going to say this but—"

I wasn't liking the sound of that. "What?"

He drew in a long, careful breath. "I think we may have to…talk about sex."

"Baby."

"Pardon?"

"Nothing." Apparently there could be a wrong time to invoke Salt-N-Pepa. "Ignore me."

"You said last night that I…that my…" He paused and went at it again. "I don't want you to feel that I am condemning your…your ease. On the contrary, I admire it greatly. And very much enjoy what we do together."

God, he looked incredibly uncomfortable.

Part of me wanted to let it go. Spare him an awkward discussion. Except that kind of thing had led us to yesterday, which—even with my zero experience—I could tell was crap. Nil points. F- boyfriending.

So we had to have this conversation. And I had to get it right this time. But I just didn't know *how*. And I wasn't inclined to trust Caspian's judgment either, because his relationship with Nathaniel had basically been a masterclass in fucking each other up.

And then it struck me: he might not have recognized it, or even believed it, but Caspian *had* shown me what to do. Every time we'd had sex: the care he'd always taken with me, his perfect blend of cruelty and mercy, of knowing when to push and when to be gentle, and when I was strong enough to hurt a little.

As he was now. For me. For us.

"Okay," I said. "Thank you."

He gave me a tense little nod. "I'm also very aware that you would like to further explore a lifestyle that I have done my best to put behind me. And while there is a part of me that would love nothing more than to take you back to that room, I cannot allow that to happen."

"Because you have to protect me from kinky shit I can't handle?"

"Because I have to protect myself from becoming someone I despise."

It had been a lot easier accepting that it wasn't my place to question his decisions when I wasn't actually faced with them. Because I was desperate to understand what was so terrible about getting his dungeon on with a fully consenting partner, i.e., me. Instead, I went with, "Do you honestly think what we're doing at the moment is vanilla?"

"Clearly it isn't." He paced again. "I know this might not seem rational to you. But the difference is the room, the implements, the toys, the tools…they take me back to a world that I never want to be part of again."

Well. That was clear cut. And there was no point making a huge fuss about him talking to me if I wasn't going to listen when he did.

"Okay," I said. "I get it."

He stilled. "Do you really, Arden? I'm telling you I might not be able to satisfy you in the ways you need."

"I've been pretty damn satisfied so far."

That won the smallest of smiles. But it didn't last. "While all relationships involve compromises, there are some that should not be made. I do not wish to be a compromise for you as I have been for Nathaniel."

This was one hell of a conversation to be having with my hair fluffed up and my nipples out. I hiked up the duvet. "Let me think a moment."

He circled back to the bed and sat down.

My head felt like it was going to explode. And, worst of all, I couldn't quite tell if we were having a breakup conversation or not. "Just to clarify: what we're doing at the moment. Like what we did on the plane. And on your desk. Is that okay or not okay?"

"Very okay."

"And we can keep doing it?"

He nodded.

Probably this was a situation when being super explicit was better than taking anything for granted. "So you're up for spanking me? And hurting me? And making me cry and beg and crawl? And maybe tying me up with items of clothing you happen to have on hand?"

"Yes. Yes. Yes, yes, and yes. And yes." He sounded very serious. But he'd also gone super pink.

"Oh, and saying I'm a slut and things?"

"Yes."

"And incredibly dirty phone calls when you tell me exactly what to do?"

"Yes."

"Then I'm in. That's not a compromise."

Various emotions flashed across his face so quickly I couldn't quite identify them. "But...the room and—"

"Well, the room is pretty cool. And if you were into it, I would be too. But, Caspian, I don't need fancy furniture. I need...well...you."

"Me?"

"Yeah. Your voice commanding me and your eyes watching me and your body controlling me."

"And that's really enough?"

"More than. Look, I'm not an expert or anything but, for me, submission is here"—I brushed a finger against my brow—"and here." I tapped my heart. "You can bring me to my knees with a word or a smile or the simple will to have me there."

He shuddered, eyes closing for a moment, but, for once, it didn't seem to be distress. "I have built a world-spanning financial empire from the ground up. I have bought and sold corporations that between them controlled the livelihoods of tens of thousands of people. I have dined with presidents and prime ministers. But nothing has made me feel as powerful, or given me such pride, as your trust, your passion, and your surrender."

"They're yours." Apparently I'd gone from stressed to lustful in 2.5 seconds. "Let me show you."

We gazed at each other across an expanse of bed. Something had definitely changed: intangible but undeniable, like the sky, and the taste of the air, on the first day of spring. But it felt fragile too in its newness. Naked skin over deep wounds.

"We shouldn't," he said. With precisely zero conviction. "I'm already late for a conference call."

Casting off the blankets, I rolled onto my knees and elbows. Arched my spine in supplicant invitation, presenting my arse in a "come and get it" kind of way.

He gave a soft, helpless groan. "My Arden."

"Yes." I wriggled shamelessly. "Own me."

We went at it no-frills. Just stripped-bare need. With Caspian not even undressing. I could tell he was trying to be careful but it stung after the pounding he'd given me yesterday.

His first shallow thrusts made my eyes water and my fingers knot in the sheets. But, being a total pervert, I was into it. There was something so primal and inexorable about his cock prizing my body open. It made me feel real again.

Once he was all the way in, and I was stretched and trembling under him, he slid a hand all the way up the sweat-damp line of my back. Cupped the nape of my neck, his touch controlling and tender and perfect.

"You're all right?" he murmured.

I bucked back against him. "God, yes."

For a man already late for a conference call, he fucked me thoroughly and languorously. And I lay among the pillows, moaning and rocking to his rhythm, my whole body alive with the raw ache of possession and the whiskey-burn of slowly gathering pleasure. I wasn't sure I'd come—the sensations were strung together too tightly—but the brush of his lips against my shoulder blade, the way he could make me feel so degraded and so worshipped at the same fucking time, sent me over.

It got a bit more explicitly *ouch* in the arse department after that. I was still okay with it, since while it wasn't good pain, it wasn't bad pain either, and I enjoyed simply being used. Except he must have figured it out because he pulled out and, from the slick sound of skin on skin, began finishing himself off.

Which I didn't have a problem with exactly. In fact, physically speaking, I was grateful. And maybe on a different day I would have found it hot. But, right now, I wasn't up for anything that put distance between us. Or made me feel uninvolved in his pleasure. I tried to roll over but his hand tightened on my neck. Time was, I would probably have taken it without question. But today I was either too strong or too weak to do that for him.

"Um," I said, in a muffled, inadvertently pillow-munching voice, "I'm all up for being objectified and wanked over, and I think I've got a pretty decent bum…but what's wrong with my face?"

A moment of silence. Then. "I adore your face. But I don't like being watched."

I put my head back down. Listened to his harsh breath. Tried, with my brain fuzzy from orgasm, to find the Robert Frost road (correct not common interpretation) between his boundaries and my own. "You can…y'know…in me."

"I don't want to hurt you."

"I don't mind."

His palm swept down my spine again, and curved possessively over my flank. "When I hurt you, Arden, it will be in a way I have chosen and can control."

And to think he kept insisting he wasn't the romantic type. I mean, yes, I was all for roses and chocolates, but there was something deeply endearing to me about a man who wanted to hurt you right.

"What," I suggested hopefully, "if I kept my eyes closed?"

Caspian made this sound—I couldn't tell if it was more exasperated or more amused—grabbed me around the waist, and flipped me over. "Happy now?"

"Yes." I tried to de-flail my limbs and arrange myself

somewhat sexily, which was actually kind of difficult when I couldn't see. And was right in the middle of my own wet spot. "It's better like this." Awkward pause. "Isn't it?"

This time his soft laugh was nothing but fondness. His fingers brushed my lips and then the tip of my nose. Tweaked at my nipple rings. Traced the tattoo at my hip. "Much." He tapped the inside my knee. "Now show me what's mine."

"All of me is yours."

Heat was trickling over me. Gathering in the places I thought he might be looking. Considering less than a minute ago I'd been lying in a wobbly heap with my arse in the air, it shouldn't have felt any more exposing to spread my legs on command but somehow it did.

Didn't stop me though. And, actually, made my cock perk back up. I just never know when to quit, that's my problem.

He gave a rough growl. And presumably got back to his masturbating.

"Sure I can't do anything?" I said. "Give you a helping—"

He put his hand lightly over my mouth. Which I entirely deserved. Giggling, I kissed his fingers, and then sucked on them.

"Oh. God. Arden."

It was such an amazing groan that I couldn't help myself…and I cheated. I peeped. The quickest glance from between my lashes. And, fuck, it was worth it. He was flushed and rumpled, his head thrown back, his neck all strong and straining, and his expression half frowning, half helpless. Completely beautiful.

And then I felt guilty as fuck because he'd trusted me and I'd epically failed to be worthy of it. What it came down to was, I was Orpheus, hanging around at the gates of Tartarus and being like "Sheesh, dude, it was only a glance" to Hades.

I squeezed my eyes tightly shut so I wouldn't be tempted again. Concentrated instead on doing the lewdest possible things to Caspian's fingers. And he came a few seconds later, with a naked cry that—for once—he didn't even try to stifle. I actually jerked when his come splashed over me, impossibly hot for the split-second of its landing.

"Can I look now?" I asked. Or, rather "Can ah ook ow?" on account of my tongue being somewhat occupied.

"If you must."

I stared at him hungrily, but he was almost back together by now. I mean, he still looked like he'd just had sex, flushed and sweaty, his chest heaving and his hair curling at the tips, but I wanted to see him in the wildness of the moment, lost and vulnerable and free. It was kind of sad-making he didn't want to share that with me. Even more sad-making that he didn't feel able to share it with anyone. Orgasms weren't supposed to be lonely.

It made me want to snuggle him without mercy. But I knew he wouldn't be into it. So I grinned up at him instead and pulled his fingers from between my lips with the wettest plop I could manage.

He winced adorably.

I let him go. Dabbed up a splash of semen from my stomach and licked it off my thumb.

"Arden…" He sounded almost shocked.

"Five-second rule. And you're delicious."

"That's ridiculous. And untrue."

"How do you know? Have you tasted?"

"Well, not myself. But I'm familiar with the...with the..."

I somehow didn't completely crack up at the sight of Caspian Hart trying to find whatever he deemed an appropriate word for come.

"...substance," he finished.

"And you're not a fan?"

Wait. Did this mean Nathaniel had funky spunk? Oh please, God, I hoped he did.

"I don't have an aversion." Caspian took off his jacket and tossed it over the end of the bed. "I just wouldn't actively seek opportunities to imbibe it."

"I didn't say I'd eat it on chips. But it's you...and I like you."

He'd gone pinkish. "Why are we talking about this?"

"You started it."

"I absolutely did not."

"Yes, you did."

He stretched himself out over me, trapping me cozily beneath his body, and kissed my nose. "No, I didn't."

"Your clothes," I protested. Though it was way, way too late.

"I would have had to change anyway."

Great. After all the trouble I went to in order to ensure nobody would have to clean my jizz off Caspian's carpet, now it was going to be someone's job to get it out of his bespoke, probably Italian suit. "Two looks in one day. You're the Kim Kardashian of financial management."

"I'm who?"

"Oh my God." My voice shook with the laughter caught in it. "You really have been in more magazines than you've read."

"That's an accurate assessment."

He kissed me again—mouth this time—and then rolled away, settling on his back beside me, one arm flung casually above his head. I curled into the space. It was something I was getting weirdly good at it: lying hopefully in the shape of a hug. I was close enough to feel the heat from his body, to smell the sex on him, but he still didn't touch me.

"Maybe," I said, "we could do a knowledge exchange."

His eyebrow twitched.

"I could teach you about popular culture…like…any popular culture. And you could—"

"Educate you on the impact of emerging economies on price movement in global equity, currency, and commodity markets."

"I was thinking more…get me into sci-fi?"

I wasn't sure how seriously I'd meant it, but he tensed right up. "I'm hardly an expert."

"It's not about expertise. So much as, y'know, sharing something with you. That you like. I mean"—I stretched an arm over the side of the bed and groped around in the box until I found *Downbelow Station*—"could I borrow this maybe?"

There was a horrible silence.

"Shit, it was your dad's, wasn't it?"

Caspian covered his face with his hands. "It's not that I don't trust you…"

"No. God. No. I know that. Don't worry about it."

"There's just…when someone dies. There's so little of them left."

"I get it, I really do." Wow. Oh wow. I was a complete fuck-trumpet. Caspian's generosity to me was boundless, ridiculous even. And here I was casually asking him to lend me his last connection to his dead father. "I'm so sorry. Forget I ever said it."

I wished I could touch him. I felt so helpless, lying there, babbling out apologies that were probably washing over him like water. When all I wanted to do was draw him close and hold him tight. Make him truly believe he was safe with me. That I would take nothing from him he feared to lose. Didn't choose to give.

Eventually, he emerged, letting out a long, careful breath. "No, it's me. I'm being foolish. Of course you can—"

"No," I cried. I mean, it was incredibly touching that he was willing. But it was the last thing I wanted now that I understood what I'd actually been asking. "I mean, sheesh. Paper books? Who reads *those* anymore? I bet I could pick this up for 99p as an epub."

He gave a slight shaken laugh.

I grabbed my phone and googled. "Well, okay, $11.99 if I pretend I'm American."

"Arden, I don't mind."

"I do. That thing's like five hundred pages. It weighs a ton." Suddenly his arms came around me and he pulled me close, turning the space into a nook, my body tucked into his. To me, at least, it felt perfect. Like I belonged there. And I couldn't help wriggling in even closer. "By the way, I think your meeting might be a bust."

"Oh fuck." Caspian swore so rarely that it always sounded extra filthy—and therefore extra sexy—when he did. He pulled out his phone and dialed with a deft swipe. "Bellerose? Cancel that call, please." A pause. "No, that's fine. Yes. Yes. I'll leave at two. Thank you."

"I'm sorry I made you miss your thing," I said, once he'd hung up, only lying a little bit. "Was it important?"

"Terribly important. But so am I. And it can wait."

I tried not to smirk.

"You know"—Caspian gave me a wry look—"you don't seem all that sorry."

"I'm *abstractly* sorry. But I like being with you too much to be *completely* sorry."

He laughed, his hand finding its way to my arse and giving it a squeeze. The fabric of his suit was slightly rough against my nipples, making me very aware of the fact he was, once again, fully clothed and I was starkers. It was kind of the way things tended to go with us. Mostly I didn't mind, and there were times when the sense of personal exposure was definitely part of the fun, but from another perspective it was bizarre. After all, I looked like me—decentish but nothing special—and Caspian was absolutely spectacular. If I'd been him, I would have been naked whenever I could get away with it.

Honestly, I'd probably never stop wanking.

While taking selfies of myself.

Narcissus for the social media age.

I snuggled in closer, just content to bask in the time that Caspian had unexpectedly given me.

"Do you mind if I smoke?" he asked, after a minute or two.

He'd told me when we'd first met—on a moonlit night in Oxford that seemed forever ago now—he allowed himself one cigarette a month. Something to do with controlling his vices, which didn't make much sense to me because if there was one thing Caspian Hart could have done with a bit less of, it was control. I wasn't entirely sure what it meant that he wanted to indulge himself here, now, with me but it was intimacy of a kind and I sure as hell wasn't going to say no. "Course not."

My bedside table was a pervert's smorgasbord of lube and condoms and exciting things to put up your arse or wrap round your knob. I didn't get much of a look in Caspian's but I was pretty sure there was nothing inside it except a book, a lighter, a saucer I guessed he was using as an ashtray, and a packet of Dunhill.

With an arm around me, he was a little clumsy lighting up. And then he lay back against the pillows, still holding me tight, and took a deep, luxurious drag. His eyes fell half closed, smoke billowing from between his parting lips. It made me desperate to kiss him. Feel the surrender of his mouth. He hadn't wanted me to see him come but he let me see this. The one pleasurable yielding he seemed able to countenance.

"Caspian?"

"Mmm?"

"What did you write on me yesterday?"

"It's from *The Lathe of Heaven*."

One of the many problems with being an English literature student, especially if you went to Oxford, was that people expected you to have read everything. Thus condemning you to a life of lying, bullshitting, and incipient shame.

I opened my mouth to do make a bland statement that implied familiarity with the text without committing myself to anything. And then I thought: fuck it, no. Caspian already knew I'd only pretended to have read *Ulysses*. He wasn't going to think less of me because I hadn't read *The Lathe of Heaven*.

And there was no reason for me to think less of myself either.

"I don't know it," I announced triumphantly.

"Why would you, since you're not into sci-fi? It's Ursula Le Guin. About a man who has the ability to change reality through his dreams."

"I can see why you might be into that."

He smiled faintly. "It's not quite what you think. The protagonist is very much a dreamer. Passive to a fault. It's other people who want to change the world, usually with disastrous consequences."

I sighed. "You know, that's another thing I don't get about science fiction. For a genre that's supposed to be all about technology and progress and the future…why does it always turn out to be a massive disaster whenever somebody tries to do anything or change anything?"

"You tell me, Mr. BA Oxon."

"I guess because a lot of genre fiction has its roots in the nineteenth century, when we had more rigid ideas about God and social order. Aaaand check out me sounding like I know what the fuck I'm talking about."

"That's because you do. Though, for what it's worth, I don't think this book is actually saying that. I think it's more about the complexities of the world and its problems, especially the problems that are connected to the complexities of people. My father…" He paused. Cleared his throat. "My father always said Le Guin was primarily interested in people."

"Isn't science fiction supposed to be about ideas?"

Caspian swallowed. "It is. But it can also be very…very human. Since a lot of the time it's concerned with human

questions. At least that's what my father believed." He shifted
and I could feel him getting self-conscious. This was usually the
moment he would pull away from me. But, to my surprise, he
gave a slightly rueful laugh and went on. "No wonder I read
PPE."

"I thought"—I gave him a naughty look—"you were lever-
aging the Oxford brand to something something the something
something?"

"That too." He let his voice slip into its driest, coolest register.
"To lead a successful life, it is vital to something something the
something something."

I giggled, hopelessly heart-eyed. I adored everything about
Caspian—his strength, his ferocity, his delicious cruelty—but
this side of him, his secret capacity to laugh at himself, never
failed to delight me.

"But I think a large part of it," he murmured, "came down
to being able to study philosophy. It gave me an excuse to keep
thinking about the sorts of things my father liked to think
about."

I was starting to wonder if maybe *I'd* developed the power to
affect reality by dreaming. Except I wouldn't have dreamed up
this in a gazillion years. I wouldn't have dared. It seemed too impossible. We'd had an argument. Fixed it. Discussed stuff. And
now we were actually cuddling. And he was talking to me, his
body warm and relaxed against mine, his eyes a darkly slumber-
ous blue, like the sea when you swam out too far. And then his
phone bleeped a reminder.

He glanced at it grumpily and sighed. "I'm sorry, Arden. I
have to get moving. Do you want anything from Paris?"

"Yes." I grinned at him. "I want you to come back super quick, and eat ridiculously expensive sushi off my restrained, naked, helplessly aroused body."

He was laughing as he caught up my hand and kissed it. "I'll see what I can do."

"You promise?"

"Promises are for children."

"And lovers."

He held my gaze for a long time, but he was the one running late and I wasn't backing down.

"Then," he said finally, "I promise, my Arden."

CHAPTER 14

Unfortunately when Friday rolled round, I was too wrecked for anything we'd planned and promised and hoped for. Instead, I was sitting on the sofa, dazed and half crying, and clutching helplessly at my phone.

It was only when Caspian said, "Arden, what's wrong?" that I realized he was there. Or even remembered that he was supposed to be coming.

I glanced up. Noted—with a terrible sense of distance—how lovely he looked just then. Charcoal gray suit, lilac shirt. And, in what must have been a moment of unusual opulence, a Liberty print tie in shades of silver and indigo. God, he'd dressed for me. And I was—

"It's Nik." The words burst out of me in a teary blurble. "He's been hit by a car or something. I don't know. He's in surgery. That's bad, isn't it? When people are in surgery?"

Caspian was silent for a moment. Startled, possibly. "Well, it depends on the surgery."

"Right. I…I…" My attention reeled from Caspian to the apartment. "I didn't get any sushi."

"Forget the sushi. I'm sorry to hear about your friend."

"Yeah." For the first time in my life, I wanted Caspian to go away. I needed to freak the fuck out. And having him standing there, all calm and pristine and vaguely concerned, was cramping my style.

"You should be with him," he was saying, with the uncertain gentleness I remembered all too well from my other crises. "What hospital? I'll call a car."

"I can't be with him. He's in fucking Boston." That was when I started crying. Properly this time. Not the anxious eye-prickling of the shocked. But the full-on wailing of the terrified and traumatized. "And I'm supposed to be his next of kin."

Caspian tugged out his pocket square—which turned out be purple and polka-dotted, unusually playful for my austere Mr. Hart—and pressed it into my hand. "What about his parents?"

"He hates them. I should probably tell them but I don't know if he'd even want them there." Words kept coming. Muddling with my tears. Until everything was a mess. "And his ex-girlfriend's in Paris and I can't get hold of her. And I have £50.56 in my bank account right now and a flight to Boston is like eight hundred quid and I don't think my family could afford it but they wouldn't say no so I can't ask and nobody over there will really tell me what's happened except there's been a crash and Nik's in hospital and he's all alone in a strange country full of Americans. And, oh God, they don't have the NHS over there and I don't actually know how insurance works. And what if he dies? What if he's already dead? Or they've thrown his broken body out of the window because he didn't have gazillions of dollars on hand to pay for medical care?"

At last I stopped talking. I was nowhere near out of panic, but I was definitely out of breath. Also most of the water in my body was erupting from my eyes. So my mouth wouldn't work anymore, except for strange, sticky gulping noises.

"Excuse me," said Caspian. "I have to make a call."

He stepped briskly away from me. I heard his footsteps carry him down the hall. The click of a door closing. The soft murmur of his voice. He could have been saying anything. Like *please get me away from this crazy, weeping person.*

I…I couldn't blame him. He'd come here for sexy funtimes. Not deal-with-hysterical-breaking-Arden-times. But seeing him turn away like that? It had hurt. A dull pain upon a deeper one. A careless knock against already bruised flesh.

I was calmer though. Not particularly in a feeling better way. So much as hollowed out. His pocket square was still crumpled in my sweaty fist so I used it to wipe my face. I'd cried so hard it was like I'd exfoliated *myself* and even the silk felt rough against my skin.

Also. Snot. There was a quite a lot of that. Caspian must have really enjoyed the sight of me tonight. And why the fuck was I worried about looking disgusting when Nik was—

At that moment, Caspian came back in.

Oh God. I was ugly and awful and he'd *seen* me.

"Sorry about that." I make a valiant attempt to pull myself together. "I was just a bit…anyway. Do you want to get that sushi?"

"Stop talking about sushi."

"Sorry." Usually I liked Caspian's commands, finding not harshness there, but the opposite. A kind of care-taking. Unfortunately I was in no state to be strong or understanding or react to anything except the surface of things. So it felt like a slap. Made me flinch.

He sighed. Crouched in front of me. Drowned me in the sweet familiar scents of his body and his cologne. "Look at me, Arden."

I wouldn't. I couldn't.

He caught the edge of my jaw and forced me. I didn't even have it in me right then to resent it—just blinked at him with swollen eyes. "The car will be here in ten minutes," he said. "The jet will be ready in thirty. Bellerose will meet you at Heathrow."

My brain was static. "W-wait. What?"

"I said you should be with your friend and I meant it."

"But…I can't…"

"You can. And you will. Now go and pack."

For some reason, the simplicity of that—of going and packing—cut through the numbness of my body and the emptiness of my mind. I rose jerkily and stumbled toward the bedroom.

Then something made me stop. Look back at Caspian.

I don't know how it happened. If he moved first or I did. But his arms opened for me and I rushed into them, and he held me. His embrace tight and warm and absolute, with nothing held back. It was overwhelming—overwhelming in a way I desperately needed—the purity of his affection. The ferocity of his solace.

I pressed myself against him, shuddering. And he let me stay.

His hand crept into my hair, soothing me. "It's going to be all right, my Arden."

"How do you know?"

"Because I will do everything in my power to make it so."

My eyes burned, as if they wanted to shed more tears. "You can't stop someone dying."

"No, but I can give your friend the best possible chance. And I can make sure you're by his side if the worst happens."

There was a silence. Beneath my cheek, his heart pulsed, its rhythm unwavering within its cage of flesh and bone. It seemed impossible that something so powerfully vital could ever falter. Or stop altogether.

"I got snot on your pocket square," I mumbled.

"Then I will have it dry cleaned." He unpeeled me carefully. Stroked the moisture from my cheeks with his thumb. "Now you really do need to pack."

I nodded, bent my head to swiftly kiss the inside of his wrist—felt his responsive shiver—and went.

My sense of time was blurry but I was pretty sure it didn't take long to fling a handful of clothes into my trundly and zip it up. And then Caspian took me down to the car, steering me expertly with one hand at the small of my back like we were guests at a cocktail party. I was trying to find words to thank him—any words would do—but the magnitude of what was happening was simply too great.

And then I was in the car and it was too late anyway.

At Heathrow, I was taken to a special entrance, where I was greeted by name and whisked off to a private lounge. As promised, Bellerose was there, looking far too elegant for a man who had presumably been yanked away from his evening in order to arrange a trip to America for his boss's…his boss's whatever I was.

He took my passport from my unresisting fingers and went off to deal with the pilot for me. I perched on the edge of one of the leather sofas and stared blankly out of the floor-to-ceiling windows. Caspian's plane was waiting on the runway, a pale bird against the oily dark.

Eventually, Bellerose dropped down beside me, and pushed a cup of something into my hands. "I got you some tea. It's hot and milky and you should drink it. And then I need you to listen to me."

I nodded. Took a sip of tea. I wasn't particularly into the stuff, but it did, actually, make me feel slightly more human. Unfortunately, "slightly more human" meant full of fear and misery again. Only wanting to be in Caspian's arms, with all the badness of the world held at bay.

"I've got you a suite at the Liberty," Bellerose was saying. "It's the closest decent hotel to the hospital. I'll also arrange for a car to meet you at the airport when you arrive."

I kept nodding.

"Do you have your phone with you? The one Caspian gave you?"

Did I? Apparently I did. And my own, too. Go me, and my brief moments of competence.

"I've sent you all the details. And call Caspian when you land. He'll be worrying."

Caspian? Worrying? "Um, okay."

"I don't suppose you thought to bring the credit card

Caspian provided when you first moved into One Hyde Park?"

I honestly wasn't sure if I'd remembered to pack my socks.

"I didn't think so. Here."

Another card. Coutts again. Quietly black on the reverse. An artfully faded image of a Chinese street on the front. The logo a flash of silver. "I…I that's…You know I can't take his money."

Bellerose's lashes—which were reddish-gold, like his hair—fluttered, as if he was trying very hard not to roll his eyes. "Given you don't have any of your own, you don't really have a choice."

"I do! I have £50.56."

"There's no shame in lack of money. Just inconvenience. How are you intending to live in a foreign country on an income of nothing?"

"Very frugally?"

"Use the card." He picked it up and slid it into my jacket pocket. "If you don't take proper care of yourself, Caspian will be angry."

"W-with me?" I found myself blinking back fresh tears, overwhelmed by, at this point, basically everything.

"Much more likely with me, since it's my job to ensure you don't starve to death in a gutter in Boston."

I cringed. "I'm sorry. I'm sorry. I don't mean to be difficult."

"Then might I recommend not being?"

"Oh God," I wailed, in unfocused despair. "You hate me."

"What does that have to do with anything?"

"I d-don't like it."

"Personally, I find the way people treat you when they don't like you infinitely preferable to their behavior when they do."

I burst into tears.

There was a longish…well. Not a silence because I was sniffling into it. But a period of time in which I cried and Bellerose sat there uncomfortably.

"Please stop doing that," he murmured. "You're getting salt in your tea."

I was trying to stop crying. I really was. Unfortunately, it didn't seem to be happening.

"For heaven's sake, I'm Caspian Hart's assistant. My opinion about anything is utterly irrelevant."

"N-not to Caspian."

"Well, no. But he does not consult me about his personal life. Nor would I want him to."

"But you keep having to do all this stuff for me."

Bellerose half turned, and it was one of those moments where, despite the fact they looked nothing alike, he reminded me of Caspian. Beautiful, unassailable, and merciless. "It's not for you. It's for him."

"I'm not sure whether that makes me feel better or worse." I did my best to present the tatters of a smile. "All the same, I'm sorry I dragged you out. And on a Friday night as well."

"It's fine."

"But you could have been, I don't know, at a party or having sex."

"Actually, I was knitting."

That surprised a snuffly laugh out of me. And then I realized he wasn't joking. "You knit?"

"What I do in my spare time is none of your business."

"But knitting? Seriously? That's…you do realize that's adorable, don't you?"

"I think I preferred it when you were crying." The look Bellerose was giving me would have clotted cream. Except he'd let himself be human with me—even if just for a moment—and I wasn't sure if I'd ever be properly scared of him again.

"You're so mean. Why are you so mean, Bellerose?"

"It gets things done."

I rested my head on his shoulder. "You know, you don't have to wait with me."

"You know I do."

Time went all airporty. Dragged its feet. Slumbered in corners. But, finally, the plane was cleared for takeoff. I went through the last few checks and hurried outside after Bellerose. He'd dealt with my luggage and was waiting for me by the door of the plane, only slightly ruffled by the wind, and looking like the center spread from a *Milieu* pull-out special on private jets.

"Um." I clunked up to join him. "Thank you for doing all this. And sorry for crying and being awkward and making a fuss about the…the credit card."

I was such a nonsense person. When a man flew you across the world in his private jet so you could be with your friend, drawing a line at using his actual money was as hypocritical as it was futile. And I fully expected Bellerose to point it out, but all he said was, "You will call him, won't you?"

"Yes. As soon as I can."

"Make sure you do."

Wow. Bellerose was certainly, err, something. I grinned at him. "He must pay you really well."

"Most likely."

"Or else you really love him." Shit shit. I couldn't quite believe I'd said that aloud.

Bellerose just smirked. "Not the way you do, Arden. Have a
safe flight."

Watching him descending the stairs with the sort of grace I
could only dream of, I couldn't help thinking of Caspian. Surrounded by glass and darkness and so many walls. "You'll take
care of him, won't you?" I blurted out.

He half turned. "Always."

And then he vanished into the shadows between the runway
lights. And I was alone. Well, apart from the pilot and the cabin
crew, and all the other people Caspian was paying to attend to
my every need.

But, y'know, emotionally speaking.

* * *

We landed in Boston at around 7 a.m. Or rather at 2 a.m. EST.
Which was instant jet lag, my body insisting that there should
be morningness, when it was still the middle of the night. I'd set
an alarm for an hour before landing, which had given me time
to shower and de-rumple, but I still stumbled off the plane like
a zombie who'd partied too hard.

I couldn't tell if it was my brain being porridged or the inherent sameness of airports but it didn't really feel as if I'd flown
across the world or that I was in another country. At least not
until I had to talk to people who sounded like they'd left their
r's in seventeenth-century England. And then the realness of it
all became almost uncopeable-with.

Once my passport had been checked, luggage retrieved, and I'd been welcomed to the USA, I was whisked along gleaming concourses, past travelers and lingerers and an honest-to-goodness Dunkin' Donuts stand, and finally bundled into a limo. It was a bit like being a rockstar and a bit like being kidnapped.

Although I would make a terrible subject for a kidnapping. I wasn't famous and my family wasn't wealthy. What were the perpetrators going to demand? *Bring us one million units of your best walnut bread and your copy of Twilight Imperium?* Or maybe Caspian would have to step in. Which sounded like the plot of a five-episode, post-watershed BBC drama series. And viewers would write in and complain about the unnecessary homosexual content. Because being part of a clearly implausible kidnapping plotline was necessary. Whereas kissing a man was totally gratuitous.

Oh God. Brain. Stop. Just stop.

My head was a ceaseless whirl, disconnected frivolities flying about as chaotically as socks in the washing machine. It was probably a slightly unhinged defense mechanism. So I didn't have to think the only thought that mattered: *Nik's in hospital. Nik's in hospital. Nik's in hospital.*

Also, the whole limo deal was extra awkward when there was only you. Maybe I should have felt like Mr. Big—sweeping between skyscrapers in my long, black penis car—but I was small. So small. The corridor of the limo rolling away from me.

I tried to distract myself by looking out the window. Except it was hard to get a sense of the city beyond its difference. An alien glitterscape, languidly sprawling, up, across, around, careless of its own space. Disconcertingly uniform, too, with its neat redbrick parcels and tall silver towers. This smooth curve of history, so unlike the haphazard patchwork of London.

Ugh. I'd been in America less than an hour and I was home-sick?

The drive was quicker than I was ready for it to be. Airport, tunnel, streets. And we arrived. The hospital was this vast campus, multi-building thing, bright, shiny, and monstrous, the way that only public institutions could be.

I de-limoed near the big red EMERGENCY sign and hurled myself into the building. Everything that followed was little more than a blur of…happening. I checked in—my squeaky questions gently put aside for the surgeon—and was redirected. A horrible hell-journey of slick gray tunnels and silver elevators, my nose full of hospital smell. I had to go through another round of identification at the ICU, while I scoured my hands with sanitizer gel. Then another corridor. Past the misted glass of waiting area: huddled shadows within. My footfalls silenced by vinyl, as if I was already half ghost.

And finally I was there.

Standing in the doorway of a room.

It was a nice room. It was. If you could look past the tangle of screens and equipment and mad scientist tubing. The white walls. The white sheets.

And Nik was—oh God.

The last time I'd seen him…so banal, really. A stilted airport parting that we'd both believed and not believed was a proper goodbye. *Shit, I'd better go*, he'd said. *Travel safely*, I'd answered. And that was it. I could vaguely remember him walking away, laptop bag swung across one shoulder, lacrosse stick over the other, his shadow cast long against the epoxy-shining floor like a sundial marking the hour.

Now he was just a flop of blondish hair, cocooned in a hospital gown.

I put a hand over my mouth because I wasn't sure I could even be trusted to breathe properly right then.

After a moment or two, the doctor came. Introduced herself—Dr. Sharma, she said—and talked to me softly. There was good news. He was breathing by himself. No traumatic brain injuries. But there was other stuff. Broken legs. Broken sternum. Multiple rib and spine fractures. Bone shards embedded in the spinal cord—

"Is he going to die?" I asked.

"He's stable for now."

She said it so warily I realized I was asking the wrong thing. "Will he...he's going to get better, right?"

Except that just made her repeat everything she'd previously said. With some extra stuff about titanium plates and potential compromise to the spinal cord.

And that was when I knew I had to stop with the questions. It was too early for them. And the answers wouldn't tell me anything I didn't already guess. What mattered was the fact Nik was alive. "Can I go in?"

She nodded and stepped away.

And I...I hesitated. Like a fucking worthless coward, I stood there. Because crossing that threshold would mean this was really happening. And I didn't know how to bear it. I didn't want the future of that golden, laughing, ridiculously talented boy to be a shattered body in a hospital bed.

Except it was. And that was that.

And it didn't make him any less Nik.

Step by step, then. Step by fucking step. A far longer journey than the one across the ocean. From the door to Nik.

I slumped into the nearest chair. His hand was lying on top of the covers, looking so neat that it could only have been *placed* there. People were naturally messy. His symmetry was as terrifying as his stillness. I didn't dare actually move the hand. There were so many tubes sticking out of it I'd probably have ended up killing him. But I covered it gently with my own. He felt strange. Not warm or cold. And very smooth. Like plastic.

"Jesus, Nik." My voice came out way too loud for where I was and I had to try again. "What the fuck? I told you to travel safely. This doesn't look anything like travelling safely. In fact, some people might call getting smashed up by a car the exact opposite of travelling safely."

I don't know. It had to be wishful thinking but I was sure I felt the slightest change in the pattern of his breathing. Like maybe whatever he was dreaming had made him smile.

It was, as nights went, shitty. Though obviously worse for Nik. Or maybe not, since he was unconscious, and I was sitting there, painfully awake. He did stir sometimes, and talk to me, but he was living in fragments. The first time, he asked where he was, which scared the shit out of me, especially because when I told him—as gently as I could—that he was in the hospital, he wanted to know why. And I didn't know how to explain to someone who'd been in a car crash about the car crash they didn't remember being in. Thankfully, he drifted off again almost immediately and I ran in a panic for the doctor in case it was a traumatic brain injury thing after all. But apparently it was pretty normal.

Next time his eyes opened, he seemed a touch more lucid. "Arden?" He blinked, the motion jerky and slow, as if it wasn't a reflex for him anymore. "Dude, you look like shit."

"Dude, you're pissing into a bag."

He made a barely there noise of amusement. And then seemed exhausted by it.

"Am I on a lot of drugs?" he whispered, just when I thought he'd slipped away again. "I can't really feel anything."

"Um. Yeah. That's…that's the drugs." Oh wow. And the Award for Least Convincing Bedside Consolation Lie goes to Arden St. Ives.

Nik's throat worked laboriously. "Are you…really here? Not dreaming?"

"I'm here. Promise." I tightened my fingers over his. They twitched in response. "Can you feel that?"

"Yeah…"

"That's me."

"You…you…won't leave?"

"Only occasionally to wee and I'll have to check in to my hotel. But I'll be super quick."

He mumbled something I didn't catch and closed his eyes. But he slept more easily. And that was good, right? He needed to rest and stuff.

More than he needed the truth right then.

CHAPTER 15

By the time dawn filled the room with fresh gray, Nik was still sleeping and I was beyond exhausted. Sodden with it like heavy rain. I dozed off and on through the morning, but by early afternoon one of the nurses had pretty much ordered me out of the hospital, telling me I'd be useless if I didn't get some proper rest.

Not sure where the hotel was, or even if I was capable of walking, I got the limo back. And discovered the place was literally just up the road. Except I was too knackered to be embarrassed. I crawled out of the car and wove my way to the front desk. Signed things and received my keycard and some other shit in a blur of words I barely understood.

Lift.

Corridor.

Room.

Bed. Face.

I groped for my second phone. Hit the shortcut for Caspian with a barely functional finger.

He picked up immediately. "Are you all right?"

"I'm sorry," I slurred, "I dunno wha time it is."

I heard him murmuring, "I'm sorry, I have to take this," and then, to me, "It doesn't matter. How's your friend?"

"Kind of fucked, but alive and breathing. That's...that's good, right?"

"Very promising."

I wasn't capable of much movement, but I managed to fold part of the duvet over me with some determined feet flapping. "I'm really glad I'm here. Thank you for helping me."

"It's nothing."

"I'm too tired to argue, but it's not nothing. It only seems that way to you because you're used to being able to do stuff like this."

"Being able to do something is simply a question of resources. Being willing to do it is a matter of heart." His voice softened. "You chose to be with your friend when he needed you. I simply made it easier for you to get there."

Warmth crept into the corners of my tiredness. "I guess. It's overwhelming, though. And I'm not sure what use I am to him right now."

"Caring for others is not my field of expertise, but in Nik's place I wouldn't need you to be useful. I'd need you to be there."

He'd done it again: said the exact thing I didn't know I was desperate to hear. "You're so wrong, Caspian. You make me feel very cared for."

"I..." I heard him swallow. Caught the uncertain tapping

of his fingers against his desk. "You'll call as often as you can, won't you?"

"I promise."

"You should rest now, though."

I rolled onto my back. Let my sleep-hazy eyes take in the blandness of a hotel ceiling. "I know. But…"

"What?"

"I don't want you to go."

The words had escaped before I could stop them, and I cringed at how childish they sounded, but all Caspian said was, "Then I won't."

"You can't just sit around on the phone with me."

"I think you'll find I can do whatever I like. And besides"—I somehow knew he was smiling—"you're practically unconscious. It'll probably only take five minutes."

I laughed, or whatever passed for a laugh when you were half drunk with sleepiness, and rolled myself up in the duvet. Caspian's breath was an intimate metronome against my ear. "Tell me something?"

"What sort of thing?"

"Anything."

"That's very helpful. Thank you, Arden."

There was that self-conscious note in his voice. And, as ever, I found it a little bit adorable. "What are you wearing?"

"I'm not sure this is really the time—"

"Not in a sex way. I just want to know."

"Oh. Well…" A pause. Maybe he was checking. "A dark blue suit by Kathryn Sargent, with a white shirt, a navy tie, and a pink, polka-dotted pocket square."

"Pink, you say?"

"Dark pink. I think they call the shade French rose. Are you giggling?"

"Only a little bit. Mainly, I'm imagining how hot you look."

His tone grew stern. "You're supposed to be sleeping."

"I know. But please don't stop talking to me." Through some complicated maneuvers with my toes I managed to kick off my shoes and wriggle my feet out of my socks. "I've never actually stayed in a hotel by myself before. It feels…weird."

"You get used to it."

It suddenly occurred to me that this was Caspian's life: a string of strange rooms. "Here's hoping I don't have to."

He was quiet for a moment. Then, "You know, you're not alone. I'm only a phone call away. And, now I think about it, I could be there in a few hours. Do you want me to—"

"No," I said quickly. "I mean, thank you. But no."

"Are you sure?"

"Yes. You generous madman." I put a hand to my mouth to stifle a slightly hysterical sound. "I can't believe you were going to come out here because I implied a mild state of disorientation."

"You sounded lonely."

"I'm all right. And I've got you, haven't I?"

"Always, my Arden."

He'd made me smile. When ten minutes ago I wouldn't have imagined it was even possible. Of course, it was immediately followed by a shard of guilt that I was smiling and flirting and being comforted while Nik was alone in a hospital bed. Although I also knew that was just my brain being mean to me. Nik wasn't going to get better or worse depending on how miserable I was. But, then, thoughts were thoughts and feels were feels, and, if you were me, their power to influence each other was less than zero.

"How's London?" I asked.

"Much as you left it, I suspect it. Warmish, with some scattered showers."

"How's the humidity?"

He thought about it. "About sixty percent—now why are you laughing?"

"Because you are legit terrible at small talk."

"And you," he said crisply, "are legit terrible at going to sleep."

"You'd better get on with lulling me, then."

He gave an un-lullful snort. "Is that what I'm doing?"

"Not right now, no."

Another pause.

He cleared his throat. "Lulling is quite difficult."

"Tell me what you're looking at. What you're thinking." I closed my eyes. And let the last twenty-four hours thunder through me, and over me, until I was dust. "I just…I just want to hear you."

"Anything you need." He sounded almost as raw as I did. But his words, coming to me down a phone, took me to familiar places. To Oxford in spring when Caspian had been a stranger. And the summer night he'd first made me feel safe. "I'm in my office. Standing by the window. It's my favorite spot."

"Good view?"

"I've never noticed."

"So…you really like the frame? The floor is especially nice there?"

"No." Caspian's voice had dropped into its lowest register: the secret one, full of sex and teasing. "I kissed someone here once. Right against the glass."

"Did you now?"

"I did. And perhaps somewhat ill-advisedly. You see, I'd made the young man in question very angry—fairly, as it happens—and he burst into my place of work to confront me over it."

I squirmed. "That seems a pretty embarrassing thing for him to do."

"He has nothing to be embarrassed about. He was magnificent and fearless and, even in the midst of his own hurt, kind. I was a fool to think I could ever possess power enough to resist him."

"Why would you want to? He sounds like a peach."

"He has no idea. Sending him home was probably one of the most difficult things I've ever done. Watching the car vanish into traffic, carrying my Arden away from me, when all I wanted to do was force you down across my desk and make you mine forever."

It was, without a shadow of a doubt, the best bedtime story anyone had ever told me. I mean, it had everything. An unlikely protagonist. A dashing—if slightly tormented—hero. And all the exciting feelings.

Unfortunately, I was knackered and wrung out, and Caspian's words had wrapped me up, as warm as the coat he'd bought me, as strong as his arms around me, and so I fell asleep before I heard the end.

* * *

For the rest of the week, I spent most of my time in the hospital, popping back to the hotel to shower and sleep in rare horizontal luxury. Mostly I was floaty and dislocated, drifting through an eerie non-space where time had lost its meaning. My entire world: two rooms with beds in them. Though one of them, at least, was filling up with flowers from well-wishers. As for Nik, he was in a lot of pain and on a lot of drugs, and we had good days and bad days, just like the doctor said we would. The bad days, when I couldn't make him laugh or speak to me sometimes, were rough. But, somehow, the good days were even worse because I saw how much they took out of him, and I knew he was doing it for me, and that was…kind of heartbreaking. And made me feel more helpless than ever. Even if Caspian had said being here was enough.

And then we got the talk. The real talk.

The one about rest and rehabilitation and prognosis. And Nik said nothing the whole time, leaving me to try and ask Dr. Sharma all the useful and intelligent questions you were supposed to ask in these situations. Of course, I'd been to google, but I was rapidly coming to the conclusion there was no right way to do handle this.

To think, all that time at Oxford looking at Elizabethan politics in Sidney's *Arcadia* when they should have been teaching me what to do when your best friend was severely injured and only had a seventy percent chance of ever walking again.

Eventually the doctor left, promising to check back soon, the silence getting heavier and heavier and spikier and spikier until it was like being crushed in an iron maiden.

Nik was staring at the ceiling.

"Um," I asked helplessly, "are you all right?"

He still wouldn't turn his head. "No, I'm not fucking all right. You heard what she said."

"Yeah but…but…I mean, we sort of knew—um. We did sort of know, didn't we?"

"Of course I knew. I'm not an idiot."

Except he didn't have to tell me: this had made it real.

"It's not all bad stuff," I tried. "And it could be a lot worse."

His hand flailed around weakly. Rumpling the covers and dragging the IV line back and forth.

"Nik, don't do that. You might pull something out or hurt yourself or—"

"Shut up. Just…shut up. Shut the fuck up."

I froze. Too shocked, at first, even to be upset. He'd never spoken to me like that. But then I noticed the tears slipping from beneath his lashes. And since he couldn't very easily dash them aside or turn away, it was the most defenseless thing I'd ever seen.

"Oh Nik." My own voice broke. "Please don't cry. It'll be okay."

"Stop telling me it's going to be okay. It's not okay. It's not going to be okay. And I'm not going to pretend otherwise to make you feel better."

I knew Nik wasn't actually trying to hurt me. Or, if he was, it was more of a load-sharing exercise than anything. But the sandstorm of his anger and fear and grief still flayed me raw. Made me shed a few tears of my own.

"What the fuck do you have to cry about?" he snarled.

"Nothing. I don't know. I'm sorry." I let out a shaky breath. "It's all really scary. I mean, I could have you lost you. You could have died. That's such a terrible thing to have come so close to happening that I can't even bear to think about it."

There was a long silence.

"I'd rather be dead." He eased his head round, so that he was looking out of the window, away from me. "Just leave me alone."

I almost kicked up a fuss, wanting to stay and fix it. But even I had enough self-awareness to recognize it would be for me, not Nik—who was telling me pretty clearly he needed something else right then.

"Sure," I said. "I'll go get a drink. And if you still want to be by yourself when I'm done, I'll head back to the hotel."

Nik didn't reply.

So I slipped out, closed the door as quietly as I could, and made my way through corridors grown as familiar as unspooled thread until I came to the coffee place near the lobby. I ordered a smoothie and cream cheese bagel, and crept into a corner with them.

Silence enfolded me, soft and stifling. Hospitals were kind of like airports—sad airports—full of distilled time and echoes.

Picking at my bagel, I discovered I had no appetite whatsoever.

Welp. This sucked.

I nearly rang Caspian. Sitting there with my phone in my hand, knowing he'd pick up, and certain that he would probably make me feel better. Though, in the end, I didn't.

Not because I didn't want to. But because I didn't need to.

His strength was a powerful gift, and one he gave to me generously, without hesitation. Except, in borrowing Caspian's sometimes, I'd remembered I had strength of my own. That my sense of myself could hold steady without the flattering mirror of his affection. And that sometimes life was shitty, and the people you loved were hurting, and sad and scared and lonely were what you had to feel.

CHAPTER 16

When I got back to Nik's room, he was propped up in bed, and looking calmer—if a bit red around his eyes and nose. He gave me an awkward grin. Which I returned with an awkward grin of my own.

We'd never actually fought before, at least not about anything more serious than Disney princes, so this was all new ground. And I didn't think either of us could tell if it was solid earth or eggshells or broken glass beneath our feet.

Finally, Nik said, "I'm really sorry, Ardy."

"Honestly, you don't have to be."

"You're not the boss of me. I can be sorry if I want."

I put my hands on my hips. "I might be the boss of you. How do you know? Do you have paperwork?"

"Dude, you're barely capable of being the boss of yourself."

"So harsh."

But we were laughing and it felt...too terrifyingly fragile to be normal. But it was good too.

"I'm shit scared, you know," he said, so softly I almost missed it.

I went to sit on the edge of his bed. Slid my hand over to his and muddled up our fingers. "Me too."

"I'm not sure I'm going to be okay." He pulled an almost comically rueful face. "I think I'm fucked."

"Oh Nik, you're not fucked. Just…fondled a bit roughly."

He laughed, then winced, his free hand curling against the bedsheets. "But what am I going to do?"

"Um, same as before?"

"Like this?"

"Well, maybe not *exactly* like this."

"I might not be able to walk."

I took a breath, hoping against hope I was going to say this right. "I know, and that is the…fucking suckiest. And everything is probably going to be really hard for a long time. But—"

"If you tell me life goes on I'm going to yank out this catheter and wee on you."

"I guess…it's more that your life isn't over?"

"Are you sure? Because I saw this movie about how it's now my social duty to euthenate myself for the sake of my loved ones."

I nodded. "And you have to leave me all your money too."

Nik grinned, but quickly grew thoughtful again.

So I went on more seriously, "A bunch of stuff is going to have to change. But some won't. And you're still you."

"I guess."

I unleashed a melodramatic sigh. "It's a shame, really, that there's never been a single scientist ever with any sort of disability."

He glowered at me. "Stop trying to make me laugh, it hurts."

"Sorry."

In the following silence, I did some hospitally things. Topped up Nik's water. Smoothed his sheets and made sure the light from the window wasn't in his eyes.

"Anyway," he went on. "I've been thinking."

"Oh?"

"I mean, about what I should do and stuff. And"—he fell quiet a moment, fiddling with a crease in his sheets—"I think you should probably…I dunno how to say this…like, leave."

I stared at him, stricken. "I've been that rubbish?"

"What? No. You've been great. Ten out ten Nightingales. But, it's not about you. I mean, it is about you. It's just mainly about me."

"How do you mean?"

"You heard Dr Sharma." He huffed out a slightly aggrieved sigh "This is going to take forever. I have to have more surgery, and then there'll be physical therapy and all the rest of the reha-bilitation crap."

"Yes, but you should have someone with you."

"Not you, though."

I blinked, not sure whether I was insulted or relieved. "What's wrong with me?"

"Well, for starters, you're my friend, not my caregiver. And that's how I'd like to keep you."

"I am a pretty awesome friend," I conceded.

Which made him laugh and scruffle my hair. "Which is handy because I need one more favor."

"Anything." I thought about it for a moment. "Well, except give you another hand job. I'm taken now."

"Sorry, mate. I'm not that desperate. Do you think you could get in touch with my sister?"

"Hang on, you have a sister? Sheesh, I've only known you for nearly four years. Is she anything like you? Is she single?"

"I thought you were supposed to be taken."

"Doesn't mean I can't have my head turned. Although"—I gave the matter due consideration—"when I try imagining what your sister would be like, I just end up picturing you in a dress." I gave it further consideration. "Actually, that's quite hot."

"Look, Arden. My sister's. Well. She's Poppy Carrie."

My mouth fell open in such an excessive way that a tram could probably have taken a shortcut through it. "What? *The* Poppy Carrie? The model."

"She's doing more acting now. But yeah. And stop sleazing on her. She's my sister, dude."

"I'm not sleazing. I'm…I'm disorientated, okay?" It wasn't that I expected—or thought I had a right—to know everything about Nik. But this was something at once so incidental and fundamental that it felt weird suddenly discovering it. "Why haven't you ever mentioned her?"

His ears had gone pinkish. "It's complicated. She's why I don't speak to my parents."

I'd wondered what was going on there, but it had never really come up and it wasn't the sort of question you just dropped on someone. "They have issues with her?"

"Yeah. They're like these total *Guardian*-reading liberals but they got all Edwardian about it the moment their first-born son turned out to be a girl."

"Wow. I'm so sorry."

Nik picked idly at the covers. Then muttered, "Truthfully, I wasn't great either. But can you try calling her? I've got her private number."

It was kind of surreal, having to ring a stranger—a famous stranger, no less—totally out of the blue. I was starting to get nervy flashbacks to the telethon, except the stakes were way higher. What if Nik's sister thought I was a stalker or a journalist or the world's bizarrest marketing company and hung up on me?

Thankfully she didn't.

Although I emerged from the conversation with barely any memory of it. Just this *holy fuck, I spoke with Poppy Carrie* feeling.

She'd called Nik *Nikki*.

And was going to be on the next flight.

* * *

That night, feeling oddly buoyant, not sure if I had any right to feel buoyant and finally decided to go with it regardless, I treated myself to an epic bath, pouring almost all of the free Molton Brown products into it until I had my very own watery bubble cloud. Unfortunately, it was way less fun than I thought it was going to be because it was a depressingly large tub to contain a single, smallish Arden. And woke up the beast of my missing Caspian, which I mostly kept tucked up inside me while

I did other things. But sometimes, when I was alone, it shook off its lethargy and came at me with teeth and claws until I was nothing but small wounds.

Reaching for my phone, I twisted myself into what I hoped was a sultry-like position, all otter-sleek and glistening, one shoulder and my tattooed hip emerging naughtily from a shield of foam. Holding the lens above me at an angle, I gave it my biggest, best, most-inviting pout-smile. Like I was saying kiss me kiss me. Or maybe just fuck my mouth.

Snap snap. Click click.

A couple of filters.

And off to Caspian.

A few minutes later I got back: *You've lost weight. Are you taking proper care of yourself?*

One hundred percent incorrect answer, I swiped.

I'm in a meeting. Pause. *You're very enticing.*

I miss enticing you.

Another pause. Then: *Come home as soon as you can. You can entice me in person.*

The bathwater was getting cool, so I hopped out and wrapped myself in a towel. And that was when I noticed the notification light was flashing on my non-Caspian phone. I glanced at my email out of habit, rather than interest, fully expecting something along the lines of "Dear Arden, it has been eight gazillion years since you were last on Facebook. We miss you!"

But it was an email from *Milieu*.

They wanted (with some edits) to publish my article.

My article…

It just went to show how much your friend getting mushed by traffic could knock you because, for a moment, I had no idea what the hell I'd sent them. And then I remembered. Dancing with Ellery in an abandoned hospital. Another world. One where getting into *Milieu* was everything I wanted.

And I'd done it. I'd actually done it.

I couldn't feel happy about it yet, though. Nik was too close and this was too distant. But in the strangest way I could feel my future waiting for me. Like that long summer after my A-levels, with Oxford gleaming on the horizon. Except this wasn't a dream created by ten centuries of other people's expectations. It was for me. And maybe I'd fuck it up or it wouldn't work out. But that would be mine too.

Dragging my laptop out of my luggage, I plopped myself Sarah Jessica Parker style on the bed and dug into my edits. Got them off in a couple of hours, with some sweating, and only a little bit of cursing.

The reply came back as I was getting ready to sleep.

And contained the most magical words in the universe: *We'd love to see more of your writing.*

CHAPTER 17

In person, Poppy Carrie was an impossible mixture of normal and extraordinary. She turned up wearing jeans and boots, a cream cashmere-silk sweater, and Audrey Hepburn sunglasses— nothing about her at all to scream "famously beautiful person." Except looking at her for too long made it hard to breathe. She had this dreamy, summery English loveliness, all corn-gold hair and eyes like freshly turned earth, and this shy scattering of freckles across the bridge of her nose. There was definitely a trace of Nik around her cheekbones and in the generosity of her mouth.

She'd come from LA, with her…boyfriend? A six-foot-something hunk of weathered manhood called Colt Dawson, who had a ranch out in Montana, and did stuff with horses for Hollywood. Apparently they'd met on the set of *Madame Bovary*. I got all this from the internet, frantically googling something I could say to Colt as we sat together in the waiting room because we were giving Nik and Poppy time to talk.

Colt himself had said exactly zero words. And was occupying

his chair with a degree of stillness I usually only associated with the deceased.

I, of course, was wriggling. Topics flitting in and out of my brain like moon-drunk moths.

"Soooo," I said, "did you vote for Trump?"

"Nope."

"Oh yay. I mean, I guess I thought you might have what with being, well, y'know, all with the horses and the big sky and things."

"Nope."

"Not that you have to explain your beliefs or your politics or your opinions or anything to some random English guy you just met in a hospital waiting room."

"Didn't plan to."

"Well." I wheezed anxiously. "Good talk."

Eventually, we were allowed back in. They both looked a little tearful, but in a happy sort of way. Then Poppy smiled at me, and I tried not to die.

"It's Arden, isn't it?" Her voice was softly musical, deep but light somehow, and it was so nice to hear another English accent.

Nod. Nod nod.

"I'd love a cup of tea? Do you want to come with me?"

Oh. My. God. "Y-yes. That would be really nice." Great. I sounded like a robot. "There's a Coffee Central near the lobby. They do hot and cold beverages. And muffins. And smoothies. And pastries sometimes and I'm not being paid to advertise them or anything."

"Perfect."

She slipped her arm through mine and we made our way

downstairs, this new reality, where Poppy Carrie touched me as she might a friend, quietly dissolving what was left of my brain.

OMG, Arden, say something.

Actually: check that. You aren't allowed to say anything ever.

"How are you finding America?" she asked.

"Oh. Um. I'm not sure. It still feels unreal." I smiled—yep, I smiled at Poppy Carrie and she smiled back. "I mean, Boston looks like I built it last week in *Sim City*."

She laughed. "But you know in American terms, it's ancient."

"It is?"

"Yes." She lowered her voice to an awed whisper. "Nearly four hundred years old."

I put a hand to my brow. "No!"

"And, compared to somewhere like New York or Washington, far less artificial than it could be. Like Oxford, Boston was essentially designed by cows."

"Hey, I've seen the Charles. The only cow fording that is a giant space cow."

"Well, they do say everything's bigger in America."

We'd made it to the coffee place and I hadn't passed out or embarrassed myself too badly. Actually, apart from occasional flashes of *OMG Poppy Carrie*, I was feeling fairly comfortable. She vaguely reminded me of Nik. Well, if he was way prettier and way more charming. But she had his appreciation for the absurd—which might have been why they both gave every impression of liking me.

"I'm so sorry, but can I be really annoying?" Poppy was saying to the barista, who frankly looked as though her being annoying at him might be the highlight of his life. "Can I have a cup of boiling water, and a tea bag separately, and some milk in a jug? I know you must hate me right now but some rather terrible things have happened to tea out here."

"N-no, that's fine."

Poppy seemed blissfully unaware of the fact she could probably have asked for a black chicken to be sacrificed in a pentagram of blood, and would have received the same answer. "What about you, Arden?"

"Oh, don't worry about it."

"Please. My treat."

Ahhh. What was I possibly supposed to say? I couldn't enter into a battle of British politeness with Poppy Carrie. That was insane. "Gosh. Thank you. I'll have a strawberry smoothie."

A few minutes later we were settled into a corner and I was trying not to slurp my drink too noisily—which was borderline impossible because I swear to God someone had left half a banana in there. No offense to Coffee Central.

"I just wanted to thank you," said Poppy. "For taking such good care of Nik."

I squirmed. "It wasn't a big deal.

"You don't have to downplay it. Having you here has helped him a lot. And I'm so glad you called me."

"I'm glad I did too. I mean, I'd do anything for Nik but I'm not…I mean…this has all been a bit overwhelming."

She nodded, stirring her tea. "I can imagine. Which is partly why—and I hope you won't feel I'm trying to take something from you—we'd like it if I could officially replace you as Nik's next of kin. You've been wonderful, Arden, but really it should be me, not you."

"Oh God, that's fine. I'm not trying to keep your brother from you."

"I never thought that for a moment."

"Honestly, I only agreed because it seemed funny. We never actually thought I'd have to do any next-of-kinning." I grappled non-euphemistically with my banana and then gave up, as it had lodged itself immovably in the straw. "We got superdrunk once and made a pact to get married if we both turned thirty-seven and weren't with anyone else. I wouldn't hold him to that either."

She gave me a mischievous grin. "You're very cute. What if he tries to hold you to it?"

"Well, he's hot and funny and clever and nice. So I'd say yes, obviously."

"Can I come to the wedding?"

"You're welcome at any and all of my queer, hypothetical weddings."

There was a brief pause.

"I'm so glad Nikki has a friend like you," she said softly. "We haven't kept in touch since I left home and, obviously, this isn't how I would have wanted to reconnect. But I've thought about him a lot."

"From what he said, he feels bad about how things went before."

"That was partially on me. He was, in his confused, teenage way, trying to protect me. And I was—I suppose I still am—very angry."

I stared at her—so composed in her cashmere, with her tea. "You don't seem like an angry person."

"Therapy. And"—she gave a slightly wry smile—"Colt, oddly enough. He understands wild things. Sometimes he just takes me out into the middle of nowhere and I scream until there's no screams left. Then we lie in the bed of his truck and watch the sun set and the stars come out."

"That sounds way better than therapy."

"And there's always action movies." She made an absolutely ferocious face and mimed firing what I presumed was an automatic weapon. "*Eat this, motherbitches*. Very cathartic. Especially if you have an unholy vendetta against blue screens."

I burst into rapturous applause. "And the award for best motherbitches goes to…"

"Now you know why I'm an actor not a writer." She put down her gun. "But you are, aren't you? Nikki said you were a journalist?"

"Well, I'm working on it." I was doing it again. I took a breath, and went on. "Actually, I've had a piece accepted by *Milieu*."

"Congratulations. Nikki loves *Milieu*, though, of course, he pretends he doesn't read it. They approached me not too long ago. But I tend to avoid interviews wherever possible."

"Is it weird? People wanting to ask you a bunch of questions?"

She tucked a lock of hair back into the knotty thing she currently had going on. "I think it's more…it's always the same questions. I know it's very selfish of me because I do care about transgender rights. But sometimes all I want to be representing is *me*."

"I don't think that's selfish. You're a person, not a political entity."

"And the truth is"—her eyes glittered, revealing a glimpse of the person who liked to wander into the wilderness and scream at the sky—"it feels as though the rest of the world is fascinated by things I myself find unbelievably boring. Like the body I inhabit. Or the name my parents gave me."

"What would you want to be asked?"

"Oh, anything that doesn't secretly want to be 'what happened to your penis?' The same questions every other actor gets. I suppose I just want to talk about my job."

"Yeah, I get it."

And then I froze, gripped by an idea. An idea that—like my dissertation—was either great or terrible, and I wouldn't know which until I saw what people thought of it. Except did I really want to live the rest of my life as someone who'd pissed off Poppy Carrie? But, then, if I didn't, I'd have to live as someone who'd completely blanked what might have been a perfect opportunity.

"Well." Oh shit. I was speaking. "I know this isn't the best time to mention this, but you could always talk to me, if you wanted."

Her smile, if anything, grew even warmer. "I think I'd like being interviewed by you."

I sealed my lips before a startled "are you sure" could escape. And I didn't faint either (though I resolved to run mad later). But, oh fuck, what was I supposed to do now? The last interview I'd conducted had been for the Sebby Hall *Bog Sheet*. And the subject of it had been the spider plant in the Junior Common Room.

"Do I contact your…publicist to get something set up?" I asked, doing my very best impression of a professional person. "I mean, I'm freelance at the moment so I'm available whenever."

A slight pause. Then, "How about now?"

I managed an affirmative squeak.

She laughed. "I was thinking, perhaps, we could just keep on as we are. And see what comes out of it."

Holy shit. An exclusive interview with Poppy Carrie. This was probably the sort of thing that changed your life. And it was happening *right the fuck now*. Except…as much as I wanted this, I also wanted to do it right. Which would have to involve some honesty. I braced myself for disaster. "Look, I should tell you, I've never done anything like this before. I might balls it up beyond redemption."

"Maybe you will. But"—she met my eyes over the rim of her cup—"I have a feeling you won't."

I thought about it for a moment. Maybe I had that feeling too. "Is it okay if I record it on my phone?"

She nodded. "I've almost finished my tea, though. Would you like another smoothie?"

"For this?" I grinned. "I'm going to need a fucking muffin."

* * *

Afterward, I sat in my hotel room, ate my way through a king's ransom of snacks, and tried to translate recorded words into written words while keeping, somehow, the *feeling* of them. And the truth of the person who had spoken them.

And it was fucking impossible.

Give me "Ten Mineral Waters You Absolutely Must Try" or "An Intimate Guide to Tending the Boylawn" any day.

This was too vast. Too complex. Too real.

My ability to language had become this octopus, all flailing tentacles and squishiness, resisting my best attempts to corral it into the shapes I needed.

Ahhhhh.

I threw myself onto the bed and rolled about, kicking my feet, expertly converting mental distress into physical dramatics. Weirdly, it helped. Cleared my head. And, probably as a Pavlovian reaction to all the wanking I'd got up to recently, made me think of Caspian. Specifically what he'd said to me on the plane back from Kinlochbervie: that wanting something meant letting yourself be vulnerable.

And I wanted—oh how I wanted—to do a good job with this.

Not just for me and my career. But for Poppy.

She deserved an interview that captured at least something of who she was. Her anger and her kindness, her charisma and her strength.

Fuck it fuck it fuck it.

I sat up and grabbed my laptop. Slammed every door in my brain that didn't lead to Poppy Carrie.

Wrote: *Eat it, motherbitches.*

Kept writing: *Poppy Carrie isn't like you think she is. And then she's not like that either.*

Soon there was nothing but the hours passing. The words ebbing and flowing across my screen.

CHAPTER 18

The next day, I said goodbye to Nik, made sure it wasn't stupid o'clock in England, and rang Bellerose.

He answered quickly, just like always. "Hello, Arden."

"Knitted anything cool?"

"I sincerely wish I hadn't told you that."

"Do you make your own yarn and stuff as well, or do you buy it?"

"My yarn is none of your business. Now, is there something you need?"

I couldn't quite contain an eager squeak. "I'm ready to come home."

"Caspian will be delighted. When would you like the jet?"

Oh dear God. I was never going to get used to being able to order a plane like a pizza. "As soon as possible?"

There was a pause. Presumably Bellerose was...actually, I had no idea. Calculating stuff? Organizing things? "You will be departing at nine a.m. tomorrow. Be at the airport in good time."

"Yay. Thank you." Since Bellerose couldn't see me, and I was in a city where nobody knew me, I skipped about excitedly. "Will you let Caspian know? In case you see him before he picks up a message?"

"Of course. Though I should tell you he has a social engagement in the evening and therefore may not be available to meet you when you arrive."

I stopped skipping. But, honestly, what had I been expecting? That a man like Caspian Hart would have nothing on his schedule? Or that he'd be able to drop everything for me? "It's okay. I get it. Thanks again, Bellerose."

"See you soon, Arden."

Disappointment drowned me in its bitter tide. And I slumped onto the bed, on the verge of tears, trying to figure out if I was overreacting or not. I mean, I knew this wasn't Caspian's fault. It wasn't a value judgment on my importance to him or a reflection of my place in his life.

It was sucky circumstances.

But I guess I'd got used to his availability. To being busy, and hurried, and in the middle of something while he scheduled and rescheduled around me. And now the clock was striking midnight. The spell was breaking. And tomorrow I'd be in London, my time turned back into mice and pumpkins: not special at all.

Then my phone rang.

It was Caspian and, for a split second, I thought about not answering. I don't know why—just that I was feeling bad, and wanting in some hopelessly petty and non-specific way to make him be the thwarted one, the disappointed one, the one who was always waiting and dreaming and hoping. Then I realized I was being a complete wanker, and picked up.

"I'm so sorry," said Caspian, rather breathlessly, "my mother's holding one of her charity auctions tomorrow. And I can't fail to attend."

Oh great. A charity auction. Could I be any more selfish?

"I understand." I said, only lying a little bit. "It's okay."

But Caspian made a sound perilously close to a growl. "It's not okay, Arden. It's been weeks. I need to see you."

God. Had I really thought I wanted him to suffer? Because I didn't. It was awful, hearing him so frustrated and unhappy, whatever my own feelings on the matter. "Can you come round after? I'll wait up?"

"These things always run late."

"I don't care. I'll be jet lagged as fuck anyway."

There was nothing to hear exactly, but I somehow got the impression he was pacing. I could imagine it all too easily—his long strides tearing his office to shreds, turning his windows to walls, his walls to bars.

"Please," I whispered. "Please, Caspian."

"I'm sorry, I'm acting like a child. I'll be there as soon as I can."

"That's perfect." I did my happiest grin at the phone, in the hope he could sense it somehow. "I can't wait."

Another restless silence.

"What time do you arrive?"

"Yikes, I have no idea. I'm flying out at nine and the flight is, what, seven hours but then there's time zones and—"

"So you'll be back in England around eight or nine."

"I will?" I found it pretty sexy that he could figure that shit out instantly. Although it did slightly remind me of the time he'd destroyed my family at Carcassonne.

"I'll pick you up from the airport and take you home. Then I can head on to the event."

That sounded amazing. But also like it would be a pain in the arse to him. "You really don't have to do that."

"I want to. So I will."

I fell back, swooning on the bed. "Yes, Mr. Hart."

He laughed, but there was rough note at the heart of it. So I knew that, in his own way, he was swooning too.

When he was gone, I settled down with my laptop and reread what I'd written about Poppy Carrie. Unfortunately, at this point, I was incapable of assessing it with any degree of criticality. It could have been brilliant, it could have been terrible, most likely it was somewhere in the middle. At any rate, it was clear there was nothing more I could do with it. So, instead, I tortured myself over my cover letter. And, finally, sent that—along with a sample of the interview itself—to *Milieu*.

Then there was nothing for it but to have an early night. I wasn't sure what Bellerose had meant by "be at the airport in good time" but he'd sounded sufficiently ominous about it that I knew I definitely didn't want to be in bad time. And so it seemed reasonable to set my alarm for 5 a.m.

Except, when it actually went off at 5 a.m., I learned it wasn't reasonable at all.

Dragging myself out of bed like a zombie from a fresh grave,

I dressed, threw my stuff into my suitcase, and went to acquire breakfast. I was drooping over toast and orange juice when I realized my T-shirt was on inside-out.

And, y'know, I just couldn't find the will to care.

Somehow, I managed to check out, get in the car, and get to the airport. Do the airport things. In one of the special lounges I was starting to take for granted, I slipped into a weird stupor, almost halfway between being asleep and being awake, and way less satisfying than either. At the back of my mind, though, I was secretly rejoicing in my borderline comatose state. An international flight was going to be a piece of cake if I could successfully spend it sleeping.

But my brain rebelled about five minutes after take-off. And, suddenly, I was wildly alert and barely able to sit still. Bouncing off the walls of Caspian's plane.

All I could think was: I'm going home.

I'm going to see Caspian.

And I couldn't seem to make myself understand that I was, actually, very tired. And had a long journey ahead of me. Instead my heart wanted to soar through the skies and skim the ocean waves.

For seven fucking hours.

Nrrrrghhh.

I would have said it was the worst journey ever except I'd flown out in the first place because my best friend had been hit by a car. And that was the sort of thing that could really hold its own at the top of your "rubbish travel experiences" list.

By the time we were dithering about in London airspace, waiting for permission to land, I had given up on everything except lying flat on my back in the middle of the floor, just about managing not to whine audibly because the cabin crew didn't deserve that.

Internally, though? It was whine city.

I'm here, I texted Caspian. With, frankly, extraordinary dignity and forbearance.

And then, *I'm back—and in time for your birthday*, along with a flourishing collection of smileys to Ellery. *yay* was her reply.

I wasn't sure what I was expecting when I was finally back on British soil…well, British tarmac. But the moment I'd been passport-stamped and custom-checked, and released from the posh-person pen, there he was: Caspian Hart, waiting for me, among the scatter of strangers outside.

It was weird, I know, but I found him without consciously having to look. As if some part of me already knew how to find him. The rest of the world reduced to nothing but a painted backdrop.

He was wearing the midnight blue suit I'd seen first at Oxford. And I'd somehow forgotten how beautiful he was. I mean, not really. But the difference between reality and memory was like Dorothy arriving in Oz. I could see color again. Endless shades of Caspian: the twist of silver in the blue of his eyes, the not-quite-black of his hair, the pale lips that lost all their severity in the redness of kissing.

God. He made me dizzy. My stomach churn and my heart flutter. My knees literally weak. How could he be even a little bit mine? I think I might have fallen over—just reeled and flopped to the floor—if he hadn't swept me into his arms.

I felt his breath against my cheek. And all he said was *Arden*. But it was so full of longing and joy and relief and possession that it hardly sounded like my name anymore.

It sounded like *mine*.

And then he was kissing me. A full-on fuck the world, I'm never getting on a plane again *Casablanca* kiss. A kiss to break the edges of skin itself and make you two, and one, and whole, and together, and everything between.

CHAPTER 19

Come on," Caspian said, letting me go at last.

Once again, my body decided that the best place for me was in a wobbly heap on the ground, but he grabbed my hand just in time. And pulled me, along with my case, toward the exit. Into the waiting—oh fuck—limo.

And onto his lap.

Where we kissed again. Again. Again. Forever.

As the streets of London unraveled around us in ribbons of gold.

Finally, we stopped. Mainly, I think, for breathing purposes, rather than any particular desire to separate our mouths.

"I'm going to put a collar round your neck," Caspian murmured, "and chain you to my bed."

Thankfully I knew how to interpret this. "I missed you too."

I thought he might laugh. But, instead, he pulled me against him so tightly that I flailed and squeaked like a squeezy toy. "Oh Arden."

"It me," I wheezed.

"My Arden." He pressed his face against the crook of my shoulder. "You make me so happy."

I wasn't sure what to say so I snuggled. Snuggled like hell. What were ribs for anyway? And, besides, it was rare for him to let me get this close, his need to be touched, his need for me, overwhelming his need for control.

"How do you have this power?" he asked.

From anyone else, it would have been a rhetorical. But he sounded so genuinely bewildered—almost plaintive—that I did my best to answer. "We like each other. It's not magic."

"It's magic to me." He slid a palm up the back of my neck and into my hair. Made me look at him. His eyes were wild and a little shadowed. Hadn't he been sleeping well? "I don't deserve this. Or you."

Urgh. That was a mood-killer. It reminded me of some of the stuff he'd said about Nathaniel and now I knew more about their relationship it was not a comparison I relished. To put it mildly.

Since I was unusually unrestrained, I took major advantage, cupping his face gently between my hands and brushing my lips across his again. "Caspian, I love that I'm a good thing in your life. Please don't take that away from me."

"I'm sorry." A shudder ran through him and I felt it in my fingertips.

"And you deserve me. You have a right to be happy."

"I'm just...not used to it."

"Then get used to it, Mr. Hart."

My world tilted abruptly. Probably because *I* was tilting

abruptly. I landed on my back on the seat of the limo and Caspian came down on top of me. And it was ridiculous—we were all limbs and elbows, and there wasn't actually enough room, so one of his knees was on the floor and my foot was in the air, and everything was hot and clumsy and precarious and desperate. We'd gone from *Casablanca* to "Paradise by the Dashboard Light," rolling around like horny teenagers, our mouths clashing as much as they were kissing, and our hands tangled up in each other, and I loved it.

It took me somewhere I'd never been. Gave me something I never thought I'd have, since I'd spent my adolescence mostly playing board games, walking on the beach, and wanking (not all at the same time obviously). Sex wasn't really on the cards until I got to university, where being skinny, queer, and bookish wasn't an unsurmountable triple threat of nope. Also I didn't have to walk miles to find a human who wasn't related to me or in love with someone related to me or married to someone who was in love with someone related to me. Things got easier, personally and logistically, is what I'm saying. And I made up for lost time. Boy, did I make up for lost time.

But, in the strangest sort of way, this felt timeless. It didn't matter that I'd just disembarked from a private jet and we were in the back of a Rolls on the way to a luxury apartment in Kensington. This was every behind-the-bike sheds snog I'd never had. A fumbling mess of hope and eagerness and sheer impossible joy.

I wasn't sure if I was going to cry or giggle.

Or, y'know, come in my jeans. Because it was fucking

ludicrously sexy. Being kissed like you were better than dignity. More important than air.

"I'm not going to that damn party," Caspian gasped. "I'm not."

That brought me back to the here and now with a bump. "I though you said it was a charity thing your mum was organizing?"

"It is. But have you any idea how many such events I have attended over the years? I want, and will have, this evening with you."

Oh dear. Conflict.

On the one hand: Caspian being all bossy, which I found incredibly hot. On the other hand: fucking charity. And probably there was a special place in hell for people who stopped good deeds happening because they wanted to get laid.

"I'll still be here tomorrow," I said.

"It's already been too long, Arden. I'm done with waiting."

He got all with the lips and hands again, so I was pretty distracted. And, even when I remembered there were protests I ought to be making, I kept putting them off because…well… kissing was better. Eventually, though, I drifted out of the sensual haze and gave his shoulder a little shove. "Caspian. Stop. Seriously."

I'd meant stop putting your mouth everywhere while I was trying to have a conversation. Not pull away abruptly and relocate to the other side of the limo. Leaving me cold, bereft, and disheveled.

"Um." I sat up too. Made a vague attempt to do something with my hair, which had fluffed up monstrously. "I just don't want your mum to hate me."

Fuck. That sounded incredibly presumptuous.

"Not," I rushed on, "that I ever expect to meet her."

He gave me an unreadable look from across the car. "But you will. At Ellery's party."

Oh. Oh gosh. I hadn't even considered that. "Then all the more reason for me not to fuck up her event by stealing her son."

"I wasn't intending to tell her, Arden. I would have made some other excuse. My work often requires me to miss things."

"But…but…" I gazed at him, shocked. "You can't lie to your family."

"Surely you've lied to yours."

"No. Never. Why would you do something like that?"

He shrugged. "The same reasons you might lie to anyone: social nicety, personal convenience, simple necessity."

How had I forgotten Caspian was like this too? Merciless in ways I could never find appealing. Cold in ways that hurt my heart.

"Do you lie to me?" I heard myself say, in a very small voice.

"Of course not."

"Are you sure it's not just personally convenient to tell me that?"

"Not at all. It's never convenient to commit to a course of action that is limiting."

I pulled a pouty face. "I can't tell whether that's reassuring or not."

"The truth is rarely reassuring. Which is rather my point."

I…didn't have an answer to that. Damn it.

"My mother won't be upset," he went on. "She understands that I have many demands on my time."

Frankly, she sounded terrifying. I mean, all I knew about her was that she organized charity auctions—an act of moral carbon offsetting if ever there was one—and that her children were Caspian and Ellery. Because, y'know. I adored both of them but I'd be kind of worried if I'd raised them.

Also, while it was super nice that Caspian wanted to be with me, I was getting increasingly...not insulted, exactly. But it rankled, somehow, the easy way he was willing to pass me off as work. Not that I actually wanted him to declare me like he was going through customs, either. Urgh. Logic and me: not the bestest of buddies.

"Okay," I said. "But what about the people with cancer or the kids in Africa?"

"What about them?"

"Well, this auction is *for* something, isn't it?"

"Bellerose handles my philanthropic concerns. And I assure you, they are substantial."

I drew my feet up and hugged my knees—since it was clearly the only hugging likely to be happening for a while. "Very much not the point here."

"Then please enlighten me. Because I was rather under the impression you wanted to spend time with me."

"God. I do," I wailed. "I really do. But I feel incredibly weird about being the reason you're not going to do something that would help people who...well...need help."

No answer from Caspian. Unless you counted the way his fingers curled tightly against his knee.

I felt awful from about six different directions at once. "You can see where I'm coming from, right?"

"I can." He reached up and flipped on the intercom. "Change of plan, Lloyd. To the Sheldrake. And quickly, please."

Wait. What was happening? I slithered along the seat as the limo swung round. Was he going to make me sit in the car like a puppy while he went to a society party? I opened my mouth to say, well, I wasn't sure what, but Caspian looked so forbidding that all my words dried up on my tongue.

And so we just sat there in the worst silence.

Great. I'd spoiled my own homecoming. But Caspian was kind of being a dick too. Not that mentioning it to him was going to improve the situation. I wished I could turn back time to the holding and the kissing—except, nothing would change. I'd still get squicked out. Because while Caspian wanting to cast the world aside for me had the potential to be incredibly exciting, on this occasion it was simply selfish. And in the ugliest possible way.

I didn't want that for him. Or me. Or whatever *us* we were.

A glance out of the window revealed lots of Georgian geometries: pale, rectangular buildings, bristling with columns and pediments. Which probably meant Mayfair. Ho hum.

The Sheldrake Gallery—should I have heard of it? I had a feeling the answer was yes, but I didn't dare google—was a lanky, white-fronted place, its windows shining brightly, and the pavement outside thick with reporters and people in black tie.

The limo drew to a halt. Caspian eased past me and stepped elegantly out of the door the moment the chauffeur opened it for him.

I...sat there like a sad lemon.

"Come, Arden."

Normally, I would have been pretty into Caspian commanding me to come. Right now? Not so much. "W-what?"

He held out his hand to me.

Oh my God. He'd gone mad. "I can't go in there. I've just got off a plane. I look—"

"Charming. And we won't be staying long."

"If you aren't staying long, why do I have to go?"

"Because I want you to."

Well. There was no way I was going to be able to resist that. I reached out, took his hand, and fell out of the limo.

Thankfully, Caspian's body was in the way so I ended up smooshed against his side, rather than face-planted onto the pavement.

The insectoid clicking of shutters filled the air. And I was immediately camera-dazzled.

Then someone called my name. I turned instinctively and a flash went off right in my face.

"First the sister, now the brother. You do get about, Ardy baby."

I couldn't see anything except snowflakes and afterimages. Had no idea what was happening. But there was something about that voice. Like a crossword clue you always were on the brink of solving, I felt I should have recognized it.

Then Caspian grabbed my hand and strode off toward the building, dragging me along behind him as you might a recalcitrant child. Which was fair enough, since I didn't wanna go to the fancy charity event.

Even my lovely coat couldn't hide how I rumpled I was. And

I felt horribly out of place in that gleaming white gallery, among the beautifully dressed visitors. Someone shoved a guidebook in my direction, but the caterer with the tray of champagne actively turned away—clearly, he didn't want to waste the good stuff on me.

A few people greeted Caspian as he cut a swathe through the crowd. He stopped only long enough to acknowledge them before sweeping on, me still bobbing in his wake like a rubber duck after a frigate. A couple of minutes later, he was bearing down on one of the gallery assistants. At least, I assumed that was her role here, since she was wearing a classic little black cocktail dress and had the sleek, self-satisfied air of someone who could afford to do a notoriously underpaid job. Something I was sensitive to because I was probably headed that way myself.

Some of her complacency fled at the sight of Caspian. "Can I help you, Mr. Hart?"

"Yes, Lenora. I'll take it all."

"All the…all the pieces?"

"Everything." He reached into his inside pocket, produced a business card, and pressed it into her limp hand. "Contact my office. Bellerose will handle the details. Oh and"—a minuscule pause—"please apologize to my mother. I'm afraid I can't stay."

And then we were off again, Caspian in full stride and me at full scamper: back through the gallery and the people and the electric maze of cameras and, finally, into the waiting limo. Which immediately pulled away.

"What…just happened?" I asked, collapsing breathlessly onto the seat.

Caspian settled next to me, graceful and composed as ever. "You were concerned that my desire to spend the evening with you would have negative consequences for the hypothetical beneficiaries of the event. I have resolved the situation."

"But you ruined the party."

"Arden"—he gave me one of his coldest looks—"most likely there are people present who care more about the party than the charity, but they are beyond my consideration. And should be beyond yours."

"I guess." I couldn't figure out was going on in my feels. I think I was comprehensively overwhelmed. And Caspian seemed so far away—literally and figuratively—that I might as well have been back in Boston. I screwed my courage to wherever it was courage got screwed and clambered awkwardly back into his lap.

Caspian drew in a sharp breath but didn't dump me onto the floor or anything, so I counted it a win. He tilted his head slightly to meet my gaze. "Does this mean you'll spend the evening with me?"

"Did you even like the art?"

"I didn't look at it. I'm sure it's very nice."

"Caspian!"

"What?"

"You can't do things like this."

His lips twitched into the faintest suggestion of a smile. "That is demonstrably untrue."

"Gah. You know what I mean. You shouldn't."

"Will you," he said, slowly and softly and full of delicious menace, "spend this evening with me?"

I wriggled happily. "You know the answer is yes. But you have to promise me this won't happen again."

"Since you won't let me lie to you, I can't make that promise." I was going to protest again but he put his fingers gently across my lips. "I would do far more than buy some art for you, my Arden."

"But now," I pointed out irrefutably, "you own some art."

"My mother has an excellent eye. Most likely, the pieces will only increase in value. In ten years or so, I can hold another auction."

Tucking my head against his shoulder, I let myself breathe. The sweet, dark scent of Caspian's cologne wrapped itself around me, as familiar as his touch. "I still can't believe you did that," I muttered. "Just to spend an evening with me."

"I'm a very selfish man."

"Hey, you've done a really good thing for what someone referred to as hypothetical beneficiaries." I smirked into his jacket.

Caspian's fingers moved lightly through my hair, sending shivers all the way down my spine. "Dear me. What pompous friends you have."

"I"—eeeeep—"I hope he's a bit more than a friend."

"I'm sure he's quite taken with you."

Oh wow. Carve that out of stars and write it across the sky. I sat up again, regarding him gravely. "Yes. I truly believe he holds me in moderate esteem."

There was a brief pause.

Then Caspian put a hand across his face and burst out laughing. And, oh God, it was beautiful—that pure, bright sound, rare as an English spring, and the flashes of his mirth-struck mouth, half hidden behind his fingers. It made me want to kiss him. Dip my tongue into his laughing.

"I'm sorry," he said, after a moment or two, blinking the glitter of moisture from his lashes. "I more than moderately esteem you."

"You mean you deeply esteem me?"

"I more than esteem you to any measure."

"Gosh." I clasped my hands to my palpitating breast. "Can it be that you...regard me?"

"Come here, you wretched monkey. I treasure you."

He kissed me, long and sweet and thorough. And, by the time he was done, I was blissfully melted.

He nudged his nose against mine. "What do you want to do tonight?"

"Um, what are the options?" It was, honestly, dizzying. Caspian's time was so insanely valuable and here he was just pouring it into my lap, as if was as abundant as Inca gold.

"Anything you want. Do you have a favorite restaurant in London? Or is there somewhere you want to go? Paris? I understand people find Paris very romantic. I could have the helicopter readied within the hour."

That sounded...well, like something that happened to people who weren't me. And not necessarily in the "would if only I could" sense. "You know," I said, awkwardly, "I think I'd rather go home, have a long hot bath, order pizza, and maybe watch a movie."

"Oh God." Caspian drew his fingertips down my cheek. "What am I saying? You've barely got back. Of course you need time to rest." He switched on the intercom, directed the driver to take us to One Hyde Park, and settled me comfortably against his side.

Although I was starting to worry he'd missed the point.

Missed the point in a significantly major way.

"With you," I said quickly. "I want to do all that stuff *with you.*"

He looked genuinely startled. "You'd prefer me to stay?"

"Hell yes. I'm especially hoping you'll come in the bath with me."

He went little pink at that—but appeared no less confused. "If this is really how you'd like to spend the evening, then…certainly."

"You ridiculous man." I shoved my hand in his and he let me, folding his fingers tightly around mine. "I can't imagine anything I'd like more."

CHAPTER 20

Getting Caspian in the bath proved weirdly difficult. He didn't exactly refuse, so much as made about a million excuses and then got very busy around the apartment. Which, incidentally, was exactly as I'd left it: pristine, gleaming, this space preserved in amber by a ruthless designer and a dedicated cleaning team.

The bath, though, the bath was fucking amazing. I'd only used the shower before, partially for convenience, but mainly because the bath was so ludicrously vast I was afraid of feeling lonely in it. Or, y'know, drowning. And being found the next morning—all soggy and blue and floating upside-down, like a baby octopus in a bowl of udon soup—by someone who did not need that in their life.

"You're missing all the bubbles," I called out.

Caspian finally appeared in the doorway and I did my best to look tempting, rather than just, well, wet. It semi-worked because he came over, crouched down and…brushed some foam off my nose.

Sigh. Sexy really did run the other way when it saw me coming, didn't it?

Or maybe it all naturally flowed toward Caspian. Who was looking…teeth-achingly hot, right then, with his jacket off, and his shirt clinging to his arms, the tips of his hair already curling in the steam.

I peered at him hopefully. "Are you coming in?"

"I'm perfectly happy to wait. You'll be more comfortable on your own."

"No, I won't. I'm actively less comfortable, in fact, because this bath is way too big for me."

Caspian was still…hmm. In anyone else I would have called it dithering.

"What's the matter?" I asked. "Don't you want to?"

"It's not that." He wove his hands together in front of him—a gesture I was beginning to recognize as the trick it was. Stillness imposed on restlessness. "It's just not something I've done before."

Not even with Nathaniel? *God, don't be smug, Arden.*

"And so," he went on, "I suppose I'm somewhat uncertain."

I offered my most winning smile. "Nothing to it. Clothes off. Hop in. Lesbians do it all the time."

"Lesbians get in the bath with you?"

"No. With each other. On TV anyway. I don't know what they do in real life. Probably fuck?"

Caspian was looking at me in obvious bewilderment. I guess I had kind of gone astray.

"You don't have to," I told him quickly, remembering all too vividly the last time I'd pushed him too hard. I really thought he was going to say no. And I told myself it didn't matter.

But then he stood and started taking his clothes off. And, holy shit, I was rapt. Obviously I'd seen him naked and removing garments before, but I'd always been distracted. Or more naked myself. But now I got to sit there among my bubbles and watch...watch...watch.

He made no attempt to be even remotely seductive, except I was seduced regardless—he was just so beautiful, baring his skin for me without ceremony. His watch and cufflinks he left by the sink. His clothes he draped over the closed lid of the toilet.

It should have been so banal. But the steam from my bath curled around his hips. Licked at his throat. Left silver curlicues in his pubic hair. And I felt I was beholding something from a pre-Raphaelite painting. One of the racier ones. Echo peeping at Narcissus, as he lingered starkers in some verdant glen. If, that is, Narcissus had been comprehensively fucking unbothered by his own spectacular gorgeousness.

And then Caspian Hart was in the bath with me.

Caspian Hart was in the bath with me!

Hunched at one end, his arms folded tightly around his knees. "Now what?"

"We...relax? Blow bubbles. Splash about playfully. Wash each other in sexy ways."

He stared.

"How about we start with the relaxing and work up?"

"What do you propose? His tone suggested he was expecting a full market analysis and five years of projected figures.

But I guess he was just…unsettled.

I slinked toward him through the water—not quite crawling because then I would probably have gone under and that would not have been at all attractive. "How about you lie back and I go between your legs."

"You go where?"

"I said, spread your legs, Mr. Hart."

He made a wary noise but obliged. The bubbles shifted on the surface of the water, offering me hazy glimpses of his upper thighs. And, um, other exciting regions. I twisted round before he could catch me ogling and carefully reversed my arse into the space he'd made for me.

Um. No. Wow. Turned out, that was super uncomfortable. I jiggled left and right, then up and down, trying to make it work. Caspian's knees bobbed around like discombobulated sharks.

"What's next?" he asked.

"Um, can you lean against the side of the bath? Then I can lean against you?"

We flailed about, but nothing seemed to help. There was always some bit of him, or some bit of me, getting in the way. Why was it never like this in the movies?

"I think," I panted, "if we could go a little lower…"

I pushed frustratedly against his leg. At which point my bum lost all purchase on the bottom of the bath, my legs flew over my head and, with a wild squeal, I crashed backward into the water.

Well. A bit into the water. And lot onto Caspian.

Who I'd basically just reverse dive-bombed.

Shit, I'd probably drowned him. Bellerose was going to kill me. I'd completed an urgent swivel when he surfaced. Spat out a mouthful of bubbles. Pushed the sodden hair from his eyes and opened them slowly.

"Why yes," he murmured. "This is terribly sexy."

"Oh my God. I'm so sorry."

He was quiet for a long moment. And viper still. And then, with great deliberation he flicked his hand against the water… and splashed me. It surprised a giggle out of me. And then, of course, I retaliated.

And this went on until Caspian wrapped me in his arms and pulled me against his chest, and somehow that worked, and there we were, warm and entangled and floating blissfully in the water.

I made the happiest of happy noises. Even if I stretched, my toes still couldn't touch the far side of the bath. And I could feel the steady thud of Caspian's heart against my cheek. The strength of him under and around me. And also: his cock. Which apparently enjoyed me being all slippery when wet.

It would have taken a better man than me to resist. I reached into the water and closed my hand round him. Dragged my palm tenderly along the length of him. Which made him shudder and close his eyes.

"Arden, don't."

Grumble, grumble. But I let him go. And he kissed the edge of my brow, his fingers brushing a tingly path along my spine. It drew a dreamy sound out of me and I relaxed an extra half percent I didn't even know was there: completely limp and weightless, draped over Caspian. Obviously, touching him would have been wonderful. But it belatedly occurred to me that if I had jerked him off in the bath, we would probably have wanted to get out quickly. Even if—in purely rational terms—the spoodge-to-water ratio was very small.

Eventually, the bubbles had mostly dissipated and my toes were turning wrinkly. So we de-tubbed and Caspian snuggled me up in one of One Hyde Park's exceptionally fluffy towels. I was having a hard time not staring at him—I mean, even more than usual. Maybe it was my greedy desire for glimpses of damp, slightly disheveled post-bath Caspian. But, actually, I craved these moments with him. Moments when he wasn't master of a world I could barely access. Moments when he was just…Caspian. A man who laughed rarely, smiled shyly, but let himself be playful with me.

A man who was mine.

"Do you need to borrow some clothes or something?" I called out, as I went in search of a non-embarrassing pair of pajama bottoms.

He laughed. "Thank you, but no. I have lived here on occasions."

I couldn't help wondering which of his houses was home. And if I'd ever get to see it.

"Do you have any pizza preferences?" I asked instead.

"None at all."

"Do you even like pizza?"

"Probably."

My rummaging had miraculously failed to turn up some sexy

yet sophisticated lounge wear. Mainly because I didn't have any. "What do you mean probably?"

"I mean…probably. I haven't had it for a long time."

"You don't have baths. You don't eat pizza." I compromised on my CHILL OUT Olaf the Snowman trousers and my I DON'T CARE I'M A UNICORN T-shirt. Okay, okay, it wasn't a compromise. It was all I had. "What on earth are you doing with your life?"

"Well," Caspian said mildly, "I've been quite busy at work."

Wandering out of the bedroom, I found him already waiting for me. I'd seen Casual Caspian before—at Kinlochbervie when he'd come to get me back—but it was still slightly intimidating. Especially because he looked like an underwear model, in loose-fitting black sweats and a T-shirt that was practically *molded* to his torso. And I looked like a cartoon character.

But I guess this was life with Caspian Hart. And it made sense that things were a little bit awkward because our relationship was a frankly bonkers combination of distance and intimacy. We'd shared secrets over the telephone. He'd given me an apartment to live in. I'd crawled to him on my hands and knees. And, unless you counted dinner with my family, this was the first evening we'd ever spent together in a way that didn't centralize destroying each other or fucking.

Not that I minded the fucking. I was a big fan of the fucking. But it was…well. It was nice that this was an option too.

I smiled at him, self-conscious suddenly. "Any thoughts about movies?"

"None." He crossed the floor toward me, silent on bare feet, and gently turned my face up to his for the lightest of kisses. "Am I a terrible disappointment to you?"

"What? No. How could you be?"

"Because you're asking me for things I have very little experience in giving."

I gazed up at him. Fuck. Maybe I should have let him take me to Paris. "Would you rather fuck me and go?"

He blinked.

"Not in a bad way. Just, this is probably really boring for you, isn't it?"

"How could I possibly be bored?" His mouth softened unexpectedly. "You nearly drowned me in the bath."

"Yep yep. I did do that. I could also get a pizza with a topping you're allergic to, if you like."

"I'm not allergic to anything. Though I'm not especially fond of mushrooms."

For some reason, this tiny piece of random knowledge thrilled me. "I won't get one with mushrooms. If you're sure."

"Yes, I'm quite sure I don't like them."

"You know that's not what I meant." I tried to sound stern but the giggling detracted.

"Yes. I'm sure I like this. And I'm sure I like you. Now"—he turned me round and tapped me rather wickedly on the arse—"go and order pizza and then pick a film."

I gave him a fluttery glance over my shoulder. "Yes, Mr. Hart."

A few minutes later, pizza was on its way and I was wrestling my bedding onto the sofa. Caspian looked mildly confused again, but didn't otherwise comment. He might have been a super powerful billionaire but there was at least one universal truth I knew and he didn't: everything was better under a duvet.

"So, I was thinking," I said as I snugged myself up, "we could maybe watch the new *Star Wars*?"

Honestly, I was more than a little bit nerve-wracked. Choosing a movie was a serious responsibility—it not only said things about you, it said things about the way you saw someone else. Two rich veins of potential humiliation. And Caspian was extra difficult because there were graven angels more into pop culture than he was. But I thought *Star Wars* might work. Given his fondness for sci-fi. And, y'know, the fact it was awesome.

"As it happens, I've seen it." He pulled the other end of the duvet over his knees and, let me tell you, his duvet technique was majorly lacking. No curling. No tucking. Absolutely no nestling.

"You have?" The possibility hadn't even occurred to me. But he did travel a lot—maybe he'd caught it on a plane.

"Yes, I watched it with my father when it first came out. He was quite fanatical about the series."

I loved it when Caspian spoke about his father. Trusting me with the fragile origami of his memories. But at the same time, I didn't want to appear morbidly eager for dead-parent-related entertainment. So I went with a casually encouraging "Yeah?"

"Mm." Caspian smiled, one of his sweetest, rarest smiles. "The original film came out when he was about sixteen. He called it his first love."

"I guess it's pretty cool I mean, for a movie from the seventies."

"He always said that, like Bertrand Russell, three great passions ruled his life. Us—Eleanor and I—our mother, and *Star Wars*."

I suddenly remembered the dedication I'd seen in one of Caspian's books. And felt a bit sorry for *all my love, L* since they apparently ranked below George Lucas in Arthur Hart's affections. Which was when another important thought occurred to me. "So how did he find *The Phantom Menace then*?"

"Well. He did not quite burn George Lucas in effigy. But from that day forth his life was ruled by *two* great passions."

I laughed. Then winced. Then remembered why I'd suggested *Star Wars* in the first place. "Caspian. You do know there's, like, *new* new *Star Wars*, right? And it doesn't suck."

"Really?"

"Yep. Nobody says anything about midi-chlorians. And no trade routes are even remotely in dispute."

"That does sound rather more like the *Star Wars* my father enjoyed."

"Did you enjoy it?"

He gave a slightly self-conscious shrug. "His enthusiasm was always infectious. Much like yours, Arden."

If you'd asked me, as a general principle, how I felt about being compared to deceased parents, the answer would probably have been *Not so great, actually*. But in this case? I was oddly touched. Showing Caspian how to enjoy things was a good trait to share with someone he loved. On the other hand, maybe *Star Wars* wasn't the best choice in this particular context.

"Would you rather watch something else? Because I'm always up for Disney."

"No, no. *Star Wars* is fine."

Fine: the answer dreams were made of.

But it turned out to be a lie, anyway, because Caspian clearly was not fine about *Star Wars*. He was enthralled. He tried to hide it but he literally gasped when the music kicked in. It was beyond adorable.

It belatedly occurred to me that I should have warned him I'm a terrible person to watch movies with—I kind of, somehow, can't stop talking through them. Which is not, well, it's not ideal, is it? But, actually, while there were lots of things I could have said, I didn't, in the end, say any of them.

Because I didn't want to spoil anything for Caspian.

And, for me, watching him was better than watching the movie. It wasn't what I would have pictured at all. But, then, doing something like this with Caspian had always been a daydream I'd never really believed would happen, so my imagination had been hazy on the details. I guess I'd been expecting his usual careful detachment: an elegant man bathed in the silver light of a screen. What I got was a boy's wide-eyed wonder. A delight in TIE fighters, Wookiees, and lightsabers that might have started as affection for his father but was now entirely his own.

And he was sharing it with me.

The pizza came and went, and he barely noticed. And, once I'd got rid of the box, he let me rearrange the duvet over us both—for maximum coze—and squeeze right up against him. I even got to wriggle my hand into his. I didn't think I'd ever liked *Star Wars* quite as much as I did right then. I felt half drunk on his pleasure. My heart huge and soft and raw and wobbly.

Oh God. Was I in love? This vast feeling soaring and wheeling inside me. Surely it was love.

When the credits rolled, Caspian turned to me, his eyes oddly shiny in the flicking light, and murmured: "I wish my father could have seen that. But I'm so glad I got to watch it with you."

And now my heart was mush. Just red mush spilling everywhere. "Caspian." Overcome with happiness and too-big emotions, I flung my arms around him and covered him with hysterical kisses.

He seemed a bit surprised but only reined me in a little bit.

I paused briefly in my frenzy. "Thank you for tonight. I loved watching *Star Wars* with you." And, in case I was overdoing it and getting scary, I added, "You big nerd."

"How dare you." He subjected me to his most billionaire-y look, only for it to be undermined by the light in his eyes and the laughter lurking at the edges of his lips. "I simply commit fully to my every undertaking."

"Including *Star Wars*."

His smile got the better of him. "Especially *Star Wars*."

Help. I was going to explode of everything. How did people cope? Did they go about their daily lives with love inside them like a skyful of rioting party balloons? And, suddenly, I was terrified.

Because what if I told him?

Because what if I was wrong?

Because what if what if what if…

I would probably have had a panic attack on the sofa but then my dick swept in out of nowhere and rescued me by getting incredibly hard. Arousal thundered through me with the sort of conviction that hurled lions off cliffs and left their sons guilt-stricken for half a movie. Slightly shocked at the intensity of my own desire, I twined my arms around Caspian's neck.

"Take me to bed," I said. My voice was so shaky, I couldn't tell if I was asking, demanding, or pleading.

But it didn't matter anyway because Caspian picked me up and carried me off.

CHAPTER 21

It wasn't the first time he'd done that, but his strength always took me a little bit by surprise. I think because—along with so many other things, passion and joy and laughter—he kept it locked away behind his well-cut suit and his cold eyes. And there was nothing quite like being carted around by someone else to make you feel excitingly overpowered. I clung to his shoulders, my stomach doing roller-coaster swoops, even though I knew he wouldn't drop me.

He tossed me onto my duvet-less bed like I was a medieval princess and he was the dark knight come to claim my maidenhead. And then came down on top of me, kissing me hard, his tongue plunging between my lips in happy anticipation of other acts-of-plunging he might be likely to perform. I sank into sex—into that warm, thudding place of heart-to-heart and mouth-to-mouth.

But, of course, the moment I got my hands under his top and against his skin he had me by the wrists and was pulling my arms over my head. He gazed down at me—all predator-sharp and sexy-hungry. "I should get my tie."

I flip-flopped between thrilled and frustrated. Because, yes, part of me would have loved it—the part in question being my dick, which had got even harder at the prospect of me being trussed and helpless and at the mercy of Caspian Hart. But my more complicated bits had more complicated reactions.

"Let me touch you," I absolutely did not whine.

"Arden…"

"I know, I know." I pushed against his hands. "I can't help it. I just want to give you pleasure sometimes."

"You do give me pleasure. You give me so much pleasure."

"Did you hate it? In Kinlochbervie?"

"No but—"

"Please." The word burst out of me, raw with longing. "I *beg* you, Caspian."

He looked startled and I couldn't entirely blame him. I couldn't remember ever begging that hard for anything in my life—including my own orgasms.

Although, slightly to my own horror, it turned out I wasn't done. "You can still be in control. I'll worship you. I'll serve you. My hands will be your slaves."

Endless silence. I could tell my eyes had gone huge and needy. And, while I knew I gave good *pleeeeease* face, for once, I wasn't trying to be cute.

"It really means this much to you?" he asked.

"Yes. God yes."

"What"—he faltered, then recovered—"do you want to do?"

"Anything."

"That's not very specific."

"Um." He was right, but now he'd put me on the spot. And having already made a massive fuss, I felt duty-bound to be reasonable. There was, after all, no point asking for the moon when the stars were plenty shiny. "Can I give you a hand job?"

"Just a hand job?" Wow. Way to sound insultingly relieved, Caspian.

I pouted. "Hey now. There's nothing *just* about a hand job when it's from me."

"It's really what you want?"

Well. No. It was a sneaky piece of icing from the spectacular, multi-tiered cake of my wanting. But, dammit, I would take it. "Yes."

He let me go and rolled onto his back. "As long as you don't—"

"Put my weight on you. And I'll stop straightaway if you tell me."

"All right." He sounded perfectly calm, even bored, but his eyes—which held mine like a drowning man might clutch me—told a different story.

"I promise," I whispered. "And thank you."

He gave a shaky laugh. "I'm not sure I've done anything to merit gratitude."

"Oh my God." I turned and ran palm down the frankly ridiculous contours of his abdomen. "You're trusting me. And you're giving me...you. That's the most incredible gift."

"I very much doubt it."

"Don't say that stuff. You'll make me cross with you."

My caress became a well-deserved a poke. Which made

him…I didn't quite know. From anyone else it would have been a yelp. From Caspian it was probably a much more dignified sound. "I'm very sorry."

"I'll forgive you. Can I take your clothes off?"

"I presume you're intending to follow suit?"

He'd had me naked and in compromising positions pretty much constantly. But nothing—not even the threat of torture, well, okay, the threat of torture, let's keep a sense of perspective here—would have made me point it out to him.

"Course." I whipped my top over my head and wriggled out of my pj bottoms.

And, yep, there I was again: slightly cold and extremely undressed in front of the most gorgeous man I'd ever met.

But, God, it was nothing.

Barely a fraction of what I would have done to please him. To make him feel safe. Sure of his power and my so-willing supplication.

He sat up and I caught the hem of his T-shirt, drawing it up and off. A ribbon of heat spiraled down my spine toward my increasingly perky cock. He'd never let me do anything like this before. With other people, I'd dragged them out of their clothes and hardly given a second's thought. With Caspian, it was intimacy beyond anything I'd dreamed of: no longer just a recipient of his desires, I was part of them.

And there was no way I was goofing this up. No catching his ear or messing his hair or getting his arm stuck. Oh no. I divested him of his T-shirt like it was fucking cloth of gold. He emerged blinking, his freshly bared chest heaving with his quickened breath.

"See." I leaned in and brushed my mouth over the stark crests of his collarbones, remembering the way he'd responded in Kinlochbervie. He trembled now, my gorgeous man, felled by the gentlest of touches. "You can imagine you're Alexander and I'm Bagoas and I'm disrobing you after some great battle."

He cupped a hand beneath my jaw and drew me up for a brief kiss. "I think I'd rather you were Arden."

"I can definitely live with that. I'm still yours, though."

"Is that so? How's your dancing?"

"I've got some moves. How's your global conquest?"

"Largely financial."

He was stalling. It was cute stalling, but stalling nevertheless. Shuffling lower on the bed, I slipped my fingers gently under the waist of his lounge trousers and slid them all the way down. Swear to God, if I'd attempted a sexy move like that on myself, I'd have got them tangled in my knob. Or around my knees. But, for Caspian, I found grace.

And there he was: my own private centerfold. I actually groaned at the sight of him. Like when you're super hungry and somebody makes you bacon for breakfast. That kind of groan.

"You are so ridiculously hot," I told him.

And, of course, he blushed—a pinkish tinge spreading across his cheekbones and down his chest. Which made him look, if possible, even better. It gave life to that perfect physique of his. A whisper of the imperfect to make him real. And touchable. And mine.

He was only half hard. Not exactly a ringing endorsement of what was happening so far but I wasn't going to take it personally. Clearly he felt exposed and not everyone got off on that the way I did. Though I was hoping I could show him he didn't have to be vulnerable. That control and distance weren't always the same thing. And even if he was uncertain of himself, he never had to be of me. I would yield whenever he needed it.

I got settled by his side. Since I intended to be a while, it made sense to get comfy. "Can you grab some lube from the drawer?"

"Is that necessary?"

Sheesh. You'd have thought I was pulling his teeth, not his dick. "No, but it's nicer."

His knees shifted very slightly.

"I'm not going to cross the neutral zone, Caspian. That's how you start a war with the Romulans."

At last: a faint smile.

I grinned back at him. "Get me the damn lube, will you."

He turned onto his side, pulled open the bedside drawer, and froze. "Good God. What's all this?"

"Just your standard, everyday, perfectly average collection of sex toys."

"I wouldn't call this average, Arden. I would call it expansive. I mean—"

I glanced at what he was brandishing and shrugged. "Everyone needs a Fleshlight."

"And a vibrating cock ring?"

"Hell yes."

"What about…actually, I have no idea what this is."

"It's a guybrator. And that's a prostate massager. And that's a subtly but significantly different prostate massager. That one's a very basic dildo."

"And this?"

"A dildo in the shape of a tentacle. Obviously."

He covered his eyes with a hand. "I don't know what to say."

"How about: I respect your commitment to self-pleasure."

"This is quite the commitment."

Oh bless. He'd gone all pink again. So adorable. "Well, like the lady says: *If you don't love yourself, how in the hell you gonna love somebody else?*" Except now he had his *I have no idea what you're talking about* look. I held out my hand and wiggled my fingers impatiently. "Lube, please."

"Which lube? You own a lot."

"Hmm." I considered the matter. "The Boy Butter."

"Boy Butter? Really."

"It's lovely, I promise. Can you"—a sigh I couldn't quite stifle—"trust me. A little bit. Please."

He passed me the tub without further comment.

I flipped off the lid, gathered up a generous dollop of soft creamy goodness on my finger, and set about getting my hands, and his cock, all warm and slick. Then I noticed Caspian was frowning. "What's wrong?"

"Nothing. Just do you…are we…am I not satisfying you?"

"Where did that come from? I love sexytimes with you."

"Well." His frown intensified. "I can't help notice you have gathered masturbatory aids with the determination of a squirrel preparing for a long winter."

I couldn't help giggling at the image. Arden St. Ives: wank-squirrel. "I like getting myself off. I mean, not more than I like someone else doing it. I'm into both is what I'm saying."

This was not an ideal time for there to be silence. I knew because silence happened. And kept happening.

"Um." I shifted uncomfortably. "I'm feeling slightly slut-shamed here. For your information."

"That was not my intention. I'm simply…somewhat startled."

"I don't see why. Everyone masturbates."

"Yes, but I've always treated it as little more than a necessity." His gaze skittered away from mine.

Great. Now I'd made *him* uncomfortable. Turns out, talking about wanking was a hot potato of social awkwardness. Who'd have thought it?

"I'm pretty sure that's the general cultural perception," I said. "But I guess I don't really see masturbation as a lesser form of sex. Just a different one. Also you've made me say masturbation about eighty-seven times, which is embarrassing, so you owe me an apology."

He ducked his head to hide what was blatantly a smile. "I'm sorry."

"I suppose I'll forgive you."

He was quiet again. And then, very softly, "I love the glimpses of the world I see through your eyes."

Wow, this was like that scene in that movie where the guy is super moved by the beauty of a plastic bag blowing in the wind. Except it was my penis. I wasn't entirely sure how to respond, apart from, y'know, graciously because he'd given me a compliment. "Um, thank you."

Caspian gave me a tense little smile. And I was still sitting there, with his dick in my hand. So far Operation Hand Job wasn't anything close to the gently erotic experience I'd had in mind. In fact, it was hard to imagine how it could have gone worse without one of us sustaining actual physical injury. Or my mum and his mum walking in on us simultaneously. Probably the sensible thing to do at this point was give up.

But fuck sensible. And fuck giving up. I'd damn near demanded Caspian's trust. And so far all I'd done with it was intimidate him with my array of personal lubricants and get defensive about my masturbatory habits.

I had to fix this.

Obviously I needed to say something reassuring. Although the only things I could think of—just relax, it's going to be okay—made it sound like I was about to laser off a verruca or give him a colonic irrigation.

"Okay," I announced. "Hand job time."

Caspian gave a splutter of amusement.

Which, y'know, was better than nothing. I'd lost ground in erection terms, but I wasn't too concerned. If anything, it was part of the experience: coaxing him languorously to arousal between my palms. As far as I could tell, most people jerked off as if they were late for an orgasm appointment. Me, I took the scenic route. And, soon enough, Caspian was with me for the journey, his cock hot and hard, silky with lube, and shudderingly responsive to my caresses.

I didn't actually have any magic wanking techniques. And who had time for all that "make an O with your thumb and index finger" *Cosmo* nonsense? It was about paying attention. Taking your time. Enjoying what you were doing. And, God, was I enjoying myself. There was an intimacy to this that I absolutely loved.

I mean, of course there were a bunch of ways to get intimate with someone else's cock—but the thing about having one inside you was that it was difficult to really appreciate the, well, the subtleties. The flushes of color that rushed over the head. The tender stretch of the foreskin, with its dark, dancing veins. All the places he was extra sensitive. The puzzle-box of touches that made him arch and drip, and turned his breathing ragged.

"Arden?"

I glanced up dreamily. "Yes?"

"Talk to me."

For a second or two, I was topic bereft. But then I realized he probably didn't want to discuss the political situation in Syria. *Keep me with you*, he'd told me once. Slipping a hand under his balls, I treated them to some attention. "How's this feel? Good?"

"That's not talking to me. That's asking me things."

"It's engaging you in conversation. It counts." To make my point, I lightly circled the exposed delta of tissue on the underside of his shaft.

And he threw an arm across his face and smothered a groan. This lovely raw sound, too sweet for pain.

"You're still okay with this, right?" I asked.

"I am." His head moved restlessly against the pillow. "Though I'm at a loss to understand what you're getting out of it."

"Are you kidding me? I get to watch you and touch you and please you." I shifted my grip, giving him long, sensuous strokes. Building pleasure like a fire in winter. "I am pleasing you, aren't I?"

"Y-yes." He swallowed a gasp. He was such a tantalizing collection of contrasts just then: the sharp lines of his drawn-tight muscles and his bliss-softened mouth half hidden by the shadow of his wrist. I hoped he felt beautiful because he was. He so was.

He made me want to be an octopus. I mean, not actually. Japanese wood carvings aside, he probably wouldn't have been into me anymore. But I could seriously have used some extra arms. He was all ridges and grooves, sweat-gleam upon straining skin, and I yearned to stroke him everywhere. Smooth my palms over his trembling stomach. Press my fingers into the damp hollows behind his collarbones. Gentle his struggles as well as inspire them.

His fist clenched in the sheets. "Arden?"

"I'm right here. It's all right." It was an inane thing to say considering what was happening, but apparently it was what I had. "You're doing so well. You're wonderful."

Honestly, I didn't know what the fuck I was going on about. Except, with the same instinct that had once sent me to my knees on a balcony in Oxford, some part of me recognized it was what he needed.

"Look at me," I whispered.

A tremor shook his whole body. "I can't."

"Please."

"Don't."

"You need to. You need to see." I worked him steadily, lavishing him with all the care my hands could give. "You need to see what I do when I look at you."

He was right on the edge of orgasm. I could feel him there, a dancer not yet dancing, though I wasn't the one holding him back. He stirred agitatedly, his spine bowing, hips bucking, one foot braced against the bed. Until, at last, he pulled his arm away. His face was flushed with hectic pleasure and damp with desperation, moisture matted into the hair at his brow, and glittering on his lashes. Even wrecked, he was lovely—one of those naughty seventeenth-century poems I hadn't revised properly. Delight in disorder and all that.

His eyes found mine—wary enough to break my heart. But it was okay. I gazed at him, full of submission and hope and love and certainty. Because I knew that even if he caught only the reflected shadow of everything inside in me, it would still be enough. And he'd understand that I was his and he was mine, and could be everything that mattered.

"You're perfect," I told him. "I wish you knew. How beautiful you are. And how strong and kind. How *good*—"

He made a broken sound and came, trembling frantically, covering my fingers and his own stomach. And, for the briefest of moments, he let me see: his pleasure in all its nakedness, before he retreated behind his arm.

Grabbing my T-shirt from the floor, I cleaned us up and then went to retrieve the duvet. My preference would have been insta-snuggling, but I thought he might appreciate a minute or two to himself. And, sure enough, when I came back he seemed a lot more put together. Which was a shame because I liked him sex-rumpled. And a little bit unraveled.

I cast the duvet over the bed and bounced up beside him, hoping everything was still okay. The seesaw of equanimity had clearly decided it was my turn to get anxious because suddenly I was convinced he was going to resent what had just happened. Or have some terrible reaction to it he hadn't seen fit to tell me about.

Instead, he turned my face to his and kissed me. It wasn't rough, but it was bone-meltingly deep, and I surrendered to it gratefully. To the gentle dominion of lips and teeth and tongue.

When he finally let me go, I realized I was oddly wobbly. Happy-wobbly, like after he'd spanked me that time. The same sense of being stripped down somehow, as if he'd taken a pumice stone to my soul, and left me fresh and shiny and vulnerable. It made no sense because what we'd done had been so different…or, actually, maybe it hadn't.

"Thank you," I mumbled. "That was amazing. The best."

"But what about you?"

"What about me? Oh, you mean…" It seemed a bit weird to be turning down sexual attention but I kind of felt like I'd *had* sexual attention. "I'm okay."

"That doesn't seem fair."

"You gave me what I needed, just like always. How isn't it fair?"

He made an unconvinced noise.

"I'd rather cuddle and share your afterglow. Err, you do have afterglow, right? I gave you an afterglow?"

"Yes. I'm"—he blushed—"glowy."

My eyes got big and hopeful. "Is cuddling an option?"

He answered by pulling me into his arms. I tucked in as close as I dared, sinking into his warmth, and letting the scent of his skin—sweat, sex, the fading notes of his cologne, and something I recognized as purely *him*—wash over me.

"Though I think I might want a cigarette," he murmured, after a minute or two.

I partially de-nestled. "I'll go."

"I'm perfectly capable of getting them myself."

"Well, I know that. But I want to. Where are they?"

"Jacket pocket."

I kissed the corner of his mouth, scrambled out of bed, and went looking. As love-quests went it was minor—I didn't meet any fantastical beasts or get my head chopped off—but I liked being able to do something for him. It seemed…domestic. The sort of small task a partner might do. I even remembered to grab a saucer for the ash.

Wow, I was the best.

"Can I light it for you?" I asked, on my triumphant return.

One of his eyebrows twitched upward. "I think you might be overestimating the power of your hand job. It was very nice, but I'm still functional."

"I just thought it would be romantic." I grinned at him in what I hoped was an appealing fashion. "You know, like Bogart and Bacall, Davis and Henreid, Grant and Scott. I mean, unless you think I'll set your face on fire or something?"

"I don't think you'll set my face on fire." He took the packet of cigarettes I'd brought him, drew one out of the foil, and put it to his lips.

And, obviously, smoking was bad and everyone knew it was bad…but he looked so sexy. Half naked, stretched out in bed, still languid with post-orgasmic sensuality: this perfect embodiment of old Hollywood glamour, except nobody had to pretend they were straight.

I fumbled a match out of the box. "I should light one for me too, and then we could put the tips together and do it that way."

"I'm not letting you smoke."

"Um, is it up to you?"

"Since they're my cigarettes, yes." But then he smiled unexpectedly. "Besides, you're terrible at it, Arden. And I'd rather you didn't take up an unhealthy habit."

"It's *your* unhealthy habit."

"Indeed. And there are many other aspects of my life I would prefer you didn't repeat."

I blinked at him. "Really? You don't think I should aspire to be rich, successful, brilliant, and gorgeous?"

"I think you should be exactly who you are. Including all the ways you are not like me."

I couldn't quite untangle what was a compliment and what wasn't. But I was getting distracted anyway. I didn't actually want to smoke—I was just getting bratty because I'd been told I couldn't. And it was extra-nonsensical because Caspian not wanting me to get cancer and die was hardly the height of oppression. So I stopped arguing and lit his cigarette for him. And I didn't make a total hash of it. Yay.

Caspian was pretty casual about the whole thing, but I was strangely touched. Maybe because I was thinking of Oxford again. His smoking had been this private ritual then and he'd seemed like an impossible fantasy of a man, as beyond me as the stars and the golden towers. Except the truth of him was so much more.

Making sure the match was out, I dropped the box on the bedside cabinet and snugged up next to Caspian. Watched the curls of smoke drifting from between his lips. Was it wrong that I found it hot? Of course, I would have preferred him to have a non-harmful hobby, but I don't think he did it enough for it to be very damaging.

"Are you going to stay?" I said, instead.

"If you'd like to me to."

"Hmm, let me think about it. *Yes*."

He laughed, but quickly turned serious again. "I can't promise to…to be the best sleeping companion."

"I'll, um, try not to flip out this time."

"Thank you."

"I'm incredibly jet-lagged anyway. I probably won't notice if you slip out to join a mariachi band."

He stubbed out his cigarette, put the saucer to one side, and drew me fully into his arms. "Then you should sleep, my Arden."

"Will you?" I brushed a finger against the corner of his eye. "You look tired too."

"I missed you."

I was going to say something about my absence being no excuse for Caspian not taking proper care of himself. But I was too cozy. Too cozy for anything except snuggling. And a bit of happy mumble-purring.

At some point, I did become vaguely aware of being disentangled. Nudged gently across the bed and tucked up. But it was okay. I could still feel the shape of Caspian behind me. And the pattern of his breath was as comforting as the fall of raindrops against my window back in Kinlochbervie.

CHAPTER 22

Of course, I woke up alone. And, thanks to jet lag, it was still the middle of the night. I rolled about, trying to re-snuggle, but it wasn't happening. The empty space beside me just made me sad. Even though I knew Caspian wasn't trying to hurt me, any more than I was doing something to drive him away.

The last time I'd gone looking for him hadn't exactly been a rousing success, but we'd both been independently messed up, and, presumably, if I didn't descend on him wailing about Nathaniel like I'd been possessed by the spirit of lovers past it would go better. And, anyway, if I could spontaneously ask Poppy Carrie for an interview, I could go and find Caspian.

Hell yes, I could.

Throwing off the covers, I scrabbled about on the floor for my pajama bottoms and padded out into the hall. I expected he'd be in the living area, but he wasn't. It was empty, caught in the eerie half-light of the city's ceaseless glow. Maybe he was sleeping somewhere else? Except no sign of him in any of the bedrooms.

Shit. Maybe he'd left?

Fuck me sideways, he'd better not have. If he'd fucked off on me after last night I…well, I had no idea what I'd do. But I knew this wasn't the sort of thing I'd get over. My stomach knotted with a strange mixture of preemptive anger and fear. While my heart was already begging: *please don't do this to me, Caspian.*

Then I heard it: a gasping sound, almost a sob.

I turned. Followed it like a ninja. And, for the record, I wouldn't normally have burst in on someone in the bathroom, especially if weird noises were involved, but the door was half open and I could see Caspian inside. He was braced against the marble counter, head down. What I could see of his face in the mirror was pale, sweat damp like his tangled hair, and he was trembling violently.

Don't tell me I'd done this to him again.

"C-Caspian?"

He glanced up, his reflected eyes red-rimmed, damp, and desolate. Meeting mine only briefly.

"What's wrong? Are you—" I remembered just in time how he'd reacted to the word *triggered.* "Is it like before?"

"No. No. Nothing like that. I'm…oh God, don't laugh."

"Of course I—"

My assurance was lost as he rushed on. "I had a dream."

I guess maybe some people might have found it funny. He was, after all, a grown man, and a powerful one, and only children were supposed to be scared of dreams. But I'd heard my mum begging and screaming in hers way too often to take them lightly. "You mean, a nightmare?"

After a moment, he nodded.

"Do you want to talk about it? It's okay if you don't, but sometimes it helps. Was someone hurting you?"

"No. I…I…"

Suddenly he spun away from the counter and pulled me into his arms so fiercely it almost knocked the wind out of me. I hugged him back and, for once, he didn't protest or pull away, his body this tangle of physical anguish against mine, all hot, rough breath and the panicked heartbeat of a wounded beast. And then, before I quite knew what was happening, he was on his knees, clinging to me.

"I was hurting you," he whispered.

It felt about eighty-seven types of weird to be standing when Caspian wasn't. On any other occasion I would probably have hit the floor too in order to balance things out. But I knew that wasn't what he needed from me tonight. So I stopped worrying. Curled my fingers very lightly into his hair, trying to soothe him. "It was only a dream."

"You were crying, Arden, and screaming. And there was blood on your back, and you were begging me to stop. And I didn't."

"It was a dream," I said again. "Only a dream."

His fingers tightened, digging hard enough into the backs of my thighs I was sure he was leaving bruises. "It felt so good."

"Yes, but that doesn't mean anything."

He didn't answer. Just stifled another miserable sound.

"I'm serious. You'd never do something like that in real life."

"Arden"—he looked up at me with his restless ocean eyes, so full of unfathomed pain—"you have no idea what I'm capable of."

It was the easiest thing in the world, right then, to hold his gaze. "I know you'd never hurt me in ways I didn't want to be hurt. I know you'd never break my trust. And I know that, whatever you've done or whatever's been done to you, you're a good person."

I could sense the protest gathering inside him. Any second now he was going to say something devastatingly rational about how I couldn't be sure and then we were going to have a big argument because, on this particular subject, I wasn't yielding. Not for him. Not for anyone.

But I guess he was still too raw. Because he let me hold him instead. And we stayed there like that for long enough I started to worry about his knees on the marble floor.

When my mum had nightmares we turned on every light in the house. And checked every room. That wouldn't work for Caspian, though. He had different demons.

Which wasn't to say they couldn't be conquered.

I touched his shoulder gently. "Come back to bed."

"You still want—"

I knew it was rude to interrupt, but sometimes you had to. "More than anything in the world."

* * *

My body had apparently given up on time zones because when I next woke up it was still far too early, especially for a Saturday. To my slight surprise, Caspian was beside me, as close as he could get without us actually touching.

God, he must have been exhausted because he was *out*. And,

whereas when I was asleep I looked like a concussed bunny, drooling and twitching and snuffling my nose (I knew because Nik had been kind enough to record me), even after last night Caspian looked beautiful. Like he belonged in an arty black 'n' white photo series.

He was lying on his stomach, head turned to the side, one arm flung across the pillow, the other curled neatly beside him. The covers had slipped down, exposing his shoulders and the long sweep of his spine. And the teeniest hint of buttock curve. His hair was an adorable ruffle across his brow and his eyelashes were infuriating. I mean.. Did he need them that thick and dark and soft? Really? Did he? When the rest of him was so ridiculously exquisite? He could have afforded one less than perfect feature. Except I loved his contrasts: his strength and his secrets, like his lavish eyelashes, his delicate collarbones, and the enticingly tender skin of his flanks.

I stared at him creepily for a while. Partially because I could, and Caspian would never know, but also because my phone was flashing super insistently and I wasn't ready to face whatever I was being messaged about. Not when I could live in the shadows of Caspian's far too lovely eyelashes.

Finally, though, I forced myself to get out of bed, creeping into the living area so I wouldn't disturb Caspian. Strips of pale yellow-gray sunlight fell across my feet, making them look jaundiced. Oh England with your half-arsed summers. I was so happy to be home.

I glanced down at my phone. Holy shit. That was a lot of notifications. Which, once again, I wasn't conscious of having done anything to inspire. Sighing, I googled Ellery (nothing

new), myself (nothing new), and finally yesterday's event. I was
fairly reassured that I had to hunt to find it, but there it was
in a particular scurrilous gossip rag: "Keeping It in the Family:
Aloof Billionaire Caspian Hart Steals Sister's Squeeze." And
a fuzzy side-by-side of two mes—one eating strawberries with
Ellery, and one holding Caspian's hand outside the gallery.

So, yeah. That was pretty icky. And typical, honestly, that the
public record of Nathaniel's relationship with Caspian was all
glossy couples pics from charity events, whereas I was turning
into a tabloid-headline-generating floozy. But, whatever. Being
with Caspian probably meant some of this stuff was inevitable.
I forwarded the article to Bellerose just in case and turned to my
emails.

A few were related to my own writing, one was from *Milieu*
(oooh), the rest were Nik, Sophie, Weird Owen, Professor Standish, Oxford University notifications…oh fuck.

Fuck fuck fuck fuck *fuck*.

This could mean only one thing.

My results were out.

I could have put it off. Once upon a time I would have.
But not anymore. I had an article coming out in *Milieu*. A re-
spectable army of Instagram followers. A billionaire lover who
fucked me and cherished me, and let me comfort him when he
needed it. I'd danced all night at a secret rave in an abandoned
building. Flown to Boston to be with a friend. Interviewed
Poppy Carrie in a hospital café. Frankly, Oxford could suck my
balls.

I dug my password out of the sludge in the bottom of my
brain and logged into the student self-service.

And there it was.

Arden St. Ives: 2.2.

The rest of the non-work emails were mostly congratulations. Polite congratulations. Professor Standish said she hoped this wouldn't hold me back because she knew I was very capable when I put my mind to it. Weird Owen had helpfully gone to Exam Schools and taken a photo of the public list for me. I was right at the bottom. Worst mark in college. Even Druggie Matt, who had been off his face in every tutorial, had managed a 2.1.

So. Yeah.

2.2.

The result you got when you weren't competent enough for a 2.1 or incompetent enough for a third. A 2.1, said "I did what I was supposed to do," a third said, "I gave no fucks about doing what I was supposed to do," and a 2.2 said nothing at all.

It was a squeak of inglorious inadequacy.

I waited for the sky to fall. I waited to burst into tears.

But the world stayed right-way-up. And I was…totally and completely fine.

Huh.

Well, time to see what *Milieu* had to say. Which was, if anything, even more nerve-wracking. They'd got back to me much quicker than last time, which made me suspect I was either moving up in the world or about to suffer a devastating insta!rejection.

But it was good…ish…news. I think. They liked the interview, though it would need a lot of work, and to run it at the length they felt it deserved, it would have to be a main feature. Meaning, they wanted Poppy for the cover. And so, since she was essentially my contact, I had to email her. And what with it still being the middle of the night in Boston, and the weekend, it would probably sit there in her inbox for hours, if not days.

Holy tenterhooks Batman.

"Arden?" Caspian's voice startled me away from my phone.

"Sorry. Sorry. I'm here."

I ran back into the bedroom. Found Caspian sitting up and bleary-eyed, pushing the hair out of his face.

"I'm starting to see," he said, "why you object so much to waking up alone."

"Did you miss me?" I jumped back into bed.

"I wouldn't say missed you exactly—"

"Wow thanks."

He gave me a look. "Well, I knew you were unlikely to have gone far."

"You could still miss me though."

"I certainly awoke and was aware of your absence."

"If you ever get sick of being a billionaire, you could work for Hallmark." I mimed titles flying through the air. "I Am Aware of Your Absence. I May Have Mildly Inconvenienced You. My Concern on This Non-Ideal Occasion."

"Oh shush."

I'd never seen someone try to laugh while they were scowling. Or scowl while they were laughing. Anyway, it was…pretty special. Then he twisted a hand in my hair and pulled me in for a kiss that felt like reward and punishment all at once.

"Caspian," I mumbled against his mouth.

"Yes, my Arden?"

"I failed Oxford."

He drew back a little. Not in a recoiling-from-my-ignorance way. More just giving me space. "You failed? Nobody fails Oxford. You mean you got a third?"

"2.2. That's worse than a third."

"It demonstrably is not."

"You and your damn logic." I sighed. "Sorry. I guess…I don't know. I can't figure out how I feel. I'm supposed to be wrecked. Why aren't I wrecked?"

"Perhaps," he said with gentle mischief, "you've developed a sense of proportion?"

"Um. Have you met me?"

He leaned in and kissed my nose. "When you're there, Oxford seems like the whole world. And its values the only values that matter. But you've been flourishing elsewhere, and in your own way, for months now. At this point, your degree classification is largely irrelevant."

"I do"—I squirmed with an almost uncontainable sense of liberation—"feel…maybe…that I'm flourishing. *Milieu* might want my interview as well."

"I'm so proud of you. Both for what you've achieved at Oxford, and beyond."

Ahhhhh. Too much. Too much. I flumped over and pulled a pillow over my face. "Oh my God, what are you doing to meeeee?"

"What on the earth's the matter now?"

"I can't cope when you're this lovely. I don't deserve it."

"Is that so?" He wrestled the pillow away and rolled on top of me, sliding his knee between my legs. Last night's nightmare seemed very distant indeed as he gazed down at me like a wolf with an exceptionally delicious rabbit between its paws. "Because I can also be terribly cruel."

My cock got hard so quickly it practically sproinged. "Fuck yes. Please be cruel to me."

He caught my lower lip between his teeth and tugged until I whimpered. It was such a sweet, sharp pain.

"But first," he murmured, "let me make something very clear."

Some boys liked diamonds. I liked being sexually threatened. I nodded eagerly. "Okay."

"When it comes to me, I decide what you deserve. And I will feel proud of you when I damn well please." He nipped at my chin. Then moved down my neck, making the skin dance under the scrape of his teeth. "Understood?"

I tipped my head, already breathless. "Y-yes."

"Good. Now, then. Shall we see what you deserve today?"

Apparently what I deserved was to beg and moan a lot. To get covered in bites and bruises. To be sweaty and mindless and helpless. And, finally, when I was literally *crying*, to come like the end of the fucking universe.

Leaving me used and abused and sated and happy.

* * *

Caspian had to fly to New York on Sunday. But—apart from the time I spent on the phone, first to my folks, who were thrilled for me, and then to Nik, who'd got a first, of course—he was all mine for Saturday. Remembering how much he'd enjoyed our family game night, and facing up to the fact that I was never, ever, *ever* going to be remotely interested in learning how not to suck at chess (even from Caspian). I took him down to a board game shop in Seven Dials. He wanted to call a car but I insisted we walk, since it was only half an hour, through Hyde Park and Mayfair, and that turned out to be exactly the right call. Because the day was shiny with sunlight and Caspian let me hold his hand and, for a little while, we were lost together in the London crowds. Just another couple.

I thought I was never getting Caspian out of the shop but we finally settled on a few two-player games. Caspian chose Hive because the assistant described it as "like chess with insects" and I went for Fungi because it was about mushrooms. We headed home via our local Waitrose so I could buy lunch—picnic food, mainly, of the sort best nibbled between committed bouts of sex and board games—and I wasn't sure Caspian had ever been in a supermarket, or at least had forgotten how they worked, because he looked distinctly bewildered the whole time we were there.

I spent the afternoon having my arse handed to me (in a nonsexual way) by an increasingly apologetic Caspian. But it worked out okay since I was far more attracted to his ruthlessness than I was embarrassed by my own abundance of ruth. And I got to tease him about it and make him blush, which was far more satisfying than winning anyway. Then we watched *The Force Awakens* again. I tried to tell Caspian other movies existed—that even other *Star Wars* movies existed—but he said he felt he might have missed things the first time round and wanted to study the film further. Because he was a ginormous dork.

It was more *Star Wars* than I would normally have been up

for, but I liked…no, I loved being able to indulge Caspian. Draw out his tentative pleasures. Catch the gleam of happiness as it crept shyly into his eyes. Also real talk: my toenails were a complete state, and this gave me an opportunity to sort them out. Even if it meant subjecting the man I desired most in the universe to the sight of me hunched over on the sofa like an elderly baboon. Or, y'know, Yoda before he got all CGI. I went for blue-black glitter and teeny-tiny silver stars because I thought Caspian would like it. And I guess he did because he threw my freshly beautified feet over his shoulders and fucked me into a puddle of happy goo as the credits rolled.

Probably ruining the *Star Wars* theme for me forever.

Or improving it immeasurably.

I couldn't quite decide.

After that, I was pretty much done for, but it turned out Caspian wanted to take me out for dinner. As in put-clothes-on-call-a-car-spend-more-money-than-I-was-comfortable-with-maybe-we-could-just-stay-home-and-I-could-make-pasta-instead dinner. Apparently he wanted to celebrate my accomplishments and he wouldn't take no for an answer. Not that I tried to say no very hard. And it was quite a complicated no anyway, because the no-ness was largely about the fact I would never be able to do anything like this for him. But what I really wanted to say was *yes*. Because, while it involved far more chauffeuring and Michelin stars than I was used to, it was…a date. A date with Caspian Hart.

He wore charcoal gray with a slate gray shirt, a maroon tie, and dark gold pocket square. And looked, as ever, ridiculously gorgeous and well put together. So I nobly pulled on my one suit—my crappy, exam-doing suit—only for Caspian to send me back into the bedroom to change. It wasn't until I reemerged, this time in rainbow tie-dye skinny jeans, a T-shirt, and my plum velvet jacket, that I realized he'd dressed for me. Not in the sense that we looked remotely similar. But he'd clearly chosen his tie to complement my jacket, the boldest splash in his otherwise subdued palette like a private tribute to my very favorite color.

In the car, he passed me a neat little parcel, and explained, "We were instructed to bring a book."

"To dinner?"

He nodded. "I hope you don't mind that I had Bellerose provide one."

"Did he also pick the restaurant?"

"He"—Caspian got all pinkish at the top of his cheekbones—"helped me come up with something you would like."

"Maybe I should go out with him."

"I would strenuously object."

I unwrapped the book and burst out laughing. It was a folio society edition of *Rebecca*.

The restaurant turned out to be this wood cabin built on a traffic island near London Bridge. Inside, it was clean and unfussy, all grown-up shades of brown, and books everywhere—there was even one on our table, a copy of *Eros the Bittersweet*. And it turned out the whole deal was about telling stories through food. Which I…yeah. Cheesy or not, I loved it.

And, best of all, they had a tasting menu so I was saved from having to order, something I always hated. I mean, not what beans I wanted in my burrito, but there was way too much pressure in fancy places. You had to worry about the price of things, whether you were paying or not, and also what your choices might be saying about you. Like if you had the beef after the crab, did that mean you were a yahoo, and everyone was secretly laughing? And…and…on top of all that was the major commitment you were making to a large, expensive plate of food that *you might not even like*.

But this way I got to sit there and enjoy a candlelit Caspian and the food took care of itself: arriving as part of what seemed to be an endless parade of exciting nibbles. Some of which, I'll admit, were slightly challenging for a middle-class boy who grew up in the middle of nowhere, but I quickly got swept up in the drama of never quite knowing what was going to turn up next. We had savory Oreos, called Storeos, made with squid ink and eel mousse, and crispy cod skin with cod roe emulsion, and black pudding topped with pineapple. And that was before the meal had even properly started. I didn't think my bouche had ever been so comprehensively amused.

They brought us pouches of sourdough next served with condiments, and I literally squealed when it turned out the candle was made of beef fat and had been quietly forming a pool of warm, meaty deliciousness for us to dip the bread into. I did quite a lot of squealing, actually, as the various dishes appeared. Squealing, squeaking, gasping. Occasionally even waving my hands in the air. Everything was just so pretty and playful and *weird*, like the teeny-tiny mashed potato served with coal oil, or the Snow White apple that was presented to us in a bowl of billowing dry ice and opened up to reveal beef tartare and truffle, or the tiny little milk bottles that were full of rhubarb and custard soda.

And Caspian...God, I don't quite know. He was looking at me the way he looked at *Star Wars*. Which made me so happy I got scared. Because it made me realize that I'd been with Caspian longer than I'd ever been with anyone and I had no idea what it meant. Our relationship had started with a blow job on a balcony, progressed to a pre-negotiated, short-term sexual arrangement, and then exploded.. And now it was...nothing and everything and we were at a restaurant together and was he my boyfriend?

Was Caspian Hart *my boyfriend?*

And did I even want him to be? Since it generally resulted in me going off someone pretty quickly.

Eh. Was it really worth worrying about? It was obvious Caspian liked me. And liked me far more than I was used to being liked. More than any reasonable person ought to like me, in all honesty. But I couldn't help wondering: did it feel for him the way it felt for me? These Icarus wings, heavy on your back, and full of the promise of power, drawing you higher and higher and faster and faster until you couldn't tell anymore whether you were flying or falling or soaring or drowning.

CHAPTER 23

I'd meant to be delightful when Caspian left, sending him across the ocean with the sweetness of my kisses lingering on his lips, but unfortunately our parting took place at 4 a.m. And so I was mainly half asleep, mumbly, and pathetic. I think I got my message across, though, especially when I wrapped my arms around his leg and wouldn't let go.

"I'll be back next Saturday," he said, trying to sound exasperated and actually just laughing. "Please let go. I don't want to be late."

"No. I'm keeping you."

"Arden."

I whimpered tragically. "Promise you'll come and see me straight away? As soon as you land?"

"It's Eleanor's birthday. Have you forgotten?"

Oh shit. Where had August gone? "Only technically."

"How about"—he peeled my hand gently off his knee and gave it a squeeze—"I pick you up and we go together?"

That startled me almost awake. "You want to take me to…
um…a family thing?"

"Why not? You were invited."

"I know, but it seems serious, doesn't it?"

"If you're uncomfortable, I can meet you there."

"No!" Oops. Capslock! Ardy Strikes Back. It was too late to
sound nonchalant now, but I tried. "It's cool."

He smiled, and bent down to kiss my nose. "Then it's a
date."

The sheer sweetness of those words left me floating through
Sunday in a happy haze. On Monday, though, work happened
to me. I honestly hadn't expected Poppy to say yes, since all
we'd discussed was the interview. But she did—as long as I was
still involved. And from then on everything became a flurry of
agents and publicists and contracts and ahhh. It took most of
the week, untold emails and even a couple of conference calls,
all of which felt way above my pay grade. Especially because I
didn't have a pay grade.

But, somehow, by Thursday, it had all come together. And,
with the end in sight, an email plinked into my inbox that was
only to me. It was from Mara Fairfax, the editor of *Milieu*, and
it said: "Do come along to the office. This afternoon. 2?" Nine
words and the world's most unconvincing question mark—as
impenetrable as a text from someone you fancied when you
weren't quite sure if they fancied you back. Was this a casual
visit? A job interview? Did they just want to look at me like I
was a monkey at the zoo?

Still, at least I didn't have long to fret about it. A little before
two, I'd navigated a receptionist and was ascending to the

appropriate floor of a moderately ugly, portico-fronted office block off Hanover Square. A woman, a leggy brunette in pearls and ballet flats, was waiting for me at the far end of a long, white corridor, where the words MILIEU, EST 1702, was picked out in gigantic, shiny letters on the wall.

"You're Arden, aren't you?" she said, stepping forward. "I'm Tabitha. Tabitha England-Plume and, yes, I'm a real person and that's my real name. You can look me up if you like. I'm in the Bible."

I shook her hand dazedly. "Were you begat?"

"The other Bible. Debrett's."

"Oh. The thing is, I haven't actually…"

"Don't worry, Mara'll give you a copy. It's all terribly silly really."

She led me under the *Milieu* sign and into the office itself. I was braced for the full *Devil Wears Prada* but, actually, it was kind of banal. Plainly decorated, with computers tucked into cubicles, it could have been the admin block for almost anything. The Wernham Hogg Paper Company. Maybe half of the workstations were occupied. All of them frighteningly tidy.

"Mara's nuts about clutter-free working," said Tabitha. "This way."

I hurried after her down another corridor, this one lined by framed *Milieu* covers. Things gradually got shinier—through their glass walls, I caught glimpses of fancy meeting spaces and rooms so full of clothing racks you could barely have wriggled inside.

Mara's own office, when we finally got there, was large, but not swaggeringly so. It was clean and bright, austerely decorated with a few black and white prints, and what I took to be a personal photograph of a laughing girl and a horse. There was room for a sofa and glass-topped desk, and a large table, currently strewn with photographs, which was where the action seemed to be happening.

A woman, who I thought was Mara Fairfax, was leaning over the images, studying them with a focus bordered on ferocity. Her colleague, probably the photographer, had her hips braced against the edge of the table, one foot—in a perfectly polished Oxford—swinging idly. She was pretty much the picture of glamorous nonchalance, in high-waisted pinstriped trousers held up by braces over a low-cut white shirt, but then she reached out to Mara and tucked a strand of her honey-brown hair gently behind her ear. Which Mara herself hardly seemed to notice.

"Well," she said, "I think any of these three could be a cover. Or maybe just these two. I like her face in this one—there's a softness there, almost a whimsy, which isn't a side of her we usually see. But this one, the shape of her body"—her hand traced a curve—"it's pure Kate."

The photographer tapped the second. "This is it, I think."

"Let's try it." Mara straightened up. And then, with a wave of her hand, "Come in, you two. Have a seat."

"Um. Hello." I perched on the edge of one of the chairs in front of Mara's desk.

"I'm Mara Fairfax. And I'm sure you'll have heard of George, here."

Was this a test? There was really only one notable George in the British magazine photography. I'd seen what I'd assumed to be *his* name credited on so many fashion and editorial shoots. *Time Out. Skin Two. Vogue. Milieu.* "George…Chase? You're George Chase?"

"It's so convenient when one's reputation precedes one." She reached into the pocket of her trousers and pulled out a card case. Flicking it open, she extricated a business card and held it out to me between two agile, knotty-knuckled fingers.

It was matte black, faintly textured under my thumb, a barely visible circular pattern that suggested the shape of a lens. All it said was GEORGIA CHASE: LIBERTINE, ROUÉ, PHOTO-GRAPHER. And then a website.

"Anyway," said Mara, effortlessly reclaiming my attention, "thank you for coming in, Arden. You've sent us some quite interesting pieces."

"I have? Gosh. Thank you."

Mara Fairfax wasn't what I'd expected. But then my expectations had probably been thrown off by too much Meryl Streep. She was about five years older than George, maybe more, not exactly beautiful, but classically English: all strong bones and clear skin, and the sturdy athleticism of having spent most of your life on horseback. "Why don't you tell us a little bit about yourself?"

I glanced from Mara to George and back again, still not entirely sure what was happening. After a dithery couple of moments, I decided to risk a direct approach. I mean, what was the worst that could happen—apart from excruciating personal embarrassment, that is. "I hope you don't mind me asking, but why am I here?"

"I'm deciding whether I like you."

"And what happens if you do?"

"Then I offer you a job."

I successfully managed not to fall off my chair. Go me. "At *Milieu*? OMG. I mean…uh…holy shi—that would be a dream come true. But I should tell you, I…I just got my degree results and I sort of…I got a 2.2."

There was a silence. I waited to be escorted from the building.

Tabitha laughed. "I got a third."

"And Mara here," said George, grinning, "was sent down."

She shrugged. "If I hadn't been, I would never have met you."

"Oh please God no." That was Tabitha. "No more stories about New York in the eighties. It was a golden age. You once threw up on Andy Warhol. We get it."

"Alas, poor Tabs. The most exciting thing you've ever vomited over are your Jimmy Choos." George climbed lazily to her feet. "But, in any case, I should leave you all to your chat." She began gathering up her photographs, pausing only to glance my way. "I do hope we meet again, poppet."

And, with that, she sauntered out.

Leaving me genuinely unable to figure out whether I was relieved or not. She seemed kind of into me, which probably meant she was my ally in whatever was happening here. But, at the same time, she had legs for miles and a fantastic rack and she kept smirking at me distractingly.

So I guess I was overall grateful for her absence.

Especially because, so help me God, I was *not* fucking this up. It was the opportunity of a lifetime and I wanted it so badly it was making my throat tight and my mouth dry. My brain, of course, was a flurry of uncertainties. It wanted to tell me I wasn't good enough. That I didn't deserve this. That I'd only end up disappointing everyone.

But I wasn't listening. I *wasn't*.

I'd earned this chance. Worked for it. *Milieu* and me were made for each other. And I was going to land this job.

Because, let's face it, I was likeable as fuck.

* * *

Fifty minutes later, I emerged flayed, dazed, giddy, and job-having.

Junior Assistant Editor. I was a junior assistant editor.

Truthfully, I was still a bit shaky on what that actually involved. But, whatever it was, it was a real thing and I was going to be paid for it. Not, y'know, much. But I'd never been paid for anything before. Unless you counted that time Caspian had established a scholarship in my name after I'd given him a blow job.

I lurched past one of the Pitts and into Hanover Square. Slumped onto a bench, amid the swirling green, and messaged everyone I knew with shaking fingers. Caspian first, of course. And he was the first to get back to me, signing his congratulations off with an *x*, which was incredibly effusive for him, squeaking in before my family, who sang to me as follows: *We knew you could do it / Just call it a hunch / Ardy's delicious & nutritious / For dinner, breakfast, and lunch*. Rabbie and Hazel wrote music for adverts, and pined after the days of the unironic jingle, so most of my accomplishments were celebrated via cheesy earworm.

Tucking my feet onto the edge of the bench, I hugged my knees and watched the shadows of the trees dancing over the grass. I was half expecting to jolt awake and find myself back at Oxford, in my single bed, under my crappy duvet, on the morning of my first exam. Having desperation-dreamed this whole absurd fable: being with Caspian, meeting Ellery, not completely fucking up my finals, landing a job at *Milieu*.

Except no. This was my life. This was really my life.

I bounced up, flung wide my arms, and wheeled in circles, accompanied by a few startled pigeons. Well. I figured I deserved my very own Disney princess moment. Even if I did look slightly bonkers.

From there, I headed home, where I found Ellery and a bottle of scary-expensive congratulatory champagne Caspian had contrived to send me that she'd mostly drunk. Her pink tulle skirt and leather jacket combination made her look like Tinkerbell gone bad.

"Came to be all yay and shit," she explained.

I twitched the champagne from her hand and took a swig. The bubbles rushed up my nose and down my chin and left me sneezing. Gosh, I was just the coolest. "It seems like you've started the party without me."

"Haven't you heard?" She gave me her flattest stare. "I am the party."

Laughing, I went to shed my coat and shoes. When I came back, she was standing by the fridge and tearing the foil away from another bottle of champagne with her teeth.

As ever, I was mildly qualmish about taking advantage of Caspian's largesse or whatever. But technically Ellery was the one taking advantage. And I really did have something to celebrate.

Pulling herself onto the edge of one the gleaming marble counters, she popped the cork with upper-class ease. Foam surged upward, splashing onto the floor and running down her hand. I would have been squeaking and flailing for a cloth, but she only laughed and licked the champagne from her arm, spilling even more as the gesture tilted the bottle downward.

Mustering some of her insouciance, I skirted the puddles of champagne and hopped onto the counter next to her.

She nudged my knee with hers and passed me the bottle. "I'm happy for you."

"Thanks." I swigged—didn't choke myself this time—and kicked her gently back.

"Is this…what you want to do? With your life or whatever?"

"Yes. I mean, ideally at some point in a less tea-making, better-paying capacity. But this is a super exciting start."

"Cool."

We passed the bottle back and forth for a while. Ellery, though, seemed restless, her heels catching against the cabinets below.

"Are you okay?" I asked.

She shrugged. And, then, after an uncomfortably long pause, "Just thinking about shit. I was quite busy dying for a while. And then I had to not die. Now I guess I have to do something else."

"Well. Is there anything you like?"

"I liked dying. I was into that." Her mouth curled into a rare smile. "Good at it too."

I reached out and ran my thumb across the bumpy, wrong-way scar on her wrist. "I'd say you were mediocre at best."

And she threw back her head and laughed the rough, throaty laugh that reminded me so much of Caspian. Not so much the sound of it, but the way it tore itself free, like a butterfly from a cocoon. It made me want to hug the shit out of both of them.

"So how about," I said instead, "we back-burner suicide for the time being?"

She rolled her eyes. "If you insist."

"Is there anything else you enjoy?"

"Coke?"

"Seems to me you'd make a very successful investment banker."

"Nahh." She took another swallow of champagne. "My dick's too big."

Now it was my turn to giggle. "Speaking from experience?"

"City types are always the same. Fat bonus, tiny prick. Lawyers are even worse."

"I've only slept with proto-lawyers." My mind produced a hasty, semi-pornographic montage of everyone I'd bonked at university who I vaguely remembered as having been studying law. "They seemed fine."

"Maybe they shrivel away over time or something."

"Consumed from within by their own pedantry."

"Yeah." Ellery lifted the bottle in a toast of disdain. "Pompous wankers."

Her contempt, which usually hummed along at a certain comfortable baseline, had spiked noticeably. "You really don't like lawyers, huh?"

"Probably Caspian just hires the biggest twats he can find. I dunno."

"Okay. So"—I made a valiant effort to redirect the conversation—"putting aside Class A narcotics—"

"Cocaine isn't a narcotic. That's a pharmacologically erroneous legal classification."

"Thanks, Walter White."

"I told you lawyers were bullshit."

I wrestled my face into its most patient expression. "Is there anything else that makes you feel even a little bit like you don't want to die?"

She huffed out a long, aggrieved sigh. And then mumbled something.

"What?"

"Music. Music's okay."

"What about that, then? I mean, there's university or… like…music school."

Shit. I was out of my depth and it earned me a scowl. "No. I hate music like that."

"Like what?"

"In a cage." She gulped down the last of the champagne, jumped off the counter, and pulled open the fridge. Glanced over at me and grinned, feral and bright with the light shining on her face. "Another?"

My memories of the rest of evening got all bubbly. Ellery lay under the table and talked about Bartók a lot—about exile and the preservation of Hungarian folk songs. And I pitched articles to her, my ideas flowing as bounteously as the booze, though significantly poorer in quality. At some point we might have done the full Titanic pose on the balcony—with me shouting that I was king of the world to the slumbering city below. And we'd hooked my phone up to the sound system and danced and danced and danced until the stars blurred and Ellery looked almost happy.

CHAPTER 24

Oh God. I was dying.

I peeled open an eyelid and immediately regretted it. Light lanced straight through my skull.

What…what had happened to me? Had I been attacked? Hang on. No. I'd spent the evening with Ellery.

And now I was broken.

Probably the best thing to do was lie very still and pretend I didn't exist. Yep. That would work.

The sound of a door opening and closing thundered across my senses like a stampede of raging wildebeest. Must have been the cleaners. Twitching my fingers in the direction of the pillow, I mashed it protectively against my face.

"Arden?"

Wait. That was Caspian's voice. I partially self-excavated. Forced my eyes to work. Then my brain.

There was a human-shape in the doorway.

And, yep, it was definitely him. Not a hallucination. But a

vision, nonetheless, in a chocolate brown pinstriped suit and a paisley tie that made him look like something from a jazz-age daydream.

"Good God," he said. Way too loudly. His voice echoing through the spaces surrounding my wizened, dehydrated brain. "Are you ill?"

I whimpered. "No. But I wasn't expecting you till tomorrow. Unless it's already tomorrow. Is it tomorrow now?"

"I came back early. I wanted to see you." The bright blur bobbing about in front of him resolved itself into a bouquet of tulips—and not the fancy kind either, the kind you got from a stall. Just some flowers tied up with paper and string. "I texted. I didn't realize you hadn't received it."

"I'm barely receiving oxygen right now. But I'm always happy to see you."

His free hand came up in a gesture that didn't seem to be anything at all and then dropped back to his side. "This was ill-conceived. I don't know what I was…that is. I'll come back when we agreed. I'm sorry."

I tried to croak out something to stop him.

But then Ellery—who, given the vastness of both the bed and my hangover, I'd failed to notice had been sleeping beside me—poked her head up and drawled, "Well, isn't this sweet."

Caspian went white. It was awful to watch. Like when somebody gets shot in a movie and there's this silence. And then suddenly blood everywhere. The tulips slipped from his hand and scattered at his feet. Rainbow shrapnel.

Then he turned and—

Fuck.

I dived off the bed, relieved to discover I was in boxers. And a sock. For a moment, I thought I was going to throw up, but I couldn't tell if it was physical or mental distress, or a little bit of both. Thankfully the churning in my stomach and the spinning in my head briefly balanced each other out and I managed to stagger after Caspian.

He was almost *gone*. And I knew, I just knew, I couldn't let him step out that door. Because while I had no doubt he'd come to his senses, I might never forgive him. For someone so committed to seeing the best in me, it didn't take much for him to assume the absolute fucking worst.

"Don't," I cried. "Wait."

And because I had no idea what else to do I…flung myself at him. It was probably the least dignified thing I'd ever done, which, y'know, talk about stiff competition. As I moved, I caught sight of my shadow on the wall, outstretched arms doing the full 1922 Nosferatu death scene. But, somehow, I managed to get them wrapped round Caspian's waist. My cheek to his unyielding back. And there I clung.

He stopped. I guess he had to or look as ridiculous as me. "Let me go."

"What the fuck are you doing?"

"You were in bed with my sister."

"I'm cuddly, Caspian. I like to sleep with people. I mean literally sleep with them. Not have sex with them."

He didn't move. Just stood there, sucking the heat and hope out of me like an ice sculpture of a man who thought I'd fucked his sister.

"Oh come on." I squeezed him desperately. "Use that magnificent brain of yours. Putting aside the fact that I would be mad to want anyone else while I have you, do you really think I'd be stupid enough to cheat on you in your own house? Knowing you could turn up at any moment? Is that it? Do you think I'm stupid?"

His hand crept up and covered mine. His fingers were cold and trembling slightly. "I don't understand why you'd…why you'd…"

Given Caspian's own discomfort with physical intimacy, it did make a terrible sort of sense that he couldn't imagine sharing a bed with somebody without dicking them. But while that helped me understand a bit more about what was going on, it didn't make me feel any better about it.

"Why do you do this to me?" I wailed. "I've given you no reason to doubt my faith or my…my virtue." Oh God. Now I was in a Victorian sensation novel. I was probably about to discover I was my own twin brother who had been confined to a lunatic asylum. "And with your sister for God's sake. What the fuck is wrong with you?"

Of course, Ellery would choose exactly this moment to come out of the bedroom. She was wearing my CALLIPYGIAN T-shirt, a pair of cat-head thigh-highs, and a death glare. And I wanted to strongly encourage her to go away but, unfortunately, she spoke before I could. "I'll tell you what's wrong with him. He thinks everyone's like he is."

Caspian spun round so fast it centrifugal-forced me away from him and sent me crashing to the floor. "What," he asked, with hideous calm, "is that supposed to mean?"

"You don't value friendship so you don't understand why anyone would."

This was definitely one of those *stay down* situations. I huddled, wishing I had a helmet or something.

"The thing is, Caspian"—Ellery's lip curled with a frankly spectacular degree of scorn—"while fucking you up is one of the few things I really enjoy, I like Arden. And I don't want to fuck him up as well."

Caspian sighed. "You're being childish, Eleanor."

"I'm not the one freaking out because he thought someone else was playing with his toys."

"You have no right to interfere in my affairs or embroil Arden in your attention-seeking dramas. He is my partner. He is not your friend."

"He's also right here," I said. "And I'm seriously not enjoying being the stick you use to beat each other."

There was a brief, profoundly awkward pause.

And then Caspian extended a hand to help me off the ground. "I apologize for my sister's behavior. She's been impossible for years and I have no idea what makes her act like this."

My mouth dropped open. Caspian didn't so much end arguments as nuke them from orbit. I really didn't want to take sides here but he was crossing an unacceptable dick threshold. "Um—"

"It's you." Ellery wasn't breathing well enough to be yelling. Her voice sounded genuinely broken, caught somewhere between tears and screaming. "You make me act like this. You've made me invisible. You've made me worthless. You've taken away everyone who's ever cared about me. Dad.

Mum. Lancaster. Nathaniel. Even your fucking self."

If we were in a movie, this would be the moment that changed everything. They'd hug and cry and lay their feelings bare and promise to be better people and a Sam Smith song would play and everyone would go home all uplifted and shit.

Except we weren't in a movie. And what Caspian said was, "I'm not having this conversation with you."

Ellery stared at him with eyes that were so like his and so not.

Then she turned and walked back into the bedroom, emerging about thirty seconds later with her boots on and her bag over her shoulder.

She was gone without another word.

Leaving us standing in the middle of this emotional crater. At least, I was standing in an emotional crater. I had no idea what was going on with Caspian.

My voice floated out of me like a confused poltergeist. "I…I don't think I can be here right now."

"Get dressed. I'll take you out."

"Um. No? Thank you. I need to"—I made a helpless gesture—"be by myself for a bit. I might go for a swim?"

Caspian had become a stranger. Regarding me considerately. "I see. Would you like me to wait?"

"Would you like to?" Or maybe we had both become strangers, marooned on islands of courtesy.

"I'll wait."

I dug out my towel and a dressing gown, and changed into my trunks. Drank about a million gallons of water, grabbed my phone, and got the hell out of the apartment.

Say this for complete psychological devastation: it really put a hangover in perspective.

The pool was as serene as ever, the silvery light soothing my gritty eyes. Slumping down onto one of the fancy lounger things, I rang Ellery.

No answer. Of course not.

I rang again. And again. And again. And again.

Until at last, she answered. "Hi, Mum."

"No, it's me, Ard—oh wait, I see what you did there. Are you okay?"

I could almost hear her shrugging. "Sure."

"You know I'm your friend, right?"

"I know you're my friend with terrible taste in men."

"And you're okay?" I faffed miserably with my towel. "You promise."

"Yeah, Arden, I double pinky swear. And, for the record, you're being super-weird."

"I just…I don't know…I was afraid you might be…I don't want you to…"

"What?"

My mouth formed a series of useless shapes. And then I blurted out, "Kill yourself."

A long silence.

"Because of Caspian?"

"Um. Because of anything."

She laughed. "Like he'd even care. Talk soon."

And then she hung up.

I stared helplessly at my phone for a moment or two. Well. At least she was talking to me. And not…um. Dead. Sigh. Sigh forever.

Dragging off the dressing gown and leaving everything on the lounger, I plopped gingerly into the water. Only discovering how numbed-through I was when I heard my own splash before I felt the lap of heat against my skin.

And that was my body. Fuck knew what was going on in my brain.

I swam a few lengths as vigorously as I could given my general weediness, thrashing up and down the pool like a stressed-out basking shark. Not that I had my mouth wide open or anything, on account of preferring not to drown, but if it had been possible to wear my emotional state on my face that would have been me: frozen in an epic *oh fuck*.

Moving helped. Turned the volume up somehow. Though eventually I just flipped onto my back and floated listlessly. I knew this wasn't my shit. That it wasn't about me and didn't involve me. But, God, it was hard to watch. And it made me a traitor whatever happened: a bad friend or a bad…oh! Caspian had called me his partner. Which would have made me so happy if he hadn't only done it to hurt someone else. Or maybe he thought he was protecting what was his from a perceived incursion.

And, wow, was that a recipe for all the ambiguous feelings. Because I loved thinking of myself as Caspian's. I wanted to be claimed and possessed and treasured by him. But in this particular context—when it wasn't about me or us at all—it was icky. It was icky as fuck.

I lost track of how long I drifted in the water. I wasn't even sure if Caspian would still be there when I went back. Or how I'd face him. What I'd say. If, for that matter, there was anything *to* say. I mean, I knew full well that he could be like this. And also that it wasn't a true reflection of who he was. Apparently, some families could really bring out the worst in each other. It made me extra glad for mine.

Of course, plenty of people thought we had a pretty weird setup. And, in all fairness I could see that, considering Mum and I were hiding from my dad with her girlfriend and her girlfriend's husband in a majorly remote part of Scotland. But while nearly everyone I knew spoke about loving their folks as a duty they were resigned to…I actually liked mine. And I was starting to think that was a very special thing.

Back in the apartment, I found Caspian sitting on the sofa in the living area, his face turned toward the window, and his body thrown into silhouette against the gleaming afternoon.

It reminded me of the time I'd come down to London to yell at him. Before then, I'd only seen him amid Oxford's golds. But this was his world: high windows and horizons. And later, once I'd got past the anger and the crying and the being kissed and being rejected, I'd thought about how alone he'd looked. An untouchable prince, caged by his own power.

Well, he wasn't alone now.

I padded across the room and dropped to my knees beside him, a gesture not of submission but of offered closeness.

"Arden." His hand moved. Then stilled.

I smiled up at him. And very gently nudged his thigh with my cheek. "Hey."

"I owe you an apology."

"For whose behavior?"

He had the grace to blush a little. "Mine."

Silence.

More silence.

"I'm kind of waiting for it here," I said.

At last he touched me—his fingers gathering a few drops of water from the tips of my hair. "I'm sorry. I've…I've been…"

He looked like he was struggling so I got helpful. "A complete dick?"

"That seems a fair description." He went all quiet again for a second a two. "And I hope you know that I…that I don't doubt you."

"You say that, but you're super quick to think I've banged your sister."

He put his hand to his eyes, shielding even more of his expression from me. As if being in profile and tight-lipped just wasn't remote enough. "I was jealous."

"Of me and Ellery? There's nothing there to be jealous of."

"Of course there is. I'm jealous of how close you are. Of the intimacy you have."

"All relationships are their own thing." I pressed against his leg again, until his fingers curled through my still-damp hair. "We have our own intimacies."

"But I may never be as easy with you as she is. I may never be able to give you that."

"Do you want to?"

After a moment, he gave a swift, sharp nod.

"Then that's enough for me." I caught his wrist and bestowed a fleeting kiss upon his palm. "But you have to do better with Ellery, okay?"

He pulled away slightly. "I'm not sure I know how to."

"Oh come on, Caspian." I sat back on my heels. "You're not a robot or a monster. You know what you did and why it was awful. And I get you were upset but that's no excuse."

"Eleanor is different with you. She never responds well to me."

"That doesn't mean you get to be...like almost *willfully* nasty to her."

He sighed. "I have spent my life hurting my sister. I don't think either of us is prepared for that to change now."

"I think maybe you're not prepared."

"Shouting at me about all the damage I've caused is hardly an effective way to open a dialogue."

"Actually...it could be. You're the one who's refusing to listen."

"Arden, you know what kind of man I am. You've always known."

"Yes." I gazed at him steadily. "I do. I know how kind you are, for a start. And I know you don't treat people badly. So why Ellery? It's almost like you don't want to fix things. Like you're trying to keep her at a distance. Why do you want your sister to hate you, Caspian?"

"Come here, my little journalist." He reached down and pulled me onto his lap. Kissed me hard enough to make my head spin. "Always looking for an angle or a story."

"You're trying to distract me."

He pushed a hand under the dressing gown and stroked my thigh until I got the shivers. "There is no try. Do or do not."

"OMG, you are the dorkiest." He kissed me again and I felt his smile against my lips. "But I know what you're at."

"Maybe, but I came here for you, not to talk about my sister."

"And still at."

His expression was serious as he met my eyes. "Would it really be so terrible, Arden, to let me? I understand you care about Ellery, but she is not the only person who has been hurt today. And this is certainly not the afternoon I envisioned for us. With your consent, I would very much like to salvage it and celebrate your latest accomplishment."

I wanted to say yes. And Caspian was certainly doing everything in his power to make it super tempting. Except I couldn't. I just couldn't. It would have meant accepting things that I was no longer comfortable accepting.

Not after everything that had happened between us.

I shook my head. And gave him a little push, knowing how responsive he was to that sort of thing. Sure enough, he let me go at once.

Gazed at me in obvious dismay. "Arden…"

"I'm sorry. The thing is, I can't keep ignoring how much you keep from me."

"My relationship with my sister has nothing to do with you."

"I know. But"—I swiveled sideways on the sofa so I could see him better, even if it was his profile—"*I* have something to do with you, don't I?"

"Of course you do, but there are simply some things I don't wish to talk about. Surely you can respect that?"

Great. Now I looked totally unreasonable. If the carnage with Ellery had shown me anything, it was that Caspian was good at winning arguments. Maybe because he saw them as something that could be won.

Or, perhaps, had to be.

"Yes," I said. "I can't make you tell me stuff. And I wouldn't want to. I just wish you felt like you could."

His sneered with Ellery-like contempt. "One of the many toxic facets of modern psychology is the way it teaches us that sharing is inherently beneficial. When often it is selfish, hurtful, or otherwise self-indulgent."

"Okay, but if you'd told me about the nature of your relationship with Nathaniel, then I wouldn't have pushed you so hard over the room and probably…" Urgh. He wouldn't thank me for mentioning what had happened that night "…I wouldn't have made you feel so bad."

"Well, if you hadn't been so determined to pry, then the whole situation would not have occurred in the first place."

Yep. This was definitely verbal Carcassonne. And I was definitely losing. And there was nothing I could do about it, short of running out of the castle and being attacked by wolves, necessitating a rescue from Caspian that would lead to us eating soup together and playing in the snow and then he'd give me a library and—wait, that was something else.

I tried a different tack. "Look, you told Ellery I was your partner because you wanted to hurt her. Not because it's how you see me or how you treat me. That's really fucked up."

"I'm trying, Arden." And maybe I was better at Carcassonne than I thought, because he sounded genuinely shaken. "I want to be a partner to you. I want to make you happy. But at some point you're going to accept that this is who I am."

"No. It's who you say you are. That's not the same thing."

He turned sharply. "What do you mean?"

"You're not asking me to accept you as you are. You're asking me to accept the way you see yourself. Which I can't do." I had to curl my hands in my lap to stop reaching out to him. "Because that's not how I see you."

Caspian surged off the sofa, obviously frustrated.

"I'm sorry, Arden, but how many times must we have this conversation? Reach this same impasse? You're looking for something that isn't there. You must understand. And ultimately decide for yourself if this—if *I*—can be enough for you."

Wow. What? No.

How had we got here?

I stared at him in horror. "You can't just dump the whole responsibility for our future on me. There's two of us involved here."

"Yes, but I'm not the one who's unhappy." It was his gentlest voice. The voice that often cut me deepest. "I'm doing my best, but I'm tired of disappointing you, Arden."

"You don't," I cried. "You aren't. All I'm asking—"

"Is for things I can't give."

There was a long, nasty silence.

"I should go," said Caspian, finally. "You need time to think. Text me if you still want to be my date tomorrow."

I was too stunned to even try and stop him.

CHAPTER 25

Saturday dawned shittily. I hadn't slept well, and I'd done exactly zero preparation for the phenomenally posh birthday party I would have to attend, whether I went with Caspian or not.

Urgh. Caspian. What had I done?

I mean, maybe he was right. Maybe I *was* asking for the impossible. He'd told me about Nathaniel. He'd trusted me with his nightmare. It wasn't my job to fix his relationship with Ellery. It wasn't even my business.

Back in Kinlochbervie, he'd promised to try, and I'd promised to be patient. And only one of us, really, could be said to have kept their side of the bargain.

Clue: it wasn't me.

I'd been greedy, and pushy, and demanding. And not very kind. And Caspian had stuck with me, supported me, done so much for me, both practically and emotionally. And, in return, I'd made him feel like a failure. Like he couldn't make me happy.

When he did. He *so* did.

Obviously, what we had together wasn't perfect. But what was? I didn't know how to do relationships and I was starting to get the sense he didn't either. But we were trying. Faltering and fucking up, but definitely trying.

Well, except for the bit where I'd told him that wasn't good enough.

And what did I want, when it came down to it? A fairy tale? A happily ever after as smooth as glass? Or something real and messy and occasionally painful? With the complicated, damaged, fascinating man I was pretty sure I was falling in love with?

I groped for my phone, and texted Caspian: *I'm sorry. You couldn't disappoint me if you tried. Please pick me up. I would love to be your date for the party.*

As ever, Caspian's reply came quickly: *I think you've forgotten that I am capable of accomplishing almost anything to which I bend my attention. I could disappoint you comprehensively if I so desired.*

I didn't deserve to be joked at. But I laughed and felt better. Accepting Caspian's comfort because he'd offered it and I needed it.

Still had to deal with the damn party though. In the end, I googled the closest branch of Moss Bros and forked out fifty quid to hire a tux and all the fixings. Of course, everyone else was probably going to be in bespoke designer shit, but at least I was in the vicinity of appropriate. I didn't have a mask either, but anything in my budget wasn't going to work for an event like that.

Basically I'd be Kaylee in that episode of *Firefly* where she goes to a party in the best pink dress in the 'verse. But everyone is all sneery because it's off the rack instead of custom made by poor people.

Then, as I was sloping moodily home past the Mac concession on the ground floor of Debenham's, I had a eureka moment. I didn't need to buy a mask at all—I could use makeup. That way it could be as extravagant and unique as I wanted, and people would go "oh, isn't he arty" rather than "oh, isn't he cheap." I stocked up and raced back to the flat.

It took a bit of practice, some diligent eyebrow shaping, and most of what was left of my afternoon but I was pleased with how it turned out. I'd managed to give myself butterfly wings: dark pink at the inside corners of my eyes, blending into blue and yellow and pearly green as the design unfurled across my cheeks and brow. The colors seemed especially vivid against the austerity of my hired formalwear and I felt, honestly, a little bit…magical.

Needless to say, I did what anyone would have done under the circumstances and I selfied the living fuck out of myself.

And was therefore so late that Caspian had to come up and get me.

"Did you change your mind?" he asked, stepping softly in the living area. "Are you all right?"

I yelped, nearly dropping my phone. "No, I mean yes, I mean I haven't changed my mind sorry."

"What are you doing?"

As it happened, what I was doing was working a MySpace angle but there was no way I was admitting that. I lowered my arm sheepishly. "Just, um, trying to get a signal."

"Clearly." He sounded very dry. "I sent you three texts."

"God. Sorry." This was the problem with having two phones—it was double the opportunity to miss things. Closing Instagram down, I turned hastily and—

Wow. Oh wow. Caspian.

He was immaculate in full black tie. Effortless, too, nothing imprecise or overdone: just fiercely fine tailoring and the subtle sheen of matte silk from the reverse and buttons of his classic, one-button peak lapel jacket. His mask was a single strip of black satin that I could already tell would make everyone else look too ornate and tacky by comparison. And it seemed so completely miraculous right then that this man, so steeped in wealth and power, who could have anything in the world he wanted...wanted me.

My heart twisted itself into a knot so tight and tender I could hardly breathe.

Then he crossed the room and drew me into his arms. Turned my face up to his and gazed at me in a manner I'm sure Jane Austen would have described as *ardent*. "You're enchanting," he said. "I want to kiss you, but I'm afraid I'll smudge it."

"Err." I was good to take the risk but words weren't working so well. Despite the fact that a couple of minutes ago I'd been fearlessly broadcasting how hot I looked to the whole internet, his compliment had flustered me. And was probably undoing all my hard work because I hadn't factored being bright red into my mask design.

"This will have to suffice for now." He caught my hand, drew it to his lips, and kissed my knuckles. All soft and gallant and unexpectedly sweet.

I just about swooned. "How about we ditch the party?"

"I don't think Eleanor would ever forgive you."

It was the only time he'd ever spoken of her in a way that suggested he had any understanding of what she might care about. Or interest in it. And he was right too—as much as I'd have liked to unwrap and eat Caspian like a Godiva Carre, it would have been a shitty thing to prioritize on Ellery's birthday. "I don't think she'd be massively happy if you didn't show up either."

"On the contrary, I think she'd be quite pleased."

Had he even been in the same argument I'd witnessed yesterday? I made a whingey noise, wanting to protest, but also not wanting to start another fight with him about something we'd never agree on.

"And you're sure about tonight?" The question was casual enough, but his eyes were so intent on mine he might as well have been saying *are you sure about me?*

"Yes. Definitely."

Holding my hand tight to his chest, Caspian bestowed another of his fleeting kisses upon my nose, and then let me go. "Then come on. Fashionably late is one thing. Late is quite another."

We traveled mostly in silence. The car took us right into the heart of Kensington—past on-site security and into a leafy boulevard literally behind Kensington Palace itself. A street of private mansions, delicately illuminated by Narnia lampposts and patrolled by armed guards.

It was hard to process really…the existence of a place like this, right in the middle of England's capital, where the land values were unthinkable. Even One Hyde Park, with all its aggressive opulence, had been obliged to build upward. Not these languorous, three-story homes, with their wings and gardens and stable blocks. There was a quietness of conviction here, an unshakeable expectation of wealth and its advantages that was frankly kind of scary. How did you get the balls to own a place like this? To believe you deserved it?

The houses themselves, though, were just a little bit incongruous. The ornate stucco frontages, all pillars and porticos and wedding cake molding struck me as something I'd have expected to find in a Henry James novel. Status symbols of people called Vanderbilt. Not English old money.

The car drew to a halt in front of one of the mansions and I scrambled out, feeling dazed and floaty. Caspian, of course, strode straight through the swung-wide gates, past the fountain (the motherfucking fountain) and up the steps to the house, which was lit up and shining like a medieval vision of heaven. Or the Disney castle if it had been a touch more Rothschild.

Even in the moments I wasted dithering, a second car pulled up—*another* black Maybach—and disgorged a small collection of glamorous people, all of them masked, the men aloof and interchangeable in black tie, the women aloof and marginally less interchangeable in their designer frocks. Laughing, their voices entangling, they glided past me, and I realized that if I didn't catch up sharpish I was going to lose Caspian in the flow of the fabulously dressed.

I scampered after him. Clearly starting the evening as I meant to go on: looking like an idiot. And caught up just inside the entrance hall, somehow managing not to go arse up, face down on the highly polished marble floor.

Holy fuck, that house.

I mean, yes, it *had* an entrance hall, for starters. It was that sort of place. Full of stately rooms that didn't seem to be for anything. At least, nothing that normal people did like watch TV or wander round absentmindedly while chain-eating Pringles. It was all ornate plasterwork and inlaid panels, curlicues and chandeliers. Those really tall vase things that did nothing except proclaim that your house (and wallet) were big enough to accommodate them.

It all left me slightly dizzy. Too much light glinting on too many surfaces. And the inescapable truth that the only circumstances in which people like me were expected to visit places like this was with a National Trust membership card.

And Caspian had grown up here. This was *his*.

Shit. I was having a Pemberley moment.

I looked around desperately for Ellery. But unless she was wearing a particularly distinctive and Ellery-ish mask, or a name badge, maybe, I had no way of recognizing her among the guests. It wasn't a horrible crush or anything—people sort of spilled very naturally through the spacious rooms and the atmosphere was at once lively and refined (dear God, I *was* in a Jane Austen novel). But there was no getting away from the fact I'd blithely turned up at a gathering where I didn't know a fucking soul. And where the whole point of the evening was making basic interaction as difficult and obtuse as possible.

Suddenly, Caspian—who, I guess, hadn't abandoned me after all—seized my hand. I hadn't expected him to get all

PDA-ey and I would have been gratified except he was holding me so tightly that I felt my bones creak in protest.

A man and woman had disengaged themselves from another couple and were now coming toward us.

She was just…lovely. This willowy, honey-and-roses beauty and an ageless, English elegance, everything about her exquisitely simple, from the smooth caramel twist of her hair to the midnight-blue folds of her gown. Her mask was a swirl of silver filigree over navy brocade. Impossible, in the presence of such grace, not to be self-conscious about my off-the-rack tux and my visit to the Mac makeup counter. I swallowed, trying not to succumb to profound despair. *Attendee commits seppuku at high society event.*

"Caspian." She leaned in to kiss his cheek. "I'm so glad to see you." Her voice was familiar. Its rhythms and intonations—that hint of a Fanny Ardant purr.

He gave a tight little nod. "Mother."

Oh wow. I suppose I should have figured that out. I probably had. But…from the whole art auction thing and the way Caspian and Ellery talked about her, I'd convinced myself that Mrs. Hart would be a grim and heinous witch. Not a woman whose smile cut a deep dimple into her cheek and made her eyes crease at the corners.

She was smiling that very beautiful, very real smile at me now. "And you must be Arden?"

"Uh, yeah," I replied suavely.

"And this our life, exempt from public haunt, finds tongues in trees, books in the running brooks, sermons in stones, and good in everything."

My mum loved those lines. I could remember her whispering them to me, holding me tight, on the nights when—I realized with hindsight—she was waiting fearfully for my father to come home.

I nodded helplessly. It was either that or burst into tears. Vomit my life story onto Mrs. Hart's Jimmy Choos. Weirdly, I almost wanted to. For some reason, part of me was convinced she'd be really super nice about it. Her golden-hazel eyes were so full of warmth.

"Arden." Caspian's voice sliced the silence. "This is my mother, Gertrude Hart."

"Please, call me Trudy."

"O-okay." Fuck. Worst. Guest. Ever.

It wasn't so much a sense of movement but a sense of stillness that reminded me she wasn't alone. Weird, because the man at her shoulder wasn't normally the type of person you wouldn't notice. He was impressively tall and impressively attractive, in a steely, corporate kind of way, not entirely dissimilar to Caspian. Except older and sort of…*more* somehow. His mask was very plain, one side ungleaming black, the other a deep, heavy gray, almost the same shade as his eyes. It was testament to just how much I was Caspian's that, apart from a mild and largely curious stirring of my libido, I wasn't *that* into him.

"It's been a long time, Caspian." He spoke much as he presented himself: with an air of cold command. "Won't you introduce me to your friend?"

Caspian's hand was sweating in mine. "Of course. Arden, this is Lancaster Steyne. He was my father's business partner."

Steyne had barely glanced at me, which I discovered I was

actually pretty glad about. He was fashioned to hit all my *yes please* buttons, but the sexy to scary ratio was a little too far toward scary for my comfort. Of course, I was into discomfort too, but I knew my own limits. I might fantasize, sometimes, about men like Lancester Steyne doing terrible things to me. But I didn't want him to actually do them.

"Arthur always hoped you'd follow in his footsteps," he was saying. "But I knew better."

There was a pause. And it felt full of thorns.

"Why are you here?" Caspian asked, after a moment.

"Ellery invited me. So, of course, I came." Steyne smiled, a perfectly normal smile, easy, affectionate, and urbane. "It's been a welcome opportunity to renew acquaintance with your family. I was always very fond of you."

Maybe I was imagining things but Caspian seemed… flustered somehow. "I'm surprised she still remembers you. It's been a long time."

"She's very loyal. She feels both friendship and betrayal perhaps too keenly. But"—another smile—"who would know that better than you? You are her brother, after all."

A terrible shudder ran through Caspian's whole body. I wasn't sure it was visible but, God, I felt it. Something was very wrong here and I didn't know what it was or how to help. All I could do was hold Caspian's hand and hope it could be enough when it so clearly wasn't. His silence had taken on this odd, almost defeated quality. I'd never known him lost for words before and it…frightened me.

And that was when Nathaniel turned up.

I wasn't sure how I recognized him because I'd never seen

him in the flesh before but somehow—even with the top half of
his face covered by a golden mask—I did. Maybe it was the rich
copper of his hair or the expensive whiskey sheen of his eyes.
The kissable lips. The sculpted jaw of a curse-breaking fairy tale
hero.

Or maybe it was the familiar, possessive way he put his arm
around Caspian's waist and the way Caspian didn't flinch or
pull away. I'd seen them standing like that in photographs.
Friends. Lovers. Partners. Everything I still wasn't quite.

"Oh here you are," he said. "Can you come a moment, my
prince? There's been a cock up with the caterers."

It was a shock to hear him speak. For Nathaniel to suddenly
become real to me in a way he never had before, when he'd been
safely contained in pictures and in the past. In Caspian's assurances that it was me he wanted. Me who understood him. Me
who made him happy. But it was hard to remember that when
Nathaniel touched him so easily. Called him by a name that belonged to the life they'd shared.

Caspian glanced at him, his eyes too bright and desperate.
"Of course." He pulled his hand from mine, murmured something vague about being back soon, excused himself politely
to the others, and then disappeared into the sea of formalwear
with Nathaniel.

Lancaster Steyne watched him go. I had no idea what he was
thinking.

Or, for that matter, what had happened. Only that I felt horribly dislocated. Caspian had brought me with him into this
world—*his* world—and hadn't even thought to prepare me for
it. He'd just let me blunder into things, clueless and confused

and blind. Which would have been, well, not fine but typical. I'd have coped.

Except he'd needed me.

He'd needed me, but he hadn't given me the power to help him. He hadn't trusted me enough. Or believed I could.

And so it had fallen to Nathaniel.

I couldn't resent him for rescuing Caspian. But it hurt that it had been someone else. That I hadn't been able to protect my man.

I suddenly realized Lancaster was departing as well—apparently he'd seen a viscount he needed to talk to. And then everyone was gone and I was alone with Mrs. Hart.

CHAPTER 26

I mustered a pathetic smile. Tried to think of something to say to her.

Thankfully she was on the case, smiling at me as if this wasn't potentially excruciating. "It's so lovely to meet you at last. Caspian has told me almost nothing about you."

I should have been all out of hurt for one evening. But, apparently, I wasn't. Though, this little sting was at least familiar. An old friend. "I guess he wouldn't have," I managed, at last.

"I raised two extraordinarily secretive children. Caspian, in particular, holds the people he values most very close indeed."

Oh God. My heart gave a desperate a lurch. I wanted to believe her. To take the reassurance she was offering me. Take it, grab it. Squeeze it like a small child with a teddy bear. "R-really?"

"Yes. And I can see why he likes you." Her eyes had more green in them than Ellery's did but the shape was similar. I couldn't, however, imagine Ellery looking at anyone with such gentleness.

"I was worried you'd be mad at me for messing up your charity auction."

She tilted her head quizzically. "How so?"

"Well, I accidentally made Caspian buy all the art."

"Oh, I did wonder about that. It was a rather fine collection, but I was somewhat startled by his enthusiasm for it. Did you like the pieces?"

Great. Now I'd made her think he'd bought an exhibition for me as some kind of passionate love gesture. "I didn't get much chance to look around. We hadn't seen each other for a while, but I didn't want to get in the way of a good cause."

"So he assuaged your concerns?"

"He assuaged them excessively."

She laughed—and there was something about its timbre that reminded me a little bit of Ellery. If Ellery ever let herself laugh so freely. "My son is more of a romantic than I realized."

"I think he'd say he was being very practical."

"Of course he would. In any case, Arden, you made a young artist an overnight success and raised a lot of money for malaria prevention."

I cringed from approval I didn't deserve. "I didn't mean to."

"Nevertheless, good is good." She smiled at me with unabashed sweetness. "And I hope you'll ask Caspian to show you the pieces. They're by an Icelandic painter called Ragnar Vilhjálmsson. The collection is called *Let Us Compare Mythologies*."

"Is that…is that a Leonard Cohen reference?"

She nodded. "You know, if it wouldn't be the…" For the first time, her grace faltered, a delicate flush brushing the fine arch of her cheekbones. "The *uncoolest* thing in the world, would you like to come to lunch with me someday?"

"I'd love to."

"Wonderful." She leaned in and kissed me once on each cheek. It was effortless—a level of confidence and sophistication I could never imagine attaining—and it was only by holding very still that I managed not to Bork the whole thing up. "I'm already looking forward to it."

Then, with a final smile and a little wave, she was gone.

And I was left terrifyingly alone at a grand social occasion.

Snagging some champagne from a passing waiter, I scurried into a corner. Stared at the glass—the rise and fall of the little golden bubbles—so I didn't have to stare at the party. Which was nothing but strangers, and spaces Caspian wasn't.

I was already starting to give up on him coming back.

He'd just…abandoned me. And I had no idea why.

Except that Nathaniel had called his name. And Caspian had gone.

Suddenly: a click and a whirr. And a voice drawling out, "Smile, poppet. Butterflies make poor wallflowers."

I glanced up into another click and nearly dropped my champagne when I realized I was being photographed. And by George Chase no less. "Oh my God, don't. I probably have eight chins or red eye or something."

The photographer raised a perfectly arched and devastating eyebrow. "Most people get to know me before they insult me."

"No, no, I didn't mean you, I meant me—"

She silenced me with a single finger—the nail, I couldn't help noticing painted dark green—and stepped up close, turning the camera so I could see the screen. Sure enough, there was me, half in shadow, my gaze downcast, looking kind of feral and kind of fragile at the same time, with the butterfly mask a bright splash across my face.

Definitely no red eye.

Definitely only one chin.

Even my hair was behaving itself.

It was honestly best picture of me anyone had ever taken. So good, in fact, it was hard to believe it *was* me.

I couldn't help feeling a little bit flattered. I'd been on the verge of dying of nobodyness. And yet someone had seen me and found something…worth seeing. Something beautiful.

"Oh wow," I said. "That's…you've made me look amazing."

"Well, of course I have. I have two talents. Sex and art. And this one happens to be my job."

She raised the camera and snapped another picture. "Besides, you're such a pretty little thing."

"I'm not—"

"Shush, now. I don't like being contradicted."

I shushed. Mainly so I could decide whether I was annoyed or not.

A flurry of fresh clicks.

"And you like being told what to do." It wasn't even a question.

"Yes." My chin came up. "But that doesn't mean I like *you* doing it."

"Keep telling yourself that, poppet." George lowered the camera again and smirked at me. And, just for a moment,

I allowed myself to notice she was hot. In an arrogant sort of way. With those Marlene Dietrich eyes, all mockery and smolder.

She was probably about as tall as Caspian, even in flats, and her high-waisted, satin-seamed trousers made her legs look about a million miles long. No mask. No jacket. Only a cummerbund and a formal shirt with enough buttons undone to reveal the pale, upper curves of her breasts and an edge of black lace.

Okay. Upgrade to *really* hot.

"Are you going to keep calling me that?" I asked. By way of a distraction tactic.

"Maaaaaaaaybe."

I knew this game. "You're not, are you?"

"No."

"Gosh"—I gave my head a coquettish flick—"how dare you demean me in this fashion."

Her eyes flared with barely banked wickedness. "Having fun?"

I...I guess I was. Like when you passed your hand through a Bunsen burner flame trying to figure out how close to the blue you had to go to feel it. And then to make it hurt. "I'm with Caspian," I squeaked.

"I know you are. But he's foolishly left you all alone." She lifted her camera, catching what I hoped was a look of flustered outrage and nothing more revealing than that.

I actually enjoyed flirting—even if (maybe especially if?) it came with an edge of danger. Except Caspian probably wouldn't like it. "Please don't."

She put a hand flat to the wall close to my head and leaned in. I got a waft of cedar and sandalwood, spicy and rich. "Am I scaring you?"

"Not in a bad way." I tried not to look at all the interesting ways her shirt was gaping. "But I don't want to hurt Caspian."

She stared down at me for a moment. And then she murmured, in a tone both dulcet and ironic, "Sweet, loyal little butterfly."

I tried to laugh it off and blushed instead.

She shook her head. "Where on earth did he find you?" Thankfully, my three years at a world-renowned institution of higher education had taught me to recognize a rhetorical question so I kept quiet, and she went on, "In any case, I'm not going to leave you here, looking all lovelorn. Come along, poppet. You're going to be my assistant until Caspian wants you back."

"Am I?" It was a mild protest, mainly for the sake of my pride. Though, truthfully, I was relieved.

It was about time someone rescued me.

And, in practice, being George's assistant wasn't very demanding. I held lenses, passed her the occasional glass of champagne, watched and listened. She introduced me to nearly everyone—some of them were, in fact, viscounts—but nobody was awful and I did my best to be charming. I just wished it'd been for Caspian. That he could have stood at my side and been proud to be with me.

Sometimes George set up particular shots, moving people into position with terrifying efficiency, keeping up a constant flow of instructions, praise, and promises: *heads together please, turn this way, give me a smile, you're gorgeous, oh yes, show me those eyes, this is going to be perfect…* But mainly she waited, patient as a cat in the moonlight, or prowled the edges of the room, camera in hand.

"What do you look for?" I asked.

"The thing nobody else sees." She propped her hip casually against a piece of furniture I didn't have a name for—something ornate and impressive, probably a credenza or vitrine or whatever. "Society photography comes down to one very simple principle. Anyone can take pictures of Kate Middleton and Lady Gaga. The trick is getting a picture of Kate Middleton *with* Lady Gaga."

"And have you?"

"Not yet. But I'm a long way from dead, and hopefully so are they."

I laughed. In a strange way, she reminded me a little bit of Caspian. The same conviction, the same merciless drive, although focused and expressed very differently.

I guess it was becoming pretty apparent I had a type.

But mainly I was grateful. Now, when I looked across the room, I met smiles. Flashes of recognition in other people's eyes. I knew faces and names. I could have joined some of the conversations. Instead of drifting around pathetically.

Still no sign of Ellery, though. I was starting to wonder if she'd blown off her own birthday party. Which, admittedly, had a certain punkish panache. But since Caspian was still MIA with Nathaniel, if it hadn't been for Trudy none of the family would have been present at all. My mum would have skinned me alive—well, no, she would have been disappointed and Hazel would have skinned me alive—if I'd invited people to my house and either not turned up or just fucked off. I guess the rules were different for the rich. As usual.

"Um, is Mrs. Hart with Lancaster Steyne?" I tried to sound casual, which was tricky considering I'd launched myself into a total non sequitur. But clearly Caspian was never going to tell me anything ever so if I wanted to be a useful partner to him, it was going to have to be by stealth and cunning. And if I had to speculate wildly about the sort of tensions that might exist between a mother, her son, and her deceased husband's business partner, then the Hamlet Dynamic seemed a reasonable starting point.

George glanced across the room to where they were standing together. "I very much doubt it. She's a sparrow and he's no sparrow hawk."

"What's does that mean?"

"It means he's a predator who only preys on predators."

She said it matter-of-factly but I shuddered at the memory of his soft voice, slipping words into the conversation as precisely as the strokes of a razor. But before I could say anything else, we were suddenly dropped into darkness, and in the startled silence, a clock began to strike the hour.

Oxford had been full of bells, but I couldn't remember the last time I'd heard an actual clock do the *donnnnng* thing. It was such an old-fashioned sound. Eerie, and so Edgar Allan Poe–ish that I half expected there to come a tapping, as of someone gently rapping, rapping…

Instead, when the twelfth chime had shed its bronzy echo, a pale light illuminated a figure at the top of the stairs. It took me a second or so to recognize Ellery, partly because of the drama of her entrance but mainly because I'd never seen her dressed like that before. She was wearing a scarlet, floor-length evening gown, lace over satin, with a mermaid train. Intricate trails of sequins and beads shattered any light that touched them into bloody fragments. Her arms were bare and her hair was down, her lips the same color as her dress.

She was monstrous. And glorious. The only red in the room.

And then she lifted the violin she was carrying to her shoulder and began to play.

The first note fell upon the air as tenderly as tears. Ellery's eyes were half closed, the bow moving almost languorously upon the strings, while the fingers of her other hand flexed and flickered with what seemed like impossible dexterity.

My mouth had fallen open. Maybe just to get more music inside me because my ears couldn't cope with the flood of loveliness trying to flow through them.

I had no idea what I was hearing but the intensity of it never let up, the beauty becoming savage, as sharp as teeth. And Ellery played without mercy, her expression as lost, as wild as the music. Sometimes she seemed almost at war with her instrument, her hand moving upon its neck like a lover seeking one last surrender.

She could have been playing for five minutes or five hours but, somewhere in the middle of that exquisite storm, I felt a body pressed to my back. Inhaled the familiar scent of Caspian's cologne. And then his arms were around me and I was leaning into his embrace—almost drunk on the sheer relief of being his again. Safe from strangers and violins and a world I wasn't used to.

From somewhere nearby I heard the click of George's camera but I didn't care. And, from the way he clung to me and kissed the side of my neck, neither did Caspian.

I could have stood there forever now, nestled into my lover, letting the music tear my heart open, but the piece was sufficiently demanding that I had no idea how Ellery hadn't collapsed already. Pure will and ferocity, probably.

When she was done, the silence she left behind seemed to clamor. And then came an explosion of applause—which she ignored, vanishing upstairs, almost immediately after the final note was done.

CHAPTER 27

The lights came on slowly. And presumably we were expected to go back to do party things. Except I was good exactly where I was. I twisted my head so I could look up at Caspian. "What was that?"

"That," he returned, in his driest tone, "was my sister, Eleanor. I thought you'd met."

"Har har. I meant what was she playing."

"Sibelius. The first movement of his only violin concerto."

It didn't mean much to me but at least I could google it later. "She was amazing."

He nodded slowly. "She's extremely talented. She had a place at the Royal Academy of Music but she turned it down. I've no idea why."

"Did you actually ask her?"

"I...I can't remember." He frowned. "I presume I did."

I swiveled in his embrace, wanting to ask...all the things.

What had happened, where he'd been, if he was okay, what the fuck he thought he was doing—

But then I caught sight of Ellery crossing the room toward us. She was still in the dress, barefoot, and without the violin. So I had to let go of Caspian in order to give her a birthday hug.

Despite the supermodel sweep of the gown, she was still very much herself underneath it, sharp and fragile and Ellery, all jutting bones and elbows. So holding her felt a bit like wrangling a feral coat hanger.

I'd expected a brief, public occasion salute and she didn't exactly come across as the cuddly sort, so I was surprised by how tightly she squeezed me back, pushing her sweat-damp face kittenishly against my neck hard enough to leave me with a lipstick mark.

When we parted, Caspian stepped forward with a touch of awkwardness and murmured, "Happy birthday…Ellery."

She stared at him, her eyes—oddly naked without the heavy liner I was used to—bright and startled. Perilously close to pleased. Then she shrugged. "Whatever."

He didn't quite flinch but he got that look: the closed down, *I am a million miles away from you* look I knew all too well. "I'll leave you to enjoy it."

And, with that, he…went away.

Again.

I bit down on a *gah* of frustration. I wanted to kick him in the shins. You couldn't just fix what was probably years of hurt and misunderstanding with a single, and very small, gesture.

Also the fucker had barely spent five minutes with me.

But I pushed all that aside. And turned my very best and

sparkliest smile on Ellery. "So what happens next? Do we all die of the plague?"

She sneered at the room. "Mm, here's hoping."

"Wow, that's the last time I RSVP to an invitation from you."

"I don't mean it." She sighed and with the air of a small child being forced to eat Brussels sprouts added, "Thank you for coming."

"I didn't know you played the violin."

She shrugged. "I'm brilliant. When I'm not rusty."

"Well, if that's how you play when you're rusty."

"Not exactly." She looked briefly uncomfortable. "I had to practice the shit out of that thing. Worth it though. Did you see their faces?"

I hadn't, as it had happened. I'd been too absorbed by the music and then by Caspian. "I think everyone was really impressed."

"They were freaking out. I'm this total fuck up, remember? But now nobody knows what to think."

"Are you seriously telling me that you spent weeks—"

"Months."

"—months practicing a violin solo just to annoy people?"

"Yep." The corners of her mouth curled upward. "And it was awesome."

I suspected at least some of this was simply bravado. But it was her birthday and you let people get away with things on their birthdays, so I laughed. "I can't wait to see what you do next year."

"Oh there's nowhere to go from Sibelius. I'll have to auto-erotically asphyxiate or something."

"I think that's only for creepy politicians."

She thought about it for a moment. "The auto part sounds especially pathetic." Then she heaved another sigh. "You know, I don't actually hate absolutely everyone here. I should probably go and say hello and shit."

"Good plan."

"It'll suck, but you can come if you like."

It might have been delivered Ellery-style but it was still more consideration than Caspian had shown me all evening. And the fact I'd been waiting for something like it, just a fucking goddamn *hint* that he cared I was there, and it was Ellery—sulky, thoughtless, self-absorbed Ellery—who wanted to make sure I was okay, had me blinking back tears. "Thanks, but I'm going to look for Caspian."

Look for him. Find him. Shout at him.

Her only answer was a theatrical eye roll.

I spent the next ten minutes or so wandering through gilt rooms, past all the beautiful people, in hopeless pursuit of the questing beast that was Caspian Hart.

Only to discover he was nowhere.

Typical.

Ellery, however, in her red dress was as easy to spot as a flame in a forest. Remembering the theme of the ball, it was a little bit macabre of her. But I wouldn't have expected anything less and she was so clearly reveling in it. Several of her guests had even obligingly pretended to drop dead at the sight of her. It was one of the few times I'd heard her laugh without wariness.

I eventually ran out of places to look. Unless I started peering under chaises and behind curtains. Was he still dealing with the caterers? After five hours? If there'd even been something that needed dealing with in the first place. And it wasn't an excuse to fuck Nathaniel in the pantry.

Oh God, I didn't want to think about that.

Besides, I knew with the certainty of sunrise that Caspian wouldn't cheat on me.

And, actually, now the notion had sidled stickily across the threshold of my mind, I couldn't really imagine them together. They'd look beautiful—like a slightly risqué, designer underwear advert—but Nathaniel didn't strike me as someone to readily abandon his dignity.

And, in my experience, dignity was pretty much the opposite of sex.

Trying to rid myself of an image that almost epitomized my understanding of the tragicomic (though not one, thankfully, that had found its way into my apparently rubbish finals essay on the subject), I stared out at the gardens. There wasn't much to see—just the shadowy wash of a perfectly maintained lawn and the pale gleam of what was probably a gazebo or a folly, half lost amid a haze of distant willows.

Aaaaaand that was when I knew exactly where Caspian was.

I tried the handle on one of the French windows and, sure enough, it was open. A quick glance over my shoulder confirmed that nobody was paying any attention as I slipped outside.

I'd never entirely worked out what a folly actually was—or how it differed from, say, a building—but I found Caspian in this miniature classical temple type affair of slender marble pillars supporting a domed iron roof. Swept in dusty starlight and overlooking a tiny silver lake, it was an absurdly romantic spot. It looked like the sort of place where you'd sit in a crinoline, waiting to be ruined and then jilted by your no-good suitor.

Caspian was smoking.

He turned as I approached and cast the cigarette aside. I'd prepared a casual *hey you* type greeting but I never got the chance to utter it.

I was too busy being slammed up against the nearest pillar and kissed—holy fuck kissed—like he'd never kissed me before. The aggression I was used to, the will to dominate, to control, to claim. The ruthless determination simply to *have* me and wring a yielding from me that left me shaking and breathless and undone. But, this time, he was rough because he was clumsy, and he was clumsy because he was desperate.

Desperate for *me*.

He tasted of tobacco and the salt of unshed tears, and the sound he made against my lips, oh God, the sound. So helpless and naked and frantic.

And, of course, I forgot everything. I forgot my frustration and disappointment and hurt. The words I'd been going to say. All that mattered right then was that he needed me.

I reached for him, wanting to draw him close—to show him how safe he was, and how absolutely I was his. For a moment, he allowed it, shuddering against me, wrapped in my arms. But then he caught my wrists and pulled me away and I let him. Because whatever I could give, whatever he wanted to take with his cruel hands and his harsh mouth, was his.

He drew back a little, eyes wild in the uncertain light. And ran a single finger down the line of my throat, bringing with it a sharp, bright bliss. I tilted back my head and pressed into his palm. He could have that too. All my pleasure and all my pain, my heart and soul, my very breath.

"What do you want, Arden?" He sounded ragged and feral and dangerous: a beast about to snap and make me bleed.

I leaned into him as much as I dared, so he could feel the word gather in my throat before I gave it to him. "You."

It was the truth. The only answer I could give. But it made his eyes darken, the curve of his mouth turn cruel. The pressure of his hand eased. His fingertips skated over my leaping pulse. "Even like this?"

"Yes. Like this." I was trembling a little beneath his touch, but if it was fear it was indistinguishable from excitement. From love. "Like everything."

For a moment, he said nothing. Just stared at me, searching my eyes as if he wanted to crack me open like a coconut. And then, so softly, "You really want to hurt for me?"

I could have told him *I already do*. "Yes."

"Scream and weep and beg for me?"

"Fuck yes." And then because I saw no reason not to get a head start. "Please."

His fingers were still idling at my neck. He caught the corner of my bowtie and gave a sharp tug. The rasp of silk on silk made me gasp as if it was me he unraveled. "You'll let me have complete control?"

There was something about him tonight. Some edge that felt as brittle as it was sharp. I wanted to comfort him as much as inflame him—but there was no denying what he did to me, his threats as sweet as promises to my ears. And maybe the only way he'd ever let me truly reach him was through surrender. I tried to muster my usual tone of minx-ish provocation. "I'll give you anything you want, Mr. Hart."

"God." It was little more than a despairing groan. "Why? Why do you let me do this to you?"

I almost couldn't answer, my throat too clogged with tears at the thought he'd have to ask me that. "Because I like you. Because I trust you."

I took a chance and took his hand. Held him softly and gently. As if he were the butterfly tonight. And, when he didn't shake me off, drew him down to my cock. Which was hot and straining and aching for him. "Because it turns me on."

His fingers closed around me through my trousers and squeezed until I bucked and moaned. Some of the anguish faded from his face, the tight lines of his brow and mouth yielding to desire, and something tender I might have called hope. "Don't move," he whispered, as he stepped away.

"Okay." My heart thumped as eagerly as a puppy's tail. I loved the anticipation that came with his commands. And I loved pleasing him.

Of course, my nose started itching almost immediately. But I was manly and ignored it and held still as he'd told me to.

Caspian circled the pillar, leaving me standing there like Andromeda. Well, Andromeda if she'd had a massive erection. Then he drew my hands behind me and I felt the cool brush of silk against my skin.

It encircled my wrists. Pulled taut.

Oh my God.

My bowtie. He was bondaging me with my own bowtie.

I made a noise of surprise and excitement, which came out as a delirious hiccup that would have been embarrassing if I'd still had the brain space to care. I'd been fantasizing for years about what it would be like to be properly tied up and the answer was fucking amazing. Kind of like having my feet tickled. Terrifying and wonderful and just the right amount oh-no-too-much to turn my bones to treacle and fill my head with stars.

He'd pinned me with his hands and his body often enough, and I'd loved it, the weight of him and the sense of being physically overpowered. But this was different.

This was…this was special.

The care in it. Being wound inescapably in silk.

Like a gift, prepared for his pleasure.

I'd never dared struggle when he held me in case he let me go. But now I could. And so I did, simply for the visceral pleasure of feeling the knots tighten, reminding me that I was trapped. Bound. Helpless. At his mercy.

Exactly where I wanted to be.

He came back round, all flushed and wild in the moonlight, and I wriggled with wanton abandon. The *absence* of him, the handfuls of air between us, were so potent suddenly—as physical as hands upon me—all because it was beyond my power to breach them.

I felt like a heretic martyr waiting for the flames.

"Oh fuck, Caspian." Wow. I sounded half drunk. "Touch me do something please."

"Do something?" He looked gloriously wicked right then— taunting me with my own desire.

"Anything you want. Just…please."

He reached out and flicked open the topmost button of my shirt. Cool air hit that sliver of exposed skin like a blade and I whimpered. Usually clothes went quickly when Caspian wanted me, but tonight he bared me one fastening at a time. The sense of exposure was dizzying. And entirely disproportionate considering I was still mostly full dressed.

I stole a quick glance at my bare chest, aroused and embarrassed by how brazen I looked: shirt hanging open, shoulders pulled back, nipples pointy and straining toward him like they were shouting *mememememe*. Any other time I might have been irritated I was wearing the butterflies he'd seen before, but then he reached out and pulled lightly on their chains. I went up on my toes with a squeak, sharp little tingles shooting all the way to my cock.

His eyes were intent on mine as he circled me with the pad of his thumb. Circled and circled and circled. His caresses so light and so relentless, they quickly became torture. Attention and sexual cruelty: my two favorite things, especially from Caspian. It wasn't long before my eyes were wet with wanting and I was writhing against the pillar, basically attempting to fuck the air.

He paused, and I sagged, relieved and aching and disappointed all at once.

He put his mouth close enough to mine that I could feel the heat of his breath. "Say it."

Teased and tormented to the point of incoherence, I answered something like "whu."

"Ask me."

Another command, but one so filled with longing that I

finally understood. And my own voice, for once, was steady. "Give me more. Hurt me, Caspian."

Shuddering, he pressed into me with a muffled moan. A strange embrace, but perhaps one I couldn't return was the only kind he knew how to seek just then. I grazed my lips against the edge of his brow, accepting this too, letting him take whatever solace he wanted.

"Do you remember," he murmured, fingers tracing the outline of one of my butterfly nipple shields, "the last time I hurt you like this?"

I gave a shaky laugh. "I'll never forget. All I had was your voice on the phone. And I wanted you to be there so badly."

"I wanted it too. I wanted to be the one touching you. Watching you. Making you suffer."

"You can now."

He lifted his head. His face was open for a moment, full of warmth as well as passion, the upward curl of his lips unexpectedly tender. And then he put a hand across my mouth and, before I even quite realized what was going to happen, gave my nipple chain a savage twist.

The pain was shocking—a bolt of silver-white lightning—all the more intense for my powerlessness. I couldn't really move. Couldn't stop it. Couldn't control it. Couldn't do anything except feel it.

Which I did—my frantic scream muffled by his palm.

We were both panting when he let me go. And I...I started to laugh. Adrenaline, I guess. And the dizzying rush of fading hurt which was in that moment as sweet as pleasure. Perhaps sweeter.

"Arden?" Caspian's question was as gentle as his touch was ruthless.

I grinned at him, feeling rather feral myself. "Again."

He didn't, though. Not at first. Just toyed with me, tugging this way and that, turning me into a whimpering mess, want and fear feeding each other until I couldn't tell them apart anymore.

"Ohgodohgodohgodohg—"

One hand caught the rest of my wail, as he wrenched on the chain with the other. And, somehow, the pain was worse—sharper and harder and nastier—for my being familiar with it. Or maybe because it came from him, not my own trembling fingers, taking me deeper than I'd have ever dared take myself.

Maybe that should have been terrifying. And...well...yeah, in some ways it was. But mainly it was...freeing. Being able to sob into his skin while he hurt me. The twin flood of agony and arousal making me feel strong and weak and overwhelmed all at once.

And so close to Caspian I could almost taste his heartbeat.

This time, it took me a handful of seconds to realize he was done. All the borders between sensations had dissolved, and I was flying on wings of pleasure and pain.

He pressed himself against me, putting his lips to the edge of my jaw before tracing a tear track all the way to the corner of my eye. The fabric of his tuxedo was exquisitely harsh across my tormented nipples, his tongue like warm velvet against my cheek. I shuddered on the contrast and on the strange intimacy of him tasting the tears he'd caused.

"Arden," he whispered. "My Arden."

Words were so not happening with me but I moaned and nodded and conveyed my enthusiasm for the general sentiment of being his.

"You're so beautiful."

A slightly ridiculous comment coming from Caspian Hart. Especially when I was half undressed, and soggy all over from crying and sweating and leaking precome like a busted, uh, leaking thing. But he said it with such conviction that I believed it was true. Right then, anyway. For him.

He kissed my damp eyes. And, so softly I was half convinced I'd started hallucinating, murmured, "Everything I'd have dreamed, if I'd let myself."

And while I was still reeling from that, he dropped to his knees. I probably couldn't have been more surprised if he'd turned into a chicken. He yanked my trousers open so hard that I heard the button go pinging off somewhere and then he peeled my pants down my hips, freeing my painfully eager cock to the night.

So there I was: tied to a pillar with my nipples still stinging and my dick hanging out. And yet I felt…totally okay. This moment of calm at the heart of a storm.

Caspian glanced up at me. And I thought I caught the glitter of moisture on his lashes too. "You shouldn't be with someone like me."

Okay. Not…not the most encouraging thing I'd ever heard. "This," I croaked, "would be a super terrible time to dump me."

"I couldn't. I'm too selfish." He pressed his cheek to my thigh and I twisted in my bonds, wishing I could touch him. Reassure. "But I hate how much I want to hurt you."

"I love it when you hurt me. I love everything you do. And everything you are."

And that was when he turned and drew me into his mouth. It was the teeniest bit awkward—he even nicked me slightly with the edge of his teeth, suggesting maybe he didn't do this all that often. He certainly hadn't with me before. Not that I'd minded. He made me come just fine.

But...wow.

He could have been actively terrible and I wouldn't have cared: Caspian Hart was sucking my cock.

No teasing. Only his lips wrapped tight round me, his mouth soft and hot and perfect.

Ohfuckohfuckoh*fuck*.

I was...Caspian was...

I turned my head into my shoulder in an effort to muffle my noises. Which were at least as loud as when he'd been torturing my nipples, and probably even less dignified. Pain was one thing. I could take pain.

But I was pleasure's bitch.

Honestly, I put in a pretty embarrassing showing. Pleading and mewling and falling part in about thirty seconds.

What pushed me over the edge was the moment when he gagged. Just a little. My cock pushing into him past the point of comfort. It wasn't that I wanted to hurt him. That did nothing for me. Never could, never would. It was more that he wanted me so much.

So much he lost control of himself.

Let me in a little too far, a little too deep.

And it was a real humdinger of an orgasm. A balls to brain

and back again explosion that left me shaking, breathless, and shattered. And Caspian swallowed me down like he couldn't get enough.

He rose quickly afterward, reaching round me to fumble with the knots of the bowtie, managing to loosen them enough I could slip a wrist free. Turned out, freedom was what I needed right then, even though my arms were noodles and I was wibbly to my core.

Caspian caught me as I swayed. Sinking to the ground with me and holding me tight.

I was mumbling—probably trying to say thank you—and he was whispering back, my name mostly, and fractured pieces of praise.

For a few blissful, hazy minutes we were the very definition of sweet nothings. I even somehow found the courage and co-ordination to pull his face down to mine and kiss him. And for once he let me, his lips parting for me so I could slip my tongue into his mouth, and taste myself there.

God. Too much moonlight could turn a boy's head.

"Please," I said at last, "take me home."

CHAPTER 28

It took us a little while to put ourselves back together. Getting me cleaned up with Caspian's pocket square. Buttoning my shirt with tangled fingers. We abandoned my bowtie entirely in the end—it was beyond either of us but, since it was after midnight, I could get away with leaving it rakishly undone.

We snuck through the house hand in hand, as ridiculous as schoolkids playing hooky. I wouldn't normally have cared what people thought, but Trudy had been super nice to me and I wasn't sure how she'd feel about me defiling her firstborn in the family folly. I mean, it was one thing to be vaguely aware your son was having sex. Quite another to be faced with the rumpled, glaze-eyed evidence of it.

Caspian left me in a corner of the entrance hall while he went to have the car brought round. Looking back at the evening was like looking through some kind of weird distorting lens. It was hard to believe the end was connected to the middle or any part of it followed from the next. I tried to hold on to all the new faces, string together the conversations in which I'd been an active participant but, the truth was, I barely remembered anything that wasn't Caspian. His strange behavior. And then all the wonderful things he'd said to me and done to me in the garden.

I leaned against the wall and closed my eyes for a moment. Soaked in happiness like a warm bath.

And then a voice said, "You're not helping him, you know."

Which comprehensively trashed my mood.

Nathaniel Priest was standing over me. De-masked. All tall and gilded and severe. A sculpture from a classical pantheon. God of justice maybe.

"Uh, what?" Not exactly the cutting response I wanted but it was the best I could manage.

"If you care for him at all, you'll stop this."

"Um, stop what? Seeing Caspian?"

"What you're doing with him." Something flickered in Nathaniel's expression. A tinge of discomfort. Embarrassment?

And that was when I knew he'd…oh God…he'd seen us. Outrage crashed down on me. And then just this sad exposed feeling that someone who wouldn't understand had shoved their way into something beautiful and personal and special to me. My mouth opened and closed a few times as I tried to find my way to a response.

Nathaniel's expression softened. "Look, Aidan—"

"Arden," I snapped.

But he pressed on as if I hadn't interrupted. "I'm sure you think what you're doing is harmless. But it isn't."

"Yeah." Somehow I didn't punch him right in his smug face. "Thanks for the safe, sane, and consensual lecture but Caspian isn't hurting me and I have no intention of hurting him."

Nathaniel gazed at me with all this…patronizing fucking sadness in his honey-gold eyes. "Except you are."

"How?" I should have known better than to let him draw me. But: too late now.

"He's smoking again, for a start."

I pulled off a truly Ellery-worthy eye roll. "One cigarette a month is hardly going to kill him."

"Is that what he told you? And you believed him?"

Now that I thought about it…he did tend to reach for his cigarettes once we'd sexed. And he'd smoked after dinner. And during *Star Wars*. And just now in the garden. Oh fuck. Fuuuuuck.

Nathaniel was shaking his head at me. "You poor, sweet boy. You don't know him at all, do you?"

"I…I'm in love with him," I said, in the world's smallest voice.

"I can see why you'd believe that. Caspian can be quite dazzling when he chooses. But you don't understand anything about who he is. Or the damage you're doing to him."

I tried to reply…to protest…to defend myself. Defend him. Defend *us*. But I had nothing. Caspian had de-clawed me with his secrets. Left me powerless and alone.

"You deserve better," Nathaniel went on softly. "He's using you like his cigarettes. You might feel good in the moment, but you're bad for him. And don't think he doesn't know that. He won't forgive you for what you'd turn him into."

His gazed at me. I probably looked horrified. But he was

serene, his eyes unflinching, full of the fires of the just and the true. I gathered up the ashes of my anger. "Maybe," I retorted, my voice ricocheting off too much marble, "what I'm turning him into is someone happy with who he is."

For a moment, I thought maybe I'd struck him back. That he wouldn't have an answer for me this time. He even turned and started walking away. But I guess he wanted to pose, as he paused and threw over his shoulder: "He's not looking for happiness, Arden. He's looking for redemption."

I shouted "Fuck you" at his back.

But it was a storm of paper arrows. Nothing but bravado.

* * *

We were quiet on the ride to One Hyde Park. Mostly because my mouth felt like Pandora's box and I was sure only horrible stuff would come flying out if I opened it. Caspian was looking out of the window, the lights and shadows of the city dancing across the perfect sculpture of his face.

In the end, unable to bear the silence, I hit upon the cunning notion of pretending to be asleep. Except it somehow slipped into something very close to real sleep. And I was only sludgily aware of Caspian carrying me up to the apartment. Undressing me. Ineptly sponging away my butterfly wings when I had *cleanser* for God's sake. And then tucking me in. As he bent over me to kiss me, I caught his wrist.

"What happened tonight?"

He froze. "Oh, you know how it is. Families are always difficult."

"That's not an answer."

"I suppose"—He sat down on the edge of the bed, hands folded together, locked into stillness—"this evening stirred up the past a little."

"How?"

"It doesn't matter."

I'd thought I wasn't angry anymore. Apparently I was wrong. "You fucked off and left me in the middle of a party and I have no idea why. You don't get to tell me what matters."

"Arden—"

"And you don't get to *Arden* me either. Something was really wrong tonight and Nathaniel knew what was going on and I didn't."

"How many times must I tell you?" He didn't quite roll his eyes but, by God, he came perilously close. "This isn't about Nathaniel."

"I know," I…well…I kind of yelled. "It's about you. The only reason he could help you when I couldn't is because he understands things about you that I don't. And that's only because you won't let me. Which is your choice. Yours. You chose to make me worthless to you."

He drew in a sharp breath.

And I steamed right on. "This has nothing to do with accepting you. It's about accepting a lesser place in your life. And I'm not going to do that, Caspian. Because I love you and I've held nothing back from you and I deserve the same in return."

We stared at each other, both a little shocked. I felt like a cartoon character who'd run off a cliff, legs pummeling empty air, only beginning to fall when I noticed there was nothing beneath me.

Caspian was frowning, eyes glacier pale, and just as bleak. "You don't know what you're asking for. There are some truths that change too much."

"For the record, my patience for ominous pronouncements is at an all-time low. What truths? What do you mean?"

"Well. Reverse it. Think of the thing you're most ashamed of. And imagine telling it to me. The man you claim to love."

I did it. I thought about it. And he was right: it was awful. This searing combination of unfading remorse and utter, ugly nakedness.

"Fine." I swallowed. Blinked back tears. "When I was, like, thirteen or something I tried to get in contact with my dad. He's...not a good person, and he's obsessed with Mum, so if he'd found us, it would have been really, really dangerous for her."

Caspian looked genuinely flustered. "I didn't mean for—you didn't have to..."

"And"—a weird little giggle clawed its way out of my throat—"he's one of those borderline personality types so probably he doesn't give a fuck about me anyway."

A hideous silence.

I did some jazz hands. "So. There you go. Now you know just how stupid and selfish I can be."

"Don't say that." He pulled me into his arms and I went gladly enough, letting him enfold me. "You were a child. You wanted to be loved by the people who were supposed to love you."

"Don't make excuses for me."

His breath was warm against my cheek. "I'm not. But you don't deserve condemnation either."

"I fucking hate myself for it."

"You shouldn't." He turned his head and kissed the side of my brow. "There is nothing in you worthy of hate, my Arden. And I'm so sorry I made you tell me that."

I glanced up. "I'm not. I mean, it wasn't fun. But I trust you. With the worst of me, as well as the best, and all the squishy ambiguous bits in between."

"Thank you," he said, unexpectedly grave. "I hope to always honor that trust."

"As I will for you."

He didn't respond.

"So, y'know"—I nudged him gently—"your turn."

It took a long time, but he did eventually speak. The words coming slowly and painfully, like razor blades from his lips. "If I tell you, you'll know what Eleanor said about me is right. That I'm sick and twisted and I ruin everything that's good."

"She only said that because she was angry."

He shook his head. "No, she said it because it's true. You see, I learned who I was when I was fourteen years old."

"What happened when—wait. When your father died?"

"After that. When I seduced his business partner. His best friend."

I...I genuinely had no idea what to say. Too much clamoring in my head. Nausea churning my stomach. And the memory of Lancaster Steyne's cold gray eyes. The way they had lingered on Caspian, possessive and predatory and cruel. Oh God, how had I ever thought he was hot? And should I have…seen this? Guessed at something like it? At the very least? How fucking stupid and blind and ignorant was I?

"You seduced him?" I repeated carefully.

"Yes. I was angry with everyone, especially my mother who was close to Lancaster then. I felt she was betraying my father." He uttered a soft laugh, devoid of mirth. "She wasn't. I did that."

"For fuck's sake." I was drowning but thrashing doggedly regardless. "I don't see how a fourteen-year-old could have seduced anyone."

He went rigid in my embrace. "You don't believe me?"

"No, I believe you. But as far as I'm concerned, if an adult sleeps with a child, that's abuse."

I waited for him to accept my unassailable logic.

But all he gave me was another one of those hollow laughs. "You're so sweet, Arden. But I wasn't a child."

"Are you seriously telling me"—my voice rose a little—"that if I went out and banged a fourteen-year-old you would be okay with that? You wouldn't think it was deeply fucked up and wrong?"

"To say nothing of illegal," he added for me. "No, of course it would be wrong. But it was different for me. I knew exactly what I was doing."

I suddenly realized I was meant to be comforting him and, instead, we were sort of having an argument. But I didn't know how to let it go. Hell, I didn't *want* to let it go. How could he believe these things? How could he think I would? "You were a grieving teenager. He was an adult. Even if you *thought* you were consenting, it was his responsibility to…Jesus, Caspian. To look after you."

Caspian shook me off impatiently, and rose. He seemed very tall just then, in his barely rumpled black tie, while I huddled naked in bed. "I know what you're doing. I know this would be more comfortable for you if it was some heartrending tale of a vulnerable boy and a wicked uncle, but that simply isn't true."

His voice lashed at me and his words hurt. The injustice of them. I wiped away fresh tears with the heel of my hand. "It's not about my comfort."

"He didn't force me. He didn't rape me. He didn't make me to do anything I wasn't willing to do." He gazed down at me and it was like looking through the bars caging a wounded beast. "You may be sure I experienced pleasure with him, Arden. On many occasions."

"That's still not the s-same as consent," I said in a small voice.

"We were together a long time. Beyond any point that would absolve me of responsibility on grounds of age. I could have left him. And I chose not to."

"Yes," I protested, "because this stuff is complicated. My mum stayed with my dad for *years*. Half believing that if she could only be better and do things right, she could change him back into the wonderful, adoring man she married."

He turned on me, almost snarling. "Don't compare me to your mother. It does not reflect well on either of us."

I held his gaze, shaky but committed. "You're never going to convince me that a relationship between a fourteen-year-old boy and a grown man was the fourteen-year-old's fault."

"Then what if I told you how he cultivated my darkest desires. Nurtured my cruelty. Encouraged my worst impulses. How he taught me and indulged me, and brought me lovers to break like toys."

"I'd say he was a sick fuck."

Caspian threw back his head, and covered his face with his hands, more of that strange laughter bursting from between his fingers. "Now you sound like Nathaniel. But I was no sacrifice to Lancaster's degeneracy. I was his acolyte."

"You were his victim."

He made a noise of frustration—maybe even anger. And spun away from me. "Stop it. I don't want to hear this." He curled his hands into his hair. "Why won't you understand? Can't you see? I'm ruined and filthy and fucked up. I want the people I love to suffer. Because that's what turns me on above all else. Control and pain and degradation."

"Yes. I know." I steadied my breathing. Tried to meet the storm of his fury and pain with gentleness. "You're a sadist and dominant. And yes, you've hurt me sometimes—"

"It's the price of being with me."

Okay. Screw gentle. "Let me fucking finish," I yelled. "Yes, you've hurt me but I *wanted* you to hurt me in the ways you did. It's not a price to me, it's a privilege. I *like* it. Don't you get it? And if you're going to sit…well, stand…there and claim—fucking erroneously, by the way—that a child can meaningfully consent to sex, then you don't have any right to tell me, a fully legal and empowered adult, that I can't consent to control or pain or even degradation…from the man I…the man I love."

Silence came down like steel. I gasped, suddenly breathless.

"You should be disgusted by me," said Caspian, at last. "You should want nothing to do with me."

I swayed exhaustedly where I knelt. "Well, I'm not. And I don't. How many times are you going to ignore me telling you that I love you? Because I do. I really do. And you can think all these awful things about yourself if you must. But nothing—*nothing*, do you hear me—will make me believe them."

"You can't love me. You don't know me."

"You mean, because I didn't know about this? That's only because you lied to me about it."

He paced restlessly, up and down that pristine room. This lost creature in Caspian Hart's skin. "I didn't lie."

"I asked you outright. In Kinlochbervie."

"No. You asked if someone had hurt me. And they haven't."

"Oh fucking hell." I rubbed my hands against my burning eyes. "*I* could have hurt you. Don't you realize how completely fucked it feels looking back at all the times I've pushed you on sex stuff with no clue about what happened to you?"

"Well," he drawled, "I did warn you that I'm a cruel and selfish person."

"Why didn't you tell me?"

He paused. And gazed down at me with eyes that had nothing in them at all. No light. No warmth. Nothing. "Because I didn't want you to know. I wanted you to see me as you did. Not as the monster I am."

"God, Caspian. You're not a monster. You're an abuse survivor."

There was a long, long, increasingly unpleasant silence.

Then, in his coldest, sternest voice, "This isn't working. I've enjoyed our time together, but we're done."

"Wait. *What?*"

But it was too late. He'd turned on his heel, and was fucking gone.

I threw myself out of bed and pulled on the nearest pair of pajama bottoms. Ran after Caspian into the hall.

"What the fuck?" I cried. "Seriously, what the fuck was that?"

Caspian's attention flicked my way. He was utterly calm, but there was something terrible about it. Like shatter-proof glass, holding its shape when it's nothing but cracks.

"You're leaving me because I won't tell you you're evil?"

"No, Arden. I'm leaving you because you want me to believe things I cannot believe. Accept things I cannot accept. Be someone I cannot be."

No. No. This couldn't be happening. The world had gone slow and watery. I felt like he'd hit me. Except, y'know, inside. Right where there was nothing to protect my most naked, tender parts.

Tears were slipping down my cheeks and stinging the corners of my lips. "That's not true. I just want you to see that you're kinky, not twisted. And hurt, not broken."

"You may use the flat for as long as you like," he said. "And if you need money—"

"Shut up about the fucking flat and your fucking money."

"Very well."

Oh God, how could he look so perfect, arranging his cuffs like he was goddamn stock art: handsome young businessman in formal wear adjusting sleeves while standing in luxury interior.

And I still couldn't quite believe this was happening.

Except Caspian was walking away from me.

I lunged after him and caught his arm. Spun him round. Gazed up at him pleadingly, my eyes heavy, and my face hot and wet and sticky from crying. "I don't understand."

"There's nothing to understand." His expression didn't change. His tone gave me nothing. "I can't do this, Arden."

"Please, can't we—"

"I thought you would hate me and there could be nothing worse. Instead you pity me and that I cannot bear. I will not have you make me weak."

Very gently, he peeled my hand away. Turned. Walked.

My skin burned from his already fading touch. "Caspian?"

He paused.

I could barely speak, my mouth was so full of tears, and my heart this helpless lump of rubbery meat flopping in my chest. "Can you promise me one more thing?"

"I very much doubt it."

"Can you maybe…think about seeing a counselor? Nobody should feel the way you do."

He half turned, his face all shadows and blade-sharp angles. "How I feel is not your concern."

"You need to talk to someone. Please give yourself that."

"Therapy is not a magic spell. But for your information, Nathaniel arranged for me to see someone when were together."

"Really?"

"Yes."

"And you did it?"

"Weekly for over a year."

My head was full of white noise. Every breath I took snapped like icicles in my throat. "Well, y'know something? Whoever you saw? They did a piss-poor job."

The door opened. Closed.

And that was it. We were done.

CHAPTER 29

Everything hurt.

The hours were wild horses. Dawn broke around me. I spent most of the day on the sofa, crying myself out of tears, watching the sky turn tauntingly through shades of silver and gold.

I tried to be brave. To be strong. To be less fucking pathetically embarrassing.

But my inner Scarlett O'Hara was AWOL—tomorrow being another day seemed scant fucking consolation.

And while I sometimes tormented myself with idle fantasies of Caspian coming back, of sweeping me into his arms, full of sorrow and declarations of eternal devotion…I knew it wasn't going to happen.

I wasn't sure I could ever bear pain like this again.

* * *

Later…later…later…

My phone bleeped.

And, like a fool, I scrabbled for it. Wrecked with hope with fear with hope.

It was Nik: *I MOVED MY FOOT!!!!!*

* * *

I slept and didn't sleep and the hours sped and sluggished by.

And, finally, I rang home.

Hazel picked up. "What's wrong?" she said, before I even had a chance to speak.

I took a deep breath, then another. Terrified of saying it. Of making it real. Of breaking the strange, still twilight of my grief. "He left me."

It was all I managed before I started crying again.

The line crackled as Hazel shouted: "Rabbie, get the car." And then to me, "You sit tight, Ardy. We're on our way."

I didn't tell them they didn't need to come.

Because they did.

They really, really did.

* * *

The next day, I took a shower. The water hardly touched me. It just ran over my body.

Afterward, I put clothes on.

Because I vaguely remembered that was the sort of thing people did.

* * *

Text from Rabbie: *nearly there!* They must have driven for twelve hours straight.

It didn't take me long to pack. I briefly considered breaking everything in the apartment. But then I didn't.

I rang Bellerose. "I'm moving out."

"Arden…"

"I'll leave the phone and the credit cards and everything on the table." I sounded weird, even to me. Like one of those *Star Trek* episodes where a crew member gets taken over by an alien brain parasite.

"All right."

"And thanks for…y'know."

"I was simply doing my job. You don't have to thank me."

"Well, I just did, motherfucker."

He made a sound that might have been a laugh. "I'm sorry, I'm not the most socially adept of people."

"You don't come across as socially inept. You come across as really mean."

"I'm that too." He paused. "In any case. You have been…that is…you are…a person in my life toward whom I did not feel… complete revulsion."

"You what?"

"Keep my number."

The line went dead.

* * *

I thought about calling Nik. But I wasn't ready to talk and he had enough going on.

* * *

I texted Ellery, though.

No way was I letting her find me gone for the second time.

* * *

I was standing on the pavement with my bags at my feet when Rabbie and Hazel arrived. The car, which looked dingy in Kinlochbervie, looked borderline derelict in the middle of Kensington. But I'd never been so fucking relieved to see it.

We were strictly business. No questions asked. Just getting my stuff piled into the boot. And then Hazel and Rabbie swapped sides, and I crawled into the backseat. One of Mum's quilts was waiting for me there and, never mind it was the middle of summer, never mind the glass-ricocheting sun glare, never mind that it was already stifling in the car, I wrapped myself up tight-as-tight. And I swear to God, I could smell the sea.

And then we were off.

Hazel opened the glove box and a dusty jumble of CDs clattered onto her lap. "What have we got, then? *Lord of the Rings*? *Hitchhiker's Guide to the Galaxy*? *Winnie-the-Pooh*? *The Code of the Woosters*? *Murder Must Advertise* with the last disc missing?"

I thought about it a moment. "*Lord of the Rings*, please."

The familiar music washed over me. And then the equally familiar words: *Long years ago, in the Second Age of Middle-earth, the Elven-smiths of Eregion forged rings of great power.*

I closed my eyes.

I was home.

* * *

Hazel must have texted ahead because, when we wheezed into Kinlochbervie some twelve or thirteen hours later, Mum was waiting for me on the doorstep.

And I dived straight into her arms.

* * *

I spent a lot of time in the attic room—Mum's room—curled up in the bed under the eaves. The first place I'd spent the night with Caspian Hart. I listened to the whispers of the sea. Caught the dapple of the fairy lights in my cupped hands.

And cried and ached and grieved.

Tried to let Caspian go.

Honestly, I wanted to hate him. But how could I, when he already hated himself? And with such unassailable fervor that he'd rather believe he was a monster, than accept he could be hurt.

I'd probably watched too much Disney. But wasn't love supposed to be strong?

Except I'd loved and loved and loved.

Loved with all my heart.
And lost long ago.

* * *

Every night, Mum came in with our old copy of *Father Brown*.
Read to me until I fell asleep, just like when we used to wait for
my dad to come home.

It was weird, at first, not having to whisper.

Not having anyone to fear.

* * *

Eventually I remembered there were things I should have been
getting on with. I was starting a new job in a couple of weeks—a
job I'd been incredibly happy and proud to get—and I had
nowhere to live.

So I sat down with Rabbie, and he helped me figure out
my tax bracket and what my take-home pay would be and all
that stuff. I thought I could stretch to around seven or (at a
push) eight hundred a month for rent, and still leave enough
for grown-up things like bills and travel and food and tooth-
paste.

Not much for fun, though.

But I guess this was life when you weren't dating a billionaire.

In any case, I thought eight hundred quid a month would be
loads. I wasn't expecting to move into a palace or anything but
I thought it might stretch to a nice little apartment somewhere.

That could, hypothetically, look similar to the one Sarah Jessica Parker had in *Sex and the City*.

Unfortunately, I hadn't quite accounted for London. And the fact I wasn't the quirky protagonist of an American TV show. It turned out there were garages—and not even *nice* garages—beyond my budget. And the only residential properties I could afford were spurious house shares or dreary little studio flats. Places with only one or two pictures on RightMove—usually a bare mattress jammed against a stucco wall or an exterior shot of a concrete block or, in particularly dire cases, a photo of the loo. Seriously? Those were the best images somebody could find? I mean, maybe if I'd been an Elizabethan time-traveler the fact I didn't have to poo out of the window would have been a major wow factor. But, child of the post-Bazalgette era that I was, I was inclined to take indoor plumbing for granted.

Oh God. Caspian had spoiled me. He'd made ordinary life look…really rubbish. And left me stranded between worlds. Alone.

* * *

I was sitting on the swing, swaying in a desultory fashion, and watching the horizon eat the waves. And then the back door opened.

My heart shattered like someone had thrown a rock through it.

But it was Ellery who stepped into the garden. She clomped toward me, hands in the pockets of her hoodie. Scotland suited her. Made her eyes as clear as the sky and the sea.

"What are you doing here?" I asked. Surprised I was even capable of speech.

"Taking in an exhibition at the Tate Modern." She heaved an exasperated sigh. "Came to see you, dipshit."

"You didn't have to do that."

She shrugged. "Guess Caspian fucked you over, huh?"

For a moment or two I didn't say anything. The wind was sharp and salty-clean like the first sip of an exceptional margarita. It felt good simply to breathe. Let the air scour you. "Well, we're not together anymore."

"You're better off without him."

"I don't think it's a question of better or worse. But not being with him hurts." I toed the ground, pushing myself a little higher. "You know about Lancaster Steyne, don't you?"

"Yeah. They didn't even try to hide that shit from me."

"But none of it was Caspian's fault. You get that, right? He was young and vulnerable and messed up. And betrayed by someone he trusted in the worst way possible."

Another Ellery shrug. "Sure."

"Sure? Is that all you can say?" My voice cracked. And, suddenly, I was back at One Hyde Park with Caspian. Losing him all over again.

"What the fuck do you want from me?"

"I don't know. Understanding. A little compassion, maybe?"

"Screw compassion. I mean, if what happened to him was *soooo* terrible, why wouldn't he put a stop to it now?"

"What do you mean?"

She gave a nasty laugh. "Oh come on, Arden. He's probably already with him. He always goes back to Lancaster."

I stopped swinging. I wasn't going to cry. I wasn't going to cry anymore.

Ellery's hand brushed my shoulder briefly. "He's fucked up. He fucks everyone up. I'm sorry."

"He's so unhappy," I mumbled.

"You're not the first person to try and fix him."

"I just wanted to be with him." I leaned into her and while she made an irritated noise she didn't move away. "And it seems cruel beyond reckoning that a man with such power over his world could have so little over himself."

She rolled her eyes. "Yeah. Tragically ironic. And you know what else is tragically ironic?"

"What?"

"The fact you're sitting here in the arse-end of Scotland, with nothing, and nowhere to go, and probably no clue about anything, trying to make me feel bad for the guy who treated you like shit."

"Hey now," I protested. "He offered me money and the apartment."

"Like you were going to take it. How long was he with you? Did he know you *at all*?"

"We were kind of in the middle of an argument at the time."

"Right. But it's been over a week."

It had. And I'd told myself I wasn't hoping for anything. Except I must have been. Because now I felt silly.

Ellery kicked the tree moodily. "Stop feeling sorry for him. I expect he's feeling sorry enough for himself. Or Lancaster's found him a new whipping boy."

"Don't."

"Sorry."

"Did you really come all the way to Kinlochbervie to say I told you so?"

"No." She pulled her hood up and disappeared into its shadows. "I came to ask if you want to live with me."

I nearly fell off the swing. "Live with you?"

"Yeah. Thought I should move out. Do some shit with my life or something."

"What sort of shit did you have in mind?"

She kicked the tree again. And then, apparently finding the shelter of her hood inadequate, caught the strings and yanked them so tight that only a tiny window was left for her face. "Thought I might go Bartók on some English folk songs. Try to bring them back into the popular consciousness or whatever."

"Um. How?"

"Well. I thought I'd start by playing them."

I gazed at her, slightly shocked. "That sounds amazing."

"Right? I found one about baby murdering."

"Wow. Yes. People need that in their lives." I clutched my chest. "How can we, as a culture, have let our babymurdersongs whirl away upon the slipstreams of time?"

She made an odd muffled noise. I think she might have been laughing. "Is that a yes, then?"

"Do you even have a house for me to move into?"

"Yeah, I do. Just bought it. Although it's not…exactly a house. It's more of a space."

Oh dear God. I was going to end up living in a derelict power plant or a disused Tube station. "You should charge me rent, though."

"Hell yes, I will." She emerged slightly from her hoodie. "I'm not Caspian. You don't get to pay me in sex."

I gave an outraged squeak. "That was not our arrangement."

"Rent's £750 a month, bills included."

It was so perfect for me I suspected she'd put far more thought into this than her manner suggested. "That seems unreasonably reasonable for London."

"Yeah, well. It's going to need some renovation. And there'll be a lot of babymurderingsongs happening."

"I guess…I guess I'm in."

She gave me a flat look. "Okay then."

"You know what this means, right?"

Now her gaze became distinctly wary. "No. What?"

"Hug time." I bounced off the swing.

"Oh don't. Do you have to?"

She grumbled, but she let me hold her. Even gave me a brief, grudging squeeze in return.

And, afterward, we sat on the grass together. Watched the sunset crack the sky like an egg, spilling gold and scarlet and purple across the shifting waves.

I still felt miserable. Lessened. Turned into ribbons of myself: thin enough for the light to shine through.

But I also knew that I was going to be okay. Maybe not today or tomorrow or even the day after that. Probably not for a long time. But it was there. Waiting for me. Just a step beyond the horizon.

When Caspian left me, I thought I'd lost so much that I'd lost everything.

Except I'd found something too.

A piece of truth, as smooth and bright as sea glass.

For all his wealth and power and beauty, I had something Caspian Hart would never have. Would never be able to accept.

It was the simplest thing in the world. And the most precious.

I knew I was loved.

Acknowledgments

I would like to thank the usual people for doing the usual things for which I usually thank them. My partner (for putting up with me), Courtney Miller-Callihan (also for putting up with me), and my #iconic friend Kat (yet again for putting up with me). Finally my gratitude to my editor, Madeleine, for your continued support and patience. And, of course, to everyone who reads my stuff.

DON'T MISS THE FINAL INSTALLMENT OF
ARDEN AND CASPIAN'S STORY,

COMING SPRING 2018!

SEE THE NEXT PAGE FOR A PREVIEW.

CHAPTER 1

Stop me if you've heard this one before.

Boy meets billionaire. Billionaire offers boy short-term pre-arranged sex contract. Boy runs away from billionaire. Billionaire comes after boy. Boy and billionaire get back together. Billionaire sends boy to America on account of boy's best friend having been in horrendous car accident. Boy comes home again. Billionaire freaks out because of abusive history he never fucking told boy about. Boy blows it with billionaire.

Boy gets on with life.

And, you know something? Boy's life wasn't too bad.

I'd moved in with Ellery—into what I'd thought was going to be a converted warehouse for Spratt's Patent pet foods, but turned out was a warehouse she blatantly had no intention of converting into anything. Looking back, I wasn't sure why I'd expected otherwise. But I had the loft, and we mostly had electricity and running water, so it was actually pretty romantic in a writing poetry and fucking Kerouac kind of way. Well, except when I came home drunk and walked into a girder, and Ellery had to take me to A&E. But that was one time.

As for Ellery, she came and went at all hours, shamelessly ate my food, and sometimes crawled into my bed to sleep curled up next to me. It was like having a cat, if the cat also took a lot of drugs and threw wild parties. Not that I think Ellery meant to throw wild parties—they just sort of happened around her, especially now that her band, Murder Ballad, was taking off, or at any rate accruing a devoted cult following. I had no idea *how* because they didn't seem to advertise their gigs or hold them at, y'know, venues (the last one had been in a derelict church) but, somehow, the word got out.

Because apparently songs about child murder, sororicide, and accidentally cheating on your husband with the devil performed in abandoned buildings were less nichey than the elevator pitch suggested. Or maybe it was Ellery. She was electric on stage. As far as I knew, she arranged most of the music herself and she was in every swoop of the soprano, every cry of the violin, every beat of the drums: savage and mournful and free.

I was still at *Milieu*, though it would have been damning if I hadn't been. An ouchie in the heart region made time drag itself along like a dying cowboy in a western, but it had been a mere handful of months since Caspian had left me. The longest autumn of my life. The coldest winter.

Or else that was non-metaphorical cold because the heating had gone off again. I pushed my sleep mask onto my forehead and poked my nose out from under the quilt Mum had made. Immediately regretted it and vanished back under my pile of blankets. This was a major disadvantage of being a proper grown-up: you had to get out of bed. Not that I had a bed. I couldn't afford a bed. I had a mattress on the ground. But it was probably really good for my back. And at least I wasn't living on Coco Pops in a hovel by myself, which was all I could have managed on my salary without Ellery.

I would have done it, though. Because deep down I knew that no matter how sharp and real and inescapable my pain felt right now it would fade. My life was more than Caspian. Weird as it seemed, he'd shown me that.

Shown me how to fly, then pushed me through a window.

Some days, I was epically pissed about it. Others I was just sad. But, occasionally, I'd wake up in the rose and silver haze of a London dawn. Sit there on my mattress, wrapped in the quilt that still smelled of home, watching the light gleaming on the mist that coiled off the canal and be…almost okay.

Living in a warehouse intermittently full of musicians wasn't the most convenient arrangement I'd ever experienced but, damn, the views were spectacular. Especially from my loft with its huge, semi-circular window, like the apex of an industrial cathedral.

This morning, however, I wasn't feeling so appreciative. In fact, I was all for sticking my head under the pillow and pretending I didn't exist.

Except then I'd be late for work.

I got out of bed and, whimpering softly, peeled off the two pairs of socks I was wearing. The floor was hideously cold against my bare feet, but it was better than slipping on twisty little stairs that led to the main level, and ending up in A&E.

As I'd discovered a couple of weeks ago.

The bathroom was this a long corridor that had been partitioned off, with a shower over a drain at the far end. Ellery, with the air of someone defiantly uninterested in interior decor, described it as Shawshank chic. And, truth be told, it was a bit of a shock to the system after the pristine marble palace that was One Hyde Park. But I adapted. I'd washed in way worse places when I was student.

Morning ablutions complete, I spent some time picking out clothes and making my hair super cute. Life as a junior editor wasn't actually that glamorous—mainly I made tea, wrote the boring sort of copy, proofed other people's more interesting copy, and did what was called "gathering assets," which really meant googling shit—but you still had to turn it out. Basically you had to look like the type of person who worked at a high society lifestyle magazine. Not posh, exactly, but as if you knew what you were doing fashion-wise.

Thankfully I'd emerged from the womb serving manic pixie dream queer.

I went for some skinny leg, windows check trousers and a chunky cable-knit jumper, also courtesy of Mum, and my very pointiest shoes. And then hurried downstairs to see if Ellery had eaten all the Coco Pops.

Which, apparently, she had. Or rather was about to, as she tipped the last of the packet directly into her mouth. She was wearing an oversized T-shirt, which simply said "BASTARDS and some stripy thigh highs, and sitting cross-legged in the corner of the vast L-shaped sofa that was pretty much our only item of furniture. I mean, unless you counted the table I'd made out of wine crates. And the taxidermy walrus that…actually,

I still had no idea about the walrus. Ellery said he was called Broderick.

The rest of the band were scattered about in various states of consciousness. The drummer—Osian Ap Glyn—was facedown in the middle of the floor in a tumble of red hair. For a moment, I thought he might be dead, but then he twitched and I heaved a sigh of relief. Innisfree, who did keyboard and soulful vocals and was essentially the anti-Ellery, was sitting in the lotus position with her face turned ecstatically toward the sunrise. And Dave, the guitarist, was, as ever, just kind of there, looking as if he'd blundered into Ellery's life by mistake and couldn't think of a way to politely excuse himself.

"Innis made you a packed lunch." Ellery smirked as I edged carefully round Osian.

"Oh wow." My heart sank. "She shouldn't have."

Innis turned briefly in my direction, like a more serene version of that scene in *The Exorcist*. "It's my pleasure, Ardy. Healthy body, healthy soul. And compassion in every bite."

"There's a quinoa salad," Ellery told me sadistically. "With kale and avocado."

"Yum."

"And dried beetroot crisps."

"Whoopee."

Innis smiled, showing her perfect, shining teeth. "And, as a special treat, some of my handmade protein balls."

"Thank you." I squirmed miserably.

"Don't forget your tea."

I was so very doomed. "You made tea too?"

"Nettle and fennel."

"Ardy's favorite," exclaimed Ellery.

Very much earning the betrayed look I cast in her direction. And receiving absolutely no repentance in return.

I gave her the middle finger, picked up the eco-friendly silicon storage container Innis had left me, along with the bamboo fiber travel cup, and made for the door. Closing it firmly on both Ellery's laughter and Innis reminding me to buy a coat.

Because, as it happened, I had a coat. A really fabulous one. But it had been a gift from Caspian. And while I was sure one day it would be a welcome reminder of a man I'd loved once, right now it just hurt too fucking much to wear it.

Besides, I grew up in Scotland. Southerners knew nothing about cold.

CHAPTER 2

I hurried along the canal and then up the steps that took me to street level so I could cross the bridge. And, right there, slumped against the railing so inconveniently that I nearly tripped over his feet, was Billy Boyle, Ellery's stalker-paparazzo. I'd only met him a couple of times before and on each occasion I'd afterward found myself the subject of some nasty column inches, mostly speculating about which Hart I was banging. I didn't like him, is what I'm saying.

He used his teeth to pull a Lucky Strike from the packet he was holding and lit it with a flick of his lighter. "All right, Ardy?"

"No comment."

"You know nobody really says no comment, don't you? Only Tory MPs when they've been sending pictures of their willies to fourteen-year-old girls."

"Thanks for the tip."

I did my best to evade him, but there wasn't much I could

do short of running into traffic, so he fell into step beside me. His cigarette smelled different—nastier—to whatever Caspian smoked. But still. It was familiar enough to make my heart ache afresh.

"You back with Ellie, then?" he asked.

There was no way I could answer that question without it implying something I didn't want to imply. Which was probably the whole point. "No comment."

"Good choice, mate." Boyle grinned wolfishly. "She's by far the best of them. Can't beat sticking your dick in crazy."

"You're disgusting."

He shrugged. "Just telling it like it is. But what a family, eh?"

I walked a little faster. There were people around and cars on the road so I had no reason to feel threatened. Which I didn't really—more sort of fucked with and prodded at and imposed upon. And I wasn't sure what I could do about it in any case. Since I was pretty sure being icky wasn't breaking any laws.

"The dad was a Boy Scout. The mum's a snooty bitch. And the brother...well, you'd know more about that than me, wouldn't you, Ardy baby? But the stories you hear."

I knew he was trying to get a reaction. So I gritted my teeth and refused to give him one.

"That's the rich, though. Think they can do anything."

I kept my head down. Kept walking.

"You should think about telling yours." Boyle cast his cigarette butt carelessly into the gutter. "Story, I mean."

Startled, I stopped a moment. "Wait. What?"

"Thought that'd get your attention."

"Not in a positive way."

"Don't be like that. I'm trying to help you."

"No, you're not. You're trying to exploit me."

Normally, I cut through Tower Hamlets Cemetery Park on my way to the station—which probably sounds a bit morbid, but it was actually a lovely place, full of grass and stone and quiet, especially in the morning—but the prospect of Billy Boyle chasing me through a graveyard, or lurking there on future occasions, was seriously non-ideal. I turned onto Bow Common Lane instead, stifling a sigh when Boyle turned with me.

"Could you go away," I said, figuring it was worth a shot. "Please?"

But the man was as relentless as a piece of chewing gum stuck to the sole of my shoe. "I'd get you one hell of a deal, Ardy. And it'd be classy. Sunday magazine classy. You should think about it."

"Okay. I'll think about it."

"Chance to tell your side of things. Completely sympathetic to your point of view. And, of course, I'd make sure nothing too complicated got in the way of that."

I gave him an incredulous look. "Are you threatening me?"

"I wouldn't say that. I'd say"—he stroked his chin thoughtfully—"I'm acknowledging the infinite subtleties of human nature. I mean, you haven't exactly been a saint, have you, mate? And a story like this—if we play our cards right—could be worth a couple of mil at least. Imagine that. You'd never have to work again."

"No, thanks."

"Aw, come on, Ardy." Boyle sounded genuinely bewildered— even a little hurt. "Why not?"

"Um, how about because I'm not a total shithead?"

There was a brief pause. And I thought he was going to give up, but no. He kept talking. "Do it for Ellie, then."

"Right. Because she'd really appreciate me making her brother the subject of public speculation."

"Bit of payback for all the shit he's put her through."

That made me laugh—in a mean, skeptical way. "You can't expect me to believe you're doing this for Ellery and not the money."

"Like I said"—he shrugged—"the infinite subtleties of human nature."

I rolled my eyes.

Boyle reached into an interior pocket of his brown leather jacket and pulled out a scrap of paper with something scribbled on it. "Take my number, at least."

"Fine." I didn't actually want his number—or anything to do with him—but it was clearly the only way I was going to get rid of him.

"Don't wait too long, yeah? You always want to be ahead of a story, not behind it."

And now he was probably just digging. Trying to freak me out. Unfortunately it was working. "What story? There's no story."

"Thought you were supposed to be a journalist." He flashed his yellowing, pointy-toothed smile at me. "You should know by now there's always a story."

"Well…well…there isn't."

"Whatever you say. See you around, Ardy baby."

He gave me a mocking, two-fingered salute and sauntered

off. Finally, fucking finally, leaving me alone. Not feeling great, in all honesty, and also running slightly late.

I made a dash for the station and made it just in time, leaping between the Tube doors the instant before they closed, and then wriggling and squishing my way through a forest of armpits until I was able to wedge myself into a nook at the back of the carriage.

It wasn't a long journey—only about fifteen minutes, if there were no delays—but I felt kind of ridiculous looking back on the time I'd spent at One Hyde Park, believing I lived in London. That wasn't London. *This* was London. Long dark tunnels, strangers diligently not looking at each other, and the scent of soot and sweat.

Maybe I was a complete weirdo but I liked it more.

It was real to me in the way that Caspian's cold, beautiful, sealed-off world could never be.

Although, I will admit, I missed being able to call him the moment something went wrong. Not because I wanted him to fix all my problems for me, but because having him on my side—knowing he cared for me and wanted the best for me—was its own magic. Like Queen Susan's horn, he let me find my way through life, sheltered by the promise that help was always close by.

Though most likely all I had to do with Boyle was ignore him. Count on my own irrelevance and the fact Caspian was already well guarded from this nonsense like this. I'd as good as resolved on a course of resolute non-action as I elbowed my way off the Tube, but then I remembered that I still had Finesilver's business card in my wallet. He was the Harts' lawyer and, from what

I'd been told, he specialized in reputation management. Frankly, he was terrifying in this smiling, silk and steel kind of way. But he'd been nice enough to me on the one (also Boyle-related) occasion we'd met. And since this involved Caspian indirectly, maybe he'd be able to give me some advice.

I still had a few minutes before I needed to be in the office, so I nipped past the now-familiar statue of William Pitt the Younger and sat down on one of the benches in Hanover Square. I'd texted Caspian from here when I first got the job at—

Goddamn it.

Why was he everywhere? No wonder I loved the Tube so much. Some days, it felt like it was the only place he wasn't. As if my memories of him had wrapped themselves up in the whole fucking city. And my love was a dog off its lead. Wandering by the roadside, getting ragged and thin, sniffing every street corner for just a trace of Caspian, trying to find its way home.

With shaky fingers, I dug out Finesilver's card and dialed the number. Of course, he was too important to pick up his own phone, so I ended up having to introduce myself to an assistant and explain, not very coherently, who I was and what I wanted. Then, already convinced that this had been a terrible idea, I waited on hold for an uncomfortably long time. And finally:

"Mr. St. Ives." Finesilver sounded very, very different on the phone. Sharper, colder, and a hell of a lot meaner. "How can I help?"

"Um, you remember that reporter guy? Boyle?"

"I'm aware."

I flexed my fingers, horribly aware I was sweating over my phone. "Well, he's been hanging around again. He wants me to sell my story."

"I see. And I presume this call means you're amenable to a counteroffer."

"What? No—"

"You're not amenable?" He cleared his throat. "Mr. St. Ives, I understand that you may be carrying some resentment toward my client, but any attempt to hurt him will cause far more damage to your reputation than it ever could to his."

This was giving me serious déjà-vu. Not only was this the second nebulous threat I'd received today, but it wasn't the first time I'd been accused of trying to spill Caspian's secrets to the press. And it was unbelievably depressing to discover that you could apparently get used to it.

"I'd never do anything to hurt Caspian," I said.

"And your circumspection will be generously recompensed, pending the proper legal assurances."

"Legal assurances?"

"Just a few standard and nonintrusive nondisclosure agreements."

The conversation was getting away from me—thundering off like an out-of-control train down unintended tracks. "You don't understand. I don't want money and I will never, ever go to the papers."

A very slight pause. "Then why are you calling me?"

"Because Boyle's hanging around again. I thought you needed to know this stuff."

A longer pause. "Arden"—Finesilver's voice softened—"I

cannot help Miss Hart unless she allows me to do so and you are no longer under Mr. Hart's protection."

"But—"

"You may, however, be certain that I will continue to safeguard my client's interests. And I recommend that you continue to ensure that yours align with his."

"I told you," I muttered, "I won't go to the papers."

"Forgive me, but my profession does not reward the assumption that people will keep their word. Which is to say, if you find your morals wavering, you shouldn't hesitate to contact me, and I will shore them up with material benefit."

Boyle, with his sly glances and nasty insinuations, had made me feel pretty fucking dirty. But this was *way* worse. "Right. Okay."

"Was there anything else you wanted, Mr. St. Ives?"

I should probably have escaped with what remained of my dignity, but bitterness got the better of me. "No, thanks. You've more than satisfied my need to feel cheap and blackmaily."

"That was not my intention."

"Then I guess it's just a bonus." Finesilver started to say something else, but I cut him off. "But for the record I only phoned because I wanted to get rid of Boyle."

"I'm afraid I'm not in a position to advise you."

"Yeah, you've made that very clear."

He sighed. "Start on the IPSO website. Clause three of the Code of Practice. Goodbye, Mr. St. Ives."

With a click, he was gone. And I was left in a park, in silence. This was turning into an incredibly shitty morning and it wasn't even nine o'clock yet.

God, I wished I hadn't called Finesilver. Not only because he'd treated me like shit—which, admittedly, was his job—but because it had reminded me how far away Caspian was. I mean, I knew he was. I'd long since stopped harboring secret hopes he'd come for me again, the way he had once upon a time as I sat on a swing in Kinlochbervie. But the gulf between us had grown so impossibly vast that I wasn't a person to him anymore. I was a problem to be contained.

A mistake he'd made once.

And that hurt most of all.

CHAPTER 3

I pulled myself together, put on my happy face, and bounced into the office. Said my hellos. Did a tea round. Then got sucked into a really intense conversation with Tabitha England-Plume (the Features director) about her mum's artisanal marmalade. It was made from the fruit grown in the orangery of their stately home and named—in acknowledgment of the fact Tab came from legit aristocracy—Lady Marmalade.

Finally, though, I made it to what had become my work-space. As was the *Milieu* way, it was clutter free except for a copy of *Debrett's*, which I'm glad to say I'd never looked at. Not even when I was super bored. That was the weird thing about living your dreams: sometimes the living part was just kind of routine.

I logged into my email and got stuck in. And then began circling the issue of actual work. There was this piece on micro bags I was supposed to be writing copy for. Except I couldn't think of anything witty or interesting to say about them. *These are very expensive and unfit for purpose.* Hmm, wait. Maybe there was something about lack of adequate storage being a status symbol. Too small for convenience. Too rich to care.

Hurrah. I was a genius.

Or, at least, adequate at my job.

"Smiling, poppet?" drawled a voice. "Thinking of me?"

I glanced up to find George Chase, photographer and self-identified rake, leaning in the doorway, watching me with her usual air of faint amusement. And, in high-waisted, wide-leg satin trousers, a white shirt, and purple jacket thing with black velvet lapels that was practically frockcoat, looking so fabulous it hurt.

"Teeny tiny handbags, actually."

She laughed. "You need to get out more."

"Tell me about it."

"Oh, I can do far better than that."

"Can you?"

"Always." She twitched a wicked eyebrow at me. "Get your coat. We're going on an adventure."

A major component of my job was doing what people needed me to do—whether that was grabbing someone lunch, or finding a prop for the cover shoot, or compiling a top list of llamas who looked like the Duke of Edinburgh—and I'd played assistant to George a couple of times now. Much to the chagrin of some of the associate editors, since "gay for George" was pretty much an office meme. Not that anybody was mean to me about it—*Milieu* wasn't that sort of place. Although I can't say I was massively delighted when I discovered there was a wager for when I'd sleep with her. I was semi-tempted to bet on myself for *never.* Except George was ridiculously hot and never was a long time to wait for a payout.

* * *

A few minutes later, I was sitting next to George in her classic Jaguar roadster as she drove slightly too recklessly for my comfort through the London traffic.

"Where exactly is this adventure?" I asked.

"It's a shoot for next year's *List.*"

I gave her a severe look. "I'm starting to feel this excursion has been over-sold to me."

"Don't count on it, poppet." There was something in her tone I couldn't quite read—a touch of regret, maybe? "I'm taking the pictures, you're doing the interview."

"Okay. Sure."

It was actually a fairly straightforward assignment. The top ninety of Britain's most eligible people required only a couple of sentences, usually about how good they looked in a top hat or what dukedom they'd inherit, and a photo dug up from the *Milieu* archives. But numbers one-to-ten got their own a little feature. And the questions were standard, so as long as I didn't call someone my lord, instead of your grace, or break a Ming vase on my way out I'd be unlikely to fuck things up.

George drummed her fingers lightly against the steering wheel. "Look, I'm sorry to spring this on you. But it's Caspian Hart."

There was nothing in my head but silence, like when a

grenade goes off in a movie, and then everything explodes. Except without the explosion. Just the moment before stretching forever. "Oh."

"He's gone from seven to three."

"Yeah. Well. I guess not being with someone would help with that."

"You know something? You don't have to do this. I'll tell Mara to back off."

Mara Fairfax was the editor-in-chief. She'd hired me, and was always friendly when our paths crossed but, given she was the most important person at *Milieu*, and I was the opposite of that, I wasn't sure there was all that much off to back. "This was her idea?"

"Obviously, Arden."

"And she knows I used to, um, date Caspian?"

"Do you really think," said George with an affection so comfortable, so unabashed, I wondered if she'd even noticed it was there, "she got where she is today without the will to exploit every opportunity revealed to her?"

An ache in my shoulders made me realize I wasn't just tense. I was *braced*. For an emotional reaction that wasn't coming. "But...but...wouldn't I be the worst person in the world to send? There's no way he'd want to speak to me."

"He probably wouldn't *want* to, no." She shrugged. "But giving people what they want rarely yields interesting results."

"And this would be interesting?"

"Well, it couldn't be more boring than his usual interviews. Have you read any?"

I shook my head. I'd seen a couple, here and there, but I'd

never managed to actually get through one. Too much business talk.

"He gives so little of himself away. My gas bill has more humanity."

For some reason, this made me smile: it was so like Caspian. "He's different when you know him."

George's expression grew wry. "You've just made Mara's point for her. Thankfully, my priorities are different."

"I thought your priorities were sex and art."

"And not traumatizing poppets unnecessarily."

I wasn't sure whether I felt patronized or protected. Maybe both. "I have to ask: what would necessarily traumatizing me entail?"

"That's for me to know, and you to find out."

"I can never tell," I grumbled, "if you're threatening me or flirting with me."

She shot me an alley-cat grin. "Fun, isn't it?"

"That's for me to know, and you to find out."

"You little minx."

We'd reached the financial district. Not my favorite bit of London, I had to admit. It was almost as if the centuries had been smoothed away with the buildings themselves, leaving nothing but smooth glass, like blinded eyes, reflecting the steel-gray nothing of the sky. Or alternatively: it reminded me of Caspian, so all I was seeing was my own emptied-out heart.

George pulled over in the Barad-dûr-esque shadow of Hart Financial Services. "So what's it to be?"

"I…I don't know."

"Nobody'll think less of you, either way."

I peered up at Caspian's place of business. His twenty-first-century fortress, coldly gleaming. "*I* might."

"There's no shame in love or pain."

"Well"—I pushed open the car door and scrambled onto the pavement—"I'm sick of both."

And I marched in like I fucking owned the place.

The effect of which was slightly diminished by the fact nobody really noticed or cared, and I had to stand in the lobby like a lemon while George got her camera bag.

But then we were in the lift, being whooshed up to Caspian's floor in that tiny glass bead. And it was impossible not to remember the first time I'd done this. I'd been furious then, but so full of hope.

No hope today.

Just the determination to look Caspian in the eye, and feel whatever I felt, and know I'd keep living after.

That I was okay.

George nudged her shoulder gently against mine. "If you need to run away screaming, pull your ear or something, and I'll cover for you."

"I won't need to."

"What can I say?" She smirked me. "I'm a fan of safewords."

And so she managed to make me laugh as the doors opened, admitting us into the vestibule outside Caspian's office.

It hadn't changed. Which was to say, it was still as intimidating as hell. Glass and marble and blah blah blah. And Bellerose, at his desk, looking like a terribly severe angel.

"Hi." I waved in a *check me out not being totally destroyed* kind of way.

His head snapped up. And, wow, he was looking rough: dark circles under his eyes, cracked lips, acne rashes across the tops of his cheeks. "Arden. I…"

"We're here from *Milieu*. We've got an appointment."

"Yes, I know. It's …" He scraped a lank lock of hair away from his brow. "Actually, it's fine. Go right in."

I should probably have been squirrelling my emotional energy away for, well, myself. But, for all his sharp ways, Bellerose had been oddly kind to me.

"Are you okay?" I asked.

He frowned, reverting to his more typical mode of Impatient with Arden. "Of course I am."

"Are…are you sure?"

For a moment, he stared at me, his expression almost pleading. But all he said was, "Mr. Hart's in his office."

And so I had no choice but to let it go.

Press forward.

Caspian's door loomed. I took a deep breath, pushed it open, and stepped boldly over the threshold.

Or, at least. That was the plan.

What actually happened was that I contrived to trip over, well, nothing. I tried to catch myself but to absolutely no avail. And one startled yelp later I was facedown, arse up on the ground.

"Arden?" Oh God. That was Caspian. I hadn't spoken to him for months and yet his voice—so familiar with its upper-class vowels and its secret promise of warmth—pulled at me like an unfulfilled *geas*.

Footsteps.

Then someone reaching for me. And I let myself be helped before I realized it wasn't Caspian.

You see, I knew his hands. Knew their strength, their elegance, and their restless vulnerability. They'd touched every part of me. Claimed me, in both pleasure and pain.

But this was a stranger's hands. And a stranger's touch. And it was almost impossible to imagine that these cool, perfectly manicured fingers—the fourth circled by a milgrain platinum band—could ever falter or flinch or reveal too much.

I made it back to my feet. Looked up.

And died in Nathaniel's honey-golden gaze.

"Are you all right?" he asked, with the easy solicitude of the victorious. "Did you hurt yourself?"

I opened my mouth and waited for words to happen. They didn't.

George stepped forward, her body briefly blocking mine. "Your assistant said you were free. We're here about the interview."

"Darling"—Nathaniel cast a look of amused exasperation in Caspian's direction—"I thought you canceled that?"

He frowned. "So did I."

"Well," said George, "you didn't. And I'm a very busy woman, so can we get on with it?"

Holy shit. This was the bit in a mafia movie where all the characters started pointing guns at each other and yelling. I mean, apart from the guns and the yelling. We were all too British for that.

But some pretty frosty looks were happening, let me tell you.

Nathaniel aimed his at George. "Do you talk to all your subjects like this?"

"Only the very special ones."

"I must apologize." It was odd to hear Caspian being concili-atory but, I guess, someone had to be. "The thing is, I…that is…I'm afraid I'm no longer an appropriate topic for this par-ticular article."

"What do you mean?" Oh. That was me. In the world's small-est voice.

He'd been standing behind his desk, crisscrossed by silver-edged shadows. But now he stepped forward, his hand coming up self-consciously so he could adjust his tie when it didn't need adjusting. And there it was: a dull gleam on his fourth finger. A ring to match Nathaniel's.

"I'm…we're…"

"Engaged," I said.

"Bellerose should have told you. I mean, your magazine."

My world was a platinum circle. It was manacles on my wrists. A vise around my heart. "Congratulations."

"Thank you, Arden." Nathaniel, soft-footed, came to stand beside Caspian. Took his arm. "A shame about your wasted trip."

They already looked like a magazine cover. Caspian, exquisite in dark blue pinstripes, and Nathaniel, tastefully casual. A per-fect match, equal in beauty and poise and sophistication.

And so wrong in every other way.

I was completely fucking furious with him. And desolate all over again. How hurt did you have to be, how terrified of who you were, and what you wanted, to do something like this? Not just to himself.

But to me. And to Nathaniel.

"We'll get out of your way." George gave my shoulder something between a pat and a shake. "You must have a lot to do."

Except I was stuck. Staring helplessly at Caspian.

Waiting for him, somehow, in a handful of seconds, with nothing but silence between us, to trust, to understand, to change. And at the same time knowing it was utterly beyond him. I'd lost Caspian before we'd even met. To Lancaster Steyne. The man whose cruelty would possess him for the rest of his days.

And Nathaniel was more fucked up than any of us if he didn't see it too.

"How about a different interview," I heard myself say. "The two of you together."

Caspian gave a convulsive start. "No."

The smile I produced felt like an alien's impression of one. "It'd make a wonderful story."

"Absolutely not."

"Let's not be so hasty, my prince." Nathaniel pressed in closer, and whispered something in Caspian's ear. And then, "I think it could be rather romantic."

I shrugged. "Well, have a think about. I'll leave my details with Bellerose if you want to set it up."

Then I wheeled round.

And, on barely functioning legs, got the fuck out of there.

About the Author

Alexis Hall was born in the early 1980s and still thinks the twenty-first century is the future. To this day, he feels cheated that he lived through a fin de siècle but inexplicably failed to drink a single glass of absinthe, dance with a single courtesan, or stay in a single garret.

He did the Oxbridge thing sometime in the 2000s and failed to learn anything of substance. He has had many jobs, including ice cream maker, fortune-teller, lab technician, and professional gambler. He was fired from most of them.

He can neither cook nor sing, but he can handle a seventeenth-century smallsword, punts from the proper end, and knows how to hot-wire a car.

He lives in southeast England, with no cats and no children, and fully intends to keep it that way.

To learn more, visit:
quicunquevult.com
Twitter: @quicunquevult
Facebook.com/quicunquevult

Made in the USA
Middletown, DE
27 May 2021